T0243158
DALLAS
KNIGHTS
63
DALLAS
KNIGHTS

THE PUCKING WRONG SERIES

The Pucking Wrong Number

The Pucking Wrong Guy

The Pucking Wrong Date

The Pucking Wrong Man

The Pucking Wrong Rookie

A Pucking Wrong Christmas

THE PUCKING WRONG MAN

THE PUCKING WRONG BOOK #4

C.R. JANE

Cover design by Cassie Chapman/Opulent Designs
Photography by Ren Saliba
Editing by Stephanie H./Hannotek, Ink

ISBN: 978-1-0394-8648-5

Published in 2024 by Podium Publishing
www.podiumentertainment.com

Podium

*To my red flag renegades who know "Yes, Daddy"
and a spanking are both signs of a good time.*

Dear Red Flag Renegades,

The Pucking Wrong Man is my thickest book to date, and that's largely because I couldn't get myself to say goodbye. I swooned as I wrote Camden and Anastasia's relationship. His love for her, how careful he is in winning her heart . . . how much he would do to get her. I love them, and I'm hoping you love them too.

In this book, the focus is on the aftermath—or ramifications—of the loss of a dream. Camden is an NHL player who, while still young by most people's standards, is moving to the latter stage of his professional career. Anastasia is a ballerina trying to work her way to the top—with a huge impediment standing in her way. The question I started with was: What do you do when you lose your dream? When you lose what you've been working toward for your entire life? Is it a quiet acceptance? Do you roar and gnash your teeth and curse the world? Do you hide away and think about how unfair it is?

Or do you get a new dream . . . ?

This book isn't just about Anastasia's tragic past and how she overcomes it though. If you've been with me since the beginning, then you know this series also places a high premium on the themes of found family and brotherly love. The moments where we really see these two themes in action helped me to perfectly balance the highs and lows of the story. The "circle of trust" is out in full force and playing the different characters off one another was so much fun. I laughed at myself, so I'm hoping you laugh too.

I've been living in the Pucking Wrong world for a long time now, and I'm pretty sure these boys have become my new personality. Is it weird that I have conversations with Ari Lancaster in my head? No? Okay, good. Because it's happening.

As always, I pinch myself every day, wondering, as Anastasia does by the end of this book: How is this my life? I'm so grateful you all let me live my dream.

♡ CR Jane

TEAM ROSTER

LINCOLN DANIELS	CAPTAIN, #13, CENTER
ARI LANCASTER	CAPTAIN, #24, DEFENSEMAN
WALKER DAVIS	CAPTAIN, #1, GOALIE
CAS PETERS	#42, DEFENSEMAN
KY JONES	#18, LEFT WING
ED FREDERICKS	#22, DEFENSEMAN
CAMDEN JAMES	#63, DEFENSEMAN
SAM HARKNESS	#2, GOALIE
NICK ANGELO	#12, DEFENSEMAN
ALEXEI IVANOV	#10, CENTER
MATTY CLIFTON	#5, DEFENSEMAN
CAM LARSSON	#25, LEFT WING
KEL MARSTEN	#26, DEFENSEMAN
DEX MARSDEN	#8, CENTER
ALEXANDER PORTIERE	#11, RIGHT WING
LOGAN YORK	#42, CENTER
COLT JOHNS	#30, WING
DANIEL STUBBS	#60, WING
ALEX TURNER	#53, CENTER
PORTERS MAST	#6, DEFENSEMAN
LOGAN EDWARDS	#9, DEFENSEMAN
CLARK DOBBINS	#16, WING
KYLE NETHERLAND	#20, DEFENSEMAN

COACHES

TIM PORTER, HEAD COACH
COLLIER WATTS, ASSISTANT COACH
VANCE CONNOLLY, ASSISTANT COACH
CHARLEY HAMMOND, ASSISTANT COACH

THE PUCKING WRONG MAN PLAYLIST

"THE PROPHECY
Taylor Swift

FRAGILE
BLU EYES

HERO
Enrique Iglesias

MESSED UP AS ME
Keith Urban

LET IT HAPPEN
Gracie Abrams

MY HERO
Foo Fighters

GUILTY AS SIN?
Taylor Swift

PINK SKIES
Zach Bryan

SLOW BURN
Kacey Musgraves

FIX YOU
Coldplay

MATCHBOX
Ashley Kutcher

INFINITELY FALLING
Fly By Midnight

I'LL BE YOUR HOME
Phillip LaRue

NEVER ALONE
Garrett Kato, Elina

NEVER LET ME GO
Florence + The Machine

LOOK WHAT YOU MAKE ME DO
Taylor Swift

THE MACHINE–SPED UP
Reed Wonder, Aurora Olivas

MASTERMIND
Taylor Swift

SCAN CODE TO LISTEN ON SPOTIFY

TRIGGER WARNING

Dear readers,

Please be aware that this is a dark romance, and as such, contains content that could be triggering. Elements of this story are purely fantasy and should not be taken as acceptable behavior in real life.

Our love interest is possessive, obsessive, and the perfect shade of red for all you red flag renegades out there. There is absolutely no shade of pink involved when it comes to what Camden James will do to get his girl.

Themes include ice hockey, stalking—by the MC and the bad guy—and manipulation, somnophilia, attempted kidnapping, dark obsessive themes, sexual scenes, alcohol and prescription drug addiction, cynophobia, dog attacks, reference to prior underage sexual abuse, blackmail, death, gore, psychological, physical, and domestic abuse—note from the love interest—and references to previous sexual assault references—not involving the love interest. There are no harems, cheating, or sharing involved. Camden James only has eyes for her.

Prepare to enter the world of the Dallas Knights . . . you've been warned.

THE PUCKING WRONG MAN

"I HAVE 3,000 PENALTY MINUTES. I DON'T NEED PEOPLE DICTATING ME HOW TO DO MY JOB."

—Tie Domi

···

Bunnies, better grab some tissues, because rumor is, our hottest hometown hero is off the market. #weneedahero #icanbeyourherobaby Knights star defender @camden_james1 supposedly has a new roommate, and they don't have separate bedrooms if you catch out meaning... #LoveOnIce James was seen around town with a local ballerina, and she apparently is pirouetting off with his heart. Looks like those dreams of being rescued by our ice knight in shining armor are skating away... #HeroNoMore #PuckBunnyBlues

5:49 PM · Jul 19, 2024

2.5K Retweets **834** Quote Tweets **15.7K** Likes

PROLOGUE

ANASTASIA

Ten Years Old

"You were fantastic today, Ana. You've almost got it down perfect," Miss Gallagher murmured. I beamed under her praise. She rarely gave it, but when she did, it was *magical*. "Have you thought about the extra class I suggested? A contemporary class would be very helpful in getting you to the next step."

I ducked my head, not wanting to look her in the eyes. I *had* thought about it.

A lot.

I wanted it so badly.

But I was already on scholarship here. I was afraid to ask if they could cover a new class too. The girls already made fun of me enough. The kids in the contemporary class were older . . . they would probably be even more mean about it.

"Ana," Miss Gallagher said knowingly, her finger tapping on my chin so I had to look at her . . . she hated when I wouldn't.

"Yes?" I asked, ignoring the shakiness in my voice. She always said there was no crying in dance.

But I was really close to crying right now.

"If you need something, you just need to ask. This dance studio is very invested in you. We *want* you to succeed."

"Yes, ma'am." I sniffed, wiping at my eyes frantically because I couldn't stop my tears.

There was a pause, and then her voice lowered even more. "Is everything alright at home?"

I stiffened.

Why did adults always ask this question, like I could actually tell them the truth?

Dad would get so mad if he knew I was even talking to her.

And when he got mad—really, really bad things happened.

I held in my shiver and tried my best to keep my face blank.

She was just trying to help. They all were.

But there was no one that could help me. I just had to be okay until I was grown up.

Or at least that's what I told myself.

"Everything's fine," I said, my tone suspiciously high and squeaky. I tried to put on the dance smile that they'd taught me in my first class.

"Happiness needs to beam out of your eyeballs," Miss Franca had told us that day.

Staring up at Miss Gallagher with all the fake happiness I could muster . . . I wasn't sure she was falling for it.

Miss Gallagher sighed like I'd disappointed her and patted my shoulder. "Someday, you will trust me, ma chérie," she said before she glided away, her posture elegant and confident, and everything I wanted to be.

I wanted to run after her and tell her all about Dad and how mean he'd gotten the last few years since Mom left. I wanted to tell her how alone and scared and *hungry* I was all the time.

But the last time I'd told someone, he'd hit me so hard, my head cracked open. I still got headaches all the time from it.

Nope. I wanted to sprint after her, throw my arms around her waist and beg her not to let me go home.

But I didn't let myself.

I grabbed my bag, and I walked out of the dance studio, dread building in my stomach with every step I took.

Trudging to the bus stop, I did my best to keep the happiness with me. Dancing was the only time I felt happy. The only time I felt like everything was going to be okay. My life didn't have to turn out horrible just because *now* was really hard.

The sun dipped low on the horizon, casting long shadows across the cracked pavement as I stared at the concrete, trying not to catch anyone's attention. The regulars who caught this bus were used to seeing a ten-year-old riding by herself by now. But the new riders never were.

I nodded at the driver, a sweaty man with hair coming out of his squished-up nose and pit stains under his arms that went halfway down his shirt. He didn't nod back, he just made sure I swiped my bus card before his gaze moved to the person climbing on behind me.

The bus was like a giant metal oven, baking us in the heat of the dying sun. But instead of cookies, it smelled like a mix of old socks and moldy cheese. Every time someone opened a window, it just seemed to make things worse, bringing in a blast of hot air and even more funky smells.

I tried to ignore it, pressing my face against the cool glass and watching the world pass by in a blur of colors.

I should have gotten used to the stench by now—I probably didn't smell very good either after hours of dancing. I usually would shower at the studio, but with Miss Gallagher stopping me, she'd taken the extra time I had before I needed to get to the bus.

Dad was usually passed out or at a bar. But if he was awake and I happened to be late . . .

That would be really bad.

I fingered the shiny, pink burn mark on my arm where he'd held my arm to the gas stove six months ago.

I had only been a few minutes late that day . . .

Staring out the window, I took in the "nice" part of town as we passed through. There was a line in this city, invisible but noticeable as soon as you crossed it.

The rich and the poor side.

Unfortunately for me, I didn't live in just the poor side. I lived in the so poor everyone forgot about you side, where they didn't even bother to send buses because very few people—if any—were ever leaving there. Thus, the bus stop was a mile from my house.

I watched as the shiny buildings and storefronts, the manicured lawns and towering mansions disappeared . . . making way for crumbling buildings and litter-strewn streets.

It was symbolic of what it felt like to go from my dance classes to home.

Glittering, gleaming dance studios to boarded-up windows and struggle.

I didn't understand how in the same world, there were people that had so much . . . and others that had so little.

The bus shuddered to a stop, the squeak of the breaks making me wince as it assaulted my ear drums. I threw out a "see you," to the driver, knowing he wouldn't say anything back.

But sometimes I liked to pretend that we were friends.

"Ana!" a familiar voice called, and I sighed before straightening my face and turning around.

Michael Carver gave me the creeps. That was the only way to describe it.

And that was saying something with where I lived, where down-on-their-luck men seemed to haunt every street corner.

Maybe it was how he looked.

So perfect. So clean. Not a hair on his head out of place.

No one else looked like that around here, like they had stepped out of a *Brady Bunch* episode.

Even in my dance outfit I didn't look like that.

Maybe it was the fact that he was a sophomore at the local high school, and I'd heard rumors already in middle school about how he was selling drugs.

Or maybe it was the fact that he always seemed to be lurking around, popping up every time I was outside my house, even though I knew he lived nowhere near here.

That was probably it.

"Hi, Michael," I said politely. "I don't have time to talk today. I need to get home."

He smirked and made a disgusting show of dragging his gaze up and down my body, like I wasn't just a kid.

I was at the age where I was definitely noticing boys, even if I was staying far away from them.

But my boobs hadn't even come in yet. I didn't eat enough to have the curves that boys were already talking about at school.

The way he stared at me . . .

Creepy.

It didn't help that his eye color was what I would describe as "watery blue." For some reason that color had always given me the shivers. I'd seen a character described like that in a book once and it had always stuck with me. Michael's eyes looked empty . . . that was the word. Like he was wearing a mask and there wasn't actually anything inside of him.

A shiver crept up my back and I held it in.

"I don't know why you try so hard to not be friends with me, Ana. I could really help you out." He brushed some invisible hair from his face, trying for a hot guy move that was never going to work for him—at least not in my eyes.

"Anastasia," I said stiffly.

"What?"

"Anastasia. My name's Anastasia."

He snorted. "I've heard other people call you *Ana* before."

I opened my mouth to answer—to tell him that the only people who called me that were people I liked—or at least tolerated.

Snapping my lips closed, I didn't say anything. But somehow the words still hovered in the air between us, and the smile he'd been sporting transformed into a dark frown.

"Okay, well, nice to talk to you," I said instead, turning to step away. I really did need to get home. And it said something about how uneasy Michael made me feel that I would rather be at home than talking to *him*.

It said a lot actually.

His hand shot out and grabbed my arm.

Tightly.

"Ouch," I growled, trying to pull away.

"*Ana*," he answered, emphasizing the nickname in a calm voice that somehow made me flinch. "You just need to accept that we're going to be friends. And that it *will* be a good thing for you."

"Uh huh," I answered, finally succeeding in pulling my arm away. I could feel the lingering pressure of his grip as I backed up, not taking my eyes off him.

He didn't lunge after me or do anything else, though.

Michael did something scarier instead.

He smiled.

There were a whole bunch of promises in that smile that I wanted nothing to do with.

As soon as he turned, I sped toward home, thinking that someday I wasn't going to run from anything that scared me.

But that *someday* was definitely not today.

I dragged my tired feet up the overgrown gravel drive. It was a tangled mess of weeds and thorns and neglect.

Home sweet home.

Well, it was more of a shack really, with its sagging roof, but it kept the rain out.

Sometimes.

Somehow it looked even more run-down than it did this morning when I left. The paint peeled in long, jagged strips, revealing the decaying wood beneath. The windows were smudged with grime.

I pushed open the creaking front door, its hinges groaning in protest. I winced, wishing there was a quieter way to get in the house. It was best for me to stay as unnoticed as possible.

One step inside, and the familiar stench of alcohol hit me like a punch to the gut. I turned the corner and screeched to a halt. Dad was slumped in the armchair, the one that was so faded, and worn, and dirty, you couldn't tell what color it used to be.

He wasn't snoring yet—which wasn't good. He snored when he was in a really deep sleep. I had a test to study for, for tomorrow's history class, and I didn't want him waking up and messing that all up.

I watched him for a moment, making sure he wasn't going to jump up when I passed. His skin was a ruddy red color beneath a tangled mass of unkempt, greasy hair. His clothes were stained and wrinkled from days spent in a drunken stupor.

Even in sleep, his face was contorted with anger and bitterness, the lines etched deeply into his brows like a road map of the demons that haunted him.

As I watched him, fear and loathing curled in my stomach.

There were bottles all over the floor glinting in the dim light. I winced when I saw them because they weren't there this morning when I left, and that meant he'd spent money we didn't have. I would have my free lunch at school tomorrow, but it would make it really hard for me to get through the day. I danced for so many hours that I burned a lot of calories. A slice of plasticky pizza and a carton of milk just didn't do it.

I didn't bother picking them up, I just focused on not tripping on them.

Sometimes I thought about what would happen if he just *died.* If one day he drank so much, he never woke.

And then I felt bad, because I knew that Mom leaving him really messed him up.

But he'd told me he would never leave me that day she'd disappeared.

He'd lied.

He'd left me every day. With every drop he drank. With every step he took from who he'd been to who he was now.

So it felt like it was okay that sometimes it was hard for me to keep my promises to him too.

My stomach grumbled as I reached the hallway, and I bit my lip as I stared into the kitchen.

Maybe . . .

I tiptoed into the room, noting the dirty dishes in the sink . . . and the pizza box.

Had he ordered us dinner for once?

I scrambled toward the box like someone possessed . . . I hadn't had Papa Johns in forever.

Flipping open the lid, I could have cried.

It was all gone. Every last piece.

Forgetting I was supposed to be quiet, I threw open the fridge door, staring at the one expired bottle of mustard on the shelf, a strange numbness flooding my limbs.

I'd eaten nothing but school lunches and stale bread for weeks . . . and he'd ordered a pizza . . . and eaten the entire thing.

A tear slipped down my cheek, and I let it drip to the ground.

My stomach grumbled again, and I rubbed at it, grabbing the cup I kept clean in the cabinet and filling it to the brim with water. If I drank enough water, sometimes my stomach wouldn't hurt as bad.

I would just have to try and charm the lunch ladies out of some extra food tomorrow to help me get through the day.

Making it to my room without waking him, I collapsed on my bed, trying not to wince as a spring dug into my back. I stared up at the ceiling, at the water stains and the cracks that I'd memorized.

Someday I'd be the greatest ballerina the world had ever seen. I would dance on the stage with the New York Ballet and the entire audience would give me a standing ovation.

Everyone would know my name.

They'd throw flowers on the stage and they would love me.

I would *make* them love me.

A crashing sound echoed from the living room, and I scrambled up from the bed, preparing myself . . . just in case.

Tiptoeing to the door, I carefully placed my ear on the worn wood, listening to what Dad could be doing out there.

There was nothing but silence.

Maybe he'd just had one of his fits he sometimes got, when he thrashed in his sleep and made a mess, but somehow stayed asleep.

Another minute of listening, and I decided that must have been it, and I started to study.

After I'd finished, I got into bed, pulling up my threadbare comforter, my eyes growing heavy almost the second my head touched my pillow—one good thing about dancing for hours, no matter what, it was easy to fall asleep.

Tomorrow would be a new day . . .

My door slammed open and crashed against the wall with a bang that had me gasping for breath as I was dragged from sleep.

I blinked, trying to get my bearings, and when I did, I was immediately awake.

And terrified.

Dad was there, his body swaying in place as he stood in the doorway.

I didn't say anything. I didn't move. Like he was a predator that maybe couldn't see me if I didn't move at all.

"Demon," he growled suddenly.

I started shaking, because sometimes when he drank a lot, he started imagining things that didn't really happen, and that was always when the worst things *had* happened.

Slowly raising my hands in front of me, I tried to calm myself and think.

"Dad, you should go back to your chair. Everything's alright," I began, keeping my voice as soothing as possible.

"Demon!" he raged, and he lunged toward the bed, his movements clumsy and erratic, the rest of his words slurred and incomprehensible.

"Dad! No!" I shrieked, trying to escape the covers that were tangled around my legs.

He grabbed my wrist and pulled me toward him, his breath hot and putrid against my face.

"I won't let you get me," he spit, throwing me to the ground.

Dad fisted my hair, his knee digging into my neck. I coughed and thrashed under him, struggling to breathe.

"Dirty little devil. Demon!" he screamed, spittle showering my face with every word.

"Pl . . . ease," I tried to choke out.

His foot connected with my leg with a sickening crack. Pain exploded through me like fireworks, and I crumpled to the ground, clutching my shattered limb as tears blurred my vision.

I blinked up at the ceiling as shock settled over my skin. He stood over me and leaned down, his breath reeking of whiskey as he glared down at me in disgust.

"You're a pretty thief," he murmured as he squatted down.

And another tear slid down my cheek, because suddenly he didn't sound nearly as drunk as he had before.

His palm caressed my face, and my head slid to the side, vomit launching out of my mouth because everything was too much. The pain, the nausea from the pain, *everything*.

He staggered away, leaving me writhing on the floor, flayed open and broken.

Eventually, I glanced down at my leg, my breath scattering as I saw that there was a bone popping out of my skin.

My head dropped back to the floor as blood seeped out around me.

It was so cold.

I didn't want to die.

I wanted to live.

I wanted to dance . . .

CHAPTER 1

ANASTASIA

I opened my eyes slowly, the harsh lights of the hospital room blinding me for a moment before my vision cleared.

Where was I?

The room swam, and I winced, quickly closing my eyes again and taking a deep breath.

My entire body hurt.

Okay, I could do this, I told myself, opening my eyes just a crack this time so I could get used to the light.

Finally able to open my eyes wide enough, my gaze immediately fell on my leg . . . which was encased in a giant cast from my ankle to my thigh.

What had happened?

It took a moment, but then it all came back, my own personal horror story playing out in a macabre technicolor in my head. My father lunging at me, the sharp crack in my leg, and pain like I'd never experienced before.

My chest tightened as I stared at the cast, my breath coming in shallow gasps as an icy hand seemed to clutch at my heart.

Was I ever going to be able to dance again?

The edges of my vision were darkening, a panic attack fully setting in. And then a hand landed gently on my arm, causing me to jump in surprise. I turned my head to see . . . Michael? He was standing next to the bed, his too-perfect smile immediately making bile clog my throat. What was he doing here?

The sight of him on top of everything else made me want to scream, but all I could manage was a strangled gasp.

"Hey, hey, it's okay," he said, his voice unnervingly calm. "You're going to be alright, Ana."

I shook my head frantically, tears stinging my eyes as I tried to make sense of what was happening. Michael was the *last* person I wanted to see. What was going on?

"Why are you here?" I managed to choke out, my voice barely above a whisper.

But Michael just smiled that same too many teeth—psychopath smile, his eyes shining with a glint that made me want to jump off the bed and run down the hallway as fast as I could . . . to anywhere but here. "You've been injured badly. I just wanted to be here for you," he answered, his voice almost . . . mocking, like he knew something I didn't. "I didn't want you to be alone."

I still didn't understand what was going on. How had I gotten to the hospital? Where was my dad? Why would Michael, of all people, be here?

He reached down as I watched . . . and pushed my foot to the side.

I screamed.

It was like I was being torn apart, the pain radiating up my leg, through every fiber of my being.

The door burst open, and a team of doctors rushed in, their voices a blur of urgency as they worked to calm me down. I felt hands on my shoulders, holding me in place as they injected something into my IV, the world around me growing hazy and distant.

I tried to tell them what he'd done, but I couldn't form words around the fog of pain and medication. Michael's face hovered above me, his eyes filled with *terrifying* satisfaction. Darkness closed in, and I couldn't help but wonder if one terrible thing had become something far worse.

"Goodnight, little bunny," he whispered as I lost consciousness.

Things hadn't improved when I woke up, although the pain was at least tolerable enough that I'd stopped screaming.

Michael was still there, hovering close to me. Most of the time his hand was on my shoulder in what would have looked like a comforting gesture to anyone else—but to me was definitely a threat. I'd spent the last year shying away from his touch, only for him to touch me constantly for the past hour.

Nurses had been in and out, but none of them had caught my desperate looks. I was going to have to say something—but would anyone believe me?

A sharp rap on the door jolted me in the bed, the sound echoing through the sterile hospital room like a gunshot. The medicine they'd given me still had me off my game, and I jumped at any sudden sound or movement.

The door swung open without me saying they could come in, revealing two imposing figures in police uniforms and a stern-looking woman in a stiff skirt suit. Their presence immediately filled the room with an oppressive weight, and I shrunk back instinctively, my eyes wide with apprehension as they entered. A knot of dread coiled in my stomach as I watched them.

"Hello there, Anastasia," the taller officer greeted me with a somber nod, his voice surprisingly gentle despite his imposing figure. "I'm Officer Rodriguez, and this is Officer Thompson. We're here to talk to you."

The woman in the skirt suit offered a strained smile as she stepped forward next. "And I'm Ms. Jenkins, your caseworker. How are you feeling, dear?" She was trying to sound kind, but she wasn't very good at it. I also hadn't missed how she had called herself *my* caseworker. What was that going to mean for me?

I swallowed hard, my throat suddenly dry as I struggled to find my voice. "Everything hurts," I mumbled, my gaze flickering nervously between the three of them. "What's going on?"

Officer Rodriguez exchanged a glance with Officer Thompson before he spoke again. "Do you remember what happened to you?" he asked, his warm brown eyes filled with sympathy.

I shrunk further into the bed, scared to answer them, because I'd heard horror stories at school of what happened to kids when they were taken from their parents.

Worse things than what I had experienced with my dad.

"Anastasia, it's okay," Officer Rodriguez soothed.

"My dad was drunk. He thought I was someone else and he—he hurt me," I finally whispered, my gaze focusing on my leg. No one had explained yet how bad the injury was. I needed to know.

"Thank you for being brave and telling us. He's been arrested, but we needed to hear you say that so we can keep him from ever hurting you again," the other officer said, his voice gravelly and authoritative. "What he did, Anastasia, he won't be getting out of prison anytime soon."

Even at my age, I obviously knew you couldn't just hurt your kids as bad as my father had hurt me without consequences. But it still felt as though the ground had been ripped from beneath me, leaving me flailing in uncertainty. "What does that mean for me?" I managed to choke out, my voice barely above a whisper.

The officers exchanged a look. "That's where I come in," Ms. Jenkins interjected, her tone falsely cheerful as she stepped forward. "You'll be staying with the Carvers for the time being. You won't even have to switch schools! They're a *lovely* family, and I'm sure you'll be very comfortable there."

"What?" I gasped as Michael's fingers dug into me. I glanced up at him, flinching at the smirk playing on his lips. My stomach started to hurt as reality set in.

I froze, terror seeping under my skin, and Michael's fingers tightened, but I shook my shoulder, and he finally let go, probably wanting to play nice in front of these people.

The caseworker's friendly mask dropped when she saw the expression on my face. "Anastasia!" she said, sounding appalled. "I don't think you understand the severity of the situation. You should be over the moon that we don't have to put you in the system! The Carvers are absolute angels for taking you in. We're just lucky that they are already on the approved state list to be foster parents. There are a million children who would give anything to have such a generous offer. You should be *grateful*!" Shaking her head, her face changed back into a picture-perfect look of concern.

"The medicine and your injuries are obviously confusing you. We should let you get some rest, and we can discuss this later, when you're not in so much pain." Sighing as if she was trying to pray for patience to deal with me, she gestured to the officers. "Let's let her rest. The poor dear needs time to heal."

The officers nodded.

"We'll have some more questions to ask later," Officer Rodriguez told me. I nodded numbly, and then he and his partner left the room.

"Michael, dear. Why don't we go talk to your parents and leave Anastasia to get some rest," Ms. Jenkins simpered. She was obviously already under Michael's gross spell, showing she was a terrible judge of character—a trait probably needed for a caseworker.

"Of course." Michael smirked, giving my shoulder a squeeze for good measure before he headed for the door. "I'll see you later, *sis*." He threw the words over his shoulder, his smile reminding me of the Joker's.

And then I was alone. Nothing but numb silence surrounding me.

A tear slipped down my cheek, and I angrily brushed it away.

But it was a useless effort, because there were a million more tears that came after that.

Another knock sounded on the door, this one soft and non threatening.

"Come in," I called in a hoarse voice, rubbing at my face frantically just in case it was the caseworker . . . or Michael. I didn't want either of them to see me cry.

But it wasn't them. Thankfully. Instead, a kind-looking woman with a neat bun and a white coat slowly opened the door and popped her head in. Unlike with the caseworker, the doctor's concerned look seemed genuine. I wasn't sure how I could even know that—it was probably wishful thinking. But the soft smile she was giving me still somehow made me feel calmer.

"Hello, Anastasia," she greeted me softly. "May I sit?"

I blinked at her question, and then nodded numbly, watching as she pulled a chair up to my hospital bed.

"I'm Dr. Patel. I'm in charge of the team helping you while you're with us."

I returned her smile weakly, feeling a sense of relief wash over me at her calming presence. "Hi, Dr. Patel," I replied, my voice barely above a whisper.

She settled into the chair beside me, her expression gentle. "May I?" she asked again, nodding her head at the IV in my arm. I liked that she kept asking my permission, even if it was just a formality.

I nodded, and she carefully checked where it was protruding from my arm before sitting back in her chair.

"I'm afraid you suffered a concussion from the . . . incident," she said, her words careful. "You also have a bruised spleen, which is why you're feeling so sore."

I nodded like I understood what all that meant. There was only one real injury I was concerned about, though. "And my leg?" I asked, my voice trembling as I stared at the cast.

"Your leg," she began, her voice softening even further, "it's broken in two places. You had two surgeries while you were out—" My head jerked up at that news. She held up a hand like that would calm me down. "We had to set the bones back in place. They had broken through the skin, and it was an emergency situation."

I was feeling lightheaded at that news. I remembered the snap and the sharp pain . . . and then the numbness that had spread through my limbs.

"The good news," Dr. Patel continued, "is that you shouldn't need to have any more surgeries unless the hardware gives you trouble."

I nodded slowly, my mind reeling as I tried to process everything she was telling me. A concussion, a bruised spleen, a broken leg. That was—a lot.

"Dr. Patel, how long do you think it will take for my leg to heal?" I asked. "When can I get back to my dance classes?"

Her brow furrowed slightly, and she hesitated before answering, her expression somber. "Well, Anastasia, injuries like yours are quite serious," she began carefully. "Usually, people with these kinds of injuries are lucky if all that's left when it heals is a limp."

My heart dropped, and it was suddenly hard to breathe.

"I can't dance anymore?" My voice was high-pitched and squeaky, and the lightheadedness was getting worse. This wasn't happening. I was going to wake up and this was all going to be nothing but a bad dream. I had to dance. I had to. I was either dreaming or she was lying.

I wanted to scream or cry or rage because I would be alright with anything else being taken away from me.

Anything but losing the ability to dance.

I was faintly aware of Dr. Patel's hand on my arm. "Anastasia, *usually* doesn't mean *always*," she said gently, her voice infused with reassurance. "And things could be different for you, if you follow directions and work hard at physical therapy and anything else we ask you to do." She paused. "You also have youth on your side. Things could end up better than if this injury had happened later on."

I nodded, her words giving me a spark of hope that I was going to hold on to for dear life.

I would do whatever she said. I *was* going to dance again.

The door opened then, and Michael popped his head in, not bothering to knock. I tensed up.

"Can I help you, young man?" Dr. Patel asked.

"Just checking on Anastasia. My family will be taking care of her," he said, his face the epitome of concern.

Dr. Patel clapped her hands together. "Oh, that's wonderful. I'm so glad she's going to have a support system."

That numbness, the one I'd experienced as I lay on the floor of my room, it was spreading through me again.

But this time, I embraced it.

I stayed numb when they discharged me a week later, wheeling me out to Michael's smiling parents who shared the same watery-eyed cold stare as their son.

I stayed numb when they locked me in my new room.

I stayed numb when they made me ask permission for any food I wanted to eat in their home.

I stayed numb when I had two more surgeries on my leg, and an infection set in that made me sick for weeks.

But I gritted my teeth when I took my first step in physical therapy, and it hurt so bad I felt like I might die.

I forced myself to walk, and then to walk even farther, and then to run.

And when it was finally time, I forced myself . . . to dance.

CHAPTER 2

CAMDEN

"Fucking hell, Rookie. If you miss another pass, I'm going to have Camden fuck your grandma," Ari yelled as Logan skated after the puck.

I scoffed, tracking the puck as Detroit's defensemen sent it across center ice.

"Why did I get volunteered for the job?" I griped.

"Logan can't fuck his own grandma, James. And you're the only one of us currently unattached."

I huffed right before I slammed one of Detroit's forwards into the boards, the sound of his answering groan music to my ears.

"You're also the only one on the team who's age appropriate for my grandma," Logan helpfully added, because he never missed a chance to point out that I was almost ten years older than him.

Asshole.

At least he hadn't called me "Grandpappy" today. That was an improvement.

"Rookie, when you score more goals, you can talk shit," Ari commented as Logan lined up for a face-off.

The whistle blew and Logan wrestled the puck away and tried to pass it to Lincoln . . . only for it to get stolen and sent back toward our goal.

Typical for the game, actually.

It was the final period and we were down by one against Detroit.

Embarrassing really, since Detroit was one of the worst teams in the league.

We were the fucking Knights. We didn't lose to teams like Detroit.

Or at least we weren't supposed to.

"Hey, ref," Ari called as the whistle blew for a penalty . . . again. "Does your wife know you're screwing us?"

That got a small smirk out of the ref, which wasn't helpful since he still sent Logan to the penalty box.

We were now playing with one man down. Perfect.

Coach's booming voice echoed across the ice, cutting through the chaos of the game. "New line! New line!" he bellowed, his words ringing out loud and clear above the roar of the crowd. Lincoln shook his head and skated off the ice with Jones as Turner and Larsson took their place.

"Really, we're taking Lincoln out?" Walker snarled from the goal behind me as play started again.

"He can't hear you, Disney," Ari called as he chased down the puck. "No need to simp."

Walker groaned behind me as Ari sent the puck to Turner, who then started for the net.

"Fuck yes!" I screamed when Turner shot and it slid past Detroit's goalie. The buzzer blared and the goal light went off as the crowd screamed like we'd won instead of just tied.

Ari and I jumped on Turner, celebrating his goal, and then Coach was yelling for us to get on the bench as Peters and Fredericks jumped over the boards.

We sat down, watching as Detroit was immediately by our goal, firing shots at Walker. There wasn't a substitute for the best, and Ari and I were . . . the best.

"If that popcorn guy passes by Monroe one more time," Lincoln suddenly growled from my other side. "She doesn't need any fucking popcorn!"

"Huh?" I asked, not expecting popcorn to be in the conversation at this point of the game.

I did a fist pump as Walker made another save while Ari cursed at Fredericks to get his ass moving.

"He's fucking walking by again!"

"Linc, Golden Boy, Captain, oh, Captain. There's a terrifying bodyguard between my bestie and 'Popcorn Boy.' She's going to be fine," Ari muttered, shooting his own glance over to the girls, probably to make sure that "Popcorn Boy" wasn't actually a threat. His wife, Blake, was also sitting over there.

Tearing my gaze off the ice, I glanced into the first row where the "first ladies" of the team were sitting. Monroe, Blake, and Olivia seemed to be popcorn-free at the moment.

I couldn't imagine caring enough about a girl to worry if the concessions guy was within fifteen feet . . . but maybe it was a circle of trust thing.

The circle of trust was . . . well, I wasn't quite sure what it was, yet. It seemed to consist of my teammates Lincoln Daniels, Ari Lancaster, and Walker Davis—all stars on the team and in the league—and it seemed to be some kind of group for men scarily obsessed with their girls.

But again . . . I wasn't quite sure what it really was.

I only knew that I *kind of* wanted in.

"James and Lancaster, go!" Coach Porter yelled, and Ari and I jumped onto the ice immediately and launched ourselves into the fray.

I slammed Detroit's center into the boards, and Ari whooped loudly as he sent the puck out from behind the goal.

Walker crouched down and hit both sides of the goal, tracking the puck.

"Good fucking boy," Lincoln screamed as Walker blocked a shot.

I swear Walker preened.

He definitely had some kind of man crush on Lincoln Daniels.

I wasn't too big of a man to say that I *kind of* felt the same way.

Maybe it was another circle of trust thing.

The crowd booed when one of Detroit's defenders smacked his stick against Lincoln's legs—sending him sprawling to the ice. No whistle from the ref, of course.

Another thing that was typical for this game.

"Hey, ref, you pregnant? You've missed two periods," I sniped as I skated past.

"James, that was actually funny," Ari said as he skated past me.

I snorted and flipped him off.

"Quit your chirping. There's two fucking minutes left," one of the assistants screamed.

As if we didn't know that.

I swore every second on the game clock was ticking down in my fucking brain. Every inch of me very aware of every passing second.

I grunted as I was body slammed going for the puck. "Your mama hits harder than that," I gritted out as I gained control of the puck and passed it to Jones.

I may be thirty-one years old . . . but "Yo Mama" jokes definitely still did it for me.

Couldn't get tired of a classic.

The score was tied with a minute left, and we couldn't seem to find the back of the net.

At least they couldn't either—thanks to Walker's stellar performance between the pipes . . . and Lancaster and my supreme talent at defending, of course.

Ten seconds to go, desperation set in as we scrambled to make one final push. I skated furiously up the ice, the roar of the crowd ringing in my ears as I searched for an opening.

Out of the corner of my eye, I saw Lincoln streaking toward the net, his eyes locked on the puck. I sent a pass his way—perfect, of course—my heart pounding in my chest as I watched him line up the shot.

Lincoln reared back, the puck sailed through the air, and . . . GOAL!

The crowd erupted, so loud that I was sure I was going to need hearing aids in the near future. That would be helpful for the old man jokes.

"Fuck yes!" Ari screamed, tackle-hugging me before lunging toward Lincoln.

I raised a fist in the air and took it all in.

The crowd, the adrenaline singing through my veins, the sound of the buzzer, my teammates going nuts . . . .

There wasn't a better feeling in the world.

"Oh, hey . . . let me help you with that," I said, bending down to grab the water bottles strewn all over the bench that one of the assistant trainers was trying to pick up.

Her face went a dark shade of red, and she dropped the bottle she was holding, fumbling words trying to come out of her mouth.

Hmmm.

"Come on, *Hero*. Leave the poor girl alone," Ari huffed with a laugh, slapping me on the back.

I picked up one water bottle—for good measure—and handed it to her, pretending I didn't notice when she dropped it.

Again.

Somehow I'd picked up the nickname "Hero" in the group.

Did I have some sort of problem where I had a compulsive need to help women in distress?

Yes.

Was I ever going to admit that out loud?

No.

I'm sure a psychologist would have a field day with that particular personality trait. I had no intention of finding that out for sure, though.

"Please, tell me you didn't sleep with Becky," Logan said as he ambled up next to us as we walked down the tunnel.

"Becky?" I asked, trying to attach a face to that particular name.

Logan snorted. "The assistant trainer. The one who about orgasmed when you gave her a water bottle?"

Ohhh.

"Yeah. No. Haven't slept with *Becky*," I answered dryly. "But thanks for telling me her name."

Ari chuckled, and I shot him a glare . . . because we didn't need to encourage Logan.

My thoughts went back to the girl—Becky. She was cute . . . but definitely too young for me.

Also something I wasn't ever going to say out loud, especially in front of the rookie. He'd never let me live it down.

"Now he *will* sleep with her is what he's not saying," said Walker as he plopped down on the bench in front of his locker and wiped his face with a towel.

"I actually prefer to stay away from stage five clingers, Disney," I drawled as I bent over to undo my skates. "Fuck!"

Logan had snapped my ass with a fucking towel. Glaring at him, I thought about punching him or doing anything in retribution.

But I was too tired.

Next time, though.

"That mean we're going out tonight, my guy?" Jones asked from across the room as he unsnapped his chest protector.

I opened my mouth to make up an excuse, something I had been doing more often the last couple of months. What sounded much better than going out, was sleeping in my bed. Even my dick seemed to have been tired lately.

If that was a thing.

My phone buzzed, and I picked it up, groaning inwardly when I saw it was a reminder from Geraldine about our date tonight. Not that I didn't love Geraldine, but I was fucking exhausted. I couldn't cancel, though. I was going to have to suck it up.

"Sorry, Ky. I've got a hot date tonight," I told him as I finally got my skates off, keeping my ass away from Logan's reach as I did so.

"Oooooh," the whole locker room taunted, almost at once, like I was surrounded by junior high girls.

"Who's the lucky lady, Hero?" Logan called. "Some single mom you helped change her tire? A recent divorcee you helped jump her car? A lonely widow you gave an oil change?"

"Why, in all of these examples, is he helping these women with cars?" Lincoln asked, cocking his head. The wise one as usual.

"Yeah, I'm not really in the car business, Rookie. I got a mechanic for that," I told Logan seriously.

He flipped me off, evidently disappointed I wasn't hiding a mechanic kink from the group.

"My date tonight is actually seventy-five. Her gray hair is hot, but it's the dentures that really get me going," I joked.

The room went dead silent at that pronouncement.

"Well, I mean . . . " Logan stuttered.

"Whatever gets you going," Walker finished supportively.

My mouth dropped open, and I stared at the group in horror.

"I was kidding, you assholes. I told my neighbor I would take her to some dance thing. You guys actually thought I was taking a grandmother on a date?!"

"Well you are nearing that age," said Logan, his face completely void of any suggestion he was joking. After a second, a sly smirk crept across his face, and I braced myself for what I knew was coming. "Grandpappy . . . "

"I'm not even the oldest on the fucking team," I griped.

The whole locker room burst into laughter, and this time, I was the one flipping them off with both hands.

Because apparently, I was a junior high girl, too.

Better than being a "grandpappy," I guess.

CHAPTER 3

ANASTASIA

I woke up, the sterile smell of disinfectant assaulting my senses as I blinked away the remnants of sleep. Staring up at the white ceiling, I listened to the sounds of people getting up for the morning.

Their waking sounds were much better than the sounds they made when they were sleeping.

A lot of them cried out in their sleep. Their tragic days creeping into their nights like sinister centipedes walking through their brains.

Crying was a demonic lullaby at this point. Pain and despair my constant bed companions.

I hated that their nightmares had become my own.

I had enough of my own to deal with, thank you very much.

Yawning, I stretched my arms above my head, trying to get the kink out of my neck and wake up. I glanced at the people milling around the room, most of them looking as out of it as I probably did in the mornings.

There was a strict curfew to get in the shelter, and a specific time that you had to be up for the day and out of here.

I was used to it.

But someday, when I figured out my life, I was going to sleep in. Maybe all day.

Just because I could.

I rolled over on the thin mattress, the springs creaking beneath me.

Someday I was also going to have a bed that I actually wanted to spend all day in.

With a heavy sigh, I swung my legs over the side of the cot, wincing as the familiar ache shot through my leg. It was always worse in the morning, the stiffness and pain a cruel reminder of the past that I could never escape . . . because it was always with me.

Turned out when your father broke your fibula and your femur in multiple places, and you didn't get to the hospital for nearly twenty-four hours—and you almost died . . . your injury didn't heal right.

And you got to be in pain . . . forever.

With a deep breath, I pushed myself up onto my feet, bracing myself against the edge of the cot as I stretched. Each movement was slow and deliberate and *agonizing*.

My leg protested with every stretch, a sharp pang of pain shooting up from my ankle to my thigh. I cursed under my breath—I hadn't had a chance to ice last night after dance like I needed to. Some days, if class ran long and I didn't finish mopping in time, it was hard to get back in time for curfew, so I had to skip.

That seemed to be the theme of my life, never enough time, never enough energy at the end of the day to take care of myself.

As I finished stretching, I gritted my teeth and forced myself to stand upright, ignoring the throbbing ache. There was work to be done, rehearsals to attend, money to save up . . . I couldn't afford for a *little* pain to hold me back.

I bent over to touch my toes . . .

Okay, it was actually a lot of pain.

I grabbed my bag from underneath my bed, checking to make sure that none of my belongings had disappeared during the night.

If you got caught stealing, you were immediately banned from coming back. But that didn't mean it didn't happen.

We were all desperate here.

Desperate to survive. Desperate to exist.

Desperate.

Someday I was going to have a place to keep all my stuff, too. Here, everything I owned had to be packed up every day and taken with me, nothing left behind.

Someday I'd have a room, a closet, and a place for all my things.

Someday.

That was the word that kept me going. And usually, dreaming about the future helped.

But other times, like this morning, when my leg felt so fucked-up I wasn't sure how I was going to walk, let alone do a freaking plié, I wondered if my "someday" would actually ever be a reality.

I made my way to the communal bathroom, passing by some of the other regulars, their tired eyes and hollow cheeks a reflection of their own struggles. We exchanged nods of recognition, but no words were spoken. Besides the staff, no one here bothered to talk to me. It was lonely, but I got it. When you were just trying to get by, it seemed like too much to ask to get to know someone.

What if they wanted to talk to you? What if they told you their troubles? No one in this room could take on any one else's burdens. They had too many of their own.

Like the main room, the bathroom was clean, but the tiles were worn and cracked.

I'd take clean and old over dirty and new any day, though.

The Carvers' opinions on "gratefulness" splashed through my mind like spoiled wine.

I was sure they'd approve of that line of thinking.

Splashing some water on my face, I tried to wash away the lingering remnants of sleep, but it was no use.

Because the soundtrack of misery I heard every night . . . I was a part of it. And even now, the memories of last night's nightmares clung to me like a second skin, refusing to let go.

Hopefully I hadn't screamed too loud. There had been a mom with her two little kids in the cots next to me last night.

Staring into the mirror, I sighed, feeling so fucking resigned. Was my life going to be this terrible forever?

That attitude isn't going to get you anywhere, Anastasia, I swore at myself fiercely.

With grim determination, I slung my bag over my shoulder and hobbled out of the bathroom, steeling myself for another day of struggle.

I got up to the front desk and my first, and perhaps only, smile of the day slid across my lips.

"Ana, girl, how are you this fine morning?" Montana said warmly, smiling at me like she always did—like she was happy to see me—like I wasn't a burden.

I'd been coming here for the last three years, and she had worked here the entire time. She was *always* in a good mood. She was *always* smiling.

Maybe one day I'd ask her how she managed to do it in the face of so much misery.

"Great," I said, my voice almost sounding cheerful . . . it was kind of hard to be dreary in the face of such positivity.

Someday I was going to be like Montana for someone, a burst of sunshine on someone's cloudy day.

There was that word again.

"I'm having a lot of luck this morning. It was the craziest thing, but Sonic gave me an extra breakfast burrito when I stopped through the drive-thru. I thought maybe you would want it . . . " she said innocently, her dark red corkscrew curls bobbing around her head like they were waving at me or something.

"Bless you," I gasped, a little embarrassed about the squeal in my voice right then.

This was a familiar routine for us. She would pretend that she'd been given extra at some place and give it to me. And I should have felt guiltier about greedily taking it *every* time considering there was no way they paid her very much for working here.

But as I'd said before . . . I was desperate.

"You are a literal angel, Montana Thatcher," I murmured, carefully taking it from her like it was actually gold. I would have to eat it slowly, because I'd only had a piece of bread and some peanut butter yesterday . . . which I'd burnt off in about ten minutes of class.

My stomach was to the point of cramping, and eating it too fast might make me throw up.

On the positive side, no matter how much my stomach ached . . . my leg pain always hurt worse.

"Have a good day, sweetheart," she said, her brown eyes crinkling at the edges as she gave me another full-faced grin. "I have a feeling today's going to be a lucky day for you."

"I'm performing tonight," I admitted shyly, not sure why I was saying anything, but wanting to tell someone . . . anyone . . . about the fact that I'd gotten a leading role again after years of being relegated to the background after my injury.

"Sonic must have known," she said with a wink, and I did my best not to cry.

You weren't supposed to cry about Sonic.

"Must have," I told her in a surprisingly steady voice before I slipped out the door, eagerly tearing open the wrapper and biting into the burrito with a groan.

It was still freaking hot.

I savored every bite the entire walk to the bus stop. The resulting stomachache was completely worth it.

Stepping into the dance studio, I breathed in the familiar scent of sweat and new ballet shoes hanging heavy in the air. No matter what had happened to me, this place, this smell.

This.

It had always been my one constant.

The ache in my leg pulsed with each heartbeat, reminding me what the doctor had said a few months ago . . . but it was easier to ignore the pain when I was here.

We'd be practicing for our performances for the rest of the day, and pain wasn't going to hold me back.

I approached the barre to begin my warm-up, biting down on my lip as I sunk into the movements, all of them engrained so deeply into my consciousness, it was like they were engraved in my soul.

Except . . . fucking hell, my leg hurt.

The familiarity of the routine felt more like torture.

"Anastasia, mon dieu, what do you think you're doing?" Madame Leclerc barked, her accent thick with disdain as her eyes widened owlishly. "You look like a baby cow. What is that posture? Get lower!" She rapped her cane against my leg, and the only reason I didn't fall to the ground was because of how hard I was holding on to the bar. Her withering glare made me wish I had fallen, though—straight into a hole in the ground.

"I . . . I'm sorry, Madame," I stammered, sinking lower. She held my gaze, a challenge clearly there as I held my plié. The seconds seemed more like years as she watched me, daring me to break form. Just when I thought I was going to collapse, she *finally* huffed and went to destroy someone else.

I quickly straightened as soon as she turned away, a traitorous tear slipping down my cheek from the pain shooting through my leg.

"Ana, are you alright?" Clara whispered out of the side of her mouth as she moved next to me. "You're looking a little . . . pale."

"I'm fine," I said quickly. I liked Clara, as much as I liked anyone, really. But we had never been friends. Clara was so bright and shiny and perfect. From what I'd heard her talk about in passing conversations, she had a loving family, and an even more loving partner.

It didn't really seem like someone like that could be friends with someone like me.

A nobody.

"I have some Advil in my bag," Clara offered. "Or something stronger if you need it." She winked.

"Thanks, but I already took some—Advil, I mean," I added quickly. As much as I liked Clara, I didn't trust anyone. All I needed was for someone to tell Madame or one of the other instructors that I was coming to class *high.* I'd add that to the list of things that I hoped *someday* could happen—that I could trust someone.

"Okay," she said with a small frown. "But I'm here if you ever need anything."

I gave her what I hoped looked like a real smile, because I wasn't trying to hurt her feelings.

And then I got back to warming up.

Before my accident, the morning "company class" had been a chance to get ready for each day. It was when the entire group got together and worked on refining our skills outside of our preparation for a particular show. It was a time I could turn off my mind and slip into my rhythm.

It had been years since that was the case, but I still missed the feeling of having a set time of day I could let go of my worries.

Without that time, all I *had* were my worries.

Madame Leclerc's cold and disapproving gaze brushed over me again, and I quickly dipped down into a plié. The last thing I needed was for her to voice concerns on if I was ready to perform my piece or not.

"Shoulders back, chin up," she barked at us. "Plié, plié, demi plié and rise, demi and rise, demi into grand plié. Hold!"

My muscles trembled as I obeyed her instructions.

"Téndu en second to coupé, extend, extend!"

"Grand battement, higher, higher!"

Her eyes scanned the room for any signs of weakness, falling on me the most.

I gritted my teeth and forced myself to push through, each step sending shockwaves of agony up my leg.

After barre warm-ups, we moved across the floor and every leap felt like a death sentence, the strain and pressure of the movements threatening to tear me apart from the inside out.

But I couldn't stop. I wouldn't stop. I refused. Not when the stage called to me like every dream I'd ever possessed for this life, the only time I ever found release, the only time I ever felt . . . free.

The music swelled around me, and I lost myself in the dance, my body moving on autopilot despite the protests of my leg. I was teetering on the edge of oblivion, every movement a tightrope walk between ecstasy and agony.

There were hundreds of eyes on me, but I blocked them all out, soaking in the lights and the sounds and the passion that throbbed in my soul.

I danced with a desperation that bordered on madness. There was no greater high than the rush of adrenaline that flooded my veins when I stepped onto this stage. There was no pain that was too great, no sacrifice too large.

The only pure moment of bliss I would ever get in this life.

I danced.

I danced until my muscles screamed in protest, and my breath came out in ragged gasps. I danced until the world faded away and all that was left was the music and the movement.

As I leapt across the stage, I finally let myself soak in the audience's gaze.

On this stage . . . I wasn't poor. I wasn't homeless. I wasn't the daughter of a drunk father and a mother who never wanted her.

I was perfect up here in front of them, someone they admired. Someone they *respected.*

I was something more.

I soared through the air with reckless abandon.

I was alive. I felt nothing else but that.

And although the strain on my body might kill me someday.

I danced.

CHAPTER 4

CAMDEN

"Thanks for coming with me, sweetheart," Geraldine said as she smoothed the pink cotton of her sweater, a much more conservative outfit than she usually wore.

"Of course, Mimi. Nothing I like better than a date with my best girl," I answered, giving her a wink that brought a flush to her wrinkled cheeks.

"Such a charmer, you are. Such a nice boy. The girl that catches you will be a lucky woman, Camden."

I patted her hand, laughing inwardly that she always called me "boy." Geraldine had been my neighbor since I'd moved into my penthouse. Her husband had owned an exclusive jewelry store in Dallas that a bunch of celebrities had come from all over the world to visit. He had passed, but had left her loaded. She'd charmed me the first day I'd moved in when she'd brought me some homemade macarons. I'd since learned that macarons were the *only* cookie she approved of, as she thought they were the classiest cookie out there—and she considered herself very classy.

Worked well for my stomach.

"One day, Mimi," I told her before I glanced at her suspiciously. "You didn't bring any third wheels on our date, did you? Wouldn't want them getting jealous when I give you all my attention."

Geraldine and all her friends happened to be obsessed with matching me up since they couldn't marry me themselves—their words. And I couldn't even count all the times I'd gone over to help one of them with something and there'd been a smiley, dressed-up girl trying to get a ring out of me.

Geraldine's smile grew, and I became even more suspicious.

"Gerald—" I began.

She tsked, cutting me off. I'd always wondered what that word actually sounded like in real life, and there it was. "I would never surprise you like that."

"The fact that you actually sound legitimate when you say that is terrifying, Mimi."

She was giggling like a far younger girl as we got to our seats, and I helped her sit down.

Her blue eyes were bright with excitement as she stared around at the crowd and the empty stage. We were here for some kind of dance performance—I had no details beyond that. All I knew was that I was in for a boring night. I just couldn't seem to say no to Geraldine when she asked me for a favor.

Glancing down at the program someone at the door had handed me, I tried to find something that would get me excited.

There wasn't one word. Not one.

Taking a quick glance at Geraldine to make sure she was distracted, I pulled out my phone and sent off a text to the guys.

Me: SOS

Ari: Sexy Ombre Sausages.

Me: What? That's what you came up with?

Linc: I don't know him.

Ari: Look at this guy. Pretending he could think of something better.

Linc: I don't have to come up with something better. It already has a meaning.

Walker: It's an international distress signal.

Ari: The simp would say that.

Me: I think we missed the fact that I sent an international distress signal in the first place.

Linc: Are you dying?

Me: I hope that I would say something better than SOS if I was dying.

Ari: . . .

Linc: . . .

Walker: . . .

Me: I hate you all.

Ari: You're on a date with a seventy-five-year-old woman with dentures. How much trouble could you be in?

Walker: Good point.

Ari: That was very good simpage, Disney. I approve.

Walker: Why is it that any time I agree with anyone, I'm "simping"? You guys agree with me on things all the time.

Ari: Do we, though . . . do we?

Me: . . .

I pocketed the phone in disgust . . . and amusement that my teammates were not taking my distress call as seriously as they should have been. That last " . . . " I sent showed them, though.

At least I think it did. I wasn't quite sure yet what it meant. The meanings seemed to change in every conversation I found myself in with those guys.

The lights dimmed and Geraldine gripped my arm excitedly. Dang, she was freakishly strong for a seventy-five-year-old. "It's starting!"

I did a fist pump of excitement for her, and she snorted in amusement. "Cheeky boy."

The fact that I didn't give her an exasperated eye roll showed how "unboylike" I was, I decided.

Music began and some women dancing in pink tutus started leaping across the stage. Oh, alright. Ballet. She'd never dragged me to one of these before. Maybe it would be interesting.

"Aren't they wonderful?" Geraldine practically cooed.

I nodded exaggeratedly. The jumps and leaps were impressive.

But not quite doing it for me.

I really wished I had some snacks. I eyed Geraldine's purse. She probably had something in there.

I just couldn't trust it was from this decade.

The ballerinas finished, and I clapped along with the crowd absentmindedly, eyeing the program and checking my phone to see what time it was. These things couldn't go for hours, right? People could only dance for so long.

Or at least that was my hope.

A troop of cloggers came on the stage. At least, I thought they were cloggers. I wasn't exactly an expert on the art of clogging.

Was it called clogging?

I thought this was a ballet?

I glanced at the program.

Nope. Definitely called clogging.

I sent a text because this seemed noteworthy.

Me: Cloggers. That's how much trouble I could get into with a seventy-five-year-old woman.

Ari: Is that some kind of kinky sex position, Hero?

Scoffing, I threw my phone back in my pocket.

I sat through five more performances, jerking awake in the middle of a particularly enthralling jazz routine.

Or at least they were using a lot of jazz hands, so I figured it must have been a jazz routine.

Or did jazz routines have anything to do with jazz hands?

My hands itched to text the guys again. I could see Ari knowing about jazz hands and jazz routines—but Geraldine was side-eyeing me like she could see in my mind.

Something about silver-haired women with spectacles had the ability to make you feel like an errant schoolboy.

Focus, Camden. Don't let her down.

The performances continued and finally . . . it was the last one.

I'd dozed through the last few, but the energy in the room seemed to shift as the stage went dark, like the entire audience was holding its collective breath for what was about to happen.

I sat up in my seat, wondering what I was missing. Surely the cloggers weren't getting this reaction. No offense to anyone who clogged.

A single spotlight lit up the stage.

And I saw her.

Her.

A vision that I wasn't sure was real.

There were other dancers around her, but she might as well have been the only person left in the world.

Her body moved with a fluidity that defied description, commanding the attention of everyone in the audience as she danced. Each movement was a fucking revelation, changing my life and my focus with every step she took.

I tracked every sway of her hips, every twist of her torso. I memorized every step she took, knowing that it would consume my thoughts until maybe the end of time. The music swelled around her, every gesture imbued with emotion and intention. She danced with a fervor that seemed to consume her, her body a vessel for the raw passion that seemed to be flowing straight through her veins.

With each leap and turn, she cast a spell.

My life changed.

There was only before her, and after her.

And I was solidly in my "after her" era, a world I didn't recognize. My pulse was racing, my heart beating out of my chest. I was afraid to blink because I didn't want to miss a moment of her.

"She's good," Geraldine said, her hands clasped in front of her as she bobbed along with the music.

"Understatement of the century. She's incredible," I whispered.

I could feel her eyes boring into the side of my face, but I couldn't tear my gaze away from the sight in front of me.

The dancer's long, white-blonde hair cascaded down her back, swaying with each graceful movement as if it were a part of the dance itself. With each step, it felt like she was casting a net, taking me and everyone else in the audience captive.

Her movements seemed effortless. Every extension of her leg, every point of her toes, drew me in until I was forgetting basic things about myself . . . like how to breathe.

As a professional athlete, I'd thought I knew what passion looked like . . . certainly what it felt like.

But she was blowing my mind.

I'd never seen so much passion in a human being, it seemed as if she would die if she wasn't out on that stage. Instead of dancing to the music, the music was playing for her. Like it was made for her.

Or something like that.

I'd never been a particularly fancy-worded guy, *eloquent* I guess was the word? But I was sitting here waxing poetic about this girl like nobody's business.

She danced the same way I played hockey.

As if nothing else mattered to her in the world but that dance.

Except decades of me feeling a certain kind of way about hockey seemed to be fading as I sat in that seat. And I wasn't sure what to think about that.

She threw back her head, her entire face visible under the lights . . . and holy fuck.

I thought I knew what pretty was. Beautiful girls were throwing themselves at my feet constantly—I wasn't being a shitty prick when I said that. It was just facts. When you had a face and a body and a *job* like I did, it was kind of par for the course.

But fuck.

Her face.

She was a fucking masterpiece. I'd never seen anything in my life as beautiful . . . as perfect as . . .

Fuck! I glanced around, a strange heat clawing up my neck. Everyone was seeing her like this. Everyone was seeing what was mine.

I was strangely proud and outrageously upset about it at the same time.

What was happening to me?

She spun and the light danced across her features again. I'm sure I looked like a fool, my mouth open in complete shock and amazement and awe as I watched her expression jump from joy and sorrow to longing and desire.

I glanced down, realizing that I'd moved to the edge of my seat, my hands gripping the edge like I was trying to stop from lunging after her.

I thought I had cared about hockey more than anything, but staring at her, I wasn't sure that I'd ever cared about anything—not if this was what it looked like.

I was mesmerized by her every gesture, every flick of her wrist, every tilt of her head.

Maybe magic was real. Maybe she was a witch. Maybe I'd fucking died and this was heaven.

Whatever was happening, it was outrageous and terrifying and I was pretty sure . . .

I was in love.

Holy shit . . . I was in love?

"Are you alright, Camden?" Geraldine's voice cut through the haze. She'd noticed I was gripping the armrests like I was scared the chair was going to buck me off.

And fuck.

I was hard.

Not just hard, I had an erection that could cut glass. I was pretty sure that all the blood in my body was currently residing in my dick and that's why I couldn't think straight and I could pass out at any minute.

And I could feel Geraldine still eyeballing me.

I quickly tried to conjure up the image of Geraldine's teeth floating in a water glass, bits of spinach still stuck between the crevices.

But not even that was enough to talk the big man down since I still hadn't been able to unglue my eyes from my dancer.

What was I going to do?

I couldn't have an erection around Geraldine.

It was a life rule in general, you should never have an erection around someone named "Geraldine."

Especially the king of all erections. The record-breaking, baseball-bat-sized, swing-for-the-fences kind of erection.

Fuck, why was I using baseball references? I would blame *that* on the fact that my stepfather had called and left a voicemail for me earlier today. He'd always been a huge fan, trying to get me to play baseball instead of hockey all growing up.

Couldn't think about *him* either. The idea of my stepfather and the girl on stage—my girl—was enough to make me want to punch someone.

I had lost my fucking mind.

As the final notes of the music faded away and she took a bow, a deep sense of panic . . . of loss washed over me. I didn't want her to be done . . . to disappear from my view. I didn't know what to do with myself if I couldn't see her.

The curtains closed and I felt sick, as if I was coming down from some sort of high. Like the room had lost all color.

Like life had lost all meaning.

That may have been a little dramatic, but it was how I was feeling at the moment.

The feeling only worsened when I frantically glanced down at the program again and flipped through the pages. Past the cloggers, past the jazzers, right there to the finale. But then my stomach dropped when I realized . . . it didn't list her name.

"Well, I've lost fifty dollars," Geraldine muttered as the lights went on in the auditorium.

"What?" I asked, distracted as I glanced around the room, trying to figure out how to get backstage without actually jumping on top of the stage to get there.

"Maisy swore you'd fall for one of the ballet gals. But I had you pegged for the cloggers, personally."

That was enough to finally get my attention as I turned to stare at her incredulously.

She smirked and gave me two finger guns, and honestly, I couldn't have been more confused. "Gotcha! You think I'd ever bet on cloggers?" she huffed. "I knew it was ballet all the way."

"What are you talking about?"

"You think I didn't see you shooting those bedroom eyes at the stage like a damn fool that entire last dance?"

"I will never doubt you again," I said wryly.

I couldn't even argue with her or tell her she was imagining things. I was gone. Destroyed. Shows over. Lights out. She was the one.

"Well, what are we waiting for?" Geraldine scoffed, straightening her sweater and fixing her glasses before she looped an arm through mine. "Let's go get your girl."

"Right now?" I asked, an edge of panic riding me hard all of a sudden. Did I look okay? This wasn't even my nicest suit.

"You look like a studmuffin of the highest order," she said with a scoff, starting to drag me out the doors, through the throngs of people clearing out of their seats. She really was freakishly strong for a woman her age.

But also . . . could she read my mind?

I glanced back at the stage. The lights had been dimmed, the curtains pulled forward. There were no dancers anywhere to be seen. "We're going the wrong way," I said, my panic worsening as I contemplated scooping her up so we could get back to the stage faster.

"Men," Geraldine said, shaking her head as she continued to walk away from where I wanted to go. "She's not going to be backstage. She's going to be at the after-party. And your very hot date happens to have passes."

I could have kissed her.

"Passes? You have passes for us?" I asked, sounding a little crazed. I took the lead, hurrying her forward, vowing to make sure that Ari Lancaster never found out that I was using my seventy-five-year-old neighbor to pick up the future mother of my children. Geraldine would brag about it for sure if she got the chance. "I'm never doubting you again."

We were ushered out of the theater, but instead of streaming out the front door with the throngs of people, we veered left, where there was another set of double doors, actual security guards posted outside of them, like a horde of fans were going to try and rush the doors to meet the cloggers.

I frowned. On second thought, maybe there wasn't enough security. That angel on the stage probably had rabid fans stalking her everywhere.

I would know, I was about to become one of them.

"Step aside, gentlemen. Geraldine is in the house," she pronounced, lifting her chin in the air like she was royalty and holding up her passes.

They stepped aside, giving me a look like they suspected I was about to abscond with one of their dancers.

Hopefully I didn't look like a kidnapper in this suit. I glanced down with a frown again, wishing I'd had more time to prepare.

But was there ever enough time to prepare for the love of your life?

Stopping in my tracks, I took a deep breath. What. The. Fuck.

I pulled Geraldine to the side. "Hit me with your cane," I told her, sounding as crazy as I felt.

"What?"

"Hit me with your cane, Geraldine Burton. I've lost my mind."

She snickered, completely ignoring the fact that I was going through a life crisis. "Come on, lover boy."

People were staring as we started through the crowd. Usually it was at me, but with Geraldine's hot-pink flamingo cane, I couldn't be sure.

I craned my neck, trying to find her. The room was filled with people, dancers still in their costumes and audience members giving them flowers and congratulations.

Should I have brought flowers? I was starting to sweat. I didn't sweat like this when I was getting ready for Game 7 of the Finals four years ago. And now, I was dripping like a fucking pubescent teen.

Where was she?

"Mimi, I'm just going to drop you off at the drinks and do a loop, alright?" I asked, not proud of how frantic I sounded. Three people had tripped over her cane so far, and if I had to wait any longer to find my girl, that cane was going to become even more of a hazard . . . because I was going to start beating people upside the head if they got in my way.

"Go get your girl, Camden James." She leaned forward and got way too close to my ears with those dentures of hers. "After this, no one's going to be listening to Agatha bragging about her cat flushing the toilet. As if anyone cares what that old liar has to say, anyway. My news will be much more exciting."

"That's nice," I murmured as I scanned the room, trying to find *her*.

After leaving Geraldine by the bar—where she immediately started flirting with the twenty-something bartender—I pushed through the crowd like my ass was on fire.

My phone buzzed repeatedly in my pocket, and I cursed in frustration as I glanced around one last time before pulling it out.

Logan: Hey, Grampalicious, how's the hot date going?

I snorted, hating the small smile on my lips. But that was kind of funny.

Ari: Who put Rookie in this chat.

Logan: Can I have a cooler nickname? Like Super Stud or Sir Scores-a-Lot.

Ari Lancaster removed Logan York from the chat.

Ari: Who the fuck keeps adding him?

Walker: I'm pretty sure you do . . .

Ari Lancaster removed Walker Davis from the chat.

Lincoln Daniels added Walker Davis to the chat.

Walker: It's good to be back.

Ari: Simp.

Ari: Thanks, Golden Boy, for the support.

Linc: . . .

I quickly typed out a " . . . " for good measure, despite still not knowing what it actually meant.

Ari: Nice try, James.

Linc: But how is the date going, Grampalicious?

I scoffed.

Me: I hate you all.

I threw the phone in my pocket, not wanting to text anymore or speak to anyone until I fucking found her.

Someone with a tight ballerina bun passed by, and I followed her desperately.

"Excuse me," I said, reaching out to tap her on the shoulder.

The woman turned, her gaze growing wide as she stared up at me, her jaw slack, and awe written all over her face.

"Wow," she muttered, her cheeks blushing furiously as she took me in.

Normally, I would have thought this girl was pretty and probably flirted until I decided whether I wanted to take her on a date or just fuck her. But right now, her eyes were making me want to throw up. I didn't want her to look at me. There was only one person I wanted to make blush and fuck and date . . . and she was not that person.

It was all I could do to put on my most charming smile, trying my best to hide how fucking annoyed I was, so I could get the information I wanted out of her.

"You were great out there tonight," I told her, lying through my teeth since I couldn't think of any performance—or performer other than my little dancer.

I was definitely going to be examining the crazy thoughts in my head . . . later.

But right now I was just going to run with them.

Her blush deepened, and then she coughed and the blush was replaced by a weird look on her face. Kind of like she'd been constipated for weeks and was about to burst.

"Thank you, hot stuff," she said in a deeper voice.

Alright then . . . this was getting weird.

"The last dancer that performed . . . do you know where she is? I'd like to congratulate her too," I told her quickly, before anything else happened . . . like she jumped me.

That had happened before.

The girl's face fell, and her shoulders stiffened.

"I'm sure she left," she replied in a flat voice.

Alright then. Apparently, they weren't friends. Not that this woman seemed like a barrel of fun, but I couldn't help but wonder why.

She was probably jealous of my girl because I was sure she couldn't dance even one-tenth as good as her. No one could.

I guess the angel on stage could be a brat . . . or a bitch . . .

With talent like that, there was usually an ego.

I really didn't fucking care, though. I'd fuck the brat right out of her if I needed to.

"She left?" I realized quickly that I sounded . . . desperate when the girl frowned and began to back up like she'd catch something nasty from me if she stood too close. "That's just surprising she wouldn't want to celebrate," I added quickly.

She rolled her eyes and scoffed, and I felt overwhelmingly defensive at her reaction considering I haven't actually met my girl yet. "Come find me when you realize how disappointing ‘little miss perfect’ is in bed,” she threw over her shoulder.

Resisting the urge to tell her to fuck herself, I frantically searched the room for someone else to give me details about my girl.

The crowd parted and my eyebrow raised when Geraldine walked toward me next to an elegant older woman who moved like a stick had been shoved up her ass. I’d never seen someone with posture that straight.

My phone buzzed again, but I ignored it.

“Madame Leclerc, this is Camden James,” said Geraldine.

The woman eyed me speculatively, a gleam in her gaze that kind of made me want to run. She screamed “cougar” . . . a dangerous cougar judging by how tight her damn bun was. The uptight-looking ones were always the scary ones.

I cocked an eyebrow at Geraldine, wondering what she was up to, and then I shot Madame Leclerc a smile.

“Camden James,” she purred. “It’s such a pleasure to meet you. I’m a big fan.”

Oh, that was unexpected. This woman didn’t exactly scream hockey fan.

“Dallas Knights fan?” I asked as I shook her cold, claw-like hand.

“Jockey fan, actually,” she corrected, and my smile froze.

One of my sponsors was Jockey briefs, and one of my jobs for them was posing in their . . . apparel.

So she was a fan of my dick was what she was saying.

Perfect.

“Camden was in awe at the performances tonight, Madame. You must be so proud,” Geraldine prodded, her warm blue eyes gleaming with laughter.

“Is that so?” *Madame* simpered.

“Especially that last dance. The main performer was so talented. What was her name?” Geraldine pressed.

Fuck, I loved that old genius of a bird.

Like the woman I’d just talked to, Madame Leclerc’s lips pursed . . . and it felt like half my life had passed before she finally answered and gave me what I was looking for. “Anastasia Lennox is quite talented,” she said begrudgingly.

Anastasia Lennox.

The name carved itself into my veins.

A beautiful name for an exquisite creature.

Madame Leclerc said something else, but there was a ringing sound in my ears, and my blood seemed to be bubbling.

"Camden . . . " Geraldine's voice cut through whatever madness I was experiencing, and I blinked at her, noticing that she was laughing at me and that Madame Stick-Up-Her-Ass was nowhere to be found. "I'm ready to go home. You can start your search for your girl in the morning when you don't look like a lunatic."

I opened my mouth to tell her I would have to call her a cab because there was no way I could leave until I found out more about *Anastasia* . . . but she whacked me with her cane before I could get a word out.

"Ouch," I griped for half a second before I found myself following her out to the parking lot where I did indeed help her into my truck.

Geraldine fell asleep five minutes into the drive, and I was tempted to turn around and sneak back inside while she was sleeping. Every time I got to an intersection where I could do a U-turn, she would stir, though.

This happened so many times, I was pretty sure she was fucking with me.

Such a Geraldine thing to do.

We pulled into the underground parking lot, and her eyes popped open the second I turned off the truck, scaring me half to death when she lurched out of her seat, muttering something about needing to take out her teeth.

With the threat of seeing that sight again, I hopped out of the truck and jogged over to the other side to let her out.

"Such a nice boy," she crooned, patting my arm muscle like she liked to do as we got into the elevator and began our ascent to the top floor. "Thanks for the date."

I smiled, trying not to look too anxious about how slow the elevator was going, or how long it took to get her to her front door.

"I'll see you later," I told her, desperate to get back even though I was sure the event was over. I turned to leave and all of a sudden she was yanking me down by the collar of my dress shirt like she was She-Ra.

Geraldine was a little terrifying.

"Once you find that spark with someone, you do everything to keep it. Ya got me?" she asked fiercely, peering into my eyes and giving me a little shake.

I smirked, because this was one thing I didn't need any encouragement for.

"I got you, Mimi," I told her, giving her a kiss on her wrinkly cheek and heading to the elevators to get back to my truck.

Driving like a bat out of hell, I quickly arrived at the performance hall only to see that it was closed down for the night.

Tension buzzing along my skin, I sat in the parking lot, content for the moment just to be near where she had been.

I took a deep breath, my tense shoulders settling back. My eyes went steady, determination filling me, replacing the frantic nerves from before.

It was going to be alright. I had always been the type of guy to get what I wanted. If not by talent alone, then by sure force of will. I also had a group of guys, in a certain circle, who'd managed to find their girls.

Anastasia Lennox had no idea what was coming.

CHAPTER 5

CAMDEN

I was edgy when I arrived the next day at the community kitchen where I volunteered once a week. For the first time that I could remember, I had no interest in being there. I wanted to be out *there*, stalking the dance studio, waiting for Anastasia to get there. It wasn't a want at this point, it was a physical *need*, a desperation that sat under my skin.

I hadn't slept last night, or if I had, it had felt like a fevered dream, replaying how she'd been on that stage.

Searching for her on the internet had been . . . disappointing. She didn't have Facebook, and her Instagram had been a public account with five fucking posts. The five pictures were all black-and-white shots of her, one of her stretching in front of a floor-to-ceiling mirror, her shirt oversized and slipping off her shoulder. Another had been her dancing on her tiptoes—a move I was really going to have to research because it was fucking impressive.

Unfortunately, the three hundred followers she had were all men. So, I'd spent thirty minutes reporting all of them—and then reporting her account, too, because it was nothing but a thirst trap for horny assholes. We'd be having a discussion about privacy and who to accept as friends at a later date.

I wanted to hunt down whoever had taken her profile picture. She was sipping coffee in a sports bra, both hands holding the plain white mug, squeezing those perfect tits together as she smiled softly at the camera.

I'd saved that picture as my screensaver. I wanted that look. I wanted her to stare at *me* like that every fucking morning for the rest of our lives.

It was a goal for me.

"Hey, Camden!" Freddie said as I walked through the doors.

I threw up a hand, forcing a smile. Freddie had been an alcoholic for years and had lost his family along the way. He was three years sober now, trying to make penance to the universe for that lost time. I liked the guy, but I didn't want to give him any reason to try and corner me for a lecture about "having a positive attitude," or "searching for the good in every day." I'd endured one of those after a particularly bad game where I'd spent half of it in the sin bin, and I wasn't looking to repeat the experience.

Pulling on my gloves, I glanced over my station, making sure it was ready. The doors would be opening to the public any minute now, and it was usually a mad rush after that.

This place was one of the nicer ones that I volunteered at. Twenty-five volunteers were scattered all over a spacious room filled with long stainless steel countertops. A set of double doors behind me held a few industrial-sized stoves and ovens as well as food prep areas. There were cafeteria tables set up to the right and left of the stations where people could eat. Not sure the motivational posters on the walls really did anything, but I was positive that the shelves stacked with neatly organized cans and dry goods did.

Everyone who came today would be able to get a meal and then take some groceries home with them to help get them through the week.

Fluorescent lights buzzed overhead, casting a harsh glow over everyone as volunteers in aprons hurried to their stations with trays of food. The air was a strange mix of bread and Lysol. Not such a bad smell, actually.

"Heads up, doors unlocking now," a voice called over the speakers, seconds before security opened the entrance.

I could see the parade of people through the windows, stretching around the block. My stomach clenched uncomfortably as I fought back memories I wished I could forget. My mom had tried to leave my stepdad once, a brief moment of lucidity where she'd realized she deserved more. We'd gone to a place similar to this for a couple of months.

And then she'd gone back to him.

The line shuffled in, a procession of broken dreams and forgotten hopes, many of them regulars that I saw every week.

There was Mrs. Jenkins, her wrinkled hands trembling as she reached for a bag of chips and let me put a sub sandwich on her plate. She worked as a checker at Target, but it wasn't enough to pay for rent and food with the hours she could handle at her age. Broke my heart every time I saw her.

Behind her came Mr. Thompson. He was polite but never made eye contact with you. His whole persona radiated despair. I was quite confident that his posture came from defeat and not scoliosis. I'd heard he was once some kind of executive, and through some mistakes—or maybe just a lot of unluckiness—he'd lost it all and now had to come here for food once a week to make ends meet.

I always gave him an extra cookie. He looked like he needed it.

"Hi, Mr. James!" an eager voice called out. I glanced down, a smile already on my face when I saw Sean, a nine-year-old who was here every week with his mom.

"What's up, buddy?" I asked, holding out my fist so he could give me a fist bump. His mom, Stacey, was sporting a black eye, and I instantly frowned as I looked at her.

When she noticed me staring, she self-consciously covered her damaged eye and slowly shook her head, silently urging me to let it go. I bit down on my tongue so I didn't ask about it in front of Sean.

That was one thing they told us here before every volunteer session. Don't get involved. They had resources to get help, it was up to them to use them.

But fuck was that a hard rule to follow.

"I'm sorry you're hungry, sweetheart," my mother had whispered as we stood in line. "Just a couple more people in front of us and we can get some dinner." I huddled in the cold against her jeans, trying not to cry. She always got so sad when I cried.

We had been waiting for what seemed like forever, and the smell of something good coming through the doors in front of us was driving me crazy. Mom had been looking for a job every day while I was at school, but they'd all said no so far. She'd told me it was only a matter of time, though, and then we'd have regular food again. I was just lucky I had free lunch at school every day. I always saved something from my lunch for her. The animal crackers especially made her smile.

Not being around my stepdad anymore also *made her smile. So it was okay that I was hungry.*

When we got to the front of the line, one of the workers I'd seen in previous visits stopped us before we could get in. "I'm sorry, but we're out for the day," he said gently.

My mom stiffened, and when I glanced up, I could see she was freaking out. "But we've been standing in line for three hours. Why wasn't there an announcement? I could have taken my son somewhere else. Now they'll be closed, too." I could hear muttering behind us from other people who were upset, and I shifted uncomfortably, my stomach growling loudly and making Mom wince when she heard it.

"Please," she whispered. "There's got to be something he can have . . . "

I blinked, coming back to the present hearing Sean rattling on about a recent game we'd won.

"Oh man, your game the other day. You guys are so freaking good. Lincoln Daniels scored that goal and . . . " Sean was bouncing in place as he went over our game against Detroit, play-by-play.

I hoped he applied that much memory recall to his schoolwork, because it was impressive.

"When I grow up, I want to be just like Daniels," he was saying. I scoffed, holding my chest and pretending to falter.

Sean stopped talking, and stared at me sheepishly.

"Daniels, bud. What about me? *Defenders* have a way harder and cooler job. We have to stop them from scoring, and we have to hit people. Linc's got nothing on us," I told him, winking at him so he knew I was joking.

Forwards, always getting all the glory. So showy.

"You call him Linc," Sean whispered, like he was in awe of the fact that I could shorten Lincoln's name.

I was never telling Daniels about this. His head was too big already.

I should bring Ari in here, though, he would be able to straighten Sean out on what was the coolest position out there.

Disney would be useless. He would just agree with Sean because it was about Lincoln.

Such a simp.

Sean was wearing a Knights jersey I'd given him a few months ago, and judging by the stains on it . . . he wore it every day. I made a mental note to bring another one for him.

"Ooh, is that peanut butter?" Sean asked, bouncing up and down as he eyed the cookies in front of him.

I gave him three.

His mom pretended not to notice; a soft, sad smile on her lips that made me a little sick inside.

My mom had that kind of smile constantly, when she was trying to be brave amidst all the shit that was happening to her.

I shook my head, trying to clear out the echoes of the past battering around in my skull.

Now was not the time for that.

"Here's two cookies for you, ma'am," I drawled, ignoring the faint blush to her cheeks.

I liked single moms with the best of them, but I wasn't going there.

Plus, there was the whole fact that something had happened to my DNA last night, and suddenly, all my dick was attracted to was a ballerina who looked like an angel and danced like sin.

For all I knew, she *could* be a single mom . . . but for her, I'd go there.

I'd let her call me Daddy any day.

Alright, crazy. Don't get a woody in the community kitchen line.

I waved goodbye to Sean, promising to stop by his table in a bit, and I turned and glanced down the line to see how long it had gotten. I wasn't the speediest at this since I liked to talk to the regulars.

And holy fuck.

I blinked, and my tongs clattered to the table, because there was no way that my eyes were working. There was no way that this was real life.

Right there, like some kind of mirage . . . was my dancer. Anastasia Lennox was standing in line just a few feet away from me.

"Freddie, pinch me," I muttered and I could feel him look over at me like I was insane.

Good old Freddie, though, he did in fact pinch me. Hard.

"Fucking hell," I muttered, rubbing my arm because that had fucking hurt.

I couldn't even drag my gaze away to glare at him, though—it was stuck on her.

I hadn't thought it was possible, but she was so much better up close. Her hair was a cascade of white-blonde waves, shimmering even under the harsh fluorescent lights of this place. Each strand seemed to catch the light in a way that made her appear almost ethereal, a creature born out of my dreams and moonlight—

Dreams and moonlight?

What was I even saying right now?

I rubbed at my still sore arm absentmindedly as I took in the rest of her features. Her skin was tan, like she spent her days outside. And the effect of her light hair and light eyes against the dark tan was mind-blowing.

She was smiling at the person helping her—Tony—one of the nicest guys I'd ever met, and I wanted to chuck my tongs at him for getting her attention.

But then I really saw her eyes, and all the anger immediately drained away as her pools of light aqua reminded me of the Caribbean Sea.

I'd never seen eyes like that before.

She was without a doubt the most drop-dead beautiful girl I'd ever seen in my entire life. No comparison. No question.

This girl was the stuff of legends.

I had to have her.

Alright, play it cool. You're an NHL studmuffin.

My heart was hammering in my chest, and I was feeling queasy all of a sudden. Was this what love felt like?

You felt sick?

Someone cleared their throat. One time. And then again.

I had to forcibly drag my gaze away to the very annoyed-looking Mrs. Partridge, who had clearly been waiting for her cookie and sub sandwich for quite some time based on how severely her lips were pinched together.

"I'm sorry, Mrs. P. Let me get you the best cookie I've got."

She sniffed at me, not taken with my charm, and now I was starting to doubt myself. Was I off my game? Did I forget my aftershave this morning?

I quickly handed her a cookie—only one because of the bad attitude—and her sub, and sneaked a glance at my girl.

She was getting some salad. Two more stations and it would be my turn.

Was it hot in here? Because I was feeling a bit faint. We needed to get some air conditioning in this place.

Fuck. Did I smell? Sometimes I smelled when I sweated.

"Freddie, switch with me," I hissed. I needed more time to get my shit together. This had to be perfect.

He glanced at me, his freckled nose scrunching up toward his auburn eyebrows like I'd lost my mind. "Why?"

Fuck, she was moving to the next station.

"Because . . . because I'm allergic to peanuts. I can't handle them anymore."

"Pssh. You're not allergic to peanuts, Camden James. I saw you eating a Snickers last week."

I snarled at him before peeking to see that she was now only one station away

If I switched now, she'd notice and probably think it was weird.

Freddie followed my line of sight, leaning forward as a big smile appeared on his ruddy-cheeked face. He was staring at her, a big smile stretched across his lips.

He was *also* tilting forward a little precariously. I could just push him—a light push really—and he would stop grinning at my girl.

"Stop looking!" I hissed, trying to block his view. Freddie chuckled, shaking his head at me before he leaned back and widened his eyes dramatically.

I swung my head back around to find her again . . .

And then she was there.

Her plate outstretched as she stared at me politely.

Politely.

Like I was nobody.

Here I was, having the most visceral reaction of my life, and she was staring at me as if I was paint drying on a friend's wall that she was forced to look at.

"Hello. I mean, hi. I mean . . . do you want a cookie?" I was fumbling all over myself trying to hand her a cookie and a sub at once, but really, who could blame me for the fact that my fucking brain was short-circuiting.

She was flawless, stunning, so perfect that she couldn't possibly be real.

There had to be a flaw somewhere. Was there a hairy back hiding under the oversized sweatshirt she was wearing?

No. Fuck. She'd been wearing a low-backed spandex-looking outfit while she'd performed last night.

Definitely no hairy back problems.

"A cookie and a sandwich would be great," she murmured, her voice a soft caress against my . . . dick.

Thank fuck this table was pretty high, there'd be no hiding the baseball bat in my jeans right now. Why had I worn jeans this tight to begin with? I was throwing every pair of these things away the second I got home. They were strangling my dick.

The only thing I was interested in strangling my dick was her pussy.

Fuck! Stop thinking about your dick, Camden!

"Here you go, Ms. Anastasia," Freddie said, handing her one of the cookies from my tray because evidently I'd forgotten how to be a functioning human being.

Anastasia. I repeated the name in my head like a prayer, ready to worship at its altar. I hated that it was coming from another man's lips.

"Thanks, Freddie," she said sweetly, and I almost bit his arm off.

"Here's another one!" I said frantically as I all but tossed it onto her plate.

The cookie began sliding off, but right before it could fall, she snatched it and plopped it back on her plate.

"Thank you." This time her angelic voice was directed at me . . . and I melted.

"Camden," I blurted hopefully. "Camden James."

I looked for any spark of familiarity, but her smile was formal, stiff, the kind you gave to a person on the street that you'd never seen before.

Not a hockey fan evidently.

Well, that was unfortunate. But . . . fine. I'd just have to impress her with something else.

Freddie reached for a sub sandwich, and I lunged toward the pile and grabbed one, too. We both held out our hands to her. I looked like a fucking idiot . . . and I did not care one bit. Her clear blue eyes flicked between us, confused.

Freddie turned to me with a grin. "She likes turkey, bro," he announced proudly as he gave her a different sub.

I filed that away. Turkey over ham. I'd never make that mistake again.

"Anything else you like that I should remember?" I asked, trying to put a little flirt in my voice, distracting her from the fact that I'd thrown a cookie at her plate and shoved a six-inch sub into her face. I was usually a lot more smooth than this. But she was perfect . . . and all that perfection was making my brain malfunction.

I mean, I was so interested in this girl I might as well have a neon sign over my head that said "pick me, choose me, love me," like I was an intern on *Grey's Anatomy*.

Except, she didn't seem to be picking up on that at all.

"She doesn't like lemonade," Freddie answered for her. "Who doesn't love lemonade? Very suspicious, Anastasia."

"Lemons aren't supposed to be sweet, Freddie," she teased. "That's literally the whole point of a lemon."

"I agree," I said, even though I loved lemonade. One of my earliest memories was sipping lemonade out on Grandma James's front porch.

For her I could hate lemonade, though.

She eyed me curiously, and I stood up straighter. *Give me a sign*, I was pleading. Lust after my body at least. Fuck.

Nope. Nothing. She didn't even look at my biceps or anything.

My angel girl just said thank you again before scurrying away. She went too fast for me to even think of what else to say to her.

I'd fucking blown it.

"That was embarrassing, James," Freddie snorted as we watched her weave away through the throngs of people in the room, heading to a table against the wall. She slid into a chair elegantly, her posture perfect. Her chin up, her head held high.

Alone.

"Indeed," I said.

I handed him my tongs. "Cover for me, will ya? I need to make some . . . rounds."

He laughed at me as I marched past. I made a detour to say hello to some of the other regulars first. Didn't want to make it too obvious that I'd left my station immediately to go talk to her.

But I couldn't help but sneak glances at her as I said hello to everyone. Anastasia's perfect posture had slumped and now looked a bit defeated. Her face held the kind of sad look that had me wanting to punch something because it didn't seem fair that such a perfect being could look like that. I wanted to know what was wrong, to know what was going on inside that head of hers. I also wanted to stride right over there and tell her to let me fix it.

But I held myself back, hitting up Sean's table first where he proceeded to walk me through the entire first period of our last game before I could drag myself away.

Then Ms. Nesbitt and Mr. Thompson and then . . .

I sauntered up to her table, coming from the side so that I didn't scare her. I knew a lot of women had triggers about that—especially here.

"How's that turkey sub treating you?" I mused, wanting to drop-kick myself in the face because why was my voice coming out that deep and weird-sounding?

She nearly dropped the sub in question at the sound of my voice—the first semi ungraceful thing I'd seen her do. Her eyes were wide and confused-looking, and she glanced around as if she thought I wasn't talking to her.

I wasn't sure what was so shocking. Any man on earth would be following her around like a lost puppy.

Anastasia finally tipped her gaze up to mine, realizing there wasn't anyone else around I could be talking to. Her lush lips parted for a moment, like she was having trouble finding words. I held her gaze and she cleared her throat slightly. "The turkey sub is great," she finally murmured as she took a big bite for good measure.

I awkwardly stared at her, continuing to take in all her glorious details.

She was young, I was really getting that now. Her face was completely void of any lines or blemishes, and wide-eyed innocence was written all over her. Over eighteen, though, because this particular place didn't allow unaccompanied minors. They were sticklers about it.

Still. What was she? Nineteen? Twenty? And I was thirty-one-fucking-years old.

Well, that was fine.

I tended to go for older women, but there was something about Anastasia that drew me in. Not just her talent or the way she'd performed like she'd die up there on the stage because she was giving it her all.

There was also the vulnerability in her eyes; it pulled at something inside me. I wanted to protect her. To make her mine. It didn't matter that I was probably quite a bit older than her. Something told me my baby girl needed that.

Besides, as I was constantly telling Logan, our cheeky, arrogant little rookie. I wasn't an old man.

I was *seasoned.*

I could be the best kind of seasoning for her.

"Did you need something?" she whispered, her gaze falling to the table. She fiddled with the bun on her sandwich, crushing the edges as she bit down on her plump lower lip that I had the urge to lean forward and take between my own teeth.

I was making her nervous. Fuck. How long had I been standing here without saying anything?

"I . . . I just haven't seen you around here before."

"Hmm." She pushed a tendril of her white-blonde hair behind her ear and gifted me her crystalline gaze. Anastasia eyed me thoughtfully for a moment, like she was deciding my fate. It kind of felt like she held my entire life in her pretty hands as I stood there and waited for whatever was going to come next.

"You must be a Wednesday volunteer," she finally said. "I usually come in . . . another day." She'd cut herself off before she said "another day," which meant that she was probably thinking I was some kind of demented stalker and didn't want to give me too much information.

I would have told her I wasn't a stalker, but overnight, that had become one of the untruest things that could be said about me.

I was a stalker.

Her fucking stalker.

And I didn't see that changing. Because by the looks of things, fate was decidedly onboard with that new life calling since it had brought her to me today.

"Yep, Wednesdays are my day," I said, wondering if I'd be able to sneak in some other days here and there. It's just that I volunteered at the nursing home on Mondays with practice right after, and I had games usually on Tuesdays and Fridays. Thursday we had weights and then practice.

Fuck. Well, I was just going to have to figure something out. If I was going to be her stalker, I was going to be good at it.

It was needling at my insides, though . . . why was someone her age needing to come to a community kitchen for food in the first place?

My eyes roamed over her, delving past the beauty, and seeing what I hadn't before. She was thin—overly so I would say, even though I didn't make a habit of judging women's bodies. I'd thought it was from dancing . . . but maybe it was because she didn't have anything to eat. Fuck. And those slight circles under her eyes . . . maybe they weren't from just a busy dance routine, but a deeper stress in her life.

Now that the shock of seeing her had worn off, the fact that she was here . . . really fucking bothered me.

I didn't want her to struggle. I needed to help my little dancer.

"Do you need anything else?" she pressed.

She was trying to act like she was annoyed, but no. Now that I was studying her more closely, I could see her fidgeting, the way she'd stopped eating, and how she could barely meet my eyes . . .

I made her nervous.

Most girls just looked at me like eye candy, and were very forward with their attraction. Anastasia was . . . shy.

Her eyes darted to my face, then to my chest, and a blush rose to her cheeks before she jerked her eyes back down to her tray.

A grin spread across my face.

She was attracted to me. She just hid it well.

I could work with that.

I liked a challenge, and her reaction was adorable.

I took a step closer to her, intentionally forcing her to meet my eyes—or else she'd be looking straight at my dick.

I liked this vantage point, her staring up at me.

She was going to be absolutely exquisite on her knees.

"You should eat up," I told her, glancing at everything on her plate and fighting the urge to feed it to her by hand.

Too soon. That would definitely be crossing the line.

"Yes, sir," she murmured, her breath hitching as soon as the words had come out of her mouth.

Fuck. I liked that.

"Good girl."

Her eyes widened, her blush spreading down to her chest. I watched as she obediently took a bite of the sandwich.

"Want another peanut butter cookie?" I rasped.

She paused and bit down on her lip. I leaned in, wanting whatever she was about to give me.

"I thought you were allergic to peanuts," she whispered, and a flare of mischievous amusement lit up in her eyes.

I pulled back, my mouth open in complete shock.

She had heard me.

I was slayed. Destroyed. Gone.

A smile spread across her gorgeous face. "See you around," she said brightly, clearly dismissing me, even though she'd just knocked me to the ground.

"Umm, yeah. Bye," I stuttered, my cheeks burning.

Forget thirty-one years old. Right now, I felt like I was about ten.

But I didn't care. Didn't care that I looked like an idiot right now, or that I had been completely off my game all night. Because now I knew one thing.

She had noticed me.

Anastasia stayed at the table eating her dinner for another half hour. I stayed too, a lot longer than my usual shift because I wasn't going anywhere while she was still in the building.

I couldn't tell you exactly what I did . . . I may have filled some mustard bottles. Or maybe I didn't.

And when she left . . .

I followed.

Because I was fully committed to the stalker thing now.

She left on foot—completely expected since most of the people visiting the community center relied on walking or public transportation rather than cars to get around. I left my truck behind at the shelter and trailed after her, staying a half a block or so behind her as she went along. This part of town was definitely on the rougher side of things, though—so that we could be close to the city's occupants without them needing cars.

Which meant that she wasn't safe . . . and I couldn't take that. I *needed* to make sure she was safe.

It was a compulsion at this point.

Some men sitting on the street corner of a closed-down gas station called out to her, and I plotted their deaths.

She went under a fucking bridge, and I almost had a heart attack.

And when she cut through an alleyway, I almost snatched her up to take her home with me.

There wasn't very much housing around here. It was mostly boarded-up buildings and smaller stores that were hanging on for dear life.

Where was she going?

I knew I was going to have to find a way to get into her place. I wanted to know everything about her. Where she lived.

Who lived with her . . .

Alright, I wasn't going to think about that right now.

She turned another corner, and I got even more confused—there was nothing here but the . . .

My stomach dropped as she walked up the steps of Haven . . . a homeless shelter for women and children.

She was fucking homeless.

There was a strange feeling in my heart—a mix of anger and sadness and fucking devastation as I pictured her laying on a cot, a thin blanket and flat pillow all she had for the night. She'd be sleeping in the same clothes she'd worn today, lucky if her things didn't get stolen during the night.

I knew from those couple of months with my mom, you didn't get much sleep in a place like that . . .

No wonder she had dark circles under her eyes.

While Haven was better than most, it was still dangerous. Despair and desperation and finite resources tended to do that.

What if something happened to her tonight? Even with all the connections I'd made volunteering with most of the organizations in the city—I couldn't get into that place.

I paced up and down the alley, my heart feeling like it was going to pound right out of my chest.

I had to get her out of there. I took a step toward the stairs, even knowing it was pointless. A guard stood up from the security desk behind the doors, watching me sternly, and I sighed and turned around. They weren't going to help me, no matter how charming I was. That was the whole point of these kinds of shelters.

How had Anastasia ended up in a place like this? Why was she getting food from a community kitchen . . . weekly? But yet also dancing for a fancy studio?

I couldn't take it. I was going to go insane from worrying about her.

One way or another, I was going to find out everything about Anastasia Lennox.

And then, I decided . . . .

I was going to save her.

CHAPTER 6

ANASTASIA

Anastasia," a voice called, and chills immediately cascaded down my skin.

Michael.

Taking a deep breath, I slowly turned to find him. He was leaning against the brick wall of the store next to the dance studio, his arms crossed in front of him.

Back in school, we'd once studied serial killers in psychology class. The teacher had taught us how they could blend in, how they were often attractive and agreeable, luring you in until it was too late.

My foster brother reminded me of that.

The charming teenager had become an even more charming man with his carefully parted hair, a handsome face, and a pleasant smile. When he talked to strangers, his voice was even a different pitch, unassuming and unthreatening.

Not showing you who he was . . . until it was too late.

"What are you doing here?" I asked, keeping the fear out of my voice, because he'd always fed on it.

"Just a little visit for my favorite sister," he said mockingly, his eyes tracking down my body in a way that made me want to peel off my skin. "I thought I would stop by to see when you were coming to dinner."

My breath hitched at that. I wasn't ever coming to dinner again. I could picture his little photography setup in my head, the blankets he would have spread out on the floor. The way his knife had felt scraping threateningly across my neck before I stripped.

Bile rose in my throat, and I was suddenly lightheaded.

He'd forced me to the last dinner. I couldn't let it happen again. I glanced around, hoping that other dancers had filed out behind me somehow. But no, I was out here alone. I'd had to stay later than usual to scrub the dance studio floors, so everyone must have left while I cleaned.

"I don't have time for a visit tonight, I'm afraid," I said, wincing inwardly as my voice trembled. Sometimes I wondered if he was even human or if demons were actually real, and there was one standing in front of me right then.

He sighed, shaking his head disappointedly at me as he pushed away from the wall and straightened. "No time for dinner. That's over a month now where you've said that. I'm beginning to think you're avoiding me, Ana."

He was using the same light tone as I was—so why was I shaking at his words?

Spread your legs, Ana . . . just like that. I blinked, trying to push the last dinner out of my head. I needed to focus so I could get away from him.

"I'd never do that," I said softly, desperate to keep him calm.

If I thought that his calm was scary . . . his anger was even worse.

Even in my fear, though, I had to resist the urge to correct him for the millionth time that I didn't want him using that nickname.

It wouldn't have done any good—I knew that from experience.

"We'll catch up soon," I lied. "I'll go over to Mom and Dad's house, and we can all have dinner."

Calling them "mom" and "dad" felt like ash on my tongue. His parents had never been those words. They'd given me a roof over my head, yes, but they'd also let their monster of a son torture me for years. They'd turned a blind eye to everything he did to me . . . and others.

I hated them almost as much as I hated him.

Almost.

"Will you, though, Ana? Because I feel like you've told me that before."

His blue eyes gleamed, and it was all I could do to hold in the terrified sob that wanted to squeak out.

He took a step toward me, and I didn't bother trying to stand my ground. When something that evil comes toward you, it's stupid to try and fight back.

The correct action is always to try and run.

The dying sun cast dark shadows across his face and across the concrete, making him seem even more sinister than usual. He was staring at me with dark possession, dark madness—a look that never faded no matter how much time had passed.

"There's no getting away from your family, Ana. You're a bad little girl for ever wanting to." The word *family* dripped from his lips, heavy with sarcasm. *Family* was the last thing that Michael thought of me as.

"Of course," I said appeasingly, as I continued to back away from him, side-eying my surroundings, desperate for someone to appear and save me. He usually behaved in public places, but this late, this part of town wasn't very "public."

Belatedly, I realized he'd backed me into a corner, nowhere to escape to thanks to the narrow spacing of the two buildings behind me. My hands fisted at my sides as his slow, steady . . . menacing steps grew closer.

"Say thank you to your brother for helping you to see the error of your ways, Ana."

"Thank you," I said automatically, trained from years of him forcing me to thank him for abusing me.

"Tell me you're not going to let me down anymore, little bunny," he ordered in that scary, soft tone that always came before something really bad happened.

"Don't call me that," I said in a cracked voice as I took another step away from him, memories I did my best to bury coming to the surface.

"Little bunnnnny," a voice whispered as something sharp slid down my arm.

I whimpered and woke up, blinking as I stared around the darkness, trying to figure out what was going on.

It took me a second to realize that I didn't have any clothes on.

And I'd definitely had on leggings and a T-shirt before I'd fallen asleep.

I let out a whimper, my eyes searching the dark corners of the room as I grabbed for my sheet so I could cover myself.

I could hear his heavy breathing, but for some reason I was having trouble finding where he was. Maybe it was because of the adrenaline surging through my veins, clogging my throat and making me dizzy.

It felt like I was trapped in some kind of nightmare. And why was my arm still stinging?

Slapping my arm, I tried to stop the weird stinging sensation.

I gasped when I felt something warm, wet . . . and sticky.

He'd cut me.

"Little bunny," he whispered from somewhere close by again.

"But isn't that what you are?" Michael asked, bringing me back from the horror-soaked past with a placid laugh that would sound normal to anyone else. They would miss the absolute evil threaded through its every decibel.

"My little bunny? You really should stop delaying the inevitable, Ana. You belong to me; we both know it." He extended his hand, and I'd never wanted something less.

"Stay away from me," I told him, my spine straightening, resolve flooding my insides, even though I knew I was provoking him even more.

"You know I can't do that," he smirked, mockingly shaking his head.

His muscles tensed, and just as he was about to lunge, a girl came out of the dance studio. I'd never been more happy to see someone in my entire life.

"Lacey!" I called out, my voice sounding frantic and weird enough that she stared at me like I was insane. "Let me walk with you."

We had literally said maybe ten words to each other during a class last year, so she was definitely thinking I'd gone crazy . . . but the alternative was staying here alone with Michael.

Lacey's steps slowed, and her gaze bounced between Michael and me, hesitation and confusion all over her face.

Michael had paused at her appearance, his body stretched with tension as he stopped just an arm's length away from me.

"Anastasia, I was just looking for you," Lacey said in a flat, almost reluctant tone. She was eyeing Michael nervously now, obviously having felt that innate female intuition that told her he was someone to stay away from.

"Ana—" Michael warned, his arm reaching out to me.

I sidestepped him and hurried toward Lacey, fear hammering at my insides. Lacey held out her hand, and I grabbed it, shocked and immeasurably grateful as she hurried us down the streetlight-lit sidewalk. It was opposite the bus stop I usually took to get to my next job, but I didn't care. Anywhere that was away from Michael would work for me.

We made it to the edge of the block, neither of us having said a word yet, and I glanced back at Michael.

He was standing in the shadows of the dance academy, in the same spot I'd left him.

Even from here, there was a dark promise in his gaze that spelled nothing but danger for me.

And in the back of my mind, pushed away so that I didn't think about it, I wondered when he would make that promise come true.

I didn't know how much longer I could keep this up. I was exhausted. The kind of exhaustion that felt like your body was dying, like you had no hope.

Wiping the table, I forced myself not to cry.

Just like always.

I couldn't control anything that happened in my life, but I could control my reaction to it.

Or at least that's what I always tried to tell myself.

I didn't think any part of me actually believed it.

It would be easy to let that first tear fall, maybe it would even feel good. But it was what came after that first tear that I was truly afraid of.

I wasn't sure I'd be able to stop once I started.

Sighing, I finished wiping the table and stacking the dishes in the plastic tub, then heaved them up so I could carry them back to the dishwashing station and get them cleaned.

Charlie had told me that if I bussed tables at his restaurant for a month, he would move me up to being a server.

Unfortunately, like most men, Charlie was a liar, and I'd now been bussing tables for six months with no end in sight.

Not only was bussing way more physically taxing than being a server, it also meant that I was being paid pennies because the servers had no interest in sharing their tips—even though they were supposed to.

I needed to find another job. But the thought of going to the library to use the computer and submitting applications, or going from restaurant to restaurant, or store to store handing out my pitiful resume . . . well, I couldn't quite comprehend it at the moment.

I might be twenty-one years old, but I hadn't started working until I was eighteen—Michael's parents had never allowed it. Some of the jobs after that were under the table, so I couldn't even include them in my resume to begin with. It was hard trying to get someone to hire me when I looked like I had little to no experience.

"There's another table that needs to be cleaned," Poison said in a no-nonsense voice the second I'd set down the tub next to the huge industrial sinks where she was working on getting the grease off some bowls.

Poison was a pink-haired sprite of a woman who'd evidently been working at the restaurant for over ten years. She never complained . . . and she never really talked except to tell me there was more work to do. She may have been the size of a pixie, but she was somehow one of the scariest women I'd ever met. Her name didn't help with that. I still hadn't gotten the nerve to ask her the story behind it.

"I'll get on it," I told her, giving her my fake dance smile which did absolutely nothing for her.

At least it worked for most people.

I quickly emptied the dishes from the bin and set them beside the sink, ignoring her annoyed look when one of the bowls fell into the sink with a loud *plop*, dousing the whole front of my white blouse with water.

Perfect.

Grabbing the bin, I limped back out to the dining area—my leg past the point of cooperation for the day. I'd danced for seven hours, cleaned the studio for an hour, and then hustled my way to Charlie's Diner to do this job—with the unfortunate interlude of Michael along the way.

I needed a break.

Unfortunately, I didn't qualify for a scholarship at this Company because of the liability that came with my leg—and I wasn't moving back to my old hometown, no matter how nice the instructors had been. This Company was one of the premier studios in the country, but they didn't start paying their performers liveable wages until you became a senior performer.

A saner woman would have just quit.

But I didn't know how to give up on the only dream I'd ever had.

Caught in my own head, with my own thoughts, I completely missed the leg outstretched across the aisle.

I crashed to the floor, the bin going flying, and sharp jagged pain ripping through my wrists and knees as I caught myself. The bin slammed to the floor, dishes flying everywhere, the sound of glass shattering filling the entire restaurant.

I glanced up and saw the owner of the leg, a frat-looking boy with his three friends, had just sent me to my doom . . . laughing like a pack of hyenas.

"Sorry," he snorted, obviously not meaning it. My face was burning with embarrassment as they stared at me, clearly amused at the situation.

I tried to get up, but my leg buckled with pain, sending me smacking back down to the floor. Blood filled my mouth as I bit down on my lip, trying to stop the cry that wanted to escape. I didn't want to give them the satisfaction of hearing me.

Pushing up, I tried to baby my leg, and something sliced my palm. Fuck, one of the glass shards had embedded itself in my hand.

This was the moment I broke, right? This was where I just . . . gave up?

"Let's get you up, little dancer," a deep, familiar voice murmured. There was a soft caress against my cheek and then a strong pair of arms was literally *lifting* me off the ground like I weighed nothing.

I blinked in shock, glancing up at my savior.

Him.

Camden James.

Yes . . . I'd remembered his name. Like it was tattooed in my brain as a matter of fact. Like it had melded itself to my rib cage, destined to never be forgotten or ignored.

I'd also remembered that beautiful face. Obsessed over the fact that something so perfect existed and it didn't belong to me.

As if someone like that could ever belong to anyone, though, let alone me. The idea was laughable.

I was pretty sure that men who looked like Camden James were just shooting stars in the sky that us mere mortals were destined to only be able to look at.

"Are you alright?" he asked in that same smooth drawl that sent sparks skittering across my skin because it had just become my new favorite sound.

Where the hell were these kinds of thoughts coming from?

"Embarrassed mostly," I whispered. There weren't a lot of people in the restaurant tonight, but I could still feel plenty of eyes staring.

I was fine with that on the stage—when I'd embarrassed myself, not so much.

His gaze searched my face, that same look there as he'd had at the community kitchen when I'd passed through the line. Something that almost looked like shock . . . or awe.

Obviously, that was just wishful thinking.

Then I remembered. He'd seen me getting food at the community kitchen last week.

Now, my cheeks were even hotter with embarrassment.

There wasn't anything wrong with needing extra help sometimes, but I didn't exactly want Mr. Dreamboat McDreamy Pants seeing me there.

It made me feel . . . exposed. Like he was seeing all of my struggles.

I'd been burning with nervousness when he'd come up to me at my table to talk to me. I was worried he was going to mock me, or worse, pity me. I knew I needed to get away before I saw either of those reactions on his handsome face. But right now, he was just looking at me with an intensity that had nothing to do with mockery *or* pity.

Instead, I saw something in his eyes that I couldn't quite name. It evoked a different kind of heat. This one starting low in my stomach.

"Can you stand?" he asked, his hands still grasping my hips. One of the guys at the table made a noise and Camden shot them a dark look. "Fucking idiots," he growled, and I heard one of them audibly choke.

"I'm fine. Thank you . . . I'm just going to get back to work," I said quickly, forcing my legs to work, the urge to get away from this beautiful man hitting me hard. He kept seeing me in these less than glamorous situations. I didn't know how it was possible for me to be any more embarrassed around him.

Camden turned his attention back to me, his features gentling into something so heartbreakingly caring . . . I had to yank my gaze away from him.

"Hey. Seriously. That was a hard fall. You should sit down. I'll ask for some ice," he pressed, one hand coming up to tip my chin so I had to meet his light green gaze. Sparks lit up my skin at his touch, and I found myself leaning into his hand.

Wow. I'd never seen that eye color before, like the green sky before a tornado—flakes of gold whipping in the wind in that crazy, bright green sky as the storm rolled in.

His fingers stroked across my skin, and it was all I could do to hold in a whimper. I'd never been touched like that before—I'd never *reacted* to anyone's touch like that.

I blinked, trying to get ahold of the sudden heat spiking between my legs, trying to remind myself of the one universal truth I'd learned in my twenty-one years of life.

Men were trouble.

That included men so pretty you got an ache in your belly just from looking at them.

"No—" I said sharply, jerking out of his grasp. His face fell.

"Thank you," I quickly added. "But I promise I'm fine. I can take care of myself."

He didn't look like he believed me, and there was a frown on his full lips as he took a step away, creating a distance I instantly wanted to fill.

"I'm sure you can, baby girl," his voice a low, soothing murmur. "But it's okay to have some help every once in a while."

Oooh, this man was dangerous. One *baby girl* in that smooth southern drawl, and I was rethinking my whole life . . . that's how powerful it was.

Especially that word coming from a man who *looked* like he knew how to take care of someone. His "daddy" energy was off the charts. It made me want to curl up against him and feel him wrap those muscled arms around me protectively.

I snorted to myself—I'd definitely never had that thought before.

Over his shoulder I could see Poison peeking out of the washroom—something she never did—her lips curled up over her teeth in a way that spelled trouble for me. I stepped away, even though I had to force myself to do it.

"I need to get back to work," I said, skirting a table as I intentionally went the long way around him, just so I could avoid his intoxicating orbit.

His gaze was a caress as I walked, and I swore I could feel it weaving across my skin.

I wanted to soak it up, keep it with me forever.

Besides staying away from men, I was also a big believer in not letting them know they were getting to you.

Michael had made me a master at that.

Just thinking of him was enough to throw a bucket of water on the fluttery, glittery feeling Camden had given me. Poison's glare of disapproval made sure it didn't return.

At least while I was washing dishes.

But when I saw Camden hadn't left the diner, those feelings came rushing right back.

Men were trouble.

But the question was, what kind of trouble was Camden James?

Even after I left work for the night, I couldn't stop thinking about him.

And just for the night, I didn't try.

CHAPTER 7

CAMDEN

She was trying to blow me off. It was cute, really, that she thought she could do that.

There was nothing cute about the way she was limping, though.

I turned so my back was facing the kitchen as soon as Anastasia disappeared behind the swinging doors and put all my attention on the table of assholes.

When they looked up at me, the expression on their faces changed from amused to wary.

"Did you fucking do that on purpose?" I snarled.

"Do what on purpose?" one of them asked, an edge of fear to his face. He had a patch of hair above his upper lip that he was obviously trying to grow in. It looked like a caterpillar at this stage, though.

"Don't play dumb with me," I warned.

"Look man, it was an accident . . . " another of them quivered, the red-shirt-wearing douchebag who had tripped her in the first place. There was no doubt in my mind he'd stuck out his leg on purpose. Maybe he hadn't had the intention of tripping her, but he'd definitely been trying to stop her and get her attention.

Either way, I couldn't have that.

"You have one minute to get the fuck out of here," I ground out, the threat evident in my voice.

"What?" the guys said, almost in unison like they were some kind of boy band announcing their next single on the radio. The one nearest to me suddenly gasped, his eyes flaring, and I knew he'd just recognized who I was.

I leaned over the table, my hands gripping the edge of it as I tried to keep myself from wringing their necks.

"Pay what you owe for dinner and leave. Don't make me say it again."

Red shirt's mouth hung open like he was hoping to catch some flies. "Wait a minute—you're Camden James. From the Knights!" he finally said excitedly, an edge of awe in his voice. It was obvious they'd been to games before because there was also the appropriate amount of fear that followed. I was six-four and shoved men around for a living—they should be scared.

"Yes, and yet you're not listening to me. Why the fuck aren't you moving?" I growled, losing my patience.

They stared at me again for too long, before they finally got the picture, frantically tossing bills onto the table like they were at a strip club and leaving in a hurry.

"Can I have an autograph?" one of them dared to ask.

The answering glare I gave him must have been terrifying enough, because he let out an actual squeak and started to run toward the exit like his ass was on fire. I caught his collar before he could get too far, and he let out a choking sound as I dragged him toward me.

"Don't you *ever* fuck with another woman again, you piece of shit," I hissed, shaking him once for good measure before I finally let him go.

He was trembling as he backed away, his hands up in front of him. "I promise," he cried before he stumbled out the door.

I stared after them long enough that gawkers were probably wondering if they needed to call the cops because there was about to be a homicide . . .

I hated bastards who hurt women.

I especially hated men who hurt *my* women.

Anastasia just happened to be the only woman who fell under that category anymore.

I glanced around the diner and nodded to a few of the tables, plastering on my easygoing smile so I'd look less threatening. This seemed to work, and slowly, everyone turned away and went back to their business of eating.

I went back to my business of focusing on Anastasia.

Sliding into a booth and picking up a menu, I pretended to look over it as I replayed everything that had just happened.

The way she looked when she fell . . . that flare of pain in her eyes.

Should I go back there and insist I take her to the hospital to get checked out? The fall didn't look too bad, but maybe it was worse than I thought?

No, no. I couldn't just fucking kidnap her.

Yet.

I took a deep breath, reminding myself that even being inside the restaurant where she worked was a big step. I'd been in my truck, waiting to see if she was working, when I'd seen her fall.

And then I couldn't stop myself from running in to make sure she was okay.

I'd stood in the alleyway outside her dance studio for hours after my shift at the community kitchen, more and more concerned when everyone else seemed to have left for the day but her.

When she'd finally come out, I'd followed her here where I'd hovered out of sight for another few hours, watching her and trying to learn anything I could. I'd wanted to go in, but I'd figured that showing up at her workplace right after she'd seen me at the kitchen might have sent off stalker signals I wasn't going for at the moment.

I mean, I was her stalker . . . but I didn't want *her* to know that.

Some games and practices had gotten in the way of me doing more of the reconnaissance I was desperate to do. Tonight after practice, I'd been able to hustle over to the restaurant, absolutely *delighted* that she was here and I could *finally* come in.

I'd tried to convince myself on our road trip this past week that I'd imagined her perfection, that I must've created an image that wasn't real because perfection like that couldn't really exist.

Seeing her tonight had been the same religious experience it had been when I saw her on that stage. Even clearly exhausted and done for the day—with dark circles under her eyes that had me wanting to punch something—she was, without a doubt, the most stunning creature I'd ever seen.

I'd also found out that my girl was incredibly kind.

Even worn down and working herself to death, everyone in the restaurant smiled at her as she worked. She'd stop and chat with an old guy I'd seen the last time I was here, filling his coffee when his waitress was too busy flirting with some coeds to help him. She'd crouched down and helped a mother soothe her crying toddler, grabbing a lollipop from the hostess stand and gifting it to him so he would be distracted and let his mom actually eat.

I straightened up in my seat when she suddenly reappeared, this time pushing a cart with two bins on top of it. She winced when the wheel hit something and a spray bottle landed on the floor with a clatter.

I hated seeing her work this hard. It made me sick, actually. Someone had come out to sweep up the broken plates while she'd been in the back room—so at least she hadn't had to do that.

Anastasia wasn't a waitress; that part was surprising. A face like hers would have raked in all the tips. Charlie's wasn't fine dining, but it was established in the city, enough that I'd heard about it and recognized the name.

The mysteries just kept coming. Why was my gorgeous little dancer, with one of the most decorated dance companies in the country, cleaning up tables after dancing all day and then sleeping at a shelter at night? Where was her family?

I was truly flabbergasted at this point.

Flabbergasted . . . and chomping at the bit to step in and take care of her. The way she'd stared up at me with those otherworldly eyes, soaking in the slight touch I'd given her even though I was practically a stranger—I couldn't wait to spoil her. Couldn't wait to put that dreamy look in her eyes every day because her life was so fucking good.

My dick hardened at the thought.

I was pretty sure I had some kind of caregiver kink—there was probably a weird word attached to that particular preference, but I was firmly under its umbrella.

She rolled the cart past, clearly trying to look everywhere but at me. At the last second, though, she glanced over her shoulder, squeaking and yanking her face away when she saw that I had caught her.

I grinned.

Maybe I should have been playing it cool, but I couldn't take my eyes off of her, and she knew it too. There was a cute blush to her cheeks as she grabbed a napkin from the table across from me.

Anastasia bent over to grab an errant fork, and my attention got caught on her ass.

Fuck, every part of her really was perfect.

"Hello, sir, welcome to Charlie's. My name is Whitney, and I'll be your server tonight. Would you like to hear the specials?" I blinked, coming back from wherever staring at Anastasia took me. It certainly wasn't Earth, because now that I was back in reality, glancing at the hopeful-looking waitress, I felt like I'd landed on an alien planet.

And I wasn't happy to be there.

"Just a water, please," I told her, glancing disinterestedly at the menu. Belatedly, I realized that she'd asked me if I was interested in the specials, but considering she was now blocking my view of Anastasia, my drink order was all she was going to get at the moment.

The waitress flinched at my tone, her cheeks reddening in embarrassment.

You're being a dick, a voice whispered in my head, reminding me that I was nice to women—nice to a fault.

"And the grilled salmon platter," I added, smoothing out the annoyance in my voice so she wouldn't think I was upset with her.

Her shoulders dropped and she relaxed. Great . . . and now she was going to try and stay and chat.

"Whitney!" someone called, and she frowned and gave me a longing look before turning to leave.

"I'll be back with your water in just a moment," she said before striding away.

"Take your time," I muttered under my breath, cursing when I saw that Anastasia had disappeared to the back again.

That's how the rest of dinner went. Me living for glances of my girl . . . and her doing her best to avoid me.

An encouraging sign really; the more she ignored me, the more I knew I'd gotten under her skin. She was skittish, trying her best to stay away. But she couldn't fool me. I saw the way she snuck looks in my direction. The way her cheeks blushed. She was as attracted to me as I was to her.

That was a good first step.

I finally couldn't take it anymore.

The bathroom was just beyond where she kept disappearing to, so I headed down the long hallway. Luckily, she walked out of the back room just as I came around the corner.

And then it was just me and her.

Finally.

"Hi," I murmured, taking a few steps toward her so she had to look up at me.

Her breathing picked up and she bit down on her lip as she glanced at my face. "Can I help you with something?"

I stared at her, watching as she fidgeted under my gaze, eyes darting toward the dining room and then back to me.

"Usually, Whitney's *great* at giving customers what they need."

It could have just been my imagination, but my little dancer almost seemed *jealous*. It was nice to see another sign that she wasn't immune to me.

I was over here losing my fucking mind.

It only seemed fitting that she should join me.

"I'm not here for Whitney," I said bluntly.

She pulled nervously at the apron tied around her waist. "Okay. So you're here for . . . ?"

I continued to watch her, a small smile spreading across my face.

"You."

Her eyes widened, a small gasp coming out of her mouth. She was so fucking pretty.

"Me?" she whispered.

"Yeah, you. And you're hurting my feelings, baby girl. It seems like you don't want to be my friend," I said, and then I took a chance and reached up to push a strand of hair behind her ear.

She let me, and I had to stop myself from wrapping my arm around her and pulling her in. A shiver passed over her at my touch as my fingers brushed against her neck before I pulled away.

My grin only widened.

Wait until I'm touching every inch of you, sweetheart.

With my tongue.

It was dangerous to be this close to her.

Anastasia blinked up at me, her face a little dazed. "Is that what you're doing? Trying to be my friend?"

"I've been told I'm a very good friend," I teased, not answering her question.

I definitely did not want to be *just* her friend.

I wanted to own her, crawl under her skin, protect her forever, become a part of her so she could never leave me.

Wow . . . had I really just thought that? A flicker of unease slipped through my gut. I was starting to not recognize myself. What was this girl doing to me?

"Why would someone like you want to be friends with someone like . . . me?" she asked, a hint of vulnerability in her voice. "You saw me . . . the other day. We don't live in the same world."

Ahh. At the community kitchen. She was embarrassed I'd seen her there. That needed to be straightened out right now.

"I saw you. At your performance the other night. I should be the one asking why *you* would want to be friends with someone like *me*."

Her eyes widened, her lips opening again in shock, and now I was trying to keep my dick down because all I could think about was what it would be like to fuck that pretty mouth.

She was so fucking young. At least ten years younger than me I was pretty sure. I should feel like a dirty old man right now as I brushed her bare shoulder, pretending like there'd been something there just so I could touch her again.

But I didn't, not at all.

Because I knew she was mine.

"You saw me?" She gasped, her gaze filling with suspicion and something that almost looked like . . . desperation?

"I've never seen something so beautiful in my whole fucking life," I said, my voice sounding hoarse all of a sudden. I hoped she knew I wasn't just talking about her dancing—I meant that *she* was the most beautiful thing I'd ever seen in my life too.

She dipped her eyes down shyly . . . and I knew she'd gotten it.

Anastasia took a deep, shuddering breath before she caught my gaze again. And it seemed like a switch had completely flipped.

"Well, thank you. But I really need to get back to work," she said, her voice flat as she tried to go around me.

What had just happened?

"Hey," I said, touching her again gently. She stiffened at my touch this time, and I was even more confused. What invisible land mine had I accidentally stumbled over?

"Look. I don't know who put you up to this," she told me, her eyes searching our surroundings like she was expecting someone to be there watching with a camera or something. "But it's not funny. Not only is it not funny . . . it's cruel. You—you should be ashamed of yourself." Her eyes grew shiny, like she was going to cry, and there was a quiver in her voice now that was breaking my fucking heart.

And there really wasn't anything I could do at this point. It was impossible to explain to a normal human being that they'd done something to you. That one look at their face and you'd come undone—become obsessed. You couldn't tell them that you now lived in the space between their breath and their heartbeats. I *certainly* couldn't assure her that the last thing I ever wanted to do was to hurt her because I wanted to make her mine forever.

I backed away, putting my hands up in front of me. "I promise you, there's no joke here. I happened to be passing by tonight and saw you through the window. But I didn't come here to mess with you, or whatever got you so upset just now. It's just . . . I saw a literal angel performing on that stage, and I couldn't help but want to meet you properly. Since I didn't do such a good job of that the other day."

Her gaze bore into me, and I was a little afraid she might have some sort of superpower, able to see inside me and all the sins I was willing to commit to make her mine.

"I'm sorry," she finally said, so softly that I could barely hear her just steps away. "But I'm not looking for any friends," she finished, turning around and walking back toward the dining room like her life depended on it.

I watched her go, staring where she disappeared around the corner.

Well . . . shit.

Somehow, I'd fucked that up.

But instead of wallowing or getting pissed at myself, I let determination fill me, just like I did on the ice. I didn't let obstacles kill my shot.

And I certainly wasn't going to miss my shot with Anastasia.

I knew how to work hard . . .

And I could be infinitely patient. Whether it was practicing every day so that I was good enough to get a hockey scholarship for college, or studying hard so I could get straight A's, or waiting years to finally be strong enough and smart enough to hurt my stepfather after what he'd done.

I had no problem with working hard. In fact, I relished it. I was quite sure that nothing in my life would compare to the reward it would be when I finally got her. When it came to Anastasia, I knew she was worth every bit of effort.

I was going to figure out exactly what my baby girl needed. She had demons and struggles, I could see that clearly.

But I was going to fucking fix all of it for her. She just didn't know it yet.

CHAPTER 8

ANASTASIA

Madame Leclerc entered the room, gliding regally as she walked as if she was on a wheeled platform instead of her feet. She clapped her hands loudly once, even though she'd had our attention the second she'd come into the room. "I have incredible news. The Company has procured a new donor for the upcoming show."

My heart flipped in my chest. A new donor could mean a new scholarship, potentially. With my performance the other night . . . maybe there would be a chance . . . I would just have to give the best performance of my life at the upcoming tryouts for the next showcase. With a scholarship I could maybe afford a small apartment—in the bad part of town, yes—but that would be no problem. I mentally started to go over the dance I'd put together for tryouts, tuning Madame Leclerc out until a name she was saying caught my attention.

"Camden James from the Dallas Knights has taken an interest in the arts. Evidently, he was at our performance the other night and was very impressed with our work. We haven't had this type of donor before, but I'm hopeful that it will lead to even more fruitful relationships in the future."

The room immediately erupted, everyone around me whispering in excitement.

"He's so fucking hot," Alena gasped next to me, pulling at my arm eagerly.

I gaped at her, sure I hadn't heard right. Camden James was the new donor?

And the Dallas Knights? They were a professional hockey team, right? So that meant Camden was a freaking NHL player?

The room suddenly seemed to be spinning around me.

His words the other night haunted me, walking through my head any time I wasn't distracting myself.

"It's just . . . I saw a literal angel performing the other night, and I couldn't help but want to meet you."

From the second I'd seen him, there'd been something about him that had made me feel safe.

I didn't think it was possible to be just friends with someone like that, though, and as with every other person I'd had in my life—he'd soon realize I wasn't the kind of friend anyone could ever want.

A famous hockey player . . . and me. That was the biggest joke I'd ever heard.

Nothing about us went together. Everything about me was broken.

It was a good thing that I'd pushed him away, just like I pushed everyone away.

It was the best thing for him.

And me.

I'd survived a million terrible things in my life, but I wasn't sure that I could survive *him*.

And now finding out that he was basically a celebrity . . .

"As part of this new collaboration, the Company will be attending Mr. James's match on Saturday." She clapped again—for some unknown reason—and left the room without another word.

I didn't think you called it a *match* in hockey—my French ballet instructor was definitely not an expert in the sport.

Not that I was an expert, either . . . I'd seen zero games in my entire life. The only reason I even knew the name was because of the huge parade they'd had a couple of seasons ago when the Knights had won the Stanley Cup.

The whole city had gone crazy about it.

A little thrill ran through me thinking about seeing him play. He was so big . . . so strong. I could only imagine what he would look like out there on the ice.

But, it probably wasn't a good thing for me to go—seeing as I'd decided to stay away from him. Considering Madame Leclerc saw me as a liability and a burden to the Company . . . I wasn't going to be telling her that, though.

The class was still going crazy over the news. Girls . . . and a few guys practically squealing as they talked about the game. Dallon, one of the Company's principal dancers, winked at me from across the room, and I quickly went back to stretching, nodding as Alena planned out what she was going to wear . . . in detail.

None of us were going to be able to concentrate for the rest of class.

If Camden James was doing this to get my attention, he'd certainly gotten it.

I just hadn't figured out what his angle was yet.

Every person had an angle. Every person wanted something from you.

Usually, I could figure out what that was.

Men typically wanted me for my pretty face, or they thought they could take advantage of me. In this case I couldn't even say it was for either of those reasons—a god like that could snap, and anyone he wanted would come falling to his feet, swearing eternal devotion in exchange for his attention.

So, what did *he* want?

"Do you need a ride to the game tomorrow?" Dallon asked, suddenly appearing next to me. I blinked and realized I'd been holding this stretch for an awfully long time.

Dallon was attractive. He was nice—to my face.

I wanted nothing to do with him.

"I'm good," I told him, giving him the old dance smile. No one here obviously knew my living conditions. Dallon would know that I cleaned studios after class most days just because of his position, but he didn't know where he'd have to pick me up to "give me a ride to the game."

"We could go grab a drink beforehand," he pressed, and my eyes widened.

I heard alot about Dallon; he'd dated all three of the female principals including Larissa Deletare, the Company's prima ballerina.

It had caused a lot of drama.

Good-looking or not, I didn't want any of that.

But I also didn't want to get on his bad side.

This was not good.

The last thing I needed was to piss off one of the principals. Ballet was cutthroat. No one was there to make friends. The social hierarchy started with the principals and went down from there. If he decided I was a pariah—everyone would.

Madame Leclerc had hated my guts for years. I'd been slated to be the lead in *The Nutcracker*, and unfortunately, my leg had decided to give out a few days before the first performance. No amount of *pushing through* could get it to work. The understudy hadn't been ready, and the show had been written up by a bunch of news sites as a failure.

She'd never forgiven me—as if it was my fault and I'd meant for it to happen.

A few more people like her and there wouldn't be a place for me here.

Would that be so bad, a tiny voice whispered, and I pushed that away. Without this place, without dancing . . . I was nothing.

"I don't drink," I began, noting the way his face tightened. "But I could grab something to eat." I added the last part quickly, feeling pathetic with every syllable that crossed my lips.

Dallon's eyes lit up at that. He brushed his light blonde hair out of his face, and my gaze got caught on his lean muscles.

Not nearly as sexy as Camden's.

"Oh great. There's a pizza place by the arena, *Michaelangeo's*. You like pizza?"

I opened my mouth to tell him that, actually, I hated that place. We'd once had it delivered at a Company party and I'd gotten food poisoning and been sick all night—but he cut me off before I could.

"You'll like it. I've had it before. We'll go there," he finished confidently.

My shoulders slumped. It made sense that he wouldn't care what I wanted to eat—this was, after all, a man who'd had no problem pitting our top three ballerinas against each other.

I was convinced now for sure that he'd be the type of guy to make my life hell if I rejected him.

"I'll meet you there," I told him. "Thirty minutes before the game?"

He lifted an eyebrow, his face doing that tightening thing again that told me he was annoyed. "Thirty minutes? No, meet me there at five-thirty. Two hours before the game," he said, and my stomach tightened.

Two hours? How the hell was I going to sit with him for two hours?

Before I could say anything, he walked off, dismissing me, and even as he went, I saw him smile and wink at another dancer.

Wow. What an asshole.

At least I would get dinner that day; that was my only consolation for what I'd just agreed to. I could skip the pizza and go for a salad. A guy like that—he'd probably expect me to get a salad anyway.

I went back to stretching, deciding to table any worries about my impromptu date until Saturday.

But I couldn't table thinking about Camden James.

Camden

Anastasia Lennox was a difficult woman to stalk.

I was waiting outside her dance studio, in the alleyway that had become like a second home to me as of late with how much time I spent there. I was being a creeper, hoping I could see her for even a minute. Finding out something about her that I could use to make her mine would even be better.

I'd been trying to find out more information about her every free minute I had—anything to help me win her over.

I had been very unsuccessful.

Although, I had managed to get fifty of the assholes who'd followed her removed from her Instagram profile.

So, I guess that was an achievement.

My phone buzzed in my pocket, and I leaned back against the brick building behind me as I pulled it out and glanced at the text.

Ari: Hero, there's a cat caught in a tree outside, better come over and save it.

Me: ?

Me: Where did you get the idea that I saved cats . . .

Linc: Is that a question?

Walker: It's not a very good one.

Ari: You would say that, Disney, you simp.

Walker: I was agreeing with you!

Me: I'm still waiting to understand why I would save a cat. I don't even like cats.

Ari: You take that back. Right now.

Linc: . . .

Ari: Do you have something to say, Golden Boy?

Linc: You don't even like cats . . .

Ari: Oh, right.

Me: I'm unclear what the point of this conversation is.

Ari: I'm unclear why you're in this chat, James.

Me: You literally were the one who texted me.

Ari: . . .

Me: I'm not saving a cat.

Linc: I guess you're not the hero we thought you were.

Me: Well, I could save a cat.

Ari: No. Absolutely not. There cannot be two of you.

Me: Two . . . ?

Ari: Two of you worshiping Golden Boy. It's high time someone worshiped me.

Linc: . . .

Walker: . . .

Me: . . .

Me: Did I do that right?

Ari Lancaster removed you from the chat.

I huffed, but then a second later, my phone pinged again.

Lincoln Daniels added you to the chat.

A grin stretched across my face.

Me: Thanks, Daniels. You're a man above men.

Ari: SIMP!

My phone started buzzing as Ari raged about "Golden Boy's betrayal of the Circle" or something else equally incoherent, but I was distracted as Anastasia came down the steps of the dance studio. Straightening off the wall, I took a step further down the alley so she wouldn't see me.

Fuck, she was beautiful. That tight spandex thing she was wearing should be illegal. What was that outfit called again? A leotard?

I was a big fan of leotards, I decided.

But I nearly ground my teeth down to dust when I noticed a group of guys following behind her.

I saw them also notice how good her ass looked.

One of the guys called out her name and she stopped and turned toward them. I slid to the edge of the building so I could hear what they were saying.

"Are you sure I can't just pick you up on Saturday?" one of them asked, a tall, thin asshole-looking dude.

This wasn't the first time I'd seen him talking to her.

Dallon. That was his name.

I'd searched the Company's website to find out who he was the first time I'd seen him staring at her outside. He was one of the principals of the company—one of the leads, so to speak.

I wanted to kill him.

Gritting my teeth, I glared at him even though he wouldn't notice me over here. He was leaning against the railing, staring down at her from a few steps up. I stiffened, creeping even closer, dread clogging my throat. There was a buzzing sound in my head as she smiled at him.

Her going on a date before my game was not part of the plan. How had I messed it up this badly?

It was a question I found myself asking far too often lately.

"I have a few errands I need to run beforehand, so it's just easier to meet you," she said, shifting back and forth and biting down on her lower lip like she did when she was nervous.

And yes, I already knew that about her.

I was making a point to study her every expression.

"Fine," the asshole huffed, rolling his eyes like he was a petulant teenager rather than the grown man he looked to be. "It's the pizza place on the same street as the arena. Can't miss it."

She was already backing away as he talked, giving him a quick wave before she darted down the sidewalk away from where I was standing. This place was a perfect stakeout place because no one ever seemed to come this way . . . or notice me lurking.

I glanced at my phone; she only had twenty minutes to get to Charlie's. She was cutting it close. I headed to my truck to follow after her, but then the asswipes decided to open their mouths.

"Finally got the ice queen to melt, Dallon?" one of the guys asked the tall one who had been talking to Anastasia.

I stopped in my tracks, turning slowly to look back at the group, my fists clenching at my sides.

I'd never cut out a tongue before, but I was tempted at that moment.

Once again, an impulse I'd never had before.

The dead man named Dallon smirked and nodded his head after Anastasia. "A girl like that, she'll be desperate for it. I'll pay for dinner. Buy her a few drinks at the game . . . she'll probably let me fuck her in the backseat on the way home." He snorted. "She's hot enough I might even go back for seconds."

The other two laughed like Dallon was the most hilarious guy they'd ever met, and I decided that they also looked like dead men.

Rage tore through me, and I might have blacked out for a minute. When I got ahold of myself, I realized I'd stepped out of the alleyway, ready to destroy them for talking about her like that. I held myself back as they walked off, trying to relax before I headed over to the restaurant to see Anastasia. I'd have to think of something between now and tomorrow to make sure that date didn't happen, but right now, I had to get to my girl.

Anastasia's eyes widened when she came out, and I was sitting at the table closest to the washroom.

"Oh, hi," she fumbled out, water from the bin she was carrying spilling over the edges as she came to a screeching halt at the sight of me.

"Hi, little dancer," I said, leaning back in my booth and raking my eyes over her like a man who'd been dying of thirst and finally found a pool of water. It had been eighteen minutes and thirty-two seconds since I'd seen her last.

I was fully aware that my obsession was getting out of hand.

"Stalking me now?" she asked, a small smile on her lips like she wouldn't really mind if that was the case. I highly doubted that was actually her mindset, so I just smiled in return.

"I've become particularly fond of Charlie's over the past week. I've developed a craving for it, you could say," I responded lightly.

She blushed, biting down on that plump lower lip in a way that made me want to die inside because I couldn't touch her.

"When's your break?" I asked, when she hadn't run away yet like she had last time.

"My break?" she stuttered.

"Yeah, I assume you have one of those?" I raised an eyebrow. "Or do I need to have a talk with your manager?"

Anastasia blinked at me, her eyes dazed and unfocused. "A talk with my manager . . . " She must have realized that I was not joking because she suddenly straightened. "Oh yes, I have a break!"

"Not that you should be concerned with that," she added after a couple of seconds, like she had just reminded herself that she needed to be on guard. Anastasia cocked her hip out and gave me a bratty look that had me wanting to push her to her knees and fuck her mouth to straighten out her newfound attitude.

Again . . . where the fuck had that instinct come from?

I smirked. Her attitude was cute. I had a feeling that she didn't show that side of herself very much, and I loved that something about me made her feel comfortable enough to do that.

"Maybe I'm interested in being concerned with that," I mused, unable to stop myself from gawking at her because she was so fucking beautiful. This was not the way to prove I wasn't a creeper, but technically I had been creeping after her—so maybe it was a losing effort to begin with.

Anastasia opened her mouth and then closed it, clearly at a loss for words. This was becoming a pattern for us.

"Get back to work before you get into trouble, baby girl. Come sit with me during your break," I ordered sternly. "Unless you want me to break you out of here, because then I have *way* cooler places we can hang out."

Anastasia's eyes widened, that dreamy look spreading over her features, like me getting stern was an aphrodisiac for her. She *liked* when I took charge. It turned her on.

I fucking loved that.

"Okay," she finally whispered. "I mean—that's okay. I—I'll see you at my break."

I nodded at her, trying to keep the crazy out of my eyes as I did so, and then I watched her walk away.

Two long hours later, after I'd filled my table with random food orders so they wouldn't kick me out, she was finally sitting in front of me, her fingers tapping the table softly, her gaze darting around the room like it was hard for her to look at me.

Anastasia's cheeks were slightly pink from hustling around all night, and her hair was in the same tight bun she'd been wearing at school. Pieces of her hair had fallen out, though, and my fingers itched to touch them and smooth them away from her face. I would have preferred that she sit next to me—but beggars couldn't be choosers.

"So what's your angle here, Mr. James?" she asked, cocking her head as she *finally* gave me her full attention.

"My angle?"

"You're sponsoring the Company. You gave us tickets to a game. Why would you do that?"

I was finding out more things about her every day that I was attracted to, but up close . . . her features were spellbinding. I was having a little trouble concentrating.

Camden James, pull yourself together.

I lifted an eyebrow again. "I believe that I already gave you that answer the last time you let me talk to you."

She flushed and I grinned. I loved how responsive she was. It was impossible for her to hide from me how she was feeling. I was going to take every advantage I could get.

"So, you're making a donation . . . because of me?" There was a heartbreaking edge to her tone, like the idea of that was completely out of the realm of possibility.

I leaned over the table, wishing I was closer to her, wishing I could *touch* her.

"Of course. I already told you how your dancing made me feel. Like I was dying and desperate and changing as I watched you because I'd never known beauty like that could actually exist." Her face softened as I spoke, her eyes growing suspiciously shiny, like she was trying not to cry.

"You can't say things like that," she argued, her fingers fumbling with the napkin in front of her.

"Why not?"

"Because—because it can't possibly be true!"

"Why can't it?"

"You're being difficult," she growled, reminding me of a kitten again, trying to be fierce but looking cute instead.

"It seems like you may not have had a lot of people you can trust in your life," I said softly, unable to stop myself from finally taking a chance and reaching out to touch her hand.

My dick hardened in my lap, and I scooted closer to the table—needing to make sure that she didn't see.

Not sure I'd have an adequate explanation for that.

"I haven't had *any* to trust," she muttered under her breath, before squeezing her eyes closed like she couldn't believe she'd said that out loud.

My gut tightened at her admission. It made me feel absolutely feral thinking about her being alone all this time. I was more than happy to step up, though, and be the first person to fill that role.

"Maybe it's time to let someone in, then," I suggested, pushing my luck by trailing my fingers across her smooth skin. Her eyes flew open, and I lost my breath for a second, staring into the twin pools of blue.

"Why should it be you?" she finally whispered.

The words hung in the air, and a thousand different things flew through my head. I wanted to tell her I was going to change her life. I wanted to tell her that I would take care of her forever . . . that she'd never be unhappy again as long as she gave me a chance.

I wanted to tell her she didn't have a choice.

I leaned in instead, unable to stop myself from brushing my lips across hers in a kiss that only fed the fire of the longing throbbing through my veins. "Why shouldn't it be?"

Pulling away, she seemed like she'd literally lost her breath, as she stared at me wide-eyed. I held in my smirk. "Breathe, little dancer," I urged, and she let out a long exhale, her blue gaze still locked on mine like she was afraid I'd disappear if she looked away.

"Break's over," a voice called through the charged silence between us. I reluctantly glanced beyond her to see a pink-haired woman with wrinkled skin like a walnut glaring at the two of us like we'd mortally offended her.

"I'd better get back to it," Anastasia murmured, but she was different than she'd been before, softer almost, as if I'd managed to break through some of her walls.

I'd take it. I'd just sit here while I waited for her, bathing in the memory of what her perfect lips had felt like.

"I'll be here when you're done. You're off at nine, right?"

"See, when you say things like that, I really do think you could be stalking me," she said, some of her sass leaking back into her voice.

I winked at her, once again not responding to that because what could I say? I *was* her stalker.

She went back to work, and I went back to ordering a dish every hour so that I could wait for her without causing her any issues.

It was the longest two hours of my life, made worse by the fact that I'd touched her.

I'd kissed her.

And now I wanted to do it over and over again . . . and much, much more.

Anastasia

I couldn't tell you what I did the rest of my shift. Usually, I knew what dishes I'd washed, what tables I'd cleaned, how many spilled drinks I'd mopped up . . .

I couldn't concentrate on anything that happened for the rest of the night.

All I could think about was *him*.

How he'd looked. What he'd said. The way he'd touched me.

The feel of his lips against mine.

Had that really happened? Or had I hallucinated it? Any moment now, I was expecting a camera crew to pop out and tell me that I'd been "Punk'd" or something, because things like that—fairy-tale kisses with gorgeous celebrities who said sweet things that made you melt—they definitely did not happen to girls like me.

This wasn't Hollywood.

I wasn't a princess.

And now I was quoting Taylor Swift lyrics.

That confirmed it. I had definitely imagined it all.

Except, each time I came out from the back . . . he was still there. Still gazing at me with that gorgeous face. Pulling me in with every smile he gifted my way.

I was surprised every single time I saw him.

"Ready to go, little dancer? You're probably exhausted," he said, unfolding himself easily from the bench seating despite the fact that he had to at least be six-four. That could not have been fun to sit there for the last four hours.

Camden grabbed my hand and pulled me toward the door. I got about halfway there when I woke up from whatever spell he'd had me under—because what the crap was I doing?

He was going to walk me to the doors of the shelter?

Not happening. He noticed my steps had faltered and sent me a questioning glance. I didn't want to make it a big deal since everyone in the restaurant seemed to be watching us walk out, so I pasted a smile on my face and followed him outside.

As soon as we were through the door, a chill biting into my bones as a gust of wind whipped across my face, I yanked my hand away.

"You don't need to walk me home—and I'm pretty sure that violates all the stranger danger lectures they gave us in school," I said, trying to sound like I was joking even as I started to walk away.

"Anastasia," he growled, and the sound was so sexy I felt it right between my legs.

A howl split the night air and I froze, glancing around the shadows for where the sound had come from.

Deep, rough barking followed the howl, and I screamed and jumped at Camden, clawing at his shirt—only faintly aware of how muscled his chest was.

"Do you see it? Do you see the dog? Oh my gosh. Where is it?" My voice was high-pitched and *crazy*, and I was trying to literally climb Camden's body like a tree.

But I couldn't help it.

I hated dogs. HATED them.

Camden's arms wrapped around me, his voice calm but tinged with concern. "It's probably just a stray," he reassured me, stroking a hand soothingly down my hair.

The barking got closer, and I screamed again, tears dripping down my face. "Please get me away. Please. Please. Please." I was trembling—shaking so hard that I bit down on my tongue, blood filling my mouth.

"Holy fuck," Camden muttered, adjusting my body so he was cradling me against his chest as he started walking. I kept my eyes squeezed shut, holding on to his shirt for dear life as a few more barks sounded from nearby.

My breath was coming out in gasps.

"How do you like it in there, little bunny? Gatsby looks awfully hungry," Michael grinned at me demonically through the bars of the cage he'd put me in as soon as his mother and father left for the weekend.

"Please let me out," I sobbed as Gatsby, Michael's Doberman, snarled at me from the other side of the cage. Michael had chained him tightly to the cage wall across from me, so he couldn't quite reach where I was huddled up in the corner . . . but it was only a matter of time before he let out the chain.

And the dog wouldn't stop growling at me.

"But you cry so prettily," Michael mused, settling into a chair like he was about to watch a performance.

He'd eventually gotten up because he was bored, extending Gatsby's chain so that I only had a small sliver of the cage where I could sit, and then he'd flipped off the lights. It had been pitch-black in the basement, and the dog had snarled and pulled on his chain all night, snapping at me, trying to bite me, growling. My leg had slid out from under me at one point, and he'd bit the top of my shoe when I got too close.

I'd eventually passed out from fear.

And I'd been terrified of dogs ever since.

I came back to the present in Camden's truck, the scent of nice leather . . . and him . . . flooding my senses. I'd soaked his shirt, and I was still gripping it like it held the key to redemption.

I tried to loosen my hands, but I couldn't get my fingers to work. They were trembling too much.

"Relax," he soothed.

"I'm sorry," I whispered into his chest, just allowing myself a second of this. A second of breathing him in, of feeling safe, of feeling okay.

For just a second.

There was something so . . . safe about Camden. Maybe it was because he was so much older than me. Maybe it was because of how big he was. Or maybe it was because he was holding me like I was the most precious thing he'd ever touched.

Whatever it was . . . the feeling was dangerous.

"So, I take it you're scared of dogs," he mused, his tone light. There wasn't any judgment in his tone, and he didn't seem to be making fun of me.

I breathed him in one more time, feeling like a crazy person, and then I forced myself to let him go. Once I sat up, I tried to move from his lap, but his arms pinned me in place.

"There's no hurry, sweetheart," he murmured. I finally glanced up at him, expecting to see . . . I don't know what. Pity maybe.

But all I could see was concern in his gold-rimmed gaze. Camden's thumb wiped a lingering tear from my cheek, and I watched, transfixed as he brought his thumb up to his mouth, his pink tongue darting out to lick the moisture off.

"Wow . . . that was intense," I breathed, not really knowing what else to say. I only knew that the longer I sat on Camden's lap . . . the more another emotion was building inside of me.

He didn't say anything, his gaze was focused on my lips, a charged intensity filling the cab that I wasn't sure how to handle.

Something buzzed in his pocket—his phone, probably—and we both startled.

Crap, what time was it? I glanced at the console, freaking out when I saw that I had to be in the shelter in twenty minutes, or I wasn't going to have a place to sleep for the night.

I scrambled off his lap, ignoring the giant bulge between his legs as I moved—and this time he let me.

"Can you drop me off at the corner of Clark and Fourth Street. Please." I wasn't going to let him see the shelter, but there was no way that I could get there on foot or public transportation and make it in time. That address was just around the corner from it.

"Of course," he said, not sounding happy about it.

"I'm sorry," I said quickly. "If you have somewhere to go, it's okay." It wouldn't be the first time that I'd missed curfew. A night on the streets wouldn't kill me.

Probably.

Camden scoffed. "I don't need to go anywhere," he told me firmly, but he still didn't seem happy as he drove through the streets, not even needing to reference a GPS to get to the address I'd given him. He must know this city well.

The address was an apartment building about two blocks from the shelter. I'd used it before when I'd had to get rides in the past. "This is your place?" Camden asked, peering up at the building like it had personally offended him.

What was his deal? I know it wasn't a McMansion, like where he probably lived. But still, it was perfectly nice.

Not that I actually lived there, of course.

I could only imagine what he'd think of where I really lived. He'd probably drive away screaming.

I snorted at that thought, and Camden raised an eyebrow.

How did he make that look so sexy?

A quick glance at the clock told me I only had minutes to spare.

"I've got to go," I told him, instead of actually answering. For some reason, there was a part of me that didn't want to lie to him.

"I'll walk you in," he said, moving to open his door.

"That's okay!" I squeaked. "My neighbor is kind of a psycho. Hears a mouse fart at forty feet. If she hears us, she'll report me."

OMG. DID I REALLY JUST SAY MOUSE FART?

Just let me die now.

Please.

Camden's face was carefully blank for a long moment. Maybe he hadn't heard me?

Suddenly he burst out laughing, the sound of it wrapping around me like everything I never knew I needed. I couldn't help but laugh, too, even though I wanted to find the nearest hole and jump in it.

I opened my door, and his laughter abruptly cut off, his face becoming solemn once more. "I'll see you tomorrow, baby girl. Can I send a car?"

Inwardly scoffing again, I pictured a private car rolling up to the shelter. I could only imagine what people would think if I coasted down the steps and got in.

"That's alright," I said, wincing as I remembered the unfortunate dinner plans I also had before the game.

Camden bit down on his lip, looking like he wanted to argue with me, and I had the sudden urge to bite back.

Down girl.

He reached out, doing that thing where he stroked my cheek like I was *everything* to him.

"See you later, little dancer," he murmured as I finally got out of the car.

And I loved that it sounded like a promise.

I pretended to go into the lobby, glad this place wasn't manned by a doorman. I couldn't go up to any of the floors, obviously, since I didn't have a keycard, but thankfully Camden pulled away when I walked to the elevators.

The second his truck disappeared around the corner, I took off at a sprint, my leg aching with every step, sure I wasn't going to make it.

One of the night guards was standing by the door, about to lock up when I rushed up the steps. “Cutting it close, Ana,” she chided gently as she opened the door and raised a questioning brow.

“I know. Thanks, Georgia,” I told her gratefully, breathing a sigh of relief as I passed over the threshold of the shelter.

As I hustled down the hall toward the main room where the cots were set up, I was still very sure that even if I’d had to sleep on the streets . . .

Tonight would have been worth it.

CHAPTER 9

CAMDEN

For the first time in my life, I didn't want to get ready for my game.

I had to report for warm-ups, so I couldn't personally stop Anastasia's date. But that didn't mean I wasn't going to use other means to stop it.

I mean, I was better than that.

"What's that smile on your face, Hero? You kind of look like a serial killer," Ari drawled as I changed into my uniform.

"He's probably thinking about a grandma he helped cross the road," Logan commented seriously. "Grandpappy business."

Ari rolled his eyes. "I said he looked like a serial killer, not someone helping little old ladies with their grocery bags."

"I bet serial killers do that. As a cover," Logan mused.

"Are we really talking about me being a serial killer right now? As I'm standing *right* here?"

"At least we're the kind of friends that talk about you to your face," offered Disney, strapping on his goalie pads.

"I think I'm alright with you talking about me being a serial killer behind my back," I said. "Although this conversation is completely pointless. I am *not* a serial killer, and I did not help any old ladies cross the street. Geraldine is not fond of walking across roads in general."

"Still going steady with Old Geraldine?" Ari asked.

"She must be good with her mouth," Logan said. "She probably doesn't have any teeth to get in the way."

I stared at him horrified.

"Can we not talk about James and seventy-five-year-old women," Lincoln said, wincing as he tightened his skates.

"I would appreciate that, thank you, Daniels," I said magnanimously. I ignored the little thrill that came with Lincoln Daniels agreeing with me on . . . anything.

We didn't need another simp on the team.

"Now that we got completely off track, we need to talk about warm-ups," said Ari, staring at all of us seriously like he was about to give a big speech.

"What are you talking about, Lancaster?" Lincoln asked distractedly as he stared at some kind of video on his phone. It almost looked like he was staring at a live feed of Monroe in the back of a car.

Weird . . .

"Tonight's the night. How could you have forgotten?" Ari asked, sounding outraged.

I blinked for a moment, trying to figure out what the hell he was talking about. Was there some kind of award ceremony? Kind of an odd part of the season to do that.

"Our performance!" Ari growled, throwing his hands up like we'd mortally offended him.

It took a second, but then horror hit me.

Hard.

The media had somehow gotten ahold of our little pregame ritual we did in the locker room most games—something that evidently had started when Ari and Walker were playing in L.A. and Walker got pregame jitters. That video going viral had led to our media department requesting that we perform before one of the games.

I'd blocked out the exact date since I was completely against doing it. Ari had threatened me with the circle of trust when I'd voiced an objection.

And since I still didn't know what that actually was . . . I had agreed to it.

But that was way before I'd concocted the plan to get Anastasia—to a game.

Although, the plan was definitely to get Anastasia as well.

"Can this be moved?" I asked seriously.

Ari threw an old sock at me. "No, we can't move it! This is *my* time to shine."

"You mean as opposed to the professional hockey games you play on a regular basis," Lincoln offered.

"Stop raining on my parade, Golden Boy. It's important that the world knows my secret talents."

"You could just tell them about the ring at the end of your—"

"What the hell are you all still doing in here? Get your asses out on the ice!" Coach Watts growled, popping his head in the locker room.

"We'll need to circle back to whatever you were about to say," I told Walker as we walked out of the locker room. Before he could say anything, Ari clapped his hand on Walker's shoulder. Hard, judging by Walker's wince.

"Walker 'Disney' Davis," Ari said threateningly. "Do we really want to talk about dick decorations?"

Walker grimaced, his hand hovering in front of his pants protectively, like he was in pain.

"Focus," I snarled. "We still have time to back out of this. We can still have some dignity."

"You agreed. I have it in writing," Ari reminded me as we skated out on the ice to thumping music and screams.

Shaking my head, I shot a puck at the goal, before skating around the net.

"I'd like to revoke that agreement," I hissed at Ari as I passed by him.

The asshole just laughed, like he didn't believe me.

As I continued warm-ups, all I could hope was that the other part of my plan for the night was actually going well.

And that Anastasia's "date" had never made it there.

She was here.

Alone.

And fuck, it was probably cheating to give the ballet school jerseys with my last name on them—Lancaster would definitely have something to say about that—but the opportunity to have Anastasia in a jersey with my name on it wasn't something I was going to pass up.

It was better than I'd even jacked off to.

The blue Knights logo really made her eyes pop.

Or maybe it was her perfect tits under the Knights logo that was doing that.

The only thing that would've made it better was if it said "Mrs. James." That definitely had a ring to it.

Baby steps, though.

That would come soon enough.

Anastasia was sitting at the end of the row, her eyes wide and nervous as the other dance people talked around her. I really needed to do some research on ballet—not sure it would impress Anastasia for me to call them *dance people* in conversation.

Her arms were tucked around herself, and she was watching the ice avidly—mostly me, I noticed. I couldn't wait until she was sitting with Monroe, Blake, and Olivia. I had a feeling my girl didn't have a lot of friends, and I knew those girls would scoop her right up and love her.

Not as much as I would love her, of course.

Her "date" was nowhere to be found. I guess having your car towed and an eviction notice placed on your door meant you didn't have time for a hockey game—or a date.

Thank fuck for Ryan. Ryan was a college bud who happened to be a detective with the Dallas Police Department. Since he spent most of his time with the underbelly of the city, sometimes he didn't mind doing some more questionable things when asked.

Pro tip: If you find your fraternity buddy butt naked, peeing on a snowman during Winter Carnival, get him back to his room and into some clothes before his dick freezes off.

He'll owe you for life.

"James, get back to fucking work," one of the assistant coaches growled, and I reluctantly pulled my attention back to the ice.

It was still difficult to comprehend that I had something in my life that could actually distract me from hockey. I took a deep breath, trying to center myself. I breathed in the chill of the ice, I listened to the roar of the crowd, and I took in my teammates skating around me.

No matter how hard I tried . . . it didn't quite light a fire in my bloodstream like it used to. What once was blazing color, the only thing I could see, had now dimmed.

It was terrifying.

Because it meant that I couldn't afford to lose. Hockey had always been the focal point of my life. The only thing I needed.

If I didn't get Anastasia, hockey wasn't going to fill the gaping hole inside of me.

I took a shot at the goal and then started my stretches.

One thing about hockey stretches—they're very necessary.

To be the kind of skaters we needed to be on the ice, we needed explosive hip abductors/extenders for our stride and strong hip flexors for a powerful brake.

Another thing about hockey stretches—they apparently were kryptonite for the ladies.

Although we weren't really humping the ice—and I'd never had the thought that I *was* trying to hump the ice—a few TikTok videos had shown me it perhaps could be considered that way.

Which is why, as I started my stretches, I made sure to lock eyes with Anastasia, grinning when her cheeks flushed and she couldn't take her eyes off of me.

I may have done a few extra stretches for good measure. Anything I could do to get her to picture what I could do with my hips—I was going to use to my advantage.

It was easier to really get into it with Neil Diamond blaring through the speakers.

"Trying to go viral, James? How about you grind your dick into the ice a little more," drawled Logan as he skated by. "Not exactly 'Grandpappy' behavior."

I scoffed, not ashamed at all that I was giving my girl a show.

Although, he did have a point about me potentially going viral. Now that I had dragged my gaze away from Anastasia, I could see that there were quite a bit more cameras pointed at me than usual.

I straightened up right in time to stop a puck that happened to be sliding by . . . and then I launched it at Logan.

"Hey," he growled, rubbing at his leg.

"Whoops," I responded, winking at him for good measure. "Guess that's why I'm a defender."

Logan flipped me off, and I'm sure my answering grin looked a little crazy.

"Did you have a hand in this song selection, James? Is your taste in music really this bad?" Ari asked as he skated up next to me. "Because there's no way our entertainment department picked this."

I scoffed before wiping my palms on my pants. It was almost time for our dance.

"He didn't pick it," Disney provided helpfully as he appeared next to me.

"But I think his taste in music really is this bad. He had "Go The Distance" in his top songs of the last year," offered Logan.

"Excuse me, *Rookie*. That song snaps. And also . . . get out of my fucking Spotify playlists," I hissed, thoroughly annoyed.

Logan blinked at me for a moment before laughing uproariously.

"*That song snaps*, Hero?" Ari gasped, also leaning forward and laughing like he was about to die.

"Why aren't all of you more concerned that Logan is stalking me?" I growled. "And also . . . I hate you all."

"So does that mean you're dancing by yourself—I'm positive it was your moonwalk that made this event happen," said Disney.

It was a really good moonwalk, but I still stared at him, aghast. "Of course it doesn't mean that. You think this friendship has outs like that just because I know cool lingo and you don't?"

They started laughing at me harder.

I flipped them all off, with both fingers for good measure and then went back to staring at Anastasia.

Before I danced.

Fuck. Was I really about to do this?

"Let's go, boys," Ari whooped, because sometimes he liked to pretend that we were in a Shania Twain video.

I glanced up at the official Knights DJ booth located in one of the suites and gave the DJ a head nod as I skated toward center ice. Anastasia was staring at us questioningly, her face so pretty I wanted to leap over the glass and drag her into a closet somewhere.

I willed myself not to get hard, what I was about to do was going to get enough attention.

My dick didn't need to come out and try to steal the show.

The pulsating beats of "Baby Got Back," filled the arena then, and I took a deep breath, wishing it wasn't questionable to take shots before games.

I was really going to do this, though.

Ari skated by and slapped me on the ass on the way to his spot.

Winking at Anastasia, I launched into my dance, gyrating and twisting to Sir Mix-a-Lot as I turned and shook my ass, pretending it was just at Anastasia and not an arena filled with people recording me.

Lincoln scooted me over, and I glared at him before realizing why he'd moved me. I was technically on the side of the ice closest to Monroe, and apparently, I'd gotten too close to the invisible barrier that was supposed to surround his wife at all times.

Lincoln started shaking *his* ass in front of Monroe, who was staring at him with a kind of bemused look on her face.

He was completely stealing my best moves!

I forgot about the thief, though, as Anastasia got a sort of dreamy looking smile on her face, her gaze pinned to my every move.

Everything was going well until Lancaster snuck up behind me and tried to ride me like a pony.

And then Walker was trying to ride my other side.

And everything turned to pure chaos.

The fans were screaming louder than I think I'd ever heard them, which was offensive because we were on a ten-game winning streak at the moment. There seemed to be more high-pitched screams than usual as well.

And I wasn't sure those high-pitched screams were just coming from women.

Logan did some kind of moonwalk across the ice in front of us, and hell, I was suddenly wondering if I could get away with punching my own teammate in front of an arena filled with people because obviously the only person who could moonwalk in front of my girl was me . . .

That's how we'd gotten into this mess to begin with, obviously.

The last notes finally—thankfully—faded, and I lifted my jersey to show off our finishing touches.

"Anastasia" was written in paint across my chest—fun for the uniform people to get out later. Lincoln, Ari, and Walker all had their girls' names on their chests as well. I'm sure they would have questions about who Anastasia was later on.

Logan's chest said "open for business" with an arrow pointing down . . .

Anastasia stared at my chest, her mouth gaping before she glanced up at my face. I dropped the jersey and made a heart sign before Coach began screaming at us to get our asses in gear.

"Went a little off script there, Lancaster," I muttered to him as we headed down the tunnel toward our locker room where we would no doubt get reamed by Coach until the game started.

"I'm an entertainer, James," Ari said sarcastically. "I have to do what the music compels me to do."

"The music compelled you to mount me?"

He grinned at me smugly. "Sir Mix-a-Lot demands someone be mounted."

Lincoln snorted as he passed us, shaking his head.

"Don't pretend like you don't think I'm funny, Golden Boy," Ari called after him.

"Don't pretend like you need Sir Mix-a-Lot to mount something," Lincoln shot back.

I was still shaking my head as we reached the locker room, wondering at the same time—how freaked out was Anastasia right now?

CHAPTER 10

ANASTASIA

The rest of the Company was shooting me looks, talking about me loudly as we waited for the players to come back out and the game to start. I couldn't even find it in myself to care—I was too shocked by what had happened.

Watching Camden James dance . . .

My panties were soaked.

And I didn't have a lot of extra.

The trip to the laundromat would be well worth it, though.

But the end . . . that was what had me tripping all over myself, practically falling out of my seat in a puddle of confusion and lust.

That had been my name on his chest, right? I hadn't hallucinated that?

I wanted to ask someone—check whether my eyes actually worked—but I was afraid they would think I was crazy.

It was just that the reality of what had happened seemed impossible. Because why would an NHL superstar ever put my name anywhere . . . let alone on a body part?

I'd Googled him on a library computer today. He really was a superstar. Either he or Ari Lancaster had gotten the James Norris Memorial Trophy every year for the last six years—evidently, that was the trophy for the best defender in the League.

I'd read all about all the charities he'd supported. He'd won the NHL's trophy for humanitarian work three times as well.

That was easy to believe. He'd been at a community kitchen the first time I'd met him after all, and judging by how easily everyone interacted with him—it hadn't been the first time.

I'd also come across some of the . . . campaigns he'd been a part of.

One had been a men's briefs line, and Camden James had a lot to be cocky about.

The size of his cock made sure of that.

I honestly didn't know how he fit it in his pants.

"So, how do you know Camden James?" Alena asked, sliding into the empty seat next to me. "Why didn't you mention it during class?"

"Well, I—I don't really know him."

She snorted. "Come on, Ana. He had your freaking name on his chest. Those abs," she said dreamily. "I'll never forget them."

I had the insane urge to claw her eyes out. That had been my name on his abs . . . that meant they were mine, right?

Ana, you're being crazy.

"I guess I kind of know him," I finally said.

She stared at me confused, a glint of jealousy in her gaze.

That was new. People weren't really jealous of me . . . ever.

Maybe before my injury, when my instructors had praised me over and over again and hailed me as the next big thing . . . but not anymore.

I was saved from her interrogating me any further when the lights suddenly dimmed, casting a shadow over the sea of spectators. An excited murmur rippled through the stands, quickly followed by an exhilarating cheer. I leaned forward in my seat, my eyes fixed on the ice.

A spotlight pierced the darkness, sweeping across the rink as the music crescendoed. The heavy, bass-laden beats vibrated through my chest, each thud syncing with my racing pulse. The announcer's voice boomed through the speakers, deep and resonant, filling every corner of the arena.

"Ladies and gentlemen," the announcer began, drawing out the words for maximum effect, "Welcome to tonight's game! Please put your hands together for your very own DALLAS KNIGHTS . . . "

The roar of the fans was overwhelming, the noise almost deafening. The spotlight intensified, focusing on the entrance tunnel where the players would emerge. A thrill ran down my spine as the music shifted to a high-energy rock anthem, and the tunnel lit up with flashing lights. One by one, the players skated out, their names echoing through the arena.

"Number 13, Lincoln Daniels!" The crowd cheered as he glided onto the ice, raising his stick in acknowledgment. He made a heart sign at a woman sitting on the other side of the home bench, and their cheers grew even louder.

"Number 24, Ari Lancaster!" Another wave of applause followed Ari's entrance. He was the other defenseman I'd read about. There'd been tons of articles about having Ari and Camden together when Camden was signed by the Knights last summer.

And yes, I'd done a lot of research today.

I kind of felt like a stalker.

Ari blew a kiss at a blonde woman sitting next to Lincoln's girl.

My eyes never left the tunnel, anticipation growing with each name called. Finally, the moment I had been waiting for arrived.

"Number 63, Camden James!"

I found myself screaming along with the crowd as Camden skated out onto the ice, his powerful strides confident and commanding. The spotlight followed him, casting a dramatic glow on his figure. He raised his stick high, acknowledging the fans' adoration, before he turned toward our section and pointed his stick at . . . me.

I was going to faint.

"Holy shit. Holy shit. Holy shit!" Alena screamed, her black hair whipping me in the face as she jumped up and down, grabbing onto my arm and almost pushing me into the next row.

I straightened, blinking when I saw Camden was at the glass in front of us, staring up at me, his gaze concerned and frustrated.

"Are you alright, baby girl?" he mouthed, and I nodded in shock, feeling like everyone in the arena was now staring at me.

What was this life?

Alena's hand was on my arm again, shaking me. She didn't seem to have realized that she'd almost toppled me down the rows of seats—or she might have just not cared.

The players skated back toward their bench, Camden trailing behind them, still shooting me glances as he moved. I watched as he said something to a man wearing a Dallas Knights polo, seeming to gesture over to my section as he spoke to the guy.

I bit down on my lip nervously, wondering what was going on.

Camden finished talking to the guy and joined the rest of the team before skating out with Ari Lancaster to the ice with three other players. The Dallas goalie was already in the net.

And the game began.

A few minutes in, and I was already a fan.

The game was fast and fun, and Camden had already slammed several players into the boards.

Another player had already tried to punch someone.

Absolutely epic.

"Ma'am," a voice said from next to me. I jumped in surprise, looking over to see the same employee Camden had been speaking to standing in the aisle next to me. "I'm going to need you to come with me," he told Alena.

"What do you mean?" Alena asked, staring at him confused.

"Just follow me, please. We need you in a different seat, or we're going to have to ask you to leave," the man said sternly.

"Who do you think you—"

"Next step is security, *ma'am*," he said fiercely.

Alena opened and closed her mouth, kind of like a guppy fish, glancing at me for help.

I shrugged my shoulders, giving her a sheepish look. I was honestly a little relieved she would be leaving. I'd learned Alena was dangerous when she got excited. I wasn't sure my leg could survive her reaction if the Knights actually scored a goal.

She huffed as she slid past me, muttering something about talking to a manager. The employee seemed nonplussed about her reaction, his face remaining blank as she started bitching at him.

Maybe he was used to delivering bad news to guests.

As he led her away, my gaze bounced back and forth to where Camden was playing on the ice and Alena was walking away. Did Camden have something to do with this?

I mean, of course he did.

He'd seemed like he was ready to march into the stands when he saw me almost fall after Alena had grabbed me.

A flood of warmth spread through my insides. Even out on the ice in front of thousands of people . . . he'd looked out for me.

I had the insane urge to cry.

I couldn't get used to this—having someone care about me.

It wouldn't last.

But maybe I could just savor it while it was happening. It could become a sweet memory I held on to for the rest of my life.

Biting down on my lip, I stared down at the game where a Knights player and a Chicago player were battling against the boards for the puck. Camden zoomed by my section, stealing a glance at me as he passed.

I swear he winked.

By the time we got to the third period, I'd become a big fan of hockey.

This sport was wild. Not that I had a lot of experience with other sports, but I couldn't imagine they were more fun to watch.

The Knights were up three to zero, and the other team was in desperation mode. Or at least it seemed like that. Fights were breaking out every couple of minutes, and the boards were rattling and shaking as the players slammed into them.

I watched as an opposing player tried to take the puck from Camden. He did some fancy footwork that would put any dancer's movements to shame and somehow escaped with it. Everyone around me was suddenly on their feet, screaming as Camden raced down the ice. I pushed up from my seat, ignoring the twinge in my leg as I held my breath and watched him approach the net.

Camden

With a burst of speed, I joined the rush of players skating hard toward the goal. The puck flew back and forth between my teammates, getting knocked loose by one of Chicago's defenders. The puck bounced back to where I was like a dream, a perfect setup for a shot. Without hesitation, I wound up and let loose, the puck rocketing off my stick.

It sailed through the air, the crowd holding its breath as it hurtled toward the net. Slamming into the back of the goal, the sound seemed to echo through my ears like a thunderclap.

I held up my arms, doing a little shimmy for good measure. Twelfth goal of the season, tied for most among the league's defensemen . . . with Ari.

A rush of pleasure spurred through my veins—the feeling I'd spent my whole life chasing every game.

Ari and Lincoln swarmed me, cheering and high-fiving.

"You coming for me, James?" Ari yelled, the big smile on his face saying he wasn't mad about that at all.

I gave him a little salute as they skated off toward the bench.

I didn't follow them. Instead, I skated over to Anastasia's section where she was standing, jumping up and down. Shit. Was her leg alright? Should she be moving like that? Studying her beautiful face, the big smile spread across her lips didn't seem to suggest any pain. I decided to go ahead with my next move, and I lifted my jersey, showcasing her name painted across my abs once more.

Anastasia blushed, her hands going to her cheeks adorably as she stared at me.

I could have stared at her all night. The crowd's roar grew even louder, and I knew this would be all over the Dallas news tonight and tomorrow. Maybe it would even get on SportsCenter.

Just for good measure, I pointed to the letters on my chest and then her . . . a huge smirk on my lips.

If we were going to be on the news, might as well make it crystal clear who she belonged to.

"James, get over here," Coach Porter screamed, and I cast her one more longing glance before skating back to the bench. At least Ezra had gotten rid of the girl who'd almost pushed Anastasia down the fucking seats. Having to wade into the crowd and forcibly remove her myself might have been difficult to explain to the Knights' management.

I'd spent my entire career carefully cultivating the good guy image. The All-American superstar that a team could count on.

It was crazy thinking I'd been ready to throw that all away for her by leaping up the stands and ripping that girl away.

"Is there a way to keep the four of you from making a scene?" Coach Porter hissed, smacking the helmet of Alex Turner as he climbed over the boards to finish the last minute of the game.

"Probably not, Coach," commented Ari, bouncing his head as a rock and roll song blared over the speakers. "It's a definite addiction at this point."

Coach Porter snorted and shook his head as he turned back to the game—like he didn't believe him.

I was a hundred percent positive that Ari Lancaster was not kidding. I'd watched him, Walker, and Lincoln with their wives . . . and I'd never seen anything like it. I'd never understood it. How their world began and ended with those women.

I think I was starting to get it now.

I snuck a glance over to Anastasia as the buzzer sounded, signaling the end of the game.

What?

She was headed up the stairs . . . quickly, weaving in and out of people as she made her way to the exit. I shot up from the bench, trying to figure out how I could get up to her in time to stop her. I'd totally screwed up by not making sure someone was near her to make sure she stayed.

Fuck. I looked over at the large clock above the suites and saw that it was almost ten o'clock.

Her curfew.

She only had thirty minutes to make it back to the shelter before they wouldn't let her in. I hadn't had a chance to tell her about the car I'd arranged to get her back.

And I was fucking stuck here for at least another hour with post game shit.

"Why the long face, Hero?" Walker said, clapping me on the shoulder as he made it back to the bench from the net.

"I need a favor," I told him tensely.

"Oooh, asking for favors already. You're not even in the circle yet," Ari commented, popping up like a gopher next to me. I resisted the urge to growl.

"I need you to cover with the coaches, make up some kind of excuse . . . and I need one of you to take my place in the post game press conference."

Ari groaned like I'd told him his favorite hair gel was sold out.

"Why do you need this favor?" asked Lincoln, lifting an eyebrow and staring at me in his usual intense way.

"Can we talk about that later?" I asked desperately, watching as Anastasia finally made it to the exit and disappeared from sight.

"You take two press spots next month," Ari offered.

"Done," I snapped, already making my way down the tunnel.

I stepped into the shadows of my usual hiding place outside the shelter with just a few minutes to spare before her curfew, and now I was pacing back and forth, waiting for her to appear. My breath was coming out in icy clouds, and I was fucking freezing. I'd taken one second to take off my jersey and my pads in the locker room before running out. The Under Armour shirt I wore beneath my pads was still soaked with sweat and I could smell myself, even out here in the alley where I was surrounded by trash and possibly human feces.

My wet shirt wasn't helping with the cold situation.

Okay, there was now *one* fucking minute to go before those doors locked. The security guard that I'd seen every night was standing at them right now, staring out toward the street like she was waiting for Anastasia, too.

Where was she? I'd driven thirty over the speed limit to make it here before her, so I could ensure she got inside safely. But she should have been here by now.

I hadn't seen any sign of a coat at the game. She was probably freezing to death, and once again, I hadn't thought ahead to make sure she was warm.

In the midst of my mental collapse, the clattering of footsteps finally spilled through the air. Anastasia appeared from around the corner, doing a full-out sprint as she raced toward the shelter doors, still clad in the jersey she'd been wearing at the game. There was a slight limp to her gait, and I knew that she would pay for the run tomorrow. From what I'd seen, she never took a day off from dancing.

The security guard opened the door, saying something to her that I couldn't hear, and a second later she disappeared from sight.

Self-disgust hit me hard.

I was a failure. Completely unworthy of my baby girl.

Fuck.

I'd messed up this whole night.

I needed to do better than this. I wouldn't fail her like this again.

Hovering in my hiding spot, I stared at the doors, like she was going to appear again and I'd have the chance to make up for the clusterfuck of a night I'd just let happen.

Ten minutes passed, then twenty.

A nearby neon sign flickered weakly, casting erratic shadows on the brick wall beside me.

Creeaaaak . . .

An older woman suddenly appeared on the sidewalk, wheeling herself toward the shelter, a creak filling the air with every turn of the wheel. She approached the ramp and slowly made her way up to the shelter's front door. I watched as she paused for a moment, leaning forward and staring inside. Finally, she banged on the door with her fist, over and over again until I'm sure her knuckles were aching.

No one answered.

Something in my heart tightened, the sight of the closed doors and her bowed, defeated shoulders hitting all of my triggers. I emerged from where I'd been hiding, my footsteps echoing in the quiet night.

"I don't have any money, and my vagina has dust in it and will eat your dick if you come anywhere near it," the woman croaked, turning to glare at me as I approached. One of her eyes was clouded and most likely useless to her, and her white hair was snarled and stringy.

"I'm not going to hurt you, ma'am," I said softly, holding up my hands in front of me as I cautiously approached. "But they're not going to open the doors for you. Haven has a strict curfew. *No matter what.*"

Her shoulders slumped, and any hope leaked out of her. I reached into my pocket, glad I'd at least had the foresight to grab my wallet before I left the locker room. The arena wouldn't have been open by the time I'd returned. My fingers were trembling slightly from my emotions running ragged through me. I counted out two hundred dollars.

"Here," I said, pressing the bills into her hand. "Find a hotel room for the night. There should be a Motel 6 around the corner that will let that money stretch."

The woman stared at the money for a long moment, so long I thought she was going to refuse it, and then she looked up. Her eyes were shiny, tears welling up and dripping down her wrinkled cheeks. "Thank you, young man. I don't know what to say."

"You don't have to say anything," I replied, forcing a small smile even though it felt like I was being haunted by ghosts. "Just take care of yourself."

She blinked and squeezed the money in her fist, suddenly wheeling her chair away as fast as she could. She was probably scared I'd been joking, or that I'd turn out to be some monster that would hurt her.

Watching her go, the weight in my chest grew heavier. There was a chance she'd use the money for drugs or alcohol, but I didn't care.

I couldn't *not* help.

I'd spent all those years watching helplessly as my stepdad beat my mom, stripping her of any dignity. I hadn't been able to do anything then. Even after I'd gotten older, I hadn't been able to save her.

So now I tried to do everything I could to help anyone, especially women, who needed it.

All these years later, I still felt like I had failed my mom. I refused to fail Anastasia, too.

As I walked down the block to where I'd parked my truck, each step was filled with a lingering sense of helplessness.

And I hated feeling helpless.

I couldn't take much more of this with Anastasia.

She was going to force my hand.

CHAPTER 11

ANASTASIA

My leg was ruined. Every step I took felt like my tibia was going to poke through my skin. Running was never a good idea for my body.

But running after a full day of dancing and then walking to and from the arena, taking a million stairs on the way?

Devastating.

It was one of the few times in my life, though, where the devastation had been worth it. As I limped toward the shelter bathroom, I was reliving every play, every time it seemed like Camden had glanced at me.

Maybe I didn't need a new leg, maybe I just needed Camden James. I was beginning to think he was the perfect drug. Just thinking of him made me feel better.

I pushed open the door to the bathroom, needing to wash my face before I got into my designated cot for the night. The fluorescent lights flickered above me, the smell of bleach and old, damp towels hitting my nose. As I stepped inside, my eyes adjusted to the dim light, and . . .

A girl, maybe a few years older than me, was crouched by the sinks, a needle in her arm. Her eyes widened, pupils like pinpoints, as our gazes locked.

"Shit," I muttered, instinctively turning on my heel to leave. How had she even snuck that in? Drugs were a no-no at this place, and I was sure the people in charge would find out about her soon, but I wasn't going to stick around in the meantime.

Before I could reach the door, she sprang at me like a wild animal, fear etched across her gaunt face.

“Don’t you dare tell anyone!” she hissed, her voice low and desperate as she grabbed my arm, her dirty fingernails digging into my skin.

I tried to push her off, but she was stronger than she looked. Her fist connected with my ribs, knocking the wind out of me. I stumbled, my back hitting the cold tiles. She came at me again, fists flying, and I raised my arms to protect my face. One of her punches glanced off my arm and hit my jaw, sending a jolt of pain through my skull.

“Stop!” I gasped, trying to fend her off. “I won’t tell! Just stop!”

But she was beyond reason. She seemed driven by panic and rage, and she slammed me against the sink. My head cracked against the porcelain edge, and a bright, blinding pain exploded in my skull. My vision blurred, and I felt myself slipping, the sounds of the bathroom echoing distantly in my ears.

As I lost consciousness, her terrified eyes were the last thing I saw as she disappeared from the room.

I blinked slowly, groaning because even blinking seemed to hurt. There was a buzzing sound in my head and it took me a second to realize I was hearing the hum of the lights above me.

I was still laying on the bathroom floor, no idea how long I’d been there. Not long enough that one of the staff hadn’t come yet, I guessed. I was going to get in trouble, though, if they did come in and found me like this. They’d probably think I was on drugs or something.

Like that girl . . . who’d just left me here.

Struggling to my feet, bile throbbed through my throat as the room dipped and swayed around me, and I had to stay on my knees as I tried to get my bearings. Something wet was sliding down my face, and I winced when I reached up and felt the gash right above my eyebrow. Examining my hand, I stared in horror at all the blood. The metallic scent filled my nostrils as I breathed. Head wounds bled a lot, right? So I probably only had a *minor* concussion.

Taking a deep breath, I heaved myself to my feet, staggering over to the sink so I could try and wash the blood off my face and get back to my cot.

Fuck. I looked like an extra in a zombie movie.

My white-blonde hair was matted, stained pink from the wound. Blood was smeared across my forehead where the cut was, and had trickled down my neck.

Stumbling, I turned on the tap. The water sputtered out, icy and stinging. I splashed it on my face, scrubbing at the dried blood with shaking hands.

The pain in my head flared, but I gritted my teeth and kept going. I didn't have time to be gentle.

"Come on, come on," I muttered to myself, scrubbing harder. The water ran pink, swirling down the drain. I grabbed a wad of paper towels and pressed it to my forehead, hoping to slow the bleeding. It wasn't perfect, but it would have to do.

I looked at myself again. Still a mess, but at least now I was a slightly more presentable mess. I splashed water on my hair, trying to rinse out the worst of the blood. The dizziness was still there, a constant, nagging presence, but I forced myself to stand straight.

The lights had already been dimmed when I made it out of the bathroom, my legs wobbling beneath me. I kept my head down as I limped to my cot, not wanting to draw any attention as I passed rows and rows full of sleeping women and children. A gray-haired woman with a scar across her cheek lifted her head as I passed, staring at me with vacant eyes. A lifetime later, I sank onto my cot, pulling the thin blanket around me, trying to steady my breathing. The pain in my head pulsed, but at least I was out of that bathroom.

My eyes were closing almost immediately—a sure sign I should be keeping myself awake because I knew you weren't supposed to sleep for a few hours after a head injury. The darkness behind my eyelids was a relief I wasn't going to fight tonight, though. Concussion or not.

Tomorrow, I would deal with everything.

Or maybe I wouldn't wake up.

Maybe it would be nice to not be in pain. I'd never see Camden again, though. A pang hit my heart at that thought.

I tried to be brave and positive every single day, promising myself things would get better. Tonight, though, I'd forgotten how to be either.

Camden

I practically burst through the front door of Charlie's, pissed that her shift had started an hour ago, and I was just now getting here because of practice. The scent of frying oil and coffee mingled in the air. A few people stared at me from their dinner plates. I must not have looked as crazy as I felt because they soon turned their attention away.

It felt like I was barely keeping my life together at the moment.

Turns out stalking was a full-time job and being a professional hockey player was definitely getting in the way of it.

Where was she?

I ducked into the hallway leading to the restrooms, pretending like I was going to go to the men's room, when really I just wanted to peek into the back scullery area and catch a glimpse of her.

When had it gotten to where I couldn't breathe without her? Every time she was out of my sight, I worried and stressed. I still didn't even know why she was living under the circumstances she was, but I *did* know I wanted to take her away and treat her like a princess. I just needed her to let me do that. Somehow.

She wasn't in there, and I frowned, my heartbeat thumping strangely in my chest. She was working tonight, right? If she was already in the shelter and I couldn't get inside to see her . . . I was going to lose my fucking mind.

At least a little more than I already had.

Striding back out to the dining room, I glanced around, a weird fluttering feeling taking off in my chest when I saw her bent over a table on the far side of the room, wiping it down.

Anastasia grabbed the spray bottle and stood up, anticipation growing in my gut as she began to turn around.

What. The. Fuck.

I was having trouble breathing as I stared at her.

Her face was a mess. A dark bruise shadowed one eye, and a fresh gash marred her forehead. Her white-blonde hair, usually bright and clean, was limp and bedraggled. She looked completely worn down, every bit of her energy and light sapped away. Anastasia started walking back across the dining room, headed for the hallway I'd just come from, clearly not having noticed me yet.

I practically lunged across the room.

"Anastasia," I called softly, a tremble in my voice as I tried not to startle her. Anger was bubbling in my chest, and my hands ached to destroy whoever or whatever had done this to her.

Her shoulders stiffened and she slowly turned toward me, her eyes shiny and defeated.

"Who the fuck did this to you?" I growled.

For a second, she stared at me, a slight quiver to her lips. She was exhausted, devastated, at the end of her rope . . . and she let me see it all. But then I watched as a mask seemed to slide across her features, her gaze growing hard and cold. "Leave me alone, Camden," she snapped, trying to brush past me.

"Wait, please," I insisted, stepping in her path. "Talk to me?"

She whirled around, fury and despair written all over her stunning face. "You want to know what happened to me, Camden? Do you? Really? I got beat up by a druggie in a shelter bathroom. That's right," she hissed, leaning forward so she could point a finger at my chest. "A shelter. I'm. Fucking. Homeless." She paused, her posture stiff and challenging, like she was waiting for me to run screaming from the restaurant at the news.

"Let's go back there and finish this discussion," I murmured, wanting to protect her from all the very interested eyes I could feel boring into my skull. I tried to gently grab her arm but she yanked it away from me, her hands shaking as she stalked toward the back hallway.

As soon as we turned the corner, she stopped and faced me, her hands fisted at her sides, her face reddening, the gash standing out on her forehead. "You happy?" she cried. "Now that you've discovered my dark, sad, little secret? Fun's over, Camden, right? Don't want to fuck the poor piece of trash, do you?"

Her words hit me like a punch to the gut.

I don't know what came over me then, but suddenly I was carefully pushing her against the wall and holding her wrists above her head with one hand as my body pressed against hers. I trailed my knuckles across her soft cheek as she shivered and whimpered under my touch.

Leaning forward, I brushed my lips against her ear, enjoying the way her breath hitched against me. "Let's get something crystal clear, right now, baby girl. If I ever hear you talk about yourself like that again, I'm going to put you over my knee."

She squeaked in indignation, making no move to get away from my grip, though. Anastasia's eyes were wide, a rosy blush spreading across her skin. Her tongue peeked out and licked her bottom lip . . . like she was imagining licking *me*.

"Do you understand me, Anastasia?" I growled.

I could feel her chest heaving against me, her breasts brushing my chest with every breath she took. I felt like a sick piece of trash that my dick was hardening as her black eye glared at me. But I couldn't help it.

Anastasia Lennox was a sickness in my bloodstream that I had no desire to cure.

When she still hadn't said anything, I lifted my head so I could study her face. "I'm waiting, Ms. Lennox."

She scowled at me for a long moment, biting down on her lip like she always did. I used my other hand to free it from her punishing bite.

"Yes, Daddy," she spit sarcastically. I growled, pleasure shooting through me, my dick going from half-mast to fully erect. I liked that far more than I would've thought.

Fuck, I actually loved it.

I pressed my lower half against her stomach so she could feel how turned on I was.

Her eyes widened, and I stroked her fluttering pulse with my thumb. "Now that you've decided to be a good girl, tell me what you need."

All at once her whole body fell, all the fight leaking out of it. "Why do you care?" she whispered brokenly. "You can't do anything about it."

"I want to help you more than I've ever wanted anything else in my entire life," I told her truthfully.

That seemed to be another one of those invisible land mines because she stiffened again, trying to pull away from my touch. I was afraid she was going to hurt herself, so I let her go, taking a step away so she wouldn't feel the need to fight me.

"Help?" she spat, her voice dripping with sarcasm. "Right. Like that's possible. Go back to your perfect life and forget about me."

"Impossible," I breathed, reaching forward to push a piece of hair out of her face.

"Why?" she challenged, tears welling in her eyes. "Why do you even care? I'm a mess. You can't fix me, Camden. Why do you even pay any attention to me at all? You don't know me, and you don't want to. So just stay away from me. I can't take any more disappointment."

Anastasia turned and stormed back into the washroom, slamming the door behind her. I stood there for a moment, fists clenched, but then my anger faded into a calm peace. My course was set. She needed help, and if she wouldn't accept it willingly . . .

I'd make her.

I went to follow her, and the pink-haired employee that she worked with was suddenly in the doorway, a fierce look on her face as she blocked my path.

"Don't even try it," she growled. "That girl's had enough."

The woman pulled a steak knife from behind her back and shook it at me.

Alright. I liked this lady.

I held up my hands and took a respectful step back. A steak knife to the ribs wasn't really on the docket for tonight.

But I appreciated the effort on Anastasia's behalf. It was nice to see that someone was on my little dancer's side besides me.

"You can go back out there now, fancy pants." She pointed the knife at me and slid it in the direction of thc main dining area. "Get to walking."

I shot a longing glance behind her where Anastasia was now standing, with her back to us at the giant sink, furiously scrubbing dishes.

Knowing I had a lot of work to do to get her out of the shelter, I backed away, taking a few steps before I turned around—just so I was out of reach of the pink-haired, steak knife lady.

A *rare* combination indeed—I snorted to myself at that one. Where was Lancaster when I needed him? He would have thought that comment was hilarious.

I hated every step I took away from her, but as I pushed out the door of Charlie's, my path was set.

Getting into the car, I gripped the steering wheel, wondering if my plan was stupid. Maybe I should just kidnap her . . . .

Her black eye and glistening tears filled my mind, macabre and awful and making me sick.

Memories came rushing up, to another time a woman's black eye had brought me to my knees . . .

I was huddled in the corner of my room. I was seven years old today, but instead of my birthday cake and my new toy truck Dan had promised me—he had been fighting with Mommy all day.

Their yelling was coming from everywhere, shouts and crashes that kept making me jump. Mommy had told me to stay in my room, so I did, clutching my stuffed bear tight. Sometimes it got like this, I told myself. They always made up.

It felt like forever before the house got really, really quiet. Sometimes, the quiet felt even more scary than their yells.

I opened my bedroom door slowly and stepped into the hallway, my heart pounding. The living room was just ahead, and I walked quietly, in case my stepdad was nearby.

When I reached the living room, I saw Mommy on the floor, curled up and crying. Her face was different, with a black eye and blood on her lip. I froze. She looked up and her tear-filled eyes met mine. The pain and sadness in her face made my chest hurt.

"Mommy?" I whispered, my voice tiny and shaky.

Mommy tried to smile, but it looked wrong. She reached out to me, and I ran over, wrapping my arms around her. She held me tightly, her tears wetting my hair. Mommy always gave me good hugs, like she was trying to keep me safe from everything bad. She took a shaky breath and stroked my hair, her hand trembling.

"It's okay, sweetheart," she whispered, her voice shaking but soft. "Mommy's going to be okay. Don't worry, my little brave boy."

I lay down and stared at her with wide, tear-filled eyes, not fully understanding but wanting to believe her. I could see the pain in her eyes, the bruises on her face, but her touch was warm and made me feel a bit better.

"Are you hurt, Mommy?" I asked, my voice small and scared.

She forced a gentle smile, even though it looked like it hurt her to do it. "Just a little, Camden. But I'm strong, and I'll be fine. You don't have to worry, okay?"

"Mommy, I'll take care of you," I told her, handing her Teddy so she could feel better. Teddy always made me *feel better.*

She kissed the top of my head, her tears mixing with mine. "You and Teddy are so brave and sweet, my boy. Mommy is the luckiest to have you both."

That made me smile because I wanted to be brave and sweet for her even though Dan didn't like it when I was sweet.

She didn't get off the floor all night, but she smiled every time I patted her back.

Teddy and I never left her side.

I came back to the present, squeezing the steering wheel so tightly that it made a cracking sound.

I'd failed my mother.

I wouldn't fail Anastasia.

I couldn't.

CHAPTER 12

ANASTASIA

It had been two days since I'd seen Camden.

Two days should seem like nothing in the grand scheme of things. After all, I'd been the one to tell him to leave. I'd told him who I was, how our lives could never meet because we didn't live in the same worlds.

He'd done exactly what I'd asked, hadn't he?

He'd left.

So, why did it hurt so bad?

Two days of dancing with a spinning head, throwing up in the bathroom in between classes because my head was throbbing so much from my concussion.

Two days of enduring gossip from the other dancers because I refused to talk to anyone about why I looked the way I did.

Two days of working at Charlie's without him sitting at his table and staring at me while I worked.

Two days.

I sighed as I sat on the bus, staring at my lap and the fact that my fingernails were bitten down to stumps. Between my fingers and my feet and my face . . . I really was an attractive package.

Of course he'd left. Who would stay?

The problem was that I missed him, and if I was being honest with myself, I hated him for that.

I'd gotten used to being alone, and then he'd shown up, a temporary flash of light in the sky that lit up everything around me.

And when that flash of light faded away, my world seemed darker than ever.

I trudged into Haven, giving a half-hearted smile to Clara, the night front desk attendant.

I was so fucking exhausted. And somehow everything seemed louder tonight, the children's fits, the women's cries, people arguing . . . everything was so loud. A good night's sleep was going to be impossible . . . and don't even get me started on going to the bathroom.

It had taken a herculean effort to drag myself into that restroom every day. I hadn't seen that girl anywhere since she'd left me on the floor, but that didn't mean I didn't shake every time I opened the door. I'd gone in with groups the last two nights—something I'd actively avoided in the past. But without voices surrounding me, I couldn't force myself inside.

Luckily, there was a mother and her three children headed for the bathroom at the same time as me, and I was able to follow them inside. Throwing water on my face, I hurried through my short nighttime routine, leaving the room as soon as possible.

And later, as I stared at the ceiling on my hard cot, I cursed Camden and the shooting star he'd flown away on.

"Anastasia. Anastasia. Wake up."

I blinked open my eyes, noticing that the lighting in the room was still dim. It wasn't time to wake up yet. Unless something had happened—I sat up abruptly, almost knocking heads with the night supervisor, Meredeth.

"What is it? What happened?" I asked, my eyes darting around the room as I tried to figure out what was going on. Everyone still seemed like they were sleeping—or at least the regulars seemed to be sleeping. The new women never slept the first few nights.

Meredeth's lips were pursed, her stern expression matching the tight black bun she was wearing that could rival any prima ballerina's.

"We need to search your things, Anastasia," Meredeth murmured, keeping her voice low so that she didn't disturb the people who were sleeping around us. She wouldn't meet my eyes.

"Why, what's going on?" I asked, my heart pounding in my chest from the abrupt wake-up, my brain struggling to comprehend what was happening. Why were they searching my belongings? What had I done wrong?

I slid off the cot, wincing at the soreness in my leg. My hands were trembling as I watched Meredeth and another volunteer, Conny, kneel beside my cot, their fingers digging into the space beneath it.

"What are you looking for? I don't understand," I cried. Dread pooled in the pit of my stomach as Meredeth unearthed a handful of small baggies, the white pills inside them glinting in the faint light.

"*These* are what we were looking for, Anastasia," she said, in a very disappointed voice as she slowly got up from the floor, the baggies clenched tightly in her hand.

"Those aren't mine. I swear it, Meredeth. I would never—" My voice rose in panic. The woman in the cot behind me stirred and muttered something.

I lowered my voice. "I don't know where those came from. I don't even know what they are!"

Meredeth stared at the baggies for a long moment before she finally met my gaze for the first time, her face full of disappointment.

Conny was shaking her head. Douchebag. She'd just started working here two weeks ago, and a lot of the regulars had complained of how judgmental she was. As if all of us at the shelter wouldn't have to stay here if we just tried harder.

I stared at the white pills in disbelief, trying to understand where they'd come from, how this could have happened. Tears pooled in my eyes as I realized how this looked. Glancing at Meredeth, I knew what she was going to say before the words had even come out of her mouth. "You know our policies, Ana. We have a one-strike rule when it comes to substances. I can't just ignore this." Her words were heavy with regret. "I'm so sorry, but this is your last night with us. You won't be able to come back."

Frustrated and shocked tears streamed down my face as I realized she was serious. Despite the fact that I'd had a perfect record for the entire three years I'd stayed here . . . they were kicking me out.

"What about the girl who'd assaulted me the other night after I walked in on her with a needle in her arm—did she get the one-strike rule speech as well?" I asked hysterically, searching around the room, wondering if she was sleeping peacefully in here somewhere, with the drugs swimming through her veins.

Sure there were other homeless shelters in the city that I could go to. But none of them were like this—for women only, and clean, and safe.

"Grab your things," Meredith said, not answering me, and I fell to my knees.

"Please, they're not mine. Someone planted them. Please don't kick me out tonight." I was babbling almost incoherently, but my words somehow got to Meredeth, her gaze softening. She pursed her lips and stared at the ceiling for a second before taking a deep breath.

"Because of your previous perfect record, you can stay for the rest of the night," she said, a look of pity in her gaze that I hated. "But you need to be ready to leave at seven. We'll be back in the morning to walk you out. And then you can't come back," she said firmly. I blinked at that. I mean, I had seen them do that to other people, but . . .

"You don't need to walk me out," I whispered, my ears heating up in shame.

"7 a.m.," she said firmly before she and Conny walked away.

I stared after them before I sat back on my cot heavily. What was I going to do?

And whose drugs were those? I glanced around at the cots, searching for someone who'd given me a weird vibe, or a mean look at some point. But there were only newbies around me who I hadn't really interacted with. I couldn't think of a reason that a perfect stranger would have placed drugs under my cot. If they'd been trying to hide it until later in case there was a search, their plan had backfired. Because they'd just lost their drugs.

Was it that girl? Had I somehow offended her in a past life and she'd come here to ruin me, first in the bathroom and now?

Except . . . she didn't seem to be here. So it couldn't have been her.

So how the hell did those pills get under my cot?

I rubbed my eyes, despair seeping through my veins like broken ink in a pen. The room felt too hot, hysteria crawling up my spine. What was I going to do? Where would I go?

Maybe I could talk to Montana in the morning. Her shift usually began at five. She'd known me longer than Meredeth. She'd defend me, tell everyone there had been a mistake.

I understood the reasoning behind the one-strike policy . . . but surely there had to be exceptions. Surely someone had successfully pleaded their case and the shelter let them return.

I tried to think if I remembered anyone.

And my heart sank as I lay back on my cot . . . because I couldn't think of a single one.

I was awake the rest of the night, staring up at the ceiling and counting down the hours until I no longer had a place to safely rest my head.

Going to Michael's or his parents wasn't an option.

I had promised myself I'd never go back there, and even if it killed me, I wasn't going to break that promise.

When morning came, I was sitting on my cot, my stomach in knots. Montana came through the door and I jumped to my feet as she walked down the aisle toward me, a somber expression on her face.

"Ready to go?" she asked before I could say anything. I blinked at her, the speech I'd been preparing in my head for the past few hours sinking in my chest.

"Montana, I—"

She was shaking her head before I could get the words out. "I'm so sorry, Ana," she whispered. And she did sound heartbroken. But there was also something different in her gaze, a little glimmer of doubt in me that hadn't been there before.

I slumped and stared at the floor for a second, accepting my fate. If I'd lost Montana, if she was unwilling to step in for me . . . well, then that was it.

Picking up my meager bag, I followed her through the rows of cots toward the front desk. I could feel curious gazes, but they didn't bother me.

No one who was watching me really cared.

I glanced behind me, though, thinking how sad it was that even a place like this, who took in any woman and child who walked through its doors . . . didn't want me.

"Here," Montana said suddenly, reaching behind the front desk and pulling out . . . a Sonic burrito.

I stared at it for a second, trying to will the tears away.

I'd cried for the rest of the night on my cot. I should have been all cried out by now.

"Thank you," I finally whispered in a choked, haunted voice. I took it from her hand and started toward the door.

"Be careful out there, Anastasia," she said urgently after me.

Maybe it would have been the polite thing to do to glance back at her and acknowledge what she'd said. But all I could muster was a hand thrown over my shoulder.

It was . . . bright outside, and I squinted because the sunshine of the morning seemed completely at odds with my life.

I started toward the bus stop on autopilot. I hadn't bothered to think of an action plan last night because I'd been so sure that Montana would help me—that she would believe that the pills weren't mine.

I took a deep, shuddering breath and finally glanced behind me at Haven. There was no one standing in the window watching after me. No one was running down the steps to bring me back or tell me there had been a mistake.

I bit down on my lip, telling myself I wasn't going to shed another tear for that place.

Someday, someone was going to be watching me as I left. Someone was going to care enough.

I had to believe that.

I was somewhat calmer once I made it to the dance studio. And by somewhat, I meant I was at least only inwardly crying instead of the sobfest that I could have been participating in.

I danced my heart out, pushing myself to the limit until my leg actually gave out on a turn, and I crumpled to the ground in a heap.

Everyone stopped dancing and the music abruptly cut off.

My face was beet red in embarrassment as I dragged myself off the ground, pretending like it didn't feel like a knife was embedded in my leg.

"Oops," I murmured in humiliation.

Dallon was watching me, his head cocked as he stared. He was teaching class today, because that was my luck. I hadn't spoken to him since he'd skipped out on our date—evidently I hadn't been worth an explanation.

But of course, today he would decide to talk to me.

"Why don't we call it for today, ladies," he said, his eyes not leaving mine.

The girls were chattering and tittering with each other, whispers of my name filling the air as they judged me for what had just happened.

I ignored them, like I always did when my name was on their lips.

But today it was a little bit harder.

"Anastasia, if you could stay behind for a moment," Dallon said when I'd almost made it to the door. He pushed his hair back, but the sight of his muscles did nothing for me this time.

Maybe Camden had broken me.

My classmate's whispers grew louder, only disappearing when the last of them had left the room.

"What was that?" Dallon asked, crossing his arms in front of his chest, his face the picture of disappointment.

"Just a mistake," I said, shame coating my insides at having to explain myself to *him*. Dallon was a trust fund baby whose parents had fed his talent from an early age, doing everything needed to make him into the star he was today.

He knew nothing of hardship and disappointment . . . and feeling like your whole world was ending.

"You can't make any mistakes. You can't afford them," he said. "You looked like shit out there. If you're losing your edge . . . "

The threat hovered in the air between us—the threat of being demoted to a lower rank, or even getting kicked out all together. He didn't have the same pull as Madame Leclerc, obviously . . . but any bad word from him certainly wouldn't help my case. I'd been worried about him making drama for me if I turned him down for a date—I'd forgotten he could make my life harder in other ways as well.

If they demoted me and I made even less, there'd be no way I could make up for it.

Although, that would be the least of my worries if I was sleeping in the streets.

If I lost dance after everything else that I'd lost, I would die. That was the plain and simple truth.

"It was just a bad night. I'll be better next class. I promise," I told him, averting my eyes so I could avoid seeing the pity that was probably in his gaze.

His hand went to my arm and he rubbed it softly.

Alright, I hadn't expected that. Especially with the ghosting he'd done the day of our date.

The universe must just really hate me.

Dance was very physical, obviously. Our instructors were always moving us around to show us proper technique.

And Dallon had always been . . . more physical than my other instructors.

But this was definitely on another level.

His hand went to my hip and he squeezed gently, and a nervous feeling slid up my throat.

"Is everything going okay?" He was staring at the gash still healing on my forehead and my black eye, his lips curled in disgust. I fought the urge to cover them with my hand.

This would be the time to tell someone what had happened. Not that Dallon would care, but maybe he'd know a couch I could sleep on or something. I could just tell him I'd lost my place . . . leaving out where my place actually was.

I even opened my mouth, the words at the tip of my tongue.

"I can help you with anything you need," he continued in a low voice, and his hand was almost . . . massaging my hip.

The words died immediately.

"I think I'm okay," I choked out. "A good night's sleep and I'll be right as rain."

Right as rain . . . had I really just said that?

There was a burst of thunder outside, and suddenly, I was wondering how much sleep it would be possible to get . . . in the rain.

"You know . . . I think it would be good for you to get some more private lessons. To help with the upcoming show."

I frowned. Besides that fall, I'd thought I'd been doing pretty well. How had I missed how badly I was messing up?

His hand slid lower on my hip and I stiffened.

"Free of charge, obviously. We could do it at my apartment," he continued.

I blinked, feeling a little weak at that moment. I was pretty sure what he was insinuating . . . and it would mean a place to stay for the night.

Really, who needed their virginity anyway?

I shook my head, trying to destroy the feeling.

There was weak . . . and then there was *weak* . . .

And I hadn't come this far to end up like that.

"Yeah, I—I'll speak to Madame about options for improvement," I said, shifting so he could maybe get the hint that he should let me go.

His hand squeezed my hip once and then he released me. "Make sure to ice your leg," he said in a completely normal tone, like he hadn't been massaging my hip a second ago.

I pasted a smile on my face and left, forcing myself not to limp even though every step was excruciating.

There were only a few girls left when I got into the locker room. Alena sneered at me and flipped her long black ponytail. She'd been upset with me since the game—like it was my fault she'd been "relocated."

I pretended like I always did, that it didn't hurt that these girls I'd danced with for years thought I was nothing.

Before I'd gotten hurt, it hadn't been quite as bad. They'd made fun of me at my old studio for being a scholarship student . . . but I was a star.

With my injury, I was still good. But these girls had me in their sights.

Lacey walked out of a bathroom stall, giving me a sheepish smile, but she didn't say anything before she left.

I cried again after they left, and I changed into the clothes I wore to mop the floors.

And I cried some more as I walked to the diner to start my next shift.

I always told myself I'd never give up.

But today . . . today I was close.

CHAPTER 13

CAMDEN

Anastasia Lennox was a brat of the highest order, and I couldn't wait to spank it out of her.

I sat at Charlie's table, after two nauseating days of lurking in the shadows and not being able to talk to her.

I'd seen the longing glances she'd thrown at the door of Charlie's the last two shifts, hoping I'd come in after she'd tried to push me away.

I knew she missed me.

Yet here we were, at the restaurant, and she was pretending that I didn't exist as she cleaned off the tables.

Naughty girl.

Her bruise had faded some, the dark black and purple contained more greens and yellows than it had a few days ago.

It still made me want to throw up every time I saw it.

And I'd seen it a lot.

I'd stared at it as I waited for her to leave Haven every morning.

I'd raged at it as she walked out of the dance studio and headed to work.

And I'd used it as motivation each night when I followed her from Charlie's back to the shelter.

It would certainly be more convenient when she was living with me. Traipsing all over the city on foot and in my truck had become more time consuming than my hockey schedule.

My lips twitched as Anastasia passed by me, her gaze intentionally focused straight ahead.

I'd come here tonight to give her one more chance to accept my help willingly. I *wanted* her to tell me what had happened. I *wanted* her to trust me to take care of her.

So far, all that wanting wasn't making a difference. She was trying to push me away as best she could.

My phone buzzed, and I reluctantly tore my gaze from her delectable ass as she leaned over to wipe down a bench.

Ari: From now on, I would like a six-foot radius between you and Blake.

My eyebrow raised. Lancaster was a drama queen.

Me: Huh?

Ari: Why do you always act so confused when I say things to you?

Linc: Why do you always start off conversations with random things?

Ari: This is a rule that should be applied for everyone, including my bestie Monroe.

Linc: Monroe is not your bestie, Lancaster. No matter how many times you say it.

Me: Can Monroe be my bestie?

Walker: Listen, Hero, there's only so much I can do to save you.

I could just picture Lincoln plotting my death with that comment. I couldn't blame him. I was pretty sure that I would have the same reaction to any guy wanting to be Anastasia's bestie now, too.

Me: Back to the six-foot radius thing, though . . .

Ari: She said she thought you were sweet last night because she saw you give that little kid your jersey. Absolutely unacceptable. Blake isn't allowed to think you're sweet, Mr. Gird-Your-Loins.

"Mr. Gird-Your-Loins" . . . that was a new one. I wasn't sure that I even knew what "gird" actually meant. I made a mental note to look it up.

Linc: I've instituted a six-foot rule as well. Actually, twelve.

Walker: Me, too.

Ari: You can't just agree to a rule because Lincoln does, Disney.

Walker: What if I'm agreeing with you?

Ari: That would be nice if I thought that was actually true.

I snorted at that one.

Me: Is the circle of trust just a club for crazy people who never finish their thoughts?

Ari: Wouldn't you like to know.

Me: Gasp. You mean I'm not in the circle of trust yet?

Linc: What circle of trust . . .

Walker: . . .

Ari: . . .

I really needed to figure out what " . . . " meant one of these days. The meaning seemed to change by the day, though.

Me: I've got chills, Mr. Spooky Sexy.

Me: So . . . what does one do to get into the so-called circle of trust?

Linc: You used "so" twice in that sentence.

Ari: That's not a circle of trust move.

Me: So the circle of trust involves proper English?

Walker: You used "so" again.

Me: Can everyone focus?

Linc: Well, you didn't use "so," that's an improvement.

Ari: You can teach an old dog new tricks.

Me: I'm not old!

Walker: Is there an age cap for the circle? I've never seen the rule book.

Ari: Good question, Dis.

Walker: I thought we decided "Disney" was already nickname enough.

Me: Speaking of nicknames, what's yours, Lancaster? Nicknames seem to be a theme in the "circle of trust."

Ari: Why did you put quotations around circle of trust?

Linc: Yeah, it's almost like you're mocking the circle, James.

Me: Why do I feel like I need to check if my doors are locked now, gentlemen?

Linc: . . .

Ari: . . .

Walker: . . .

Shaking my head, I set the phone down just as Anastasia slid into the bench seat across from me.

"What are you doing here?" she asked brusquely.

"Why don't you ask the question you really want to ask," I commented, tilting my head as I soaked in her beauty.

"What do you mean?" Anastasia wrinkled her nose up in adorable confusion as she stared at me, and I lost my train of thought admiring the crystal clearness of her eyes.

I'd never seen eyes like hers before.

"Camden!"

I blinked, realizing I hadn't answered her question.

"Why don't you ask me where I've been?" I said calmly.

Her cheeks flushed and she leaned forward, gripping the edge of the table as she locked eyes with me.

"I can't think of a single reason why I'd ask that. You having better things to do than stalk me at a diner seems like a no-brainer."

I huffed out an exasperated breath. She was just not going to give in, was she?

Reaching out, I grabbed her hand, slightly mollified when she didn't immediately yank it away.

"I missed you," I told her, meaning every word like they were carved into my heart. "How are you? I've been worried about you."

The look on her face told me she didn't believe me, but I couldn't imagine caring, or worrying, or stressing about someone more than I did about Anastasia Lennox.

I waited for her to tell me something . . . anything. I could see the conflict of emotions in her eyes, the inner struggle she was experiencing. She wanted to tell me. I knew she did.

But something was holding her back.

Anastasia frowned, and this time she *did* yank her hand away. I allowed it, vowing to myself that one of these days she'd want to touch me every second. "Goodbye, Camden," she murmured, a finality to her voice that felt like a knife in my gut.

I watched as she walked away.

Goodbye.

We'd see about goodbye.

It was definitely more like a . . . see you later.

I pulled out my phone and made a separate chat for Ari . . . he seemed the most up for the lunacy I was about to request.

Me: I need a favor.

Ari: Oh this will be good.

Me: Why will this be good?

Ari: Proceed.

Me: How magnanimous of you.

Ari: Better hurry. Blake is giving me the look.

I panicked. I knew what happened when Blake gave him the look . . . and it seemed to happen a lot. It also seemed to result in Lincoln having to intervene when Ari's special . . . dick decoration malfunctioned.

Me: Fuck. Don't look at her. I need you to catch some dogs for me.

Ari: . . .

Ari: I'm unclear where you're going with this. Is dogs a euphemism for something . . .

Me: Okay, I think I understand " . . . " in this context.

Ari: Congratulations. I'm still waiting.

Fuck, why did I always sound like an idiot in these conversations.

Me: Dog is not a euphemism. I literally need you to catch some dogs.

Ari: Is there more? Whose "dogs"? Where are these "dogs"?

Me: Why do you keep putting quotations around dogs?

Ari: Because it's 7 p.m. and you texted me about "dogs."

Ari: There's no other thing I could do.

Me: Okay. The dogs are nice. Kind of. They might not be nice when you have to catch them because they will be hopped up on meat.

Ari: This is literally the strangest/most fascinating conversation that I've ever had. I'm on the edge of my seat, Hero, good job.

Ari Lancaster added Lincoln Daniels to the chat.

Linc: Where am I?

Me: Why did you add Lincoln?

Linc: Trying to keep something from me, Hero?

I shivered at that.

Me: I would never . . .

Ari: He needs help with a "dog" situation. My face is too pretty to get bit.

Linc: And my face isn't?

Ari: You've got that scary energy, Golden Boy. They wouldn't dare.

Me: I'm kind of on a ticking clock here, boys. Also, they are just dogs. Not "dogs."

Ari: So he says.

Linc: . . .

Ari: Let me just catch you up, Linc. He's vaguely asked us to catch "dogs" that he says will be hopped up on something.

Me: Meat . . . they will be hopped up on meat.

Ari: The plot thickens.

Linc: Why are we catching dogs, though?

Me: We?

Linc: Obviously I'm not letting Ari handle "dogs" alone.

Me: Again . . . just dogs.

Linc: . . .

Totally knew what " . . . " meant in that context.

Me: I need the dogs to . . . scare someone.

Ari: . . .

Linc: . . .

Wasn't sure what that one meant.

Linc: Who are we scaring . . .

Me: . . .

Linc: . . .

Ari: . . .

Linc: Okay, we're in.

Me: Oh and bring Rookie. He can keep Geraldine distracted while we borrow her dogs. I know how he feels about her . . . lack of teeth.

Ari: . . .

Ari: . . . The plot thickens.

Taking a deep breath, I got up from the table and strode to the back once again.

Peeking inside, I saw that the pink-haired woman with the knife fetish wasn't back there today.

The gods were obviously smiling on me.

Anastasia's back was to the entry as she washed dishes, and I quickly glanced around the room for any belongings she'd stashed back here. She usually had her dance bag with her at the very least.

Spotting the black bag, I quietly slipped the tracking device inside, counting on her not checking her bag until tomorrow. I just needed to be able to find her tonight since she wouldn't just be going to the shelter like usual.

The thought of her being out on the street for even one minute gave me literal hives. Getting her kicked out of the shelter was a necessity, though. She never would have left on her own. I had to put her in a situation where she *had* to depend on me so I could actually take care of her.

A few hours on the street with me carefully watching over her was *necessary* if she was going to end up as my new roommate . . . *permanently*.

Backing quietly out of the room, I went back to the dining hall and then out the front door.

I had plans to make.

"Why am I here again?" Logan complained. "I had a date tonight."

"You *still* do have a date tonight, Rookie," I commented as I led them down the hall to my penthouse.

"What?"

I glanced back at Ari and Lincoln and the twin grins on their faces.

"You and Geraldine will be getting close and personal tonight. As you said, she can take out her teeth . . . so lots of benefits to that. A date to remember for sure," I commented as I waited for the elevator.

The elevator dinged as the door opened, and Ari, Lincoln, and I stepped inside.

"You coming?" Lincoln asked Logan, since he had apparently lost the ability to move after my surprise reveal.

His eyes were comically wide, and he looked a little pale now that I was staring at him. His myriad of tattoos were standing out on his skin.

"Rookie, *come*!" Ari called.

"Save the foreplay for Blake, Lancaster. I don't know if Rookie can handle it. Coming on command is next-level stuff," drawled Lincoln.

I snorted.

Ari stared at both of us in horror. "I was practicing for our supersecret mission tonight . . . .with the *dogs*. I'd like to think that I have something more creative for Blake in the bedroom," Ari snapped.

"Why are you still emphasizing the word 'dogs'? I've already told you they're *just* dogs. No hidden meanings."

"That's what they all say," Ari mused. "Until she pops out with a tail and a pink nose, and it's all downhill from there."

"I don't think I want to know that story," commented Lincoln.

"Can I trade?" asked Logan hopefully. "I'm great with dogs. Excellent, in fact."

"Nah, Rookie," I said with a yawn, staring at the numbers on the elevator impatiently because we needed to get a move on—Anastasia would be off in an hour. "Geraldine likes them younger. She'll eat you up. I'll be able to get both dogs out of her when I show up with you."

Logan side-eyed me before looking pointedly at Ari and Lincoln. "Are either of you worried about this?"

Ari cocked his head, pretending to study me before he shrugged and yawned. "He's Hero. How bad could it be? Besides, I can guarantee that whatever he's got up his sleeve . . . Golden Boy has done something *way* worse . . . so I'm not worrying too much."

Lincoln's lips twitched and I studied the star forward. If there ever was a person with Big Dick Energy . . . it was Lincoln Daniels. Didn't surprise me at all that he would be a secret psychopath. I'd seen the camera on his phone that appeared to monitor Monroe's whereabouts.

I needed to ask him what app he used as soon as I got Anastasia in my penthouse.

"I feel like there's a story there, Lancaster. Want to share with the class?" I asked as the elevator finally dinged, and I practically jumped out into the hallway, eager to get the party started, so to speak.

"Oh, there is," Ari answered mysteriously, ignoring Lincoln's scoff.

We walked down the hallway toward Geraldine's place. The building had two penthouses, mine and hers. But our places couldn't be more different . . .

Stopping by the door, I turned to face the guys. "So, I'll just warn you . . . "

"Oh gosh, this is where you tell us she has a secret sex dungeon," said Logan fearfully. It was kind of hilarious to see the six-four forward, tattooed all over man-child, looking like he was about to shit his pants.

Geraldine would love it.

"What? No. Geraldine doesn't have a secret sex dungeon." I paused for a moment, second-guessing myself. "At least I don't think . . . I just need to prepare you all for her place . . . it's a little . . . quirky."

"Oh shit. She does have a secret sex dungeon—where's Disney when we need him?" commented Ari, not sounding concerned at all.

"Lamaze class with Olivia. He's going to three different classes to make sure he has all his bases covered for the baby," I told them.

"Not sure three classes will be enough," pondered Lincoln.

Logan shook his head. "Simp."

Ari clicked his tongue at him. "Not the right context that time, Rookie."

"What?" Logan responded, sounding confused.

"Can we focus!" I said as I finally raised my hand to knock on Geraldine's door. Before I could actually touch the door, it flew open and there was Geraldine, clad in a vibrant pink and purple muumuu, a glowing purple cocktail with a pink umbrella in her hand.

This was how she normally dressed. That cardigan at Anastasia's performance had been a one-off.

"Why are you four skulking around out here? Camden, did you find these boys outside? I ordered strippers but they weren't supposed to be here for two hours." Geraldine eyed Logan like he was her new favorite candy—just like I'd hoped she would.

Logan audibly gulped.

I swore Ari licked his lips, staring at Geraldine delightedly. "Well, well, well, you must be the infamous Ms. Burton. Camden has told us *so* much about you."

Geraldine stared at him, her eyes raking over him slowly before she shook her head. "Send him back. I'm not impressed," she finally announced before she turned her back to us and strolled further inside.

Ari's mouth dropped and his eyes looked like they were about to pop out of his head. "I think I'm in love," he whispered, following her inside like the puppy dog I was trying to borrow.

Lincoln cast me an appraising look and I grinned.

"Circle of trust material, am I right?" I said.

He just shook his head and walked inside.

I was pretty sure that meant yes.

Taking a step into Geraldine's penthouse was like entering another world. The whole place was an eye burning collection of colors and textures. The walls were painted in electric blues, neon greens, and shocking pinks—that all clashed magnificently with the gaudy gold trim. Every surface was covered in something—an ornate vase, a bejeweled picture frame, or an overstuffed velvet cushion in a shade of red that could only be described as "aggressively passionate."

The real eye-catcher of the place, though, and what Logan was staring at in awed horror as I walked in—were the statues.

Life-sized, marble representations of nude men, each one modeled after her late husband, Harold. Harold lifting weights, Harold playing the piano, Harold in a heroic pose reminiscent of ancient Greek gods. It was like a very specific, very bizarre art gallery dedicated to the memory of a man who must have spent very little time at his famous jewelry store, and the rest working out or posing for these sculptures. I could almost hear her whispering, "Flex and hold, Harold, flex and hold."

Judging by the look on Logan's face, he was afraid that Geraldine was going to turn him into one of those statues if he stuck around too long.

I didn't have time for this.

"Mimi, I have a favor to ask you," I began, pushing Logan forward as an offering.

Geraldine settled herself onto a hot pink settee, propping her chin up on a pink-tipped, wrinkled hand. "I'm listening," she said, her blue eyes sparkling with anticipation.

"I need to borrow Midas and Fluffy . . . just for an hour or so. Logan here is going to stay and entertain you while I hang out with them."

I tried to make my voice as unthreatening and innocent as I could, but I was pretty sure that I still sounded a bit scary—potentially like I was going to eat her dogs or something.

Yikes.

"Should I ask you why you need them, or is this a need to know only secret mission?" she asked, gazing at me speculatively.

"Definitely a supersecret spy mission," Ari said eagerly, his head bobbing up and down like a doll.

"I don't think I asked you, young man," she said haughtily, still giving Ari shit, evidently.

Lincoln was staring entranced at the two of them. Ari getting his ass handed to him was not a sight we saw every day.

It was glorious.

"You can have both of them," she finally said, apparently deciding she didn't really care why I needed the dogs. "But I warn you, I'm getting a better deal. Fluffy shit in one of my flower pots today, the little rascal," she said, taking a big sip of her cocktail. I stared at it for a second. I was going to have to get her to teach me to make one of those. Anastasia would love that. Purple was her favorite color.

"You're a goddess," I told her, coming over to press a kiss to her soft cheek before I turned toward where the dogs hung out in the evenings when Geraldine was preparing to . . . entertain.

"Fuck," Logan suddenly griped, and I glanced over my shoulder to see him rubbing his ass, scowling at Geraldine who was giggling madly. He'd gotten too close to the couch where she was sitting; I probably should have warned him about that.

Lancaster had a sort of weird, dreamy look on his face that should never be leveled at a seventy-five-year-old woman with a fondness for strippers.

Blake would probably be very jealous right now.

Ari was trying to convince Geraldine she needed to come work at "Grandma Airlines" as I left the room. He needed to be careful. Ari's . . . dick decor might get him into a situation he couldn't get out of if Geraldine got wind of it.

I walked down a hallway to the back room where she kept Midas and Fluffy in what would be considered a dog playground thanks to the toys and the doggy tunnels and the plush beds she kept all over the room. Opening the door, I was greeted with enthusiastic barks and the sight of two enormous dogs bounding toward me like furry freight trains.

"Hello, boys," I muttered, bracing myself for impact. Midas skidded to a halt, his tail wagging furiously, while Fluffy practically pranced in place, his ridiculous poodle haircut making him look like an oversized, very enthusiastic cotton ball.

"Here you go, sweetheart," Geraldine sang out from behind me. She handed me two bejeweled collars and leashes. "Just get them collared and leashed, and you'll be all set."

I eyed the dogs warily.

Geraldine smiled and patted Midas on the head, crooning, "Oh, they're perfect angels. Aren't you, my darlings?"

Midas gave a bark that sounded suspiciously like a laugh. Fluffy just wagged his tail, looking far too innocent.

I took a deep breath and crouched down. "Alright, guys. Let's make this easy for Uncle Camden, okay?"

Easier said than done. Midas, to his credit, stood still long enough for me to slip the collar around his neck. Fluffy, on the other hand, seemed to think it was a game. He bounced around, dodging my hands with surprising agility for a dog his size.

"Hold still, Fluffy!" I grumbled, finally managing to snag him by the tuft of fur around his neck. With a quick, practiced motion that came with helping Geraldine with them many, many times, I got his collar on and attached the leash.

Glancing down at my watch, I gritted my teeth. Twenty minutes until she was done at Charlie's. We needed to get going.

"Okay, boys, let's go," I told the dogs as I tried to lead them down the hallway, toward the front door.

The moment we stepped into the hallway, Midas decided he was leading the expedition. He surged forward, nearly yanking my arm out of its socket. Fluffy, not to be outdone, pranced beside him, his leash taut as he tried to match Midas's pace.

"Ready to go?" I asked Ari and Lincoln who were both staring at the dogs.

"He really meant dogs," whispered-yelled Ari. "I thought it was a joke."

"You'll be okay, Lancaster," I told him, nodding at Logan as I headed toward the door.

"Logan, be good for Geraldine," Lincoln sing-songed, and Logan flipped us off with both hands as Geraldine rubbed her hands together eagerly.

"Maybe we can role-play," I was pretty sure she was saying as I left her penthouse.

I could just imagine Logan's reaction to that. And what if the strippers showed up while we were gone.

Epic.

"Logan might be a changed man after this," commented Ari.

"Maybe he'll score more," mused Lincoln.

Holding the dogs' leashes with one hand, I pulled out my phone and checked Anastasia's tracker. Good. She was still at the restaurant.

I didn't know about Logan . . . but I knew one thing about me.

I was definitely going to be a changed man after tonight.

CHAPTER 14

ANASTASIA

I huddled behind the dumpster, every nerve on edge.

I'd had to stay late at Charlie's, and by the time I'd gotten out . . . all the shelters had been closed . . . or full. Having someone shut the door in your face was not something I wanted to relive.

Which was why I was here. In an alleyway that was damp and reeked of rotting garbage. It had been the only place near the dance company I could find to hide, though. I wanted to be able to get up early and shower in the locker rooms before classes started, so I couldn't be too far away.

This was also a better part of town, and the streets were well lit—so less chance of danger.

Or at least that's what I was telling myself.

I shifted my bag under my head, double-checking that none of my meager belongings had rolled out as I used it for a pillow. Pulling my thin blanket tighter around me, my body trembled with exhaustion and fear. Each noise—every rustle of leaves, every distant shout—made me flinch. My heart pounded in my chest. This was how I'd felt growing up, first with my father, and then with Michael. I never knew what was going to happen when Michael would come into my room or when my father would lose his temper in a drunken rage. I'd hated feeling so vulnerable *then*, and I hated feeling so vulnerable *now*.

How did I end up here?

I tried to trace back the twists and turns of my life, every step that had led me to this godforsaken place, how I could have done better.

I could have told Camden, a voice said inside my head.

But I pushed that thought away. Now, more than ever, I was sure I was saving him from me. I was huddled against a pile of trash for fuck's sake.

He deserved so much better.

A gust of wind blew by, and I wondered if maybe I would just freeze to death tonight.

Winter was the worst time to be homeless. Even in Texas. The humidity and the cold felt like icy knives seeping into your bones.

Squeezing my eyes shut, I finally let a tear escape.

No one would even care that I was gone.

How incredibly pathetic was that?

Twenty-one years old, and the only person who might give me a passing thought was my childhood tormentor.

A dog's bark pierced the silence, loud and close. My eyes flew open as my breath caught in my throat, and I pressed myself against the cold, filthy wall. "Please, no," I whispered to myself, my voice barely audible as I peered down the alleyway, searching for where the sound was coming from. "Not now."

The barking grew louder, more insistent. I closed my eyes again, trying to calm myself down. It was just a stray. Or maybe someone immune to the cold was out walking their dog.

Nothing to be afraid of.

I wasn't in a cage. I was hidden. A dog wasn't going to attack me.

I tried to steady my breathing, but the panic clawed at my insides.

A sudden noise—a can tipping over—sent a jolt of fear through me. I peeked around the dumpster again, eyes wide. Nothing. Just shadows playing tricks on me. I forced myself to breathe, each inhale and exhale a battle to regain control.

"You're stronger than this," I whispered fiercely. "You have to be."

I wrapped the blanket around me tighter, its threadbare fabric offering little warmth and comfort. My mind drifted back to the safety of the shelter, flawed as it was. At least there, I had a roof over my head, a cot to sleep on. Here, I had nothing but darkness and fear.

A rustling sound made me jump, my heart leaping into my throat.

It was just a squirrel or something . . . right?

Or a rat.

That thought made me slightly queasy. I could just picture waking up and finding a rat gnawing on my leg.

Not that I was going to get a wink of sleep tonight.

Silence descended, the kind that felt heavy with unseen threats.

"Please," I whispered under my breath, not sure who I was begging. "Just let me get through this."

The tears continued, stinging my eyes and freezing against my cheeks.

The barking had stopped, but the fear lingered. I curled up tighter, trying to make myself as small as possible. Every muscle in my body ached, but I couldn't afford to relax. Not here. Not now.

Just let me get through this . . .

Camden

Tapping the steering wheel anxiously, my gaze was focused on the alley she'd disappeared down.

My poor little dancer. It was freezing tonight, the cold wind whipping in the air, scattering dead leaves and debris with it.

Fifteen minutes was about all I could take. Any more, and I'd be worried she was getting hypothermia.

I would have just appeared immediately . . . but that would have been suspicious, right?

Rubbing a hand down my face, I wondered why it seemed like I was fucking all of this up again. One of the dogs rattled around in their crate behind me while I stared ahead desperately, picturing her huddled against the cold.

I thought I'd lost my mind when I'd found a woman who frequented Haven, and I'd paid her to plant the drugs under Anastasia's bed. I'd snuck in the drugs with a food order I had donated to the shelter, and the woman had grabbed them and hid them while Anastasia was in the bathroom. She'd been all too easy to convince to help and didn't ask any questions when I'd offered her the money . . . or when I'd also paid for her to stay at a motel for a month while she looked for a job.

But this . . . this was what crazy felt like.

Maybe I had a recessive psychopath gene that she'd sparked to life. A psychopath gene that was completely focused on her.

But psychopath me was going to make my baby girl's life so good once I got her to give in.

Hopefully a lifetime of being a hero would make up for this little . . . pause.

Maybe that's what " . . . " meant.

It was a psychopath pause.

Although, I wasn't quite sure Disney had a psycho gene in him. Lincoln, yes. Ari, possibly. Disney?

Hard to picture.

My phone buzzed, and I glanced down, forgetting that I'd had Lincoln and Ari park around the corner out of sight.

Ari: I'm freezing my balls off right now.

Me: There's a little thing called a heater in cars nowadays. You should try it.

Not that I was using my heater. I turned it off as soon as I parked. If Anastasia was going to be freezing, so was I.

Okay, so the two weren't exactly equal, but I was trying.

Ari: Golden Boy doesn't believe in heat. Or joy.

Linc: He literally has the heat on full blast, all the vents are pointed in his direction.

Ari: Not sure how he would know since his eyes haven't left the video feed he has up of Monroe right now. She's watching TV . . . how enthralling.

Linc: Stop looking at her!

Ari: Blake's right next to her! What do you want me to do? Pretend the most gorgeous girl in the world isn't on your phone right now?

Linc: Blake's literally on your phone right now as well.

Ari: . . .

I blinked. Sometimes I couldn't tell when they were kidding, but it certainly solidified that they were the ones to talk to about . . . watching someone.

Linc: So, what exactly is the plan right now?

Ari: Yes, please enlighten us. Because so far the whole night has been the opposite of what I was expecting.

Me: I told you they were really just dogs.

Something outside caught my eye, and I looked up right as a man passed the alley where Anastasia was hiding. He had a scarf covering half his face, and I didn't take my eyes off him until he disappeared around the corner.

I couldn't take this anymore. It was go time.

Me: Your mission is simple . . . if you choose to accept it (and you have to because I'm not sure what Geraldine is making Logan do right now). I'm going to let these dogs out . . . and you're going to catch them.

Linc: Why does this not sound as simple as you're making it seem?

Me: Well, I have no guarantees where you will have to go to get the "dogs."

Ari: Now why did you type "dogs" like that?

Grabbing the Tupperware container full of raw meat that I'd brought with me, I opened the truck door, firing off one more text.

Me: Game time. The dogs will be coming out of the alleyway between the deli and that laundromat. Be ready.

My phone was buzzing frantically as I went to stuff it back into my pocket. I quickly silenced it so she wouldn't hear. They would have to figure it out.

I walked across the street, hovering by the entrance to the alley, before I carefully peeked around a corner.

She must have been behind the dumpster because I couldn't see her from here—which was good because that meant she couldn't see me.

I couldn't think about the reality of her behind that dumpster or I would go crazy. The wind seemed especially cold right here, like it was trying to push her out of her hiding spot and into my arms.

Quietly, I threw some of the meat into the alley before I jogged back to my truck, dropping small pieces of meat on the way like a cannibal's version of Hansel and Gretal so the dogs would know where to go. Once back at the truck, I cleaned off my hands with some hand sanitizer to try and block out the smell of the meat. That was all I needed, for Midas and Fluffy to make my hand a snack.

I needed that hand for many reasons.

The dogs had actually been quiet while I'd been sitting there, just the occasional whine the entire time. But they must have had super sniffers because they immediately started going crazy the second I opened the back door and held up the container.

Geraldine had originally believed that dogs should be fed what their ancestors survived on. So when she'd first gotten Midas and Fluffy—she'd fed them mostly raw meat.

She'd stopped when she realized these two dogs, in particular, became almost feral every time they ate it. Kind of like how cats reacted with catnip.

I didn't know a lot about dogs, but I was pretty sure that not all dogs had that kind of reaction.

Luckily for me, Geraldine's did.

Fuck.

I shook my head at myself, still a little flabbergasted I'd turned into this person.

What the hell was I doing? I'd just thrown raw meat into an alleyway to scare a poor girl into moving in with me. I could still picture her panicked eyes the night we'd seen that first dog. How she'd whimpered and held on to me for dear life.

And now, here I was siccing her worst fear on her.

I'd make it up to her. I knew I would.

Still, I was going to be committed if anyone ever found out.

Well, I would probably be imprisoned first. But the temporarily insane defense was going to be an option at my trial.

That was a certainty.

I let the dogs out of their crate, narrowly avoiding getting my arm bit off as Midas snapped his teeth in his eagerness to get out. Apparently, he'd already gotten a whiff of the meat.

"Fucking hell," I growled, jumping back as they flew from the crates and jumped onto the street, growling and whining—their noses glued to the ground as they sniffed out their feast.

What was the next part of the plan? My mind was completely blanking. I'd just unleashed a couple of crazed animals at my soulmate's hiding place . . .

I was still for a moment, and then I shrugged.

Ends to means or whatever that saying was.

The dogs picked up the scent and took off toward the alley, gobbling up the meat as they inched closer and closer.

Anastasia was probably freaking out just from hearing them.

Don't think about that.

Grabbing my water bottle, I splashed some of its water on my hair, because I needed to sell this next part. I was supposed to be out for a run—or at least that was going to be my excuse for being around.

Anastasia's scream tore through the night air.

Guilt lurched through me. The only screaming I wanted her to do was in my arms.

That didn't sound much better.

Screaming in my arms as she orgasmed.

There. That was normal.

Perfectly normal.

No psychopaths anywhere.

I rushed toward the alley, coming to a halt when I saw Anastasia hiding behind the dumpster.

"Anastasia?" I cried, pretending to be shocked that I was seeing her there.

She was curled up, tears streaming down her face as she rocked back and forth. Her fists were clenched in front of her as she stared horrified at Midas as he tore into a piece of meat, Fluffy snapping at him to try and steal it away.

I winced.

"Hey!" I growled, hoping that Geraldine was right that the dogs wouldn't actually eat me. Taking a step out of Anastasia's sight line, I rolled the tennis ball with meat juice and peanut butter down the street, right past their noses. They'd just finished the meat and immediately ran after the tennis ball, disappearing from view.

My eyebrows raised. I couldn't believe that worked.

Now they were Lincoln and Ari's problem.

Another loud cry snapped my attention back to Anastasia.

"Anastasia," I called again, softer this time, my hands up as I approached her slowly. She was plastered against the dirty brick wall, her eyes wide and terrified as she stared at me unseeingly.

"Anastasia, it's fine. Everything's fine, baby girl. They're gone."

She shook her head, pulling her faded gray blanket up to her chin as she whimpered.

"They went after something else. There aren't any more dogs out here."

I was literally holding my breath as she shakily stood up and carefully looked around, searching for the animals. I had to clench my hands into fists to stop myself from holding her.

That would come.

I followed her gaze, relieved that the dogs hadn't circled back. Hopefully Linc and Ari had caught them by now.

Hopefully neither of them had been mauled while doing it.

I'd never hear the end of it from Ari, and Linc . . . yeah, I wasn't going to think about that.

"Come here, baby girl," I said, proud of how sane my voice sounded.

A second later, she flung herself at me, her whole body trembling as she buried her face into my chest.

"How diiidddd you find me?" she gasped, her words shaking from the cold as they left her pretty mouth.

"Out for a run and I heard those dogs going crazy. We're only about a mile away from my place. A better question is though . . . what are you doing in this alley? Were you trying to sleep here?"

She lifted her head and met my gaze, shame coating her features. "I . . . I got kicked out of the shelter. It was a misunderstanding . . . but I didn't have anywhere else to go." Her eyes filled with tears, and she pressed her face back into my chest.

I closed my eyes, memorizing the feel of her against me, even as I willed my dick to stay down.

Nope, it was rising. Fuck.

Had to think of something else . . . Geraldine's mouth when her teeth fell out in her water, and she hadn't noticed and had kept drinking from the glass. With bits of spinach floating around that had been stuck in her teeth.

Oh good, that worked. I was limp.

That might have been a world record.

I breathed a sigh of relief, but then she nuzzled further against me, and I was having to reimagine the same scene over and over again.

I was thirty-one fucking years old. I had more control than this, damn it.

A dog barked in the distance, and she flinched, glancing down the alley in absolute terror.

"Come on, let's get you out of here," I said, beginning to lead her out to the street.

I half expected her to fight me, tell me she'd be fine on the streets or something insane like that. Which would have forced me to kidnap her for real and then it would have become a whole big thing.

The cold and the dogs must have done it, though. Because she didn't fight me at all, just cuddled closer as I led her away from the alley and to my . . . fuck . . . I couldn't lead her to my truck. I'd told her I'd been out on a run.

"Let me get an Uber," I murmured, keeping one arm tight around her as I pulled up the app.

Thank fuck. One was two minutes away.

"It will be here in just a minute," I said soothingly as I glanced down at her.

It was all I could do not to kiss her.

I mean, my face literally started to go down, and I had to yank it back.

I couldn't kiss her when I was trying to get her to move in with me. She'd go running for the hills.

"You're coming to my place. I have a guest room that I've been told is very comfortable." I was unable to keep the command out of my voice, so I tried to offset my tone with a *winning* smile.

I'd been practicing lots of different expressions today. Now that I'd become a psycho and forgotten how to do basic things like act human. I'd have preferred for her to sleep in my room, but as I kept telling myself . . . baby steps.

She bit down on her lip as she studied me, and I let her move away so that she could cross her arms around herself.

Right, it was freezing outside. I pulled off my Knights sweatshirt, and she allowed me to slide it over her arms and head.

It was huge on her, coming all the way to her knees. I pretended I didn't see how she was breathing in my scent or that I wasn't *feral* at the sight of her in my sweatshirt. I was pondering destroying all of her clothes, though, so she could only wear *mine*.

A dog—not one of Geraldine's because I would hope that Ari and Lincoln could manage two dogs by now—started barking frantically from around the corner, and Anastasia was once again plastered against me.

"Maybe just for tonight," she whispered and in my mind I was doing an inner fist pump.

I kept my face completely blank, though, like it didn't matter to me either way.

"Got any stuff in there you need to grab?" I asked helpfully, nodding toward the alley. All she had in her hand was her small bag that I'd placed the tracker in earlier.

"That's all," she said in another soft voice.

Oh, little dancer, I'm going to make your life so good. Tonight is going to be nothing but a bad dream.

The Uber arrived, and I opened the door, nodding at the driver as I turned toward Anastasia.

"Let's get you in the car," I told her.

She hesitated again, but finally let me help her inside . . . right as something moving at the end of the street caught my eye.

Ari was sprinting across the street after Fluffy.

What the fuck was he doing? He should have caught that dog ages ago.

That was definitely not circle of trust behavior.

Something told me Linc had captured his dog already, though. Daniels would never . . .

I quickly slipped into the Uber behind her before she could notice Ari.

Anastasia's hands were shaking in her lap, and there was a bluish tint to her lips from the cold.

I'd done this for a reason, I told myself.

If I hadn't come up with this crazy plan, who knows what would have happened? She could've gotten hurt again at the shelter. Or some asshole who didn't want to sweep her off her feet could have just snatched her away. Could have hurt her.

Could have stolen her away from me before we ever had a chance.

That's what I kept reminding myself as the driver took off.

"Are you sure it's okay that I stay?" she asked timidly, obviously sensing the tension threaded through my body.

I took a deep breath, trying not to come across like a psycho, even though I clearly *was* one. I wanted to tell her that I wanted her to stay . . . forever . . .

But instead I simply said "Of course" and held her for the short ride home.

CHAPTER 15

ANASTASIA

We arrived at the building where Camden lived, a glass monolith that seemed to stretch to the sky.

I instantly felt out of place.

He ushered me into the elevators, his hand warm and comforting on my lower back, and I watched as he selected the top floor. He lived in the penthouse, that's what they called the floor at the top, right?

When the elevator doors opened, I stepped into his living room and froze. It was enormous, with floor-to-ceiling windows showing off the entire city, the lights twinkling like stars. The room was filled with big, soft white couches that looked untouched, and a glass coffee table that sparkled under the lights. Tan and black, abstract paintings covered the walls, and a large, elegant rug spread out across the floor. I stood there, gaping, unable to believe I was in a place like this.

"Wow," I whispered, barely finding my voice. "This is . . . incredible."

Camden huffed, running a hand through his hair, looking sheepish as I gaped at his place. "Lincoln gave me the name of his interior decorator when I signed with the team. It's a little . . . much."

"Lincoln?" I said absentmindedly, before realizing who that was. "Oh, Lincoln Daniels."

Camden stiffened . . . and it almost seemed like he didn't like the sound of his teammate's name coming out of my mouth.

But that couldn't be it.

"Want to see your room?" he asked, and I nodded shyly, ignoring the little thrill I got when he said "your room." I hadn't had one of those in a long time.

If seeing him play in front of thousands of people hadn't cemented the fact that we lived in different worlds—seeing where he lived finished the job.

I'd never been somewhere so nice. Ever. Michael's parents had been well-off in our town in the sense that they had more than one car and a four-bedroom house. Mrs. Carver had a cleaning lady who came once a week and a gardener who would sometimes trim the rose bushes.

Their wealth was nothing like this.

My mouth dropped more with every room I passed. That had been an actual theater room, and the kitchen looked like it was literally out of a movie. I felt like I was dirtying the place just being here.

"Here we are," he said, after we'd passed what seemed like a million rooms.

I was quiet as I took in the bedroom, gingerly stepping inside.

It was like stepping into a dream.

The bed was massive, with a fluffy white comforter and a mountain of pillows that looked like clouds. Soft, warm light filled the room from elegant lamps on the nightstands. A large window overlooked the city, and I took a few steps toward it, gaping at the buildings laid before me. Tears were in my eyes as I stepped back and admired the plush rug on the floor, and the cozy armchair in the corner with a small bookshelf next to it. Everything was . . . perfect.

"I'm sorry," I whispered, wiping my eyes, completely embarrassed at the tears trying to find their way down my cheeks.

He hesitated for a moment, and then he was striding toward me, gathering me in his arms, and pressing my face against his chest so I could breathe him in.

Safe. The word echoed in my mind.

Had I ever felt safe like this before? Like my mind and my soul and my heart could actually take a breath?

I never wanted to leave his arms, and when he finally let me go, an embarrassing squeak escaped my mouth.

Camden James must have been a saint because he pretended he didn't hear it.

"There's a toothbrush and towels in the bathroom. You should jump in the shower to try and warm up. I'll bring you some of my world-famous hot chocolate and have it waiting for you."

"World-famous, huh?" I teased, managing to collect myself at least a little.

"Most definitely," he responded, a glimmer of amusement in his gaze that did funny things to my insides.

We stood there for one more long beat of silence, staring at each other. "I'll leave you to it," he finally said in a gruff voice as he backed out of the room like it was a struggle for him to turn away from me. "Let me know if you need anything."

"Wait!" I called, and his head quickly poked back into the room.

"Everything okay?" he asked, concerned.

"Thank you," I said in a trembling voice. "Thank you for saving me."

He stared at me for a long moment, his face tense, like he was struggling with something. "Always," he finally responded, before he closed the door behind him . . . and I instantly missed him.

But then, I turned to stare at the room one more time. I wanted to jump on the bed, beat on my chest, scream in exaltation.

But I also didn't want to ruin the bed with my dumpster filth.

Shower it was.

It took me at least three minutes to figure out how to work it. There were three different showerheads and a bunch of buttons, because evidently rich people didn't clean themselves like the rest of us mere mortals. There were things like steam and bubbles, and one button was even hot air that dried off your body like those air dryers in the bathroom.

I sighed as the water caressed my body. I only ever showered at the dance studio, not wanting to risk taking off my clothes at the shelter in case they were stolen or someone decided to have some fun with me.

Staring at the expensive marble tile and the soap that smelled like jasmine . . . I suddenly felt so unworthy of all of this.

Maybe it would have been better if he'd left me in that alley. I was going to have to leave tomorrow and find a new shelter.

And now I'd have this place to compare it to.

Once I was clean, I shut off the shower and slipped a towel around my body—wow. The towel bar had been heating the towel. It was like stepping into a warm hug.

In the past, I would have told myself that someday I would have a place like this, when I was a famous ballerina and the world had become my stage.

That dream had faded. The ache in my leg that never went away had chipped at that dream every day until I didn't believe in it anymore.

There was a frown on my face as I stared in the mirror and I wiped it away. I had nothing at the moment to frown about.

Tonight, tonight I could pretend my life was good.

I had a feeling I would need this in my memory bank in the upcoming weeks.

Taking out my one clean pair of clothes out of my little sack, I slipped on the oversized shirt and underwear before the scent of something *delicious* had me stepping back into the bedroom. Just like he'd promised, there was a mug on one of the nightstands, steam drifting lazily up in the air.

A little thrill passed through me at the thought of him being right outside the door while I'd been naked in the shower . . . .

I tabled that thought . . . because there was also a sandwich, three layers tall, and my stomach growled just looking at it. I practically flung myself at the food, inhaling it like a wild animal.

A knock sounded on the door, and I froze, thinking of how I looked at the moment. I frantically chewed, brushing the crumbs off my chest before realizing I'd just spilled them onto the plush carpet.

"Come in," I said in a strangled sounding voice.

Camden's face was strangely blank as he opened the door and stared at me standing there in the old T-shirt I'd pulled on. Crap, I hadn't put my leggings on yet. I'd been so desperate to find out the source of the incredible chocolate smell.

I was suddenly very aware of my bare legs as his gaze trailed along my skin, a heat in his eyes that made me hungry for *more* than the sandwich.

But I was gaping at him, too. His hair was wet and he was wearing a loose pair of basketball shorts and a tight Knights T-shirt. And holy hell, he was unfairly gorgeous. Whatever the lottery for life was—he'd won it. Hands down.

Camden shook his head slightly, rubbing a hand down his face, his cheeks tinged with color before he cleared his throat. "I'm going to be heading to bed. Just making sure you don't need anything . . . I'll be right down the hallway if you do."

I nodded shyly, shifting my weight awkwardly from foot to foot.

"Did you try the hot cocoa? It should be cooled off enough now."

"Oh! I haven't yet. I was . . . well that sandwich was amazing." Understatement, but I wasn't going to admit I'd torn into it like a bear coming out of hibernation.

"Glad you liked it," he murmured, a warm rumble in his voice that made my body flush with heat.

I picked up the mug, well aware my hand was shaking as I brought it to my lips, tentatively sipping it just in case it was still too hot.

"Mmmmh," I moaned as the rich, velvety chocolate enveloped my tongue. It was heavenly, the perfect blend of sweetness and depth, with just a hint of vanilla and a touch of cinnamon. The warmth spread through me, soothing and comforting, melting away the last of the chill and fear that had settled in my bones in that alleyway.

It was like a hug in a cup, the best hot cocoa I could have ever imagined.

"Holy cow," I breathed, and he chuckled, the sound sexy and warming me up even more than my drink.

"Did you make this?" I asked. It was probably a stupid question, but I didn't know how rich people worked. Maybe he had a cook that stayed up until all hours of the night.

He blushed at my question. And if I'd thought he was adorable before . . .

"It was my mom's recipe. Any time I was scared, or sad, or . . . well, she made it for me."

I didn't miss that he said "was" in relation to his mom. I also didn't miss how wistful . . . and sad he'd sounded just then. I studied Camden, wondering if he knew a little bit more about heartbreak than I'd first thought.

I took another sip, sighing in happiness. "You're going to have to teach me how to make this. I'm not sure I can live without it now," I joked, sneaking another sip.

"I'll make it for you whenever you want," Camden said simply, a glint in his gaze. I smiled in response.

Wouldn't that be nice.

"You have dance tomorrow, right?" Camden asked, glancing at the fancy-looking alarm clock on the nightstand.

Yikes, it was one-thirty.

I nodded, and he made a delicious growly sound, like he was upset I'd be getting so little sleep.

"Go to bed, baby girl," he said, and I squeezed my thighs together, my clit pulsing and a heat spreading through my core that I really needed to ignore.

"Yes, sir," I teased, like I had before.

And just like then, there was a tangible heat in his gaze. He stepped forward, his fist clenching at his side before he squeezed his eyes shut briefly and took a deep breath and stepped away.

Like he was trying to hold himself back.

I wasn't sure I *wanted* him to hold back, though.

Camden finally opened his mouth and hesitated, before sighing. "Goodnight, Anastasia," he murmured, and I wondered what he'd really wanted to say.

"Goodnight," I whispered as he left the room.

I kneed onto the bed, sliding beneath the covers before I grabbed the mug and sipped it greedily, staring in wonder at my surroundings.

If this was a dream, it was the best one I'd ever had.

And I really wished it didn't have to end tomorrow.

CHAPTER 16

CAMDEN

I was waiting in the kitchen with a full breakfast spread out on the counter, when I finally looked at my phone for the first time since the . . . dog incident. I scrolled through last night's messages as I waited for Anastasia to come out of her room, my amusement growing with every text.

Logan: Mayday. Mayday. Geraldine just pulled out a blindfold. Send help.

Linc: Just play along. She'll probably take out her teeth in a minute, and you'll be golden.

Ari: That's my bestie you're talking about, Lincoln Daniels.

Linc: Blake know you've picked someone up?

Ari: I'm positive she'll understand.

Walker: Why do I feel like I'm missing out tonight?

Ari: Just worry about learning the proper breathing technique, Disney. Hee, Hee, Ho, Ho.

Logan: WHY AREN'T YOU ALL MORE WORRIED ABOUT THIS. She just poured me one of those purple drinks. I'm not convinced it's safe to drink. I'm pretty sure it's just straight vodka with food coloring.

Linc: But it glows . . . so it can't be that bad.

Logan: 🖕 I will remember this next time any of you need help.

Ari: Except, I don't think you actually need help, Rookie. Geraldine seems like the kind of party you'd never want to end.

Linc: . . .

Another text had come in around when Lincoln and Ari would have been trying to catch the dogs.

Ari: Camden Motherfucking James! Fifi just fucking bit me. On the leg. She missed my dick by two inches!

Linc: Well, his name is Fluffy. So that might have been why he bit you.

Ari: Okay, Fluffy just ran away again. Was there coke in that meat you fed him? He's like a speed demon. I'm sweating, James. And it's thirty fucking degrees out here.

Ari: WHY AREN'T YOU ANSWERING?

Linc: ?

Ari: I'm on the ground on 7th Street. This is the end. You'll have to go on without me.

Linc: That's like a mile away. How the fuck did you end up there?

Ari: . . .

Linc: . . .

Linc: Did you at least get Fluffy?

Ari: If you're asking me whether Fluffy is currently eyeing me like he's going to eat me. Then yes, I did get Fluffy.

Ari: Camden James, if you're reading this, you are responsible for my death. I hope you're happy.

Ari: Also . . . tell Geraldine I said goodbye.

Linc: How about Blake?

Ari: Have a woman deliver the news to her.

Linc: ?

Ari: I've heard that sometimes widows fall in love with the first man who comforts them. You'll be responsible for instituting a large perimeter around her so that doesn't happen.

Linc: For how long?

Ari: Indefinitely, obviously! You think I'm going to allow Blake to move on? I'll just come back as a ghost and keep her company.

Linc: . . .

Ari: Are you almost here? Fuck, Golden Boy, Fifi just nibbled on my big toe.

Linc: Fluffy. His name is Fluffy. But also . . . why the fuck is your big toe out?

Ari: It's a long story.

Linc: . . .

Linc: I'm almost there.

Holy fuck. I hadn't laughed this hard in a very long time. I glanced at the hallway, making sure that Anastasia hadn't come out yet. She still hadn't appeared, so I turned back to my phone.

There was another string of messages at around three in the morning.

Ari: Hero, wherever the fuck you are, the dogs have been delivered. The package has been secured, so to speak . . . oh, and we rescued Logan.

Logan: Keep your fucking mouth closed, Lancaster.

Walker: It's three o'clock in the morning. Why are we texting?

Logan: Don't do it.

Linc: You mean don't tell them how we found you?

Logan: . . .

Hmm. Rookie was getting pretty good at the " . . . " I needed to step up my game.

Walker: I'm listening.

Ari: Of course, you're listening. Lincoln is talking. What else would you be doing?

Walker: Sleeping maybe?

Ari: I just laughed. That was a funny joke, Disney.

Linc: Logan was posing.

There was a picture after that . . . of Logan standing next to Harold's statues, flexing in a pair of tiny shorts. They must have taken that before he knew they were there.

I was howling.

Logan: You owe me for the rest of your fucking lives. Indefinitely. For infinity.

Ari: At least your dick wasn't almost bit off by an enormous poodle.

Logan: It was almost bitten off by something much, much worse, Lancaster.

Walker: . . .

Ari: . . .

Linc: . . .

I texted out " . . . " for good measure, even though I was replying hours later.

My phone almost hit the floor when I finally heard her door open. Glancing at the food, I made sure I wasn't missing anything.

6:30 a.m.

Three and a half hours of sleep wasn't ideal, but I wouldn't put it past her to try and sneak out this morning, so I'd woken up at 5 a.m. to make sure that didn't happen.

"Good morning," I said as I watched her try and sneak toward the front door, her small bag clenched in her hand. She jumped and froze before turning slowly to stare at me in surprise.

"Good morning," she squeaked adorably.

Considering she hadn't gotten much sleep, she looked much better this morning. And I wondered if she'd even slept any of those nights at the shelter.

"I made breakfast," I offered, deciding I was just going to ignore the fact that she'd tried to leave without telling me goodbye.

I knew my girl. The fact that she was here would be riding her hard this morning. She'd never had anyone to help her out in her life. She didn't know what to think about it.

That was alright. Soon enough, all of this would be as familiar to her as breathing.

"Oh, okay," she said, sounding a little dazed and confused as she walked slowly into the kitchen and stared at it.

I tried to see it from her point of view. I'd grown up with this type of wealth, courtesy of my lawyer stepdad. His money and the stability it provided had been the reason she'd gone back to him.

It was . . . a lot. Especially for one person.

But I'd obviously had great foresight because now it wasn't just one person staying here, and Anastasia deserved the very best.

"You made all this?" she whispered, gesturing at the food.

I had gone overboard. I could admit that. But I hadn't known what she would like. So, I made pancakes and waffles . . . and french toast. Bacon and sausages were stacked high on a platter, and I'd even had Mrs. Bentley, Lincoln's housekeeper, send over some of her breakfast burritos. We all liked them so much, it was basically a full-time job for her to keep us stocked up.

I probably could have just stuck with those, but the overwhelming urge to take care of her was riding me hard.

A flashback hit me. Suffocating and quick.

"Why isn't fucking dinner ready, Leslie? What the fuck has your lazy ass been doing all day? You're such a fucking disgrace. I work so hard, and this is the thanks I get?"

Smack.

Dan's hand reverberated across Mom's cheek, and she fell to the floor in front of where I'd been playing with cars while she made dinner, and my red one rolled into her hip.

I took a deep breath, trying to center myself after that unfortunate trip down memory lane. "I like cooking," I finally said, my voice thankfully even and calm. I left out the "for you" I was thinking.

"You should have let me cook or something," she said, sounding rattled. Anastasia had sweatpants on over her leotard and she'd pulled her hair back into a ponytail. She was also still holding her bag, so I grabbed it and set it on the counter for her.

"It's the least I can do after you let me spend the night."

I resisted the urge to scoff. That would probably offend her.

Over my dead body was she ever going to cook for me, though. Or clean.

Or do anything for me at all.

Except blow jobs. I decided I would make an exception for those as I got lost on her luscious lips for a moment as she slowly licked her bottom lip.

"Let me make you a plate, baby girl," I murmured, enjoying the way she blushed.

"Oh, I—" She tried to object, but I'd already grabbed a plate and was stacking literally everything I'd cooked on it.

"There's no way I can eat all of that." She giggled.

I savored the sound. I'd been wondering what this place had been missing since I'd moved in.

Her.

It had been missing her.

I led her over to a barstool and set her plate down before helping her onto the seat.

There was a small, amused smile on her face as I fidgeted with her stool until I was sure she was comfortable.

She was thin, overly so. Even for a ballerina, I was pretty sure.

I had the insane urge to pick up the fork and start feeding her, and I had to grab the edges of the counter to stop myself.

"Are you going to eat?" she asked, her fork pausing in the air as she stared at me with concern.

I'd already drank a protein shake with my trainer's prescribed vitamins ground up in it, but if eating some food meant she would eat . . . I was up for it.

I filled up a plate and settled down next to her, pretending that I hadn't shifted the barstools so that our arms were brushing against each other as we moved.

"Oh, do you need something to drink?" I asked standing up suddenly because I couldn't believe I'd forgotten. "How about some coffee?" Walking over to the counter, I started fiddling with my coffee machine.

When she hadn't said anything, I glanced over to see she was biting down on her lip shyly.

"I'm good with just water," she said softly, not sounding like she actually meant it.

I hummed as I finally got the damn thing to work, and the machine hissed as hot liquid poured into the white mug I'd placed underneath it. Then, just to show off, I poured cream and sugar into the drink, making a fancy leaf pattern.

"That's beautiful," she mused, as I slid the mug in front of her.

"Not as beautiful as you," I said, and she snorted because that was a ridiculously corny thing to say.

I was pretty sure she was still swooning, though.

"Seriously, you should drink this," she insisted, pushing it away.

"Do you not like coffee?" I asked, studying her face and committing more of her expressions to memory.

"I do like coffee," she said slowly.

"Is there a particular place you've been wanting to try? I can order it," I said quickly, wondering if she would like those supersweet Starbucks drinks—like Ari.

"I . . . I don't want to drink it because when I leave here I won't be able to afford it, and then it will make my life even more miserable than it was before." She blurted the words out, and my mouth dropped at the little nugget of honesty I'd just gotten out of her.

Her cheeks were a bright red color, and she slid her hands over her face, trying to hide from me.

She was adorable.

"Hey," I murmured, trailing my fingertips across her cheek. She shivered, and I held in a grin.

"I know what you're going to say," she rushed out before I could say anything. "You're going to be nice because, along with being beautiful, you also happen to be the nicest guy I've ever met in my whole life."

I opened my mouth to say something, and she held up a finger.

"But you shouldn't make promises you can't keep. And anything that says I'm going to be able to drink fancy coffee every day for the rest of my life—because I just know one sip will never be enough . . . it's not a promise you should be making."

This time I couldn't keep the smirk off my lips when she finished her little speech. "Are you done?"

"Done?"

"Well, I don't want to cut you off when you're on a roll."

She gaped at me. "Are you—laughing at me?" she asked indignantly.

I pushed the cup closer to her. "Drink the coffee, little dancer. Who knows, you might hate it. And then your . . . spiel . . . would have been for nothing." I dared her with my eyes, and I watched as she slowly reached for the mug. I held her eyes the entire time—as she lifted the cup to her lips, as the deep, earthy notes danced across her tongue, the bitter taste perfectly balanced with the cream and sugar I'd put in it.

She moaned softly as she swallowed it down, immediately going for another sip.

I was damn good at making coffee.

"Liked it, huh?"

She groaned, and took another sip for good measure. "See, I told you. Now, I'm going to be craving it every day."

I leaned forward, my thumb brushing some of the coffee foam off her lip, and her eyes tracked my movement as I brought it to my mouth and sucked it off.

"I'll just always have to be here to make you another one," I told her.

Her breathing stuttered and she blinked several times . . . before taking another sip.

There was a little smile on her lips now, though.

After she stopped fighting me about the coffee, she ate, and I mostly stared at her.

Best meal of my life.

She'd started out slow, but a few bites in, the floodgates opened, and she was scarfing down the food, not stopping until the plate was completely clean.

"Wow. I . . . I can't believe I just ate all of that." Anastasia stared at the plate in horror. I had to admit I was impressed and immensely happy she'd liked the food enough to eat that much.

But then a bad feeling carved its way through my rib cage.

"When was the last time you ate?" I said haltingly.

She bit her lip, looking everywhere but at me. "It's been a few days since I've eaten an actual meal. I had a piece of bread yesterday morning and some of that sandwich last night."

There was a beat of silence, and then I sprung from my plate. "I'll get you more," I said firmly.

Anastasia grabbed my arm, stopping me in my tracks because she was actually touching me willingly. "I can't eat another bite. I promise." She laughed.

I took a step toward her, and her laughter abruptly cut off, making way for a hitched breath. "You'll tell me if you're ever hungry?"

She gaped at me, and I was aware I was coming across a little intense—but I couldn't stop myself.

Thinking of her being hungry was a new trigger for me. That much was clear.

"I have to get going to class," she began, instead of answering my question. "Thank you so much for letting me stay here last night, Camden. You'll never know how much it meant to me. I'll try not to be such a nuisance in the future." Her eyes were shiny by the time she finished, and I took a chance and softly stroked her cheek again, savoring the feeling of her skin.

"We're going on a date tonight," I told her firmly, locking eyes with her and gripping her chin so she couldn't look away. "And then you're going to come back here and sleep in that room. You're going to sleep in that room for as long as you want. And you're not going to argue with me. This is going to be your home for as long as you need it."

Forever preferably.

"Do you understand?"

Her eyes were wide, and her mouth was opening and closing like she was at a loss for words.

"Besides," I continued smoothly, "how am I supposed to make you hot chocolate and coffee whenever you need them if you aren't here?"

Anastasia

It seemed like all I could do was stare at him. This was another of those moments . . . where I wasn't sure if I was dreaming or not. Had he really just offered for me to stay here . . . for as long as I needed?

I don't know what came over me next. Maybe it was the fact that I'd just eaten the best meal of my life. Maybe it was because being this close to him was a life-changing experience. Maybe it was because of what he'd just said . . .

I slid off the stool and slammed my lips against his, his body rocking backward because he was so surprised.

When he didn't move at all, I moved back, my cheeks heating and embarrassment soaking into my skin. Fuck. Why had I just done that? He'd just offered for me to live with him . . . and *that* had been my response?

I'd obviously read the entire situation wrong.

He'd just been being nice, right? That's all this was?

"I'm so s—" I began.

"Fuck," he murmured . . . and then his lips were closing over mine in a supple kiss. His hot, wet tongue was sliding inside me. He fucked my mouth; long licks that I swore had a central line to my clit. His hands were moving up and down my sides, my body pressing against his.

"I was trying to be good," he breathed in between a kiss. "But now you've done it."

I sighed against him as he dominated my mouth, his hands sliding into my hair and maneuvering me exactly where he wanted.

He broke away, and an embarrassing mewl came out of my mouth.

I needed more. I was desperate for him.

"I'm going to take such good care of you," he growled, and my heart rate spiked at the promise in his voice.

His lips went back to mine, and then I was running my hands all over his powerful chest and his shoulders, pulling at his shirt because I needed him closer . . .

He was so perfect, it was almost heartbreaking, because I'd never seen anything as beautiful as him in my entire life.

I'd been kissed before by fumbling boys and assholes like Michael who had no interest in my pleasure. All they wanted was to take from me. This was a kiss from a man—a man who knew how to play my body perfectly to get the maximum amount of pleasure for both of us.

Camden moaned against my lips, pressing his huge, hard length into my stomach as he ate at my mouth, deep, savoring licks, like he couldn't get enough of my taste.

He tugged at my hair, pulling my head back as his lips drifted down my neck, and I rubbed against him.

I didn't recognize myself as I gasped at the feel of his mouth. I'd kept any sexual desire I'd had in my life locked up tight. I hadn't had a lot of choices in my life, and keeping my virginity intact had seemed like one of the only things I had control over. Since meeting him, though, I'd found myself desperate for him. Kissing him had burst open a door inside me, and now he'd become a craving in my bloodstream. I'd take whatever he wanted to give me.

"Rub that pussy on my thigh, just like that, Anastasia." His voice was tight, pained sounding, like he was holding himself back and every second of it was torture. The sound of my name in that tone . . . I'd never heard anything hotter in my entire life.

I rubbed against him desperately, sparks shooting from my clit as my core tightened. His lips descended down my chest, and I gasped at the sensation of the cool air over my nipples as he pulled down the leotard I was wearing, baring my chest to him.

"Please," I whimpered as he pulled me closer.

I was vaguely aware that we were moving fast—zero to sixty, actually.

But I couldn't make myself stop.

A rough hand massaged my breast. "Fuck, these are perfect. I love them so much," he said in my ear, his voice rough as he pinched one of my nipples, and a dazed sob slipped from my lips. He pulled back and our gazes locked. Camden's pupils were blown out, like the taste of me had drugged him and he'd slipped into a bliss-filled high.

"You ever have an orgasm, Anastasia? Ever slip your fingers into your perfect pussy and get yourself off?"

"No . . . never," I cried as his lips descended on my nipple, sucking and biting at my chest.

"And I know you've never let some fuckwad touch you. You were waiting for me, weren't you, baby girl?"

"Yes," I whimpered as he licked the underside of my breast.

"I'm going to give you one right now, Anastasia," he growled as the combination of my clit rubbing against his thigh, and whatever magic he was weaving, sent me soaring sky-high. "Come for me right fucking now."

As if his words held magic powers—or maybe it was just his tongue and his hands . . . and him—my core clenched and pleasure surged through me. I whimpered as my legs gave out. Camden caught me, not missing a beat as he sucked my other nipple through my first orgasm. My entire body shuddered against him, and I held on to his shirt for dear life, barely able to take the foreign sensations pulsing through me.

There's nothing that can prepare you for your first orgasm. Not books, not shows. Nothing.

I think I was addicted.

I was definitely changed, unrecognizable from who I'd been just minutes before.

"Such a good girl, coming for me as I sucked on those pretty tits. How about another one? See how that pretty pussy likes to be played with?" he whispered roughly against my chest, his breath sending sparks across my skin.

"Yes," I murmured. "Yes, yes, yes." I wasn't stopping to think it through. I just knew my body wanted more. "I want that."

"Good girl," he repeated in a thick voice, lifting his face from my chest and straightening up. Camden gave me another long, possessive kiss, holding me still under his ministrations.

Camden's other hand made its way from my chest, down my side, slowly tracing the edge of the sweatpants I was wearing over my leotard. He pushed underneath the band, and I lost my ability to breathe, my clit literally pulsing as his hand slid down. Down, down, until it was running along the lining.

"Is this okay, Ana?" he murmured as he softly rubbed my pussy over the thin fabric.

All I could do was moan, and he chuckled darkly against my lips. Taking his time as he expertly rubbed along my seam, his fingers passing over my clit each time.

"Please," I begged, needing more.

The pleasure was building again; I couldn't have resisted it even if I wanted to. My breaths were coming out in embarrassing gasps, and my arousal was spiking with every swipe of his fingers.

"Does my baby girl want me to take care of her?" He smiled against my lips, seeming to find it amusing how easily he could control my body.

I wanted to be his baby girl, though. In that moment, I wanted to be everything for him, everything he'd ever wanted, everything he'd ever needed.

"Yes," I gasped. My eyes slipped closed as his fingers finally moved under the edge of my leotard, and he was suddenly sliding through my dripping wet folds with ease.

"So fucking wet," he breathed, not sounding surprised at all about that fact. But I guess the steady supply of whimpers and moans would have told him exactly what he was doing to me.

He groaned as one of his fingers pushed inside me, and I cried out at the slight pinch of pain.

"You're so tight. Your pussy is trying to pull my finger in. You're going to choke my cock, baby. I might not survive," he rasped, and my body released a full body shiver at his words.

I wanted that. His cock driving in and out of me, his body covering mine. I wanted to take every inch of him, let him do whatever he wanted—pleasure was building up again, surging to the surface as he pushed another thick finger into my core, and I lost the ability to breathe from the fullness. Almost there . . .

Camden yanked his fingers out, the leftover sensations not enough to fully push me over the edge.

"What?" I gasped, fighting the strange urge to cry.

"Shh," he murmured, bringing his fingers out of my sweatpants and up to my lips, pushing inside my mouth so I could taste myself. Camden forced me to suck them completely clean before he pulled them out and kissed me, his tongue licking inside like he was chasing the taste.

I tried to move against his leg, desperate to put pressure on my clit and finish what he'd started, but he held me tight. "I'll give you what you need, baby girl. But I want to hear you say it."

"W—What?" I asked, my brain unable to think clearly, caught in that space between pleasure and pain.

"Say you'll go on a date with me," he ordered.

"Okay," I replied immediately, moaning in relief as his hand slipped between my legs and brushed against my clit.

"Okay, what?" he pressed, stopping his hand once again.

"Okay, I'll go on a date with you," I cried, streams of whimpers falling from my mouth as he rewarded me by slowly rimming the entrance to my core.

"Now, say you'll stay here," he continued, his voice perfectly calm like he wasn't affected at all at the moment.

I squeezed my eyes shut, trying to concentrate as he pushed the tips of his three fingers inside me.

"I—"

"Say it, Anastasia. And I'll give you exactly what you need," he crooned.

"Just until I get back on my feet?" I glanced up at him, trying to keep my head on while he maneuvered and seduced my body.

His eyes flashed at my addition, but he nodded.

"I'll stay," I answered then, shocked and confused at how easily he got me to agree to things.

"That's my good girl," he groaned, plunging his fingers inside my core as his lips crashed against mine.

Yes. I panted as he finger fucked me fast and deep, skyrocketing my fading orgasm.

My cries were lost in his mouth as I came. Hard. The previous orgasm was a blip in the universe in comparison.

A tear slid down my cheek as he pulled out his fingers and sucked the taste of me off each one, holding my gaze the entire time.

"Thank you," he murmured finally, after the stillness had settled around us like a cloak.

"Hmm?" I asked, the world spinning slightly around me as I came back from a high I was worried I'd spend the rest of my life chasing.

"For giving me that," he said, the gold ring around his green eyes seeming to glow in the soft light in the room. It had still been dark when I'd come out, trying to sneak away so I didn't have to say goodbye.

Maybe a part of me had known this would happen.

That his help for one night would become . . . extended.

I didn't find myself minding so much at the moment.

Camden leaned in then and knocked my entire world off its axis with one simple sentence.

"You're going to give me all your firsts."

I gaped at him, and he smirked, grabbing a grape and popping it into his mouth and making it look way too sensual considering he was chewing.

I didn't argue with him, but I was in a daze as he straightened my clothes and then grabbed my hand, leading me to the elevator. I was still in a daze the entire drive to dance and as he dropped me off.

And as I was twirling around in class later on, feeling rested for the first time in what seemed like forever, I was quite sure that I was in *way* over my head.

CHAPTER 17

CAMDEN

DALLAS KNIGHTS

Me: I need help.

Ari: Shocking.

Logan: I do believe I said I had fulfilled all obligations for the rest of my eternity.

Logan: SHE SUCKED MY FINGER.

Linc: Whiner. A woman licks your finger, and you act like the world is ending.

Ari: This guy.

Logan: She's seventy-five years old!

Me: We don't need this kind of negativity this morning, Rookie. And don't be ageist.

Ari: Good point.

Ari Lancaster removed Logan York from the chat.

I grinned as Logan sent me a middle finger emoji right after in a different text.

Me: Sorry, CoT rules. One does not complain when a woman sucks on your finger.

Logan: I hate all of you.

Me: Why aren't you texting Ari this? He's the one who took you out of the chat.

Logan: . . .

Logan: He blocked me.

I laughed uproariously at that and then went back to the important conversation I was having in the group chat.

Me: Back to actual important things . . .

Ari: I would just like to say that a friend in need is a pest, Hero.

Walker: Agreed.

Ari: Disney. You simp.

Walker: I was agreeing with you!

Ari: Oh, right.

Linc: Can we focus? I have . . . things to do.

Ari: Would this "thing" have anything to do with the fact that Monroe has class today with a certain professor . . .

Linc: 🖕

Hmmm. I was intrigued by that story. But also a little terrified for the professor. Lincoln Daniels could be . . . scary.

A perfect use of " . . . " right there.

Me: Which one of your wives has done ballet? There has to be one of them.

Linc: Developed an interest in the arts, Hero?

Ari: Or is this one of those "dogs" things. If so, I'm out.

Walker: In all fairness, it was actually dogs.

I rolled my eyes. This was going to take forever at this pace. I added Logan back to the chat, just in case he knew something about ballet. I was quite positive one of his puck bunnies in preseason had been a dancer of some sort.

Hmm . . . maybe she had actually been a stripper.

Me: As I was saying . . . do any of your wives know about ballet?

Ari: Hero, what did I say about radiuses?

Me: What?

Ari: R-A-D-I-U-S-E-S

Logan: How long did that take you to type out?

Linc: Who invited Rookie in here again?

Walker: Not me!

Ari: You know, Disney, you don't have to be the first to respond to Lincoln.

Walker: . . .

Logan: What a simp.

Logan: Ari . . . thanks for unblocking me :)

Walker Davis removed Logan York from the chat.

Me: I believe radii is the plural of radius.

Ari: What?

Me: You spelled radiuses. That's not a word.

Linc: He was probably trying to spell radishes. That is a word.

Ari: I hate you both. And no that's NOT what I was trying to say. Who would ever put radishes in a text?

Walker: I have!

Linc: . . .

Ari: . . .

Me: . . .

Me: I did that one right!

Me: Now, what were you saying about radii?

Ari: . . .

Walker: That there's no need to involve the wives and break your six-foot radius requirement.

I frowned.

Me: Texting you about them is breaking my requirement?

Linc: Absolutely.

Well then.

Ari: But don't worry. No need for the wives. I took a ballet class in college.

Walker: What?

Ari: It helped with my footwork and . . .

There was a really long pause after that, and I was wondering if Blake had come in and distracted him. That happened a lot. He would just disappear.

While I was waiting, I checked her tracker to make sure she was still at dance. Before dropping her off this morning, I'd given her an iPhone in the car. She'd tried to refuse it—of course. But I'd told her it was an old one that someone had given me in a promo package. A lie . . . but it had gotten her to take it so she could text me when I was supposed to pick her up.

I may have also omitted the fact that I'd installed a tracking app on there, so I didn't have to worry about her finding the original tracking device I'd put in her bag yesterday.

My phone buzzed.

Linc: What Ari was trying to say was that it helped him with his footwork and . . .

Ari: Don't finish that train of thought, Golden Boy. There are no other women that exist in the world besides Blake Lancaster.

Walker: What about Geraldine?

Ari: . . .

Ari: And Geraldine.

Me: Alright . . . thirty minutes later. I doubt you will know this, but what are all the best brands for ballet dancers if I was taking a ballet dancer shopping.

Linc: I have to say, Hero. Dogs and ballet. I never would have thought . . .

I grinned, feeling strangely giddy about being such a psychopath this morning.

Ari: Capezio, Bloch, Miu Miu, Gaynor Minden. Boom. Mic drop.

Me: Alright then. I have to say that we're learning all sorts of things about each other in the circle of trust lately.

I snorted when Ari removed me from the chat and then sent me a meme with a circle labeled "circle of trust" with a dot outside of it that he'd labeled Camden.

I sent him one back with the dot firmly inside before beginning my search of where all those brands were sold.

I had a little dancer to spoil.

Anastasia

It would have been a small thing to most people, having someone waiting for me after dance. But it was a huge thing for me.

For as long as I could really remember, I'd had to get myself home after class. Walk or take the bus to whatever home or job I was going to.

It was a giddy feeling to step outside and see Camden in his lifted, fancy-looking black truck, waiting at the curb for me.

He waved the second he saw me, hopping out and jogging to where I was on the sidewalk.

I blushed as I looked at him, averting my gaze when he brushed a strand of hair out of my face that had escaped from the messy bun I'd thrown my hair up in after class.

I knew what those fingers could do now. I knew what those lips tasted like.

It was hard to meet his gaze.

He tipped up my chin so I had to look at him, pressing a soft kiss on my lips that had me melting against him with a soft sigh.

"Hi," I whispered, after he'd lifted his face away from me.

"Hi, little dancer," he murmured back, playfully batting at the mess of hair on my head. "I like this. It's sexy."

Ugh. Was I still breathing? How did I do that again? He was too charming. Too sexy. Too much.

I was in big trouble.

"Thanks," I said, my voice sounding high and breathy as he tangled his hand with mine and led me to the truck.

Is this what we were doing? Two orgasms against his wall, and now he was holding hands with me?

This was another one of those "pinch me" moments because things like this didn't happen to a girl like me.

Camden opened the truck door and lifted me up onto the seat. I stared at him, amused, as he fussed with the seatbelt, pulling it over my lap and clicking it in.

"Are you going to start getting me dressed every morning, too?" I asked, reddening all over again when his gaze heated like he very much liked that idea.

"Mmmh," he mused, smiling at me wickedly.

I was a puddle in my seat when he shut the door and walked around to the driver's side.

I can't believe I thought about not texting him when I was done with class. I would have missed out on this.

Camden started the truck and pulled away from the curb, and I got caught down memory lane, voices in the past telling me over and over again I was a burden.

"Do you know how lucky you are we took you in and kept you off the streets?" Mrs. Carver snarled as she stared down at the broken vase at my feet. I hadn't even broken the vase—Michael had and then he'd blamed it on

me. But I couldn't tell Mrs. Carver that. "We pay for food, for clothes . . . we put a roof over your head. And this is how you repay us?"

This is how you repay us?

This is how you repay us?

The words repeated in my head over and over again—though not even close to how many times I'd heard it from them.

I'd never wanted to feel indebted to anyone again.

I needed to remember that with Camden. There was always a point where things changed, when it went from a favor to a curse.

"What are you thinking about over there? You look like Geraldine when she lost her *British Bake-Off* competition against Mrs. Hennie."

"Geraldine?"

He snorted. "I forgot you haven't met her yet. I've been so wrapped up in you these last few weeks, it seems weird you don't know my whole life already."

Ugh. This was why I needed to be careful. Because he said things like *that*.

"So, where are we going?" I chirped, trying to sound excited even though that particular memory had definitely brought down my mood.

"Shopping," he said, flashing me a sexy grin.

I stiffened, my eyes widening. No. No. No. No. He was *not* allowed to take me shopping. "I'd rather not," I told him softly. "I . . . I don't want to feel like I owe you any more than I already do."

He paused, his eyebrows going up nearly to his hairline like I'd caught him off guard.

"This part of the date is actually what comes with my sponsorship of the Company," he finally said smoothly.

"A shopping trip comes with the sponsorship?" I asked dubiously.

He nodded, and I got a little lost staring at how hot he looked while driving. One thing I'd noticed about Camden, he always looked perfectly in control in every situation. Like he was the master of his domain . . . of the world.

I'd never felt like that.

"Every dancer at the Company gets a stipend for clothes. I just thought it would be fun for us to include that as part of our date," he was saying as I struggled to not picture him naked.

I guess that sounded legitimate. A hockey player sponsoring a ballet company was different to begin with, so it would make sense that maybe the sponsorship itself would have some things a little out of the ordinary as well.

"Alright, if everyone is getting a stipend," I said slowly. "Although, I'm pretty sure that your sponsorship had something to do with me as well." I raised an eyebrow, daring him to refute that.

"Anastasia Lennox, are you accusing me of not being a patron of the arts?" He placed a hand on his chest, pretending I'd hurt him.

I giggled, abruptly stopping because the sound felt so foreign coming out of my mouth.

"My second favorite sound," he mused, turning into the parking lot of a high-end shopping center that gave me hives just being near it.

"What's your favorite sound?" I asked, distracted when I saw Grand Prix, a dance store I'd only ever dreamed about going to. It had all the best brands, Capezio, Bloch, Miu Miu . . . Were we really shopping there?

I realized he hadn't answered me, and I glanced over, seeing the small, sexy smirk on his lips as he stared at me like something was amusing him. His door was open, and he had one leg out of the cab.

"Are you not going to tell me?" I asked with a laugh, going to open my door. He clicked the lock.

"Don't move," he growled, shutting his door and jogging around to open mine.

There was a glittery feeling forcing its way into my veins as he helped me out. Like I was precious. Like he was scared I would get injured and he couldn't take it.

Like I meant something.

"You wanted to know my favorite sound . . . " he murmured, pressing me against the truck as he leaned his weight against me. His lips danced across my neck, and I shivered at the feeling. I loved how much bigger he was than me. It felt like he could slay all my monsters, save me from the world.

Definite "Daddy" energy.

"Yes, sir," I gasped, unable to even care about the other shoppers staring at us right then.

"It's the sound of you coming, of course," he purred, abruptly straightening and taking a step away.

Thank fuck for my sweatpants. There was definitely a wet spot on this leotard after that little moment, and I didn't need everyone seeing it.

Or maybe it wouldn't even be a thing.

Anyone would have a wet spot when faced with a god like Camden James.

He was humming softly under his breath as he peeled me off the truck and led me toward Grand Prix, his hand once again holding mine.

What followed after that was like I'd stepped into a fairytale. Even if this was part of the sponsorship, and everyone was getting money to do this—I'd never had anything like this happen to me before.

Anything I looked at, he had the store attendant grab. Leotards and shoes, sweats and leggings, and pretty clips for my hair. Workout sets and navy-blue silk pajamas that made me want to cry with how soft they were. Camden claimed they would help me sleep better and thus dance better, and so in the pile they went.

It went on and on like this and continued after we'd left the store.

"Where are we going now?" I whisper-yelled because we'd just spent an obscene amount of money, and I was feeling a little crazy about it. I needed to get back to his penthouse and clean something or cook dinner. There was no way that all of this came with the sponsorship. My skin felt tight across my bones.

"We need to get stuff for your bedroom," he said calmly, like it was nothing as we walked to another high-end store in the shopping center.

I stopped in my tracks, and his body rocked back as I pulled on his hand—that had once again been holding mine. "What? No! Absolutely not. You may have used the sponsorship as an excuse to buy all that stuff, but there's no way that things for my bedroom are included in that."

"And by the way," I said, gesturing wildly in the air with my free hand, "that is not *my* bedroom. That is *your* guest room. Where I am staying as a *guest*." My chest was heaving, and I probably looked insane as I finished, wide-eyed and sweating slightly.

A beautiful sight, I'm sure.

"Those sheets are scratchy," he said matter-of-factly. "You can't dance when you sleep on scratchy sheets."

"I was sleeping on a cot in a homeless shelter. Those are the definition of scratchy sheets," I hissed loudly, ducking my head when I caught someone's stare.

We were standing in the tiled corridor that connected all the stores. There was a fancy fountain behind us and white lights strung everywhere.

"If you don't let me buy my favorite sheets in purple—because that's your favorite color, I'm going to put you over my knee and spank you because you're being a brat." Camden's face was perfectly expressionless as he said that, as if it was normal everyday behavior to tell another grown adult you were going to spank them.

Examining Camden's face, though . . . maybe it was.

And why was my leotard soaking wet again at the thought of it?

I bet he'd make me feel *so* good after the pain.

"Holy shit," he murmured, once again crowding against me, even though there were people passing us on the left and right. "You like that idea . . . me spanking you."

"I don't know what you're talking about," I huffed, trying to yank my hand away to hide the fact that my nipples were like diamonds popping out through my top.

As if he could read my mind, his eyes darted down to my chest, and he growled softly, his gaze searching around like he was looking for anyone daring to stare.

"Let's just zip this up," he said, as he pulled my jacket together and zipped it up to my chin.

I made a choking sound and swatted his hand away, pulling it down to a less choke-worthy level.

"Shall we proceed?" he asked, a wide, mocking smirk on his face because he knew he'd won.

I nodded, feeling like the brat he'd called me at the moment.

Normal people accepted gifts. I could do it. I could be normal.

We walked hand in hand to a home store, and I immediately messed up by glancing at a few things that had caught my eye. They somehow ended up in the basket. I wanted to object, because that furry rug and that gold frame was not a set of purple sheets. But the attendant was drooling over Camden as we walked, and I didn't want to make a scene by refusing them.

Maybe you are a user, just like Michael said . . .

The voice was loud, but I tried to block it out, just like I tried not to tear up when I touched sheets that felt like heaven.

I failed at both.

Later that night, Camden came into my room which was now stuffed full of all the new things he'd bought me. He'd also grilled me steak for dinner—that literally melted on my tongue—and cheesy potatoes that I could have eaten every day.

It had been the best day of my life.

"Goodnight, little dancer," Camden said as he literally tucked me into bed and pulled my new sheets up to my chin, his eyes burning with an emotion I didn't understand. He pressed a soft kiss against my lips, and I wanted to ask him to stay. But I didn't.

Soon.

Soon, I'd be brave enough to ask Camden James to come to bed with me.

Just not tonight . . .

CHAPTER 18

ANASTASIA

An alarm was ringing. Who set an alarm that annoying?

I blinked blearily, staring up at the ceiling. It was still dark outside. Why was the alarm going off when it was *still* dark outside?

Glancing around the room, I finally realized that the alarm was coming from the nightstand next to me; that fancy phone Camden had given me was buzzing and making the racket.

I had been the one to set the alarm.

I pressed random buttons on the phone until it finally stopped, and then I flopped back onto the bed, tempted to try and go back to sleep.

Okay, no. I'd set this alarm because I wanted to work out before Camden woke up. Rise and shine it was.

Sitting up wearily, I winced as pain shot through my leg. I hadn't stretched enough yesterday after class, and I was definitely feeling it. Leaning forward, I reached toward my toes, trying to push away the ache.

Ringggg. Ringggg.

I almost fell off the bed when the alarm started up again, the shrill noise piercing the silence of the house like a knife through butter, slicing through the tranquil morning air. It was as if a banshee had taken up residence within the walls, her wailing cries echoing off the pristine surfaces and reverberating through me.

I growled at the phone as I poked a different button than the one I'd pressed last time. I really needed to learn how to use this thing . . . even if it was just temporary. As soon as I got my feet back under me, I was going to get one of those prepaid phones, and I'd give this one back to Camden.

I didn't even want to guess how much the thing had cost. It was like a spaceship.

Dragging myself out of bed, I quickly changed into a sports bra and leggings, then headed out of the room, inching the door open so I could listen for any signs of life.

Was it ridiculous that I was checking to see if he was out there? Yes, yes it was. But since I could barely form words around him when I was fully awake, I was hoping to avoid any awkward encounters when I was half asleep.

I made my way through the penthouse, shrugging off the awkwardness I felt as I passed through it. It still didn't feel real that I was staying here. The opulence of his home was overwhelming, each room perfect and pristine. I was never going to stop feeling out of place here.

And when I moved out . . . soon . . . it was going to be painful. Because now I was going to compare every dingy and decrepit place I lived in to this place.

Just like I was going to compare every man I met for the rest of my life to the perfection that was Camden James.

I was quite sure that they would also be . . . lacking.

The hallways stretched on for what felt like miles, the sound of my footsteps echoing around me as I crept through the silent penthouse. Sunlight was starting to filter in through the windows, casting long shadows across the polished floors.

Where the crap was the workout room? He'd shown me the other day, but it felt like there were a million rooms in this place.

As I turned a corner, the sound of music caught my attention, a pounding rhythm that reverberated through the walls. Intrigued, I followed the sound, my curiosity getting the better of me as it took me right to . . . the gym I'd been looking for.

I found myself standing outside of the glass double doors, gaping at the sight in front of me.

Camden was on a bench, shirtless. His perfect chest glistening with sweat, his muscles rippling with each movement as he lifted a bar stacked with weights. The room was filled with the sound of rock music, pounding as he worked out with single-minded focus.

I couldn't tear my eyes away from him, the sight of his chiseled chest and sculpted arms sending a rush of heat pulsing between my legs. It was like something out of a dream, a fantasy come to life before my very eyes.

He hadn't noticed me, too intent on his workout to look up and see my reflection in the glass. Although my brain was screaming at me to scurry away . . . I couldn't get the rest of my body to listen.

I hovered in the doorway, unable to tear my gaze away from him.

I was used to men's bodies. While growing up, there were always quite a few male dancers in my classes, and their leotards left very little to the imagination.

But they had not prepared me for Camden. *This* was a man.

And oh my gosh he was beautiful.

The music changed to some rap song I faintly recognized, and it was enough to push me to move.

But then, just as I was about to turn and leave, our eyes locked in the mirror.

His gaze darkened, an unreadable expression settling onto his face.

"Anastasia," he said, and somehow his deep, silky voice cut right through the noise of the music, settling into my veins and sending sparks pirouetting through my bloodstream.

I was tempted to run. Embarrassing or not, it was probably safest to turn and sprint down the hall. Showing my face in a couple of hours when I had time to process the masculine hotness in front of me.

"Anastasia," Camden repeated, this time in a knowing voice, like he could see inside my brain and see all the dirty, dirty thoughts I was having right now as I gaped at him.

Speaking of gaping, I snapped my mouth shut realizing that my jaw had been hanging open like some kind of demented fish. Cheeks flushing, I finally opened the glass door and stepped inside the room.

"I wasn't expecting to see you this early," he murmured as he racked his weights and turned on the bench to stare at me appraisingly. His gaze dragged from my feet to my face, seeming to grace every curve—or lack of—on my body. My nipples hardened into tight points beneath my thin sports bra, and I swear his gaze *burned* when it brushed against my chest.

Stay cool, girl. Think of something cold. Ice. Ice . . . hockey . . . him doing stretches . . . No! Not cold. Think of something bad.

That was helpful; one thought of Michael, and my arousal went down like the air let out of a balloon.

"I thought I would get in an early workout," I said belatedly, realizing that he was waiting for a reply. I was proud of myself when my words came out in English. That was tough around him.

I wiped at my forehead, feeling simultaneously like I was wearing too much and too little clothes at the moment. Camden's gaze lingered on me, his eyes smoldering with a heat that set my skin ablaze. If he could just stop staring at me like he wanted to eat me, maybe I would be capable of forming rational thoughts.

"Have at it," he said . . . but was that a hint of a growl in his voice?

Yes, Daddy, my inner voice purred.

Holy crap what was wrong with me?

"Okay," I said, wincing at the nervous squeak in my voice. Did he hear that?

Judging by the slight smirk on his lips, I was betting he did. And could he see the way my legs were already shaking as I walked over to the mats?

This was a very bad idea.

I began some of my simpler stretches, figuring I would start slow—less chance of embarrassing myself even more. I tried to concentrate on what I was doing . . . tried to keep my gaze firmly on the floor.

But it was an impossible task.

He'd resumed his workout, his muscles flexing with each movement, and it was like he had some kind of tractor beam in his biceps because I couldn't stop myself from staring.

And that would have been fine . . .

If he wasn't staring right back.

Intensely. Like he couldn't *not* look.

His gaze stoked a fire deep within my core, and I was worried about the state of my underwear. These leggings were thinnnn. Sure to show my arousal if I didn't control myself.

My hands were trembling as I reached down for the floor, the music pulsing in the background like a heartbeat.

I twisted and turned, my body straining with the effort.

Was it hard to breathe in here . . . or was that just me? The air between us seemed to crackle with electricity, charged and tense in a way that was leaving me breathless and dizzy.

"When's your next show?" he asked casually, and I almost swallowed my tongue trying to answer him.

Show. When was my show?

What show exactly?

He grinned and my head swam.

"Soon," I choked out as he strode toward the treadmill.

An ass like that should be illegal, I decided as he stepped onto the machine.

Don't stare at his ass anymore! I hissed to myself as I jerked my gaze away. I attempted to distract myself by staring around the gym. I'd seen it briefly in that first tour, but looking at it now, it was just another reminder of how in over my head I was in this home.

The gym was a marvel, a wonderland of fitness that would fit any athlete's dream. It had everything you could possibly need or want, all neatly arranged in a space that oozed luxury and functionality. There were literal rows of gleaming equipment, like he was expecting his entire team to show up for a workout.

Hell, maybe that did happen. I couldn't imagine that their arena gym was as nice as this.

The thought made me feel a bit faint.

In one corner there was even a sauna. And was that an ice bath? My leg groaned as I pushed it, as if it were reminding me how nice that would be to soak in after a day of classes.

I was still not convinced I wasn't imagining all of this.

My gaze darted back to Camden's ass, and I decided I must be.

With each stretch, I pushed myself to go deeper, the ache in my muscles a welcome distraction from the intensity of Camden's gaze.

I turned to do another stretch—

"Fuck!" Camden cursed as a hard thud sounded in the room as something hit the floor.

Twirling around, my gaze dropped when I realized the thunk had been Camden falling off the treadmill.

"Are you okay?" I asked as I rushed to his side, my hands shaking with adrenaline as I helped him to his feet. Camden winced as he straightened up, his breath coming in ragged gasps as he rubbed his side where he had landed awkwardly.

He sighed as his head fell back, eyes glued to the ceiling for a moment before he tipped his chin down and met me gaze.

Ohhhh. I inhaled sharply at the primal lust in his eyes. Camden's lips curled into a sexy half smile. "I'll live," he finally muttered, his voice low and husky. "Maybe."

I backed away like I'd been burned, hustling back over the mats before I did something crazy . . . like jump him.

Camden

This was hell. Obviously, all those good deeds I'd done in my life hadn't held much weight because watching her in those tight yoga pants was literally going to kill me.

I'd thought I was hallucinating when I'd glanced at the mirror and saw her standing at the doors. I hadn't been able to sleep after I'd finally tasted her yesterday, and rather than break into her room and ravage her . . . I'd come down to the gym.

It had seemed like a solid plan until she'd appeared.

Anastasia's tits looked fucking incredible in that sports bra. I couldn't help but think about diving in every time I glanced over. There was no padding in that thing. When her nipples had pushed through the fabric . . . well my dirty thoughts must have been why I was being punished right now.

It wasn't my fault that I'd fallen off the treadmill. What was a guy supposed to do when faced with that kind of perfection? She'd been faced away from me, her lithe body changing my life.

I wasn't an ass or tits man anymore. I was an Anastasia man. Her body was life-altering, mind-blowing, oxygen-stealing.

Of course I'd fallen off the damn treadmill. I was just lucky I hadn't been operating any machinery or lifting weights when she'd turned and showed me that ass.

I definitely would have died.

But what a way to go . . . with the sight of her in my eyes.

CHAPTER 19

CAMDEN

I dropped Anastasia off at dance class, feeling ridiculously at the edge of panic watching her walk away from me. If I could have, I would have stitched her to my side. I wanted to do everything with her. I never wanted her to leave my presence.

Unfortunately, she wasn't ready for me to kidnap her and take her to an island where it was just the two of us forever . . . so I'd have to wait on that particular impulse.

I got back to my place, hating how *empty* it felt without her. I had practice in two hours, but not even checking the tracking app every five seconds could make me feel better.

Finally, I couldn't take it anymore. I walked down the hallway toward Anastasia's bedroom, my steps hesitant and uncertain. A very small part of me tried to turn myself around, but the rest of me was past the point of reason.

I stopped several times, my hand hovering over the doorknob. Even though I'd already done so much, stepping into her room without her permission felt like the final straw, the point where I couldn't go back.

I tried to tell myself I was better than this . . . but the pull of her presence was too strong.

Even heroes can fall, evidently.

I turned the handle and pushed open the door, the soft creak of hinges echoing in the stillness of the room. The air was heavy with the scent of her perfume, a heady mixture of orange and vanilla that immediately made my dick hard. I closed my eyes and breathed it in, letting it coat my lungs . . . become a part of me.

The room was still for the most part . . . bare. I hated that. Besides the unmade bed with the purple sheets I'd forced her to pick out, and a few other things I'd caught her looking at, there were no personal belongings for me to look through, nothing to tell me more about *who* Anastasia was.

We needed to remedy that. Immediately.

I opened the closet, peeking inside. She'd left a pair of underwear on the floor and I hesitated once again before grabbing and lifting them to my face.

Fuccck.

I knew what her pussy tasted like, but the smell of it was almost as good . . . lock me up now. It was orange and vanilla again . . . but musky. I could feel my cock weeping precum, raging to be inside her. I'd never felt lust like this before—I didn't know a human being was capable of this. It was all-consuming. I felt dizzy. Crazed. Out of my mind.

I felt like a monster.

I had to unzip my jeans, my mind filled with images of her sitting on my face, her scent and taste coating my lips as I fucked my tongue in and out of her. Or maybe I'd spread her out on the bed first, pin her legs to the bed as I buried my face in her pussy, my tongue tasting every inch of her.

My hands were on my dick before I realized drops of cum were dripping onto the carpet in front of me.

I liked it there, mingled with her scent. I wanted my cum all over her. I wanted *me* all over her.

Walking to her bed, I stared at the rumpled sheets for a moment. Stroking my hand against her pillow—still slightly indented from last night—I pictured myself touching her soft, smooth skin.

Finally, I couldn't help myself, and I slid onto the bed, breathing her in desperately, rolling around in the fabric, wanting her scent to coat my skin. Moaning, I gripped the base of my cock, my dick so hard it felt like I might explode if I didn't get some release.

I rolled back over, gulping in deep inhales of her scent; my hips thrusting against the mattress, searching for friction, like a teenager just discovering his pillow for the first time. I was driving my dick into her tight cunt, I was picturing her breathy cries as I played with her perfect tits.

Growling, I flipped over again, wrapping her panties around my cock, using the cotton to jack myself off as I pictured what it would be like to fuck her.

It wasn't something just on my wishlist—a maybe I'd spend my life hoping for.

It was a certainty, an undeniability . . . a matter of fact.

I thought of how good her pussy would taste, the feeling of her skin, the way her nails would dig into my back as she came apart beneath me and choked my cock. In my head, she was riding my dick, her breasts bouncing as she fucked herself. Her head was thrown back, her tits were thrust forward—

I came. The hardest orgasm I'd ever had in my life, pumping out in spurts until her panties were soaked and my hands were sticky from the excess. My breath was coming out in gasps. My head was floating, pleasure still simmering under my skin. I could've come again with just a few pumps—I hadn't done anything to tamper down the lust that had an iron grip on my dick.

I was out of control, and for the first time in my life . . .

I welcomed it.

Bringing the panties up to my face I breathed in our combined scents, my dick already hardening again because it was everything I wanted.

Soon, I told myself as I dragged my body from the bed, straightening the covers only a little bit.

A perverse part of me wanted her to know that I'd been there. I wanted to picture her tonight, touching that pretty pussy as she breathed in our scents, just like this. I wanted her to picture all the things I was going to do to her as she made herself come.

I left the room, the panties in my pocket. They'd be my new prized possession until I got the real thing.

This girl had ruined me.

And I couldn't wait to ruin her right back.

CHAPTER 20

ANASTASIA

"Ana, can I talk to you for a minute?" Dallon's voice floated through the room from the doorway, and I glanced up from my stretch, a thread of unease twisting its way inside of me.

What would Dallon want from me right now? I'd seen him flirting with Alena this morning as I'd walked in. I was hoping that was a sign he'd forgotten about me.

I walked across the room, aware of everyone's eyes.

"Hey," I murmured as I stepped into the hallway. "Is everything alright?"

He grinned, and the boyish prettiness of his face did nothing for me. He might as well have been a flickering candle next to a wildfire compared to Camden's rugged beauty.

Dallon glanced down at my leotard. "That new?" he asked, and I flushed, for no other reason than I was wearing one of the new ones that Camden had bought me . . . and any time I thought about Camden I blushed.

"Yeah," I said. "One of the outfits that came with the Knights sponsorship."

He frowned, wrinkling his forehead. "What?"

"Nothing," I quickly said, feeling like an idiot that I'd fallen for such a line in the first place.

Dallon would know about it if it was actually a thing.

I was starting to suspect that Camden had made the whole thing up.

Something to think about later . . .

I rubbed a sweaty palm down my tights, fidgeting as I waited for Dallon to deliver his news.

"We're doing a showcase next month, and Madame Leclerc has chosen you to perform the *Giselle pas de deux*."

My eyes widened. I'd dreamed about performing *Giselle*—or even a part of *Giselle*—since I'd started dancing. It was considered to be one of the most romantic dances in ballet. Act II's pas de deux was ethereal, supernatural . . . *perfect*.

My heart felt like it might beat out of my chest.

"Who am I dancing with?" I asked eagerly, going through the male leads in the junior ensemble.

There were a few standouts like Paul and Dameon who would be really good . . .

"You'll be dancing with me."

I blinked. "Sorry, what?"

He grinned cockily, knowing the importance of his revelation. He was a principal dancer, the male lead of the whole Company. I was still in the junior company—thanks to my injury that had set me back several years.

"You're going to have to repeat that, because I'm pretty sure I'm dreaming," I told him, trying to keep the squeal out of my voice. I should be playing it cool, but this was it. *This* was the opportunity I'd been dreaming of, obsessing over—that I'd almost given up on.

My leg chose that moment to twinge in pain, trying to remind me of my limits.

I ignored it.

"We won't go out there unless it's perfect," he told me, amusement in his gaze at my enthusiasm.

"It will be," I responded fiercely, already going through the steps in my head.

"We'll start after lunch. Until the showcase, we'll be practicing every afternoon session."

I nodded. It would be intense. Giselle would be my most difficult role thus far. If the Company was performing the whole thing, there was no way I would have gotten the role. It was always awarded to ballerinas at the height of their careers. Not only did Giselle need to be able to act, but there was a controlled technique required that was difficult for any dancer.

I could do this.

"See you after lunch in Studio B," he commented, his gaze flickering behind me as students were leaving another class.

"Yeah, see you," I said awkwardly, playing it as cool as I could until he'd turned the corner.

I covered my mouth, and I screamed, shaking a fist in the air because all the excitement had to get out somehow. Pure joy leaked out of my every pore.

I would do this. I would be the best Giselle that ballet had ever seen. It would change everything. I just knew it.

It hit me then.

I could tell Camden about this. I hadn't had anyone to tell anything . . . really ever.

Darting into the locker room, I pulled out the phone he was letting me borrow and shot off a text.

Me: You're never going to believe what just happened.

His response was instant, like he'd been waiting for me to text him.

Camden: Tell me.

I could imagine him saying it in that bossy way of his and I grinned.

Me: I was chosen to perform the Act II pas de deux in Giselle for the Company's upcoming showcase. I'll be dancing with the Company's principal male dancer!

Camden: I'm in awe of you, baby girl.

Sinking to the bench, my insides melted, my eyes growing suspiciously wet. I'd felt those words . . . everywhere.

Me: Thank you.

Camden: We'll celebrate on our date tonight.

My smile grew at that reminder. Camden had somehow convinced me to take a week off from Charlie's—to rest, he'd argued. But he'd also argued that *dates* were restful and planned one for every night this week that he didn't have a game.

Me: Can't wait.

I carefully put the phone back in the locker, and made sure it was locked up tight. I'd never had something so nice before. I was afraid to even touch it.

The Carvers had given me an old flip phone in high school—only because my caseworker had required it. But I'd left it behind when I left.

I wasn't thinking about them today, though. *Today* was a day for celebrating.

It was amazing how a few hours could change everything. Rehearsal was going . . . terribly.

To start with, Dallon had been late. I'd gotten there fifteen minutes early, stretching and bouncing with nervous energy.

And then I waited. And waited some more.

He'd finally rolled in thirty minutes after we were supposed to start, unhurried and making no apologies.

I'd put on a happy face, not daring to show him any of my annoyance.

But it had just gotten worse after that.

"Are you even trying?" Dallon snapped as I fumbled a lift. His tone was sharp, slicing through my concentration. "You're supposed to be light, not dead weight."

I bit my lip and nodded, forcing myself to stay calm. "I'm sorry," I murmured, not pointing out that it had been his wrong form that had messed me up to begin with.

He scoffed, rolling his eyes as we moved into the next sequence, where he had to lift me into an arabesque. I focused on my form, pointing my toes and elongating my limbs, but his grip was rough, and I nearly lost my balance.

"Pathetic," he muttered under his breath. "Do you even know how to hold yourself?"

His words stung, but I kept silent, knowing that arguing would only make things worse. We continued, and every step seemed to bring another round of criticism. My pirouette wasn't sharp enough, my extensions weren't high enough, my landings weren't soft enough.

"God, you're hopeless," he said during a brief break as we both gulped some water, sweat streaking down our faces. "I really thought you were better than this."

I clenched my fists, fighting back tears. "I will get better," I told him.

"'Better' isn't good enough, Ana," he shot back.

We went back to the dance, the music filling the studio. I tried to block out his voice, to focus on the rhythm and the movement. The grande jeté felt clumsy under his scrutinizing gaze, and the supported promenade seemed endless as he kept correcting me with a sneer.

"Arch your back. You're a ghost, not a fucking hippo," he growled, his grip tightening painfully on my waist during a lift.

I forced myself to hold my position, even as his words cut deeper than the physical strain on my leg that was pulsing with pain. He'd stepped on my foot at one point, and my leg hadn't recovered from the rough twist.

We finished the run-through, and I was left feeling battered, both physically and emotionally.

Dallon turned off the music, pushing his sweaty hair out of his face before he put a hand on his hip and turned toward me. "Listen," he said. "I'm doing this as a favor. I know you've been trying to get my attention, and you got it."

I blinked, trying to think of a time that I'd tried to get his attention.

I couldn't think of even *one*.

I felt gutted. Here I had been thinking that I'd earned this . . . and he was just trying to get into my pants.

Dallon's expression softened, and he stepped forward, sliding his hand to my waist . . . and then around to my ass, squeezing one of my cheeks tightly as he tried to pull me against him.

I immediately pulled away, and I watched as his face grew ugly, a sneer replacing the charming smile he'd had just seconds before.

He chased my retreating footsteps, and I shivered as my back hit a mirrored wall. "Remember, Ana, you *wanted* this. You *owe* me. Don't waste my time." His hand slid along my cheek, his gaze dripping down my form lecherously, leaving me feeling dirty and used.

I was so caught off guard, I was speechless.

A thumb slid along my lip before he pulled away, clapping me on the shoulder once like none of that had happened and we were just "bros," and then he sauntered out of the room.

You owe me.

You owe me.

You owe me.

Those words were my kryptonite, chipping away at the fragile armor I wore, and ruining every good feeling in my body. A tear slid down my cheek, and I angrily wiped it away, avoiding my reflection in the mirror.

I couldn't believe this.

I walked out of the practice room as if I were in a daze, my footsteps slow and heavy as I went back to the locker room to grab my bag. Glancing at my phone, I scoffed. We'd practiced for an hour out of the three hours we were supposed to have worked.

I didn't want to slip into my usual class. The showcase list had been posted on the bulletin, and everyone had been talking about my role since it went up.

I didn't want them to know that I was already a failure on day one.

I'd just leave, walk around for a little before I texted Camden. Maybe I'd even walk all the way to his place. That would at least give me time to clear my head, to come up with a gameplan before our date.

You owe me . . . Dallon's words beat into my skull like a sledgehammer.

When would those words come out of Camden's mouth? Today? Tomorrow? Next week?

I had a feeling it would hurt a million times worse coming from him.

Stepping out of the building, I blinked at the sun. I wasn't used to it being so bright when I left the dance studio.

I started walking down the sidewalk in the direction of Camden's building . . . when Michael stepped out of the shadows.

"Ana . . . " he called in a lilting, mocking voice.

"Michael," I whispered, taking a step back, my gaze darting around for anyone I could latch onto to get away.

But this time of day, it was almost as empty as when I got out at night on the days I stayed to clean the dance rooms. A shiver snarled its way down my spine. How long did he spend out here waiting for me? How did he always have the perfect timing to get me alone?

"I heard that you got kicked out of the shelter." He smiled, like that was funny to him, and another thread of fear crept through me.

Had he been the one to somehow organize those drugs being found under my cot? What was he planning?

"I came to fulfill my brotherly duty and offer you a place to stay." The words coming out of his mouth were all the right ones, but the way he said them . . . it made me feel dirty all over again, broken . . . terrified.

"I found a place," I told him slowly, wishing this conversation never had to happen. I didn't want to talk to him about Camden. Camden felt like a shiny, good, perfect little gift in my fucked-up life. I didn't want my psychotic foster brother to have anything to do with it.

"Oh, that NHL hockey player, right?" he asked casually.

My blood froze. I blinked slowly at him, trying to control my breathing as his smile widened.

"How did you know that?" I whispered, unable to keep the tremble out of my voice despite my best efforts.

His pale blue eyes glinted, his malicious intent peeking through as he stared at me.

"Now that you're shacking up with a rich guy, you've suddenly become a whole lot more useful, little bunny."

I stiffened, a wave of dread settling on my shoulders.

"You probably should get going. People are going to come out any minute now," I warned.

Michael's smirk widened, as if he knew that wasn't true. Knowing him, he probably did.

He made a big show of pulling something up on his phone, slowly turning it around for dramatic effect.

I flinched when I saw the picture on the screen. It was from senior year, one of the photo shoots he'd *forced* me to do for him. I was sitting on a chair, completely naked, my legs spread so he could take a closeup of . . .

Hot shame licked at my insides. He'd shoved a knife against my nipple and threatened to cut it off if I didn't cooperate.

I hadn't had a choice . . . but the reminder of those photos still made me want to *die*.

The most recent pictures had been taken six months ago at a "family dinner" he'd forced me to attend.

I'd done everything I could to stay away from him since I'd left the Carvers, but my *everything* had never been enough.

"What do you want?" I whispered in a resigned voice.

"Monthly payments," he said with a grin. "I want monthly payments to make sure that these pictures never end up in the news. Wouldn't that be embarrassing for your little NHL boyfriend to know that his girlfriend is a whore?"

"I'm not a whore," I said sharply, taking a step back at the flash of anger in his eyes at my disrespectful tone.

Michael smoothed an imaginary wrinkle from his dress shirt. "If you don't want him and everyone else to think that . . . you'd better get me that money. Five thousand dollars a month should do it. It's really not that much at all."

He smiled, laughing to himself, because he knew that much money might as well have been a *million* dollars to me.

I gasped. "I—I don't have that money. I have no way to get that for you."

Michael grinned. "Figure it out, Ana, because I can picture it now . . . your sweet pussy all over the internet." He cocked his head, like a lightbulb was going off in his brain. "Or you can just come with me right now. We could take new pictures . . . or do something else—something even more fun." He licked his lips suggestively.

I glanced frantically back at the studio doors, wishing there was at least someone to hear me scream if he tried to grab me. That's where this was headed eventually—I was sure of it.

He'd gotten off on my screams throughout my teenage years . . . I'm sure he'd missed them.

The bastard probably couldn't even get his dick up without them anymore.

I couldn't help but think of that one time . . .

"Little bunny, little bunny, let me come in," he called through the door. His parents were gone for the weekend, and I'd barricaded myself in my bedroom, the door locked and a chair pulled in front.

Even though I knew it was all useless.

I didn't answer him, I just kept my finger on my phone. I would do it this time. I'd call 9-1-1 if he came in here. I wasn't going to let him hurt me again.

"The wolf huffed, and he puffed, and he . . . "

I waited for the final words, bone-deep shivers wracking my body as tears slid down my face.

Someone, please help me.

The seconds turned into minutes . . . and the minutes went on.

Until it was hours.

Where was he? Why had he stopped? Had he gotten a phone call? Was that all he was going to do to me today?

Please, God, let that be all.

I crept to the door after two hours. He had to be gone right? I could grab something from the kitchen, enough to feed me for the rest of the day—I'd used the bathroom—and then I'd come back.

As quietly as possible, I undid the lock and slowly turned the doorknob. This was it. I'd open this door and be back in five minutes.

Or two.

Opening the door a crack, I peeked out into the hallway, listening for any sound.

It was silent.

Okay, he'd definitely left.

I slipped through the crack, stepping into the hallway.

"Hello, little bunny."

Michael touched my shoulder, bringing me back from our horror-filled past to the present—the same terror threaded through my veins. "So what's it going to be, *Ana*?" he was asking.

"Leave me alone," I told him harshly. Backing away, I held up my phone threateningly. "If you don't get away from me, I'll call the police."

"That's a fancy phone, Ana," he sneered. "Guess you haven't changed, still using any man you can. An NHL star isn't an upgrade for you, though. He'll drop you the second he realizes that you're trash. I'm the only one willing to accept where you came from."

"I'm calling," I said loudly, my fingers fumbling on the still unfamiliar screen as I tried to find the phone pad.

He held up his hands in mock surrender. "I'm leaving. No need for theatrics, little bunny. I'll expect your first payment next month." Michael gave me a little salute as he turned and started down the sidewalk away from me.

"I'll be seeing you," he promised.

I had no doubt he was telling the truth.

I watched him go, wondering how I existed in a world where I couldn't get away from him. He'd followed me into the city, sure that I would crack and beg him for help after a few nights at the shelter.

He'd been furious when I hadn't. I guess the fact that someone would rather be homeless than be with *you* was quite a hit to the ego. I'd been scared of him when I'd first moved in with the Carvers, terrified actually, with how he'd acted before, and his words at the hospital when I'd woken up.

But he'd been on his best behavior those first couple of months. Michael had lulled me into a false sense of security that maybe he wasn't that bad.

And then he'd struck, showing me exactly who he was when I'd woken up bleeding because he'd decided that cutting me while I was sleeping was fun.

I knew he was serious about the money. But even if I worked around the clock, I wasn't going to be able to get that much in time.

I could just picture Camden's disgust when he saw those pictures. His embarrassment when everyone he knew and didn't know saw my naked body. In those poses.

He wouldn't understand how I'd allowed Michael to take them. He'd hate me. He'd never want to see me again.

I couldn't take that.

Leaning over, I threw up on the sidewalk, the vomit splattering all over the concrete. I couldn't let that happen. I couldn't.

I needed to get to work.

Abruptly changing directions, I headed toward the bus stop I usually took to get to Charlie's. Why had I thought it was a good idea to take off this week? Even before what had just happened, I should have been saving money, collecting as much as I could so I could leave and not be a burden to Camden anymore. Now, it was even more of a necessity.

My phone buzzed, but I ignored it for a second until I decided it was probably the polite thing to answer Camden's text. I should let him know I couldn't make it tonight and that he didn't need to pick me up.

Me: Have to go into work. I'm sorry.

Wiping away more of the tears that had leaked out of my eyes, I pushed aside all the good things that had happened to me this past week.

They weren't for me.

This was my reality.

I couldn't forget that again.

CHAPTER 21

CAMDEN

I wish I'd taken a picture of Anastasia's face when she walked out from the back of Charlie's and saw me sitting in my usual spot.

She'd stopped midstep, her mouth open adorably.

"Hello," I said mildly.

"I—" She squeezed her eyes shut and then stomped over to me, anger in every step. "I don't have to explain to you why I needed to work tonight. I'm appreciative of everything you've done for me—but I don't *owe* you."

There was a hitch to the end of her voice as she ended her sentence, but her chin was lifted determinately, and she was just daring me to argue with her.

"That is true. You don't owe me anything," I responded.

Her eyes flashed, and she blinked a few times, searching my face to see if I was telling the truth.

"You don't actually mean that," she whispered.

I was still learning everything about Anastasia, but it was obvious that this was one of those land mines I needed to cautiously step over and avoid at all costs.

"I do mean that. Absolutely. Anything I do is because I want to help. I'm in awe of you and everything you've managed to do by yourself."

I'm obsessed with you. I . . . love you.

The words hovered on the tip of my tongue, but of course, I couldn't say them yet.

"I just think," I continued, "that it's perfectly acceptable for you to let someone else take over for a minute. For me to let you take a breath after working so hard all these years."

Before I could say anything, a woman at the table in front of us knocked her drink over, and it spilled all over the table and floor. She stared at it disgusted before she motioned at Anastasia. "Can you clean this up?" she asked in a clipped voice. "Now, please."

Anastasia threw me a longing glance before she hurried over to the table and began wiping up the mess. Once the table was dry, she kneeled down and worked on the puddle of soda on the floor.

I hated the sight of her on her knees. The only time I wanted her there was if she was kneeling in front of me and my dick was going down her throat.

Inappropriate, Camden.

It had also been inappropriate what I'd done in her sheets earlier, though, and I wasn't apologizing for that.

Anastasia couldn't work here anymore.

That was a fucking fact. She was killing herself dancing all day, cleaning the studio . . . and then coming here to scrub tables. And she was making almost nothing for all that work.

Unacceptable.

My baby girl didn't need to be working like this.

She tried to get up, and I watched as her leg gave out, her knee hitting the tile floor with a thump. A flash of nausea hit me as I imagined the amount of pain she was in. I quickly slid out of my bench seat to help her, but she held up a hand, like she knew I was coming even though her back was to me. She stubbornly pushed up from the floor and limped to the back room with the sodden rag, not looking at me once.

Anastasia was never going to agree to quit on her own.

I unfortunately was going to have to do it for her.

If I was going to take care of her how she deserved—make everything better in her life, sacrifices were going to have to be made.

Batman was just as much a superhero as Superman, right?

Even if sometimes he was the bad guy . . .

Fuck.

I was thinking in terms of DC Comics characters. Ari Lancaster was an asshole. He'd called me "Hero" so much, apparently it was becoming my personality.

Anastasia was still in the back, so I pulled out my phone to pass the time. I wasn't leaving here without her.

Me: Lancaster, I hate you.

Ari: The drama with this one. Is it because of that spin move I did today that you were so jealous of?

Ari: Or my dick.

Ari: It is my dick, isn't it?

Ari: It's alright, Hero. Not everyone can be me.

Me: That's it! From now on, no one is allowed to call me "Hero."

Linc: This guy, thinking he makes the rules.

Walker: How do you think I felt when I referred to myself in third person as "Disney?"

Ari: That's kind of weird, Dis.

Linc: Yeah, it kind of is.

Logan: Walker just let out a hitched sob and ran out of the room.

Walker: We're not even fucking together right now!

Walker Davis removed Logan York from the chat.

Ari: Touchy for a simp.

Me: So, we're on the same page, right? You can call me Camden or James.

Ari: or Hero.

Linc: Yeah, I think I'm going to stick with Hero. It's much lighter on the tongue.

Walker: Me too.

Ari: Surprise. Surprise.

Me: 🖕

Anastasia came out, carrying a bin as she limped across the room, intentionally averting her gaze from mine.

I tapped on the wood in front of me, fiddling with the silverware and feeling anxious as I watched her work.

Anastasia was cleaning a table a few down in front of me when she suddenly stopped, her eyes locked onto something outside the window. I watched as all the color drained from her face.

What the hell?

My heart skipped a beat, and I pushed up from the table, glancing out the window to see what had rattled her.

A man stood on the sidewalk, staring intently through the glass. He was tall, with a lean build. His dark hair was slicked back, and his eyes were drilling right into Anastasia.

I'd never seen him before, but I did *not* like the way he was looking at her.

Like she belonged to him.

I was the only one allowed to look at her like that.

Beyond the possessiveness of his stare, there was something off about him.

My protective instincts were on high alert as he continued to stare at her.

I walked briskly toward Anastasia, trying to keep my cool. "Hey," I said softly, placing a hand on her arm. "You okay?"

She flinched at my touch, then nodded quickly, tearing her eyes away from the window. "Yeah, I'm fine," she said, her voice shaky. "Just . . . thought I saw someone I knew."

I glanced back at the guy. He was still there, still staring. It made my skin crawl. She was lying. She knew exactly who he was. And she was *terrified* of him.

"Who the fuck is that guy?" I growled, and her eyes flashed fearfully . . . like she was afraid for me.

"Someone from my past," she whispered.

"Do you want him staring at you like that?" I asked, carefully keeping my voice neutral.

It wouldn't matter if she did, that was obviously not going to happen. But I thought I'd at least pretend to ask.

Anastasia blinked at me slowly, and I'd never seen her look so haunted.

I was out the door then, bursting into a jog as soon as I left the restaurant.

He'd already started to walk away, though. Disappearing into the crowd before I could reach him.

I searched the sidewalks for a few minutes before worrying that maybe he'd circled around and he was at the restaurant, so I hurried back.

When I got there, though, he was nowhere to be found.

As soon as I stepped into Charlie's, Anastasia was there, her face drawn and exhausted-looking. "I asked if I could leave early. I'm—I'm not feeling well," she said. "Can you take me home?"

"Of course, baby. Let's get you out of here," I said quickly, inwardly rejoicing that she'd used the word "home" to describe my place. She probably wasn't even aware she'd just done that. We stepped outside into the cool night air, and Anastasia shivered and huddled into my chest.

Leading her to my truck, I helped her into her seat, buckling her in and brushing my lips softly against hers. "I'm not going to forget that we need to have a talk about who that man was," I murmured sternly.

She sighed, and her eyes grew sad and broken before she nodded.

Which made my anger over that asshole only grow.

"Just not tonight," she said.

"Not tonight," I agreed before shutting the door and driving us home.

Anastasia was quiet when we got back to the penthouse, only nibbling at the chicken quesadilla I made her before telling me she was going to go to bed.

As she walked away, I grabbed her hand and pulled her back into my chest. "You're mine, Anastasia," I told her, loving the blush that spread across her cheeks. "Whatever you need, I'm going to make it happen."

Her eyes got wide and glossy again, and she hastily wiped at the tears before giving me a trembling smile. "We'll see," she finally said before pulling away and walking down the hall to her room.

I watched her go, wishing I could follow her, or at least make love to her to show her body what her mind couldn't seem to believe.

One thing was clear, I needed to up my game and save her from herself.

Daddy was going to take care of his baby girl.

CHAPTER 22

ANASTASIA

I couldn't sleep. Sometimes it was like this, the energy buzzed beneath my skin for hours when everything felt like too much. Sometimes it was when my body was too hurt to move, but my mind was desperate to continue. I could see the steps in my head, every inch of my soul wishing I could lose myself in them.

And sometimes it was because my sadistic foster brother had decided to torture me further by blackmailing me.

The practice with Dallon had made today a bad day for my leg—not that there were very many good days with my leg anymore. But even after icing it and taking a painkiller, it still felt like someone had jabbed a nail into my bone.

And it was too quiet. I hadn't gotten used to the lack of . . . noise in this place. The shelter had been so loud that I'd been able to block out a lot of my dark thoughts. After all, if the girl on the cot next to me had a life so bad that she had to scream in her sleep, what was mine in comparison?

In the quiet of Camden's penthouse, every depressing, morose thought and memory I'd ever had was free to run rampant in my brain. I flipped over for the hundredth time, finally burying my face in my pillow and huffing in exasperation.

What—

I lifted my head, searching to see if there was anything on my pillow that I was smelling. But there wasn't anything there. I'd helped Camden wash these sheets after he'd bought them for me.

I smashed my face into the pillow and inhaled deeply, feeling like a complete idiot as I did so. It's just that I thought that I had smelled something . . . something amazing.

The scent was oddly familiar, a smell that tugged at the edges of my memory. Where had I smelled that scent before—a complex blend of earthy musk and subtle spice that made me want to live in it.

One more inhale, and it hit me.

This was what Camden smelled like.

A whisper of a moan escaped my lips as I breathed him in.

Was this his laundry detergent that I was smelling? If so, why wasn't every person on earth using this? I'd never smelled anything so good in my entire life. That brand was really missing out.

My hand slipped into my sleep shorts, dragging down to my core to help with the sudden spike of lust I was experiencing. My fingers grazed my clit, and I bit down on my lip hard as pleasure surged through me. I pressed down and—

What was I doing? I was in Camden's house . . . as a guest . . . about to make myself come because the sheets smelled like him. In *any* circumstance that would have been inappropriate, but especially after today.

Pull yourself together, I hissed at myself, yanking my hand out of my shorts and sitting up in bed with a sigh. I was tempted to dive back into my sheets and soak up his smell again . . . but that would've been weird.

Weirder than getting off to his laundry detergent already was.

Sliding out of bed, I padded to the door, my leg groaning with every step. A glass of water would probably cure the heat between my legs.

That and a cold shower.

I needed one of those as well.

The house was silent as I walked to the kitchen.

I was tempted to turn on a radio or something, just to block out the stillness. That would be weird, though, for me to be blasting music after midnight in someone else's house, right? I could just see Camden coming out of his room and staring at me like I was crazy.

Filling a glass with water, I took a big gulp, praying that the chill of the liquid would cool me down.

It didn't work.

Sighing in frustration, I decided to walk around the house for a minute. It wouldn't help my leg, but maybe it would calm my mind.

Limping now, I made my way down the hallway where Camden's room was. The theater room was down this way as well. Maybe I would watch a movie; that would probably distract me.

My footsteps echoed softly against the polished floor as I walked down the hallway. Passing an open door, I peeked inside and caught a glimpse of Camden's room . . . and his bathroom . . . and his shower.

Which he was in.

Camden stood beneath the spray of water, his broad shoulders glistening with droplets as he ran a hand through his damp, dark hair.

Heat flooded my cheeks as I watched him, my pulse quickening with each passing second. It was like I was frozen in place, unable to tear my eyes away from the mesmerizing sight before me.

My gosh, why did he ever get dressed? It was a crime against humanity that he ever wore clothes. He had the kind of body meant to be worshipped.

I had the urge to fall to my knees.

Michelangelo would have wept to have the chance to carve him into stone.

I traced every inch of his body obsessively, the heat building in my core. This was doing absolutely nothing to help in that regard.

I really needed to yank myself away, but I couldn't seem to be able to get my legs to move.

His arm flexed as he dragged a washcloth down his chest, and then . . . the washcloth dropped.

Camden gripped his dick roughly, and I was entranced.

I honestly hadn't known that they made dicks that big. It was like he was carrying a coke bottle between his legs. How did that fit in anyone?

Don't think about his dick in someone, I hissed at myself, a little nervous I was going to squeak out an accidental moan because I was so turned on.

Even from here, I could see his swollen, glistening head, the thick veins along the length, the way his hands were closed around the rigid flesh . . . my mouth was watering for a taste.

Who even was I right now? He squeezed and pulled at his cock, sliding it from root to tip as he fucked his hand.

I pressed my thighs together, resisting the urge to touch myself because despite all the lines I'd already crossed just from watching this . . . that would be the line to stay far away from.

His ass flexed as his fist pumped up and down in long strokes, and the low groan that came from his lips had me taking a few more steps into the room—as if I just couldn't help it.

And then his head turned, and he was staring . . . right at me.

I was frozen, my gaze locked with his. This was the time for me to run, but it was as if my feet had sunk into concrete and I'd lost the ability to use them.

Camden didn't stop.

He bit down on that full, sultry bottom lip of his as his fist sped up.

I'd never be able to watch porn, because I was confident no video could ever measure up to this.

His chest was broad and defined, tattoos stretched across his muscles. The water glistened on his skin, highlighting every curve and dip, every sinew and vein that snaked its way across his torso like a map of untamed wilderness I longed to conquer.

Camden ran his free hand down his abs, a washboard of rippling perfection.

I wanted him. I wanted to touch his body. I wanted that perfect dick.

Maybe it wasn't a want. Maybe it was a need.

There was a dare in his gaze. A dare to stay. A dare to go. I wasn't sure, but I couldn't move.

He groaned again, his eyes growing hooded and dark, a faint blush to his cheeks that I was sure had nothing to do with the heat of the shower.

My hands were trembling at my sides. I'd never desired something like this before. I'd never let myself feel the kind of lust that burned your insides and put a glitch in your brain.

I wasn't human anymore. I didn't know what I was.

I just knew that I wanted Camden James with everything in me.

His gaze never strayed away from mine. I watched as his movements sped up, and his breaths came out in gasps. A moan slipped from his perfect lips when his body began to jerk.

"Anastasia," he breathed as shots of milky, white cum painted the glass in front of him. He fucked his hand through his orgasm, the head of his cock swollen and hot-looking as more ropes of his seed spilled onto the shower floor.

We stayed like that, staring at each other, long after his orgasm had ended, neither of us saying anything.

Speaking of saying anything. Had I just imagined that? Had he really said my name as he came?

That thought finally broke me from the spell I'd been under. I forced myself out of his room, sprinting down the hallway, ignoring my leg screaming at me in protest.

He didn't call after me or come rushing down the hall.

And a part of me was disappointed about that.

Once safely ensconced in my room, I locked the door behind me, leaning against it as I tried to gain control of myself. This was madness. I prided myself on control. I forced my body into submission every day, pushing myself past its limits to get what I wanted out of it while I danced.

But I couldn't control myself right then. I couldn't stop myself from crossing the room to my bed and sliding onto the sheets that smelled like him. I couldn't stop myself from yanking my soaking wet panties down to my knees and allowing my fingers to trace through my sopping, slick folds. I couldn't stop myself from pressing on my clit until pleasure was surging through me.

And I couldn't stop myself from picturing Camden the entire time that I made myself come.

The biggest thing that I didn't stop myself from doing?

Freaking out about the fact that I'd heard him listening by the door as I groaned his name.

CHAPTER 23

ANASTASIA

What?" I stared at Charlie, feeling sick.

"I'm sorry, Anastasia, but we need someone who can work longer shifts. Your nighttime shifts aren't enough anymore. The hours are too short."

I opened my mouth to argue . . . or beg. But what could I say? With my dance schedule, I couldn't go in earlier. Other employees came in at least two to three hours before me, I knew that . . . but it had *never* been a problem before this.

I was panicking, the edges of my vision darkening because this was bad, this was really bad. I had to pay Michael. Putting aside all my other expenses . . . I *had* to pay him. Cleaning the dance studio gave me a little, but it wasn't enough.

There was also the fact that I needed to find my own place. Camden wasn't going to let me stay there forever. He'd eventually get tired of me. I didn't want to go back to a shelter . . . or the streets.

And why was this such a big deal? I showed up. I worked hard. Charlie had never made one complaint about my hours. This was what we had agreed upon. He'd known this was the only way it would work from the beginning.

"Charlie, please. I really need this job," I whispered. "I'll work even harder. I'll stay later . . . please."

Charlie pushed his hair off his forehead where beads of sweat were collecting. We were back in the kitchen, and it was hot in here. I searched his face for any sign I was breaking through to him, but his usually warm brown eyes had cooled, and his lips were curled up in annoyance.

"Look, Ana, you're a good kid. But I gotta do what's best for my business, and you ain't it. You can leave your apron on that shelf over there. You're gonna be fine." He turned his back and picked up a basket of fries from a vat of hot oil, clearly signaling the conversation was over.

I stared at him for a few seconds longer, so long he was probably worried I was going crazy. I just couldn't believe this was happening.

I also couldn't understand *how* it had happened.

When he didn't turn around, and it was obvious he was keeping busy so he didn't have to—I admitted defeat.

Taking off my apron, I flung it onto the shelf and made my way out of the kitchen.

I stood at the end of the hallway, looking into the main dining hall. It was a mix of regulars and new faces. No one glanced at me.

I'd worked here for half a year, and no one would think about me after I left.

It had been like that everywhere I'd gone.

I wondered what it felt like to be memorable to someone, a ghost that lingered in their minds after you were gone because they'd actually cared about you.

What a pathetic thought.

"Take it easy, Anastasia," Poison said, poking her head out of the scullery. Those four words may have been the longest sentence she'd ever said to me. I was guessing she'd overheard the conversation—my begging had been embarrassingly loud. I nodded to her and waved before striding across the dining hall, focused on getting out of here as fast as I could.

There was a tight, panicked feeling building up inside of me as I burst out the doors into the cold night air. Glancing around at the familiar buildings . . . I was at a loss for what to do with myself.

And then Camden's giant truck pulled to the curb, his usual parking place despite the heavy traffic that went in and out of the restaurant. Just another way that luck smiled down on him.

He hopped out of the truck, and I flushed as soon as we locked eyes.

I knew what he looked like when he *came* now.

And I couldn't imagine anything hotter.

"Hey, baby girl," he said. His hair was wet and pushed off his face. He was wearing a pair of nice, black dress slacks, and a black, fitted button up dress shirt for some reason.

He looked like sex on a stick and I wanted to lick him.

Don't think about sex, I hissed at myself. *Or licking*!

"Did you hear me?" he pressed, and I realized I'd been fantasizing so hard about his dick that I hadn't heard a word that he'd said.

"Sorry, what?" I asked, trying to focus this time and not get lost in the golden flecks in his green gaze.

"I asked what you were doing getting off so early. Shouldn't you be working for at least a few more hours? Not that I'm complaining about getting more time with you," he teased, flashing a smile.

"I just got fired," I muttered, feeling embarrassed as soon as the words came out of my mouth. The list of reasons that Camden James should stay far, far away from me was growing.

Who got fired from cleaning tables?

"Are you serious?" Camden growled, and a warm feeling slid down my spine because he sounded so . . . outraged.

I'd never had someone sound like that on *my* behalf before.

"I'm going to talk to him," he said sternly, marching toward the restaurant. A giggle escaped my mouth as I grabbed his arm to stop him.

"No, you can't go talk to him!" I said, exasperatedly.

"He fired you."

"Yes, and he's allowed to do that."

"I can be very persuasive, Ana," he said, and this time his voice came out as a purr as he tangled his hand with mine and brought it to his chest. I realized he was the only one I actually liked calling me that nickname. I liked *all* the nicknames he had for me, in fact.

"I'm very aware of that, James," I responded with a smirk. Camden James must have some kind of magical powers because five minutes ago there was no way I'd have thought I'd be smiling today.

A grin stretched across his face. "Last names, Lennox? You're pulling out the big guns."

I snorted, a giddy feeling singing through me. I liked him so fucking much.

"Are you sure you don't want me to talk to him?" he pressed once more, his gaze darting around my face, that same expression there, like he thought I was some kind of miracle.

A girl could get used to a look like that.

Even if she shouldn't.

"I don't want to be somewhere where I'm not wanted," I told him simply, and he seemed to get that, because he nodded and started leading me to his truck.

"Maybe it was meant to be," he said as he buckled me into my seat.

"How's that?" I mused, my mind adding up all the money I *didn't* have to pay my dance expenses, and now Michael.

"Because now I can take you on our superspecial date." He smirked happily, completely distracting me from the frantic thoughts that had been building up inside of me.

"A superspecial date? That sounds like serious business."

His eyes heated, hunger spilling into their depths as he leaned forward and softly brushed his nose against mine.

"It is serious, Anastasia. The most serious I've ever been about anything."

I forgot how to breathe at that announcement. Because it almost seemed like he was talking about . . . us.

In what world could a man like Camden James be serious about me?

He put the truck into drive and pulled away from the curb, headed the opposite direction of how we usually got to his place.

"Sorry, I just need to make a call," he said, shooting me an apologetic glance before he put his cell phone up to his ear. "My plans for tonight got moved up a bit with your early release."

"You make it sound like I was in prison," I huffed.

He just lifted an eyebrow at me. Hmmm. I guess working nonstop was kind of like a prison sentence when I thought about it.

"Yeah, sorry. We're on our way right now. Can you move everything up?" he asked. I could hear the faint sound of a woman speaking on the other end, although I couldn't hear what she was saying. Camden was definitely being intentionally vague.

I realized my shoulders had tensed, my eyes narrowing. I didn't like him talking to another woman. I kind of wanted to grab the phone and hit End just so the conversation would stop.

No need to be crazy, Anastasia.

After a few more grunts on Camden's end, he hung up the phone and grabbed my hand, bringing it to his thigh while he drove.

If I really needed money, I could probably take a picture of him like this and put it on OnlyFans. There had to be a kink for that sort of thing.

I snorted at the thought. I could never. If I thought that listening to him have a very innocent phone conversation with a woman was bad, I could only imagine what my feelings would be if there were thousands of women drooling over him all over the World Wide Web.

Although, come to think of it . . . there already was. He was a star NHL hockey player. And I was pretty sure he'd done an underwear ad . . .

I made a mental note to not do any more research on him than I'd already done. No need to stumble on a fan site or a Reddit page.

"What are you thinking about?" he asked. "You've got that little smirk on your lips, so I know it must be good."

"OnlyFans," I said lightly. And he almost swerved off the road.

"What? Why are you thinking about that?" he asked, his voice sounding very concerned.

"Just thinking of ways to earn some money."

He made a choking sound and shook his head. "Let's table that idea for another day, shall we? A heart attack would be seriously inconvenient right now."

"I hear they pay a lot on there for feet pics," I told him, my tone very serious.

He side-eyed me, clearly panicked.

"I can definitely go back to Charlie's if this is the direction you're headed. And it's not my particular thing, but I will pay you for your feet pics if need be."

"What?" I laughed. "Is that a hidden kink of yours? I knew you were too good to be true."

His eyes flashed at that comment, and he wrinkled his nose. "Over my dead body is any person, male or female, getting pictures of you—feet or otherwise."

My stomach tightened, bile rising in my throat as I thought about the pictures someone *already* had . . .

Blinking hard, I tried to push away those thoughts. I just wanted to have a good time with Camden tonight.

Just for tonight.

My laugh was delayed as I shook my head. "I'd strip before sending people pictures of my feet. You're safe."

The truck swerved again, going into the other lane as my screech shot through the cab.

"Are you okay?" I gasped, trying to slow my heart rate down as he righted the vehicle.

"Just had that heart attack I mentioned," he growled as he pulled into a parking lot of what looked like a high-end beauty salon.

"Old man problems," I said with a nod. "Understandable."

"You just want to be spanked, don't you, baby girl?" he growled as he parked.

I ignored the way my clit was pulsing and my panties were drenched, and I peered at the building. "What are we doing here?" I asked instead of answering his question.

"Getting ready for our date," he answered mysteriously as he jumped out of the truck and jogged to the other side.

I didn't try and get out on my own—I'd learned that lesson over the last few days.

We walked hand in hand through the front doors, and as I stared around the very fancy, elegant interior, I remembered I was still in my black work uniform . . . and I was pretty sure my hair smelled like hamburger.

I was very aware of what I looked like compared to him . . .

"I look ridiculous," I hissed to Camden as he led me toward the front desk.

"Just relax, baby," he said softly, pressing a light kiss on my neck that had me almost tripping over my feet. "You're going to have fun."

Before the modelesque receptionist could even speak to us, a loud, vivacious woman bustled around the corner. "You must be Anastasia!" she exclaimed, her voice ringing through the salon. Her brightly colored dress and sparkling jewelry was almost as dazzling as her personality seemed to be. "I'm Maria, and oh my, you are a pretty, pretty girl. Perfect for our Camden here. Geraldine is going to go crazy over you." She shot a look at Camden. "Or has she already?"

There was that name again. *Geraldine*. I did not like how often Camden and Geraldine were mentioned together. At all.

"Okay, follow me. This is going to be great," she gushed, taking my hand and pulling me away from Camden. I shot him a helpless *what the hell is happening* look, but he just winked at me—the gorgeous asshole.

Maria practically pushed me into a salon chair, and then four other employees were suddenly around me, gushing and cooing as they examined me—thankfully without mentioning that I smelled like fried food and grease. Maria pursed her lips as she studied me intensely for a moment.

"I've got it!" she suddenly squawked, making me jump. "Let's begin."

I was hustled to a sink where my hair was washed, and I received what would go down as the best head massage I'd ever had in my life. It was actually my *first* head massage, but I couldn't imagine a better one. After my hair was clean, they all went to work, their hands moving skillfully through my hair, transforming it into soft waves. I closed my eyes as they applied makeup, feeling the light touch of brushes and powders. They painted my nails a delicate, shimmering shade of pink, their friendly chatter and Maria's lively stories easing some of my tension.

Maria kissed two fingers, doing a little shimmy after my hair and makeup was done. "Stunning. Fabulous. I love it." She winked at me. "He won't be able to keep his hands off you!"

I squeezed my legs together at that thought. I'd seen how Camden reacted to me in a leotard, my hair a mess.

I wasn't sure I could handle his reaction to this.

One of the employees appeared with a shiny, black garment back. She unzipped it revealing a deep-blue mini dress. I stared at it, stunned by its beauty. "For me?" I asked, my voice barely above a whisper.

Exactly what kind of date was Camden taking me on?

"Absolutely," Maria said with a wink. "Let's get you into it."

They helped me change, and when I looked in the mirror, I barely recognized myself. The dress fit perfectly, hugging my curves in all the right places. I felt like a different person. Like instead of the streets, I'd stepped off the runway.

"Shall we do the grand reveal?" Maria trilled, clapping her hands together as she looked me over one last time.

"Yes," I murmured, nervous anticipation fluttering in my stomach . . . and my core.

Taking a deep breath, I stepped out into the lobby. Camden was texting on his phone, an arm slung over the back of the chair beside him, lounging back like an arrogant god, his legs outstretched in front of him. When he looked up and saw me, a low growl ripped from his chest. The sound reverberated through me like he had a direct line to my clit.

His gaze roamed over me slowly, heating with each passing second. I did my best not to fidget.

"Give me a spin," he ordered roughly. I could hear some of the girls whispering and tittering behind me, but I slowly spun, enjoying the feel of his eyes savoring every inch of my skin.

"Incredible," he finally murmured, standing up. "I don't know if we can go tonight."

"Why?" I laughed, still wondering exactly where this date even was.

"I don't want any other man to see you like this."

I smirked, thinking he was joking.

He stepped closer, his eyes burning. "If anyone dares to flirt with you, Anastasia," he rasped, a finger trailing down my arm and leaving goosebumps in its wake. "I might have to kill them."

The intensity in his voice made me ache for him. I liked his possessiveness. I wanted Camden to own me, take care of me . . . keep me.

He grinned and it was like the storm parted, all traces of his intensity from just moments ago disappeared. "Shall we go?" he asked, offering me his hand.

Camden waved at someone behind me and I turned my head and saw Maria standing there, waving a hand in front of her face like she was burning up.

"Wow," she mouthed. "So hot."

I grinned and shrugged. She was right.

"Have fun, darlings! And don't be strangers! And Camden—" she called.

Camden stopped and glanced at her.

"Don't keep her from Geraldine for long. You know she won't like it."

He laughed with a nod, and my inner bitch growled.

Freaking Geraldine.

All thoughts of that woman disappeared when we got to the truck, and I was suddenly pushed against it, his lips smashing against mine.

"Fuck," he growled in between biting kisses. "You're so fucking hot. I'm literally dying. Where did you even come from? I can't believe you're real, baby girl."

I gasped as his lips slid down my neck, biting down on a sensitive spot right between the neck and shoulder, making me moan.

"I could ask the same thing about you," I gasped and he huffed, giving me one more soul-shaking kiss before he pulled away. His chest was heaving, and his pupils had expanded into the green—like he'd gone feral.

I loved him like that.

"We're going on this date. But when we get home . . . all bets are off," he murmured, and oh my.

I was ready for that.

We got back into the truck, a charged silence pulsing between us as we drove.

No matter what this date was, I was quite sure that the afterparty . . . it was going to be a million times better.

CHAPTER 24

ANASTASIA

We pulled up to the valet of a popular club, Allure, and I started to freak out. "What are we doing?" I asked, my voice a bit frantic. There was a line trailing down the side of the warehouse where the club was housed.

I did not belong here.

"You're going to meet my best friends," Camden said calmly.

"What?" I gasped, stiffening in my seat. "I'm meeting your friends?"

I blinked at him. Was I ready for that? Holy. Crap.

The valet opened the door and extended his hand to help me out.

I glanced at the guy in a daze; he was cute, in a boyish-looking way.

"Don't even think about it," Camden growled at him, all his *calm* leaking out of his voice. The valet startled and backed up. "Yes, of course, Mr. James. I'm sorry."

Camden huffed and hopped out of the truck, walking to my door and putting his big body firmly in between me and the young man.

"I would say someone's jealous," I whispered.

His eyes flashed. "You have no idea."

Camden tossed the keys to the valet, ignoring his apologies as he guided me toward the entrance, his arm wrapped around my waist. Heat was bursting from his fingertips, soaking into my skin and sending all sorts of dirty thoughts racing through my brain.

The brief interlude with the valet had distracted me from the reality of the moment, and I was freaking out again as the bouncers lifted the purple rope and let us in, ahead of the huge line of people that seemed to be frothing at the mouth to get in.

I wasn't the kind of girl that bouncers just let by at a club. Especially a club famous enough that I'd heard of it. This was where most of the recording artists stopped by to give small performances when they wanted an intimate setting or if it was a special event.

I'd honestly never thought I'd see the inside of this place.

"Just so we're clear . . . I'm awkward. If you didn't already know that," I whispered to him as he led me up some steps and through a door.

"You're perfect," he corrected me. "They're going to love you." He kissed the side of my head, and I instinctively melted into his side. I wasn't sure how he was able to do that. Make me feel so safe and seen . . . that whatever else was happening didn't seem as overwhelming anymore.

The space on the other side of the door was dimly lit, with warm, ambient lighting casting a golden glow over the crowd. Small, round tables filled the room, each with a flickering candle in the center. The stage at the front was modest, just big enough for a band to play, and there was a small stool set up currently with a microphone in front of it.

I glanced around, feeling a mix of awe and disbelief. The walls were lined with photographs of famous musicians who had performed here, their signatures scrawled in bold, confident strokes. The air was filled with the low hum of conversation and the occasional burst of laughter, creating an electric yet cozy vibe.

"Wow," I whispered, more to myself than to Camden. "I can't believe I'm here." I was embarrassed the second the words came out of my mouth, but he just smiled at me like I was cute and led me further into the room.

My nerves came skyrocketing back as he led me to a group of the most beautiful people I'd ever seen—besides Camden of course. These were the people Camden belonged with. The gods who walked around us mere mortals.

"Hero." A tall dark-haired dreamboat with mischievous emerald-green eyes was the first to notice us. His gaze went to me and a smirk formed. I could almost see his brain rubbing its hands together in anticipation.

This guy was trouble.

"Lancaster," Camden drawled, pulling me closer into his side. The man watched the movement, his smirk growing.

"And who do we have here?" he asked.

"Ari," a beautiful, stunning, angelic-looking, blonde woman gently chided as she smiled up at him. "Behave. I don't want you to scare off my new friend."

I seriously had never seen a prettier woman before, and she looked familiar. But where would I have seen her before? And had she just said she wanted to be friends with me?

I was swooning.

Ari's smirk melted as he gazed down at her, and suddenly I was looking at a googly-eyed, lovestruck puppy dog of a man—his mischief contained—for the moment.

"Anastasia, that's Ari. And that's Blake, his wife. Her, you can be friends with. Him, you cannot," Camden said. I glanced up at him, thinking he was obviously kidding.

He didn't seem to be, though.

Ari snorted and leaned forward, taking Blake with him as if he couldn't bear to be more than three inches away from her. "Don't listen to ol' *grand-pappy* over there. I'm sure we're going to be best, best friends."

Ari howled as Camden growled and a giggle slipped out of me. I glanced up at Camden, realizing I still didn't know how old he was. A lot older than me, but how old . . . I wasn't sure. Probably should ask that at some point.

"Did he just call you—" Camden crushed his mouth against mine, cutting off . . . grandpappy.

"Please never let that word come out of your mouth," he murmured when he'd come up for air.

"Please keep kissing me like that forever." The words slipped out and I gasped, wanting to find the nearest trash can to throw myself in because I couldn't believe I'd actually said that.

"Deal," he said, instead of running for the hills like he should've been.

I was still gaping at him when the next couple came up.

"Hi, Anastasia," another beautiful girl said. She had pin straight, long black hair and the greenest eyes I'd ever seen. She looked like she was around my age. Just like Blake, she seemed . . . sweet. Maybe you couldn't really tell that from two words, but girls who looked like her, they usually had a stuck-up aura around them, like they were doing you a favor by being in your presence.

This girl had none of that.

"This is Monroe, and that's . . . Lincoln." Camden hesitated, pasting me so close to him I might as well have been glued to his side.

When I saw the golden model of a man at Monroe's side though—I kind of got it. I mean Camden was still the most gorgeous creature I'd ever seen. But this man . . . this man was a close second.

"Oh, you guys all play on the Knights with Camden," I exclaimed, finally remembering where I'd heard these names before.

My cheeks flushed, because that probably should have been a no-brainer, but no one looked like they were questioning my intelligence . . . so that was good.

Lincoln was intense . . . like really intense. He glanced down at Monroe, and I was surprised we were all still dressed, that an orgy hadn't broken out in the room because of the pheromones coming out of the two of them.

"We're going to be even worse," Camden muttered to me, reading my mind somehow.

It took me a second to get what he was saying, and when he did, my entire body went up in flames.

He winked at me, chuckling under his breath as his fingers danced over my rib cage.

"I'm really excited about this development," Ari said and Camden scoffed.

"You just called her your new best friend. What's Geraldine going to think about that? She values loyalty, Lancaster."

Geraldine really seemed to get around.

Ari grinned unrepentantly. "I don't know, she's probably more upset with Logan over here," nodding his head at a tall blonde with tattoos going up his neck. "He didn't want to see her teeth trick."

Logan for his part, looked a little green. "She didn't want to take 'no' for an answer," he said.

"But you did keep saying no . . . right?" Ari asked.

Logan glanced up at the ceiling suddenly, refusing to answer.

There was a pause, and then the group burst into hysterics. Ari and Blake, Monroe and Lincoln, and Camden . . . who was laughing so hard, I had to practically hold up his entire weight so he didn't fall over.

Okay, now I was really confused.

Camden finally straightened and wiped his eyes. "Sorry, baby girl," he said, his body still shaking with laughter. "This will be really funny when you meet Geraldine. Just trust me."

I grinned, because the sound of him happy . . . made *me* happy.

"This is Disney," Camden said, gesturing to an attractive brunette male who had just walked up from the back.

"Walker," the man said with a sigh.

"Walker?" I repeated, confused.

"Walker is my real name. For some reason these fools decided that 'Disney' was better than the name my mama gave me." He rolled his eyes. "It's a whole thing."

Walker had the deepest southern drawl out of all of them, and I got it then. "Disney" like a Disney prince.

It was very apt for him.

"How's Olivia?" Camden asked, and Walker's answering grin was blinding.

Seriously, was there a secret society where everyone in this group drank blood and made a pact in exchange for being the hottest humans alive?

I was going to question Camden about this later, because I had suspicions.

"She's good. Nervous as usual. And the baby keeps kicking, so she's afraid she's going to mess up."

"Have you been to one of her concerts yet?" Blake asked me, ignoring the fact that Ari seemed to be braiding a section of her hair.

"Her concert?" I asked, embarrassment creeping in again because I had no idea what they were talking about.

"I wanted to surprise her," Camden said gently, brushing a kiss on my head. They all watched us, fascinated, like we were some sort of exotic animal.

I blushed, and I saw Lincoln and Ari grin at each other.

"My wife is Olivia Davis . . . formerly Olivia Darling," Walker said proudly, a dreamy look in his eyes that I swore I'd seen in Camden's when he looked at me.

Wait a minute . . .

I gaped at him, feeling faint.

This was it. This was how I knew that this new life I'd stepped into was a dream, and any time now, I was going to wake up and be devastated.

Olivia Davis was my idol. My favorite performance I'd ever done had been to a song of hers called "Bluebird." She had the best voice, the best songs . . . she was perfect.

She also had a tragic backstory, and I'd always imagined that we were similar in that way. And if she could have a happily ever after . . . maybe I could, too.

"Woah there, baby girl," Camden chuckled. "I'm getting jealous again."

"Not a surprise in this group," joked Monroe, and Lincoln made a playful growling sound before he smacked a kiss against her lips.

"I can't believe I'm going to see her. She's really performing tonight?" I glanced up at Camden, because my irrational brain was afraid this was going to turn out to be a joke.

Hearing her sing live was literally one of my life goals.

"She really is," Camden said, his eyes glittering with amusement.

I almost said "I love you."

It really almost slipped out.

I just didn't know how he did it, anticipating what I needed or wanted *every* single time. It was like he had an inside track into my mind.

Getting fired? Pshh. I'd get fired a million times if it meant getting to see my favorite artist on earth perform.

"Before she comes out, tell us more about you," said Blake, staring at me interestedly. I blinked, not understanding how this perfect creature would want to know anything about *me*.

"Have we met before?" I blurted out, sinking against Camden as he started chuckling.

Blake was the one who blushed this time. "I don't think so," she said shyly.

"Blake's a supermodel," Ari said, the pride in his voice rivaling Walker's only moments ago.

"I'm not a *super*model," Blake grumbled, putting a hand over her face like she was trying to hide.

That's where I'd seen her, in magazine campaigns. I was sure of it now.

"She's a supermodel," Ari mouthed as he lifted her up and started giving her kisses all over her face until she was giggling.

"You guys are adorable," I murmured, a strange longing hitting me.

I wanted that.

And more specifically . . . I wanted that with Camden.

I avoided his gaze—just in case he *did* have some kind of magic powers and could read my mind.

"As I was saying," Blake continued, slightly out of breath after she'd managed to peel Ari off her. "Tell us about you."

It was a little intimidating to have them all staring at me.

I opened my mouth, but nothing came out. I . . . was a nobody. A street urchin. My father was in prison and my mother had left me. I was a foster child who hadn't been wanted.

Oh, and I'd been fired from being a busser tonight . . . so there was that.

"Anastasia is the most incredible ballerina in the whole world. I saw her on stage and I was hooked. I'm serious, guys, when you see her dance, it's life-changing. I dream about her dancing. *And* she was recently picked for a showcase of *Giselle*, one of the hardest pas de deux's in ballet," Camden announced . . . and I wasn't sure how it was possible . . . but he sounded even prouder than anyone else had.

He had also completely butchered the term pas de deux.

Camden completely got an A-plus for effort, though.

"Wow."

"That's awesome."

"I can't wait to see you perform!"

They all said incredibly nice things, and I was a blushing, sweating mess because it had been a very long time since I'd gotten this kind of support from people.

I wished they could be *my* friends.

The lights dimmed, and Walker stiffened. "Shit, she's coming out. Do you think the lights will be okay for the baby? You know sometimes Olivia has red cheeks after performing. Maybe I should have put sunscreen on her belly . . . and headphones too . . . just in case it's too loud for the baby's ears."

"Is he serious?" I whispered to Camden, keeping one eye on the stage because I didn't want to miss a second of Olivia singing.

"This is tame for him," Camden muttered back, giving me another sexy wink.

I was pretty sure I was addicted to those.

I forgot all about anything else when Olivia Freaking Davis walked out on the stage. Even more stunning than her pictures and videos with her long dark auburn hair, gorgeous face, and the cutest baby bump I'd ever seen.

And we were only feet from the stage.

"My name is Olivia Davis, and I'm going to play some songs for you tonight," she said in a sweet, clear voice—the same thing she'd said at the start of every performance since her first show.

As if she needed any introduction.

"You know that phone records things, right?" Camden whispered, and I startled because I honestly had forgotten anyone else was in the room.

Some people loved chocolate.

I loved Olivia Davis.

I grabbed my phone immediately and had Camden show me how to video things because I didn't want to miss a thing.

"Looks like we have another simp on our hands," Ari commented, before he huffed in pain. I was pretty sure Walker had punched him.

"Everyone is allowed to simp on my wife. She's perfect," Walker said, and I sighed because it was so cute.

Olivia began to sing, some of her new stuff and some of her old stuff, and all of it was completely amazing and wonderful, something I would remember forever and ever.

Camden sang along to some of the songs, but mostly he watched me, holding me tight as he took in my every move. I would catch his eyes sometimes and get caught up because he looked like he liked me so much.

Some girls might have even mistaken it for love.

Along the way his hands stroked against my sides, up and down, sending sparks over my skin that only had one end in mind.

I was faintly aware of everyone dancing around me, and the trickle of sweat sliding down my spine from the mass of bodies around us heating the room. I tasted the cold drink Camden handed me, the sweetness overpowering my tastebuds.

But I was mostly aware of the fact that every love song that Olivia sang reminded me of how Camden made me feel.

"Let's get out of here," I told him, before she'd even gotten to the last song.

He looked shocked. "What? Is everything okay?" he asked, concerned.

"I want you," I rasped. "Desperately."

Camden closed his eyes, his whole body perfectly still for what must have been the longest second of my life.

When he finally opened them, the hunger in his green depths left me breathless. "Me too, baby girl," he said roughly. "Me fucking too."

"See you guys later," Camden said.

"Tell Olivia she's amazing," I added.

I never would have pictured leaving an Olivia Davis concert early. But I'd also never imagined Camden James.

So, maybe it was fitting.

And then we were off, like two school kids running through a field as his tangled fingers took me through the crowded room, both of us desperate to get out of there as soon as possible. A quick glance back at the group, and I saw they were smirking after us. I tossed a wave behind me . . . I'd really liked them.

I was against the wall as soon as we got out of the main room, Camden crowding me as he kissed me like I was the only thing that could quench his thirst. He pushed his hard length against me, and I reached down between us, stroking him through his clothes, my mouth literally watering.

A small part of me was very aware his dick was going to split me open with its size, but that particular fear was overtaken by the way his lips felt, and how his hands seemed to know my body like he'd read a book.

"Fuck," he swore, his eyes burning as he tore himself from my lips and grabbed my hand again, pulling me out into the chilly night air.

Waiting for the valet to pull around his truck, even for the two minutes it actually took, felt like a lifetime. Camden's hands were stroking me all over and I was wishing for magic that could transport us back to his place in the blink of an eye.

Or maybe the truck would work. Losing my virginity in a vehicle wasn't exactly how I'd pictured it, but I was desperate enough to go there.

I sighed in relief as the truck was pulled in front of us and Camden chuckled. "Me, too," he whispered, employing those powers again to read my mind.

He helped me inside, his hands lingering on my thighs after he'd buckled the seatbelt. "I want you so badly." Camden's voice was low and desperate, and I felt like I might melt off the seat.

"Take me home, Camden," I answered, and he growled as he pushed away from me like it was the hardest thing he'd ever done and went around the truck to get in on the other side.

The engine rumbled as we drove through the city streets, the night pressing in around us. I sat in the passenger seat, feeling the hum of the road beneath me. The cab felt small, the air charged with so much tension my skin was prickling.

Camden's presence beside me was almost overwhelming. I could sense every movement, every breath he took. I could feel the heat of his body, the subtle shift of his arm on the steering wheel. Every time our eyes met, it was like a spark igniting something deep within me. I'd never been more aware of another person in my life.

"Are you warm enough?" he asked, his voice low and rough, cutting through the silence.

"I'm fine," I replied, my voice barely above a whisper. And it was the truth. Despite the chill of the air outside, I was on fire, a heat that seemed to seep into my very bones.

I swallowed hard, my mind racing with thoughts of what was to come.

The way his hand gripped the steering wheel, the way his jaw tightened, everything about him drew me in, made me want more.

We were almost home when I decided to put my cards on the table, just so he wasn't shocked when he saw the aftermath on his sheets.

"Camden," I began, not even sure how to say this.

"Yeah?" he replied, his voice softer now, almost tender.

I turned to look at him, my heart pounding. "I've never—I've never done this."

He glanced at me, his eyes dark and intense. "What do you mean, baby girl?"

The cab of the truck seemed to shrink, the space between us crackling with electricity.

"I'm a virgin."

The words hovered in the air.

When he didn't say anything, my freak-out began. Why had I told him that? This was a thirty-something-year-old man . . . a professional athlete. I'm pretty sure their kind were taught to run to the hills if a virgin reared her head. He was probably going to kick me out once we got home. He probably thought I was going to be a major clinger. I needed to clear this up, tell him he didn't have to worry about me. That this was no big deal.

Even if it was a *really* big deal to me.

"Fuck—" the words cut through my inner hysteria. I glanced at his face, my eyes widening as I took him in. He looked like a man barely holding on to control. There was a red flush to his cheeks and he was sitting scarily still. His hands were clutching the steering wheel so tightly I was worried he was going to break it off.

"Camden—I'm not expecting anything from you," I began, completely embarrassed I'd even said something to begin with.

"I'm going to ruin you."

His words were . . . shocking, to say the least.

"What?" I asked, a little offended.

He suddenly pulled off to the side of the road and put the truck into park before facing me. Nervous anticipation was bleeding through my veins.

Camden's hands slid through my hair, and he pulled my head back so I had to look at him.

"I'm going to be your first and your last. I'll be the only thing you crave after I'm done with you. You're not even going to be able to look at another man because your body is going to know I'm the only one that can give it what it needs." There was a rough, almost manic promise in his voice and I whimpered just thinking about what he was saying.

"That sounds . . . intense," I finally murmured. My clit was pulsing between my legs, like a phantom limb was pressing on it as he spoke, every word reaching out and brushing against me.

"You have no idea," he growled, pressing a punishing kiss to my lips that was definitely an omen of what was to come. "You're going to be mine, baby. As soon as you bleed all over my dick, you're done. There's never going to be anyone else."

I gasped, squeezing my thighs together, my nipples hardened into points beneath my dress.

I couldn't wait.

Camden leaned forward and bit down on my bottom lip. Hard. Until I tasted blood. His tongue slid into my mouth, capturing the salty, iron tang as it tangled with mine.

Why was that so fucking hot?

He let me go and pulled back onto the road, and this time there was a feral energy to his actions. We were going at least twenty over as he sped through the streets, screeching around the last corner before his penthouse like a man possessed.

Thank goodness we hadn't been noticed by the cops. I wasn't sure what Camden would have done if they'd tried to pull us over.

He raced into his building's underground parking garage and was out of the truck the second he'd thrown it into park. Camden yanked open my door, his arms extended like he was going to grab me and haul me over his shoulder.

Hot . . . but maybe we needed to slow down for just a second.

"So, you're not mad about this? I promise I'm not going to need anything from you, or start acting crazy—"

"Fuck, Anastasia. Act crazy. Take whatever you want from me. Own me like I want to own you. Hearing that I get to have what no man ever will is the best. Fucking. Thing. I've ever heard in my life."

His chest was heaving, so much emotion in his gaze I almost couldn't handle it.

He leaned in close, his breath caressing my ear. "I've never wanted anything like I want you, Anastasia Lennox."

"You have me, Camden James," I whispered back. "Now, take me to bed."

A growl burst from his chest as he undid my seatbelt and scooped me into his arms, slamming the truck door behind us as we strode to the elevator.

One step inside, and he was pushing me against the wall again. My legs hooked around his waist as his lips met mine.

The kiss felt desperate and hungry, and unlike any other kiss that had come before. He fumbled with the buttons on the wall as his tongue swept into my mouth. He'd probably hit a few floors he wasn't supposed to, but I didn't care—as long as he kept kissing me like this. Like his soul was just as desperate for me as his body was.

He sucked on my tongue as his erection pushed against my core. I moaned and his grip on my hips tightened. I wanted him to hold me tighter. I wanted evidence of him all over my skin. To not only remember this when I woke up tomorrow, but to see it.

The elevator chimed and the doors opened. Camden glanced over, cursing softly as he quickly pressed the button to close the doors. "Wrong floor," he whispered as his tongue slid down my neck. My head fell back as he sucked on my pulse.

I wasn't human anymore. I was some kind of wanton creature who survived on pleasure.

We finally got to the right floor, and Camden stalked into the penthouse, still holding me tight.

Our lips were tangled together the entire walk to his room, and right before we crossed the threshold, I pulled back and took a second to stare at him. Maybe I looked deranged, but I just wanted to remember this *before* moment.

"What's wrong?" he rasped, his eyes dilated, the black bleeding into the green as he stared at me worshipfully.

"Not a thing," I answered, and he stepped into the bedroom.

As he walked us to the bed, his lips still dancing across my skin, I took a moment to reflect on the *after*.

This was probably going to turn into something tragic, a memory that would make my heart ache whenever I thought about it for the rest of my life. I'd compare him to every lover I would ever have, and the loss of him would sit in my soul forever.

I knew that. Yet I still allowed him to take me to his bed.

Because all that pain that would come, all the sleepless nights, the eating my feelings in my room alone trying to forget him, the tears I wouldn't be able to stop . . . .

I had a feeling he would be worth it.

CHAPTER 25

ANASTASIA

Camden slowly slid me down his body until my feet touched the floor, and I was standing in front of him.

He gulped, his eyes hot over my skin as he slowly turned me. His fingers traced along my shoulder, leaving goosebumps in their wake as they slid down my bare back until he got to the zipper, fingering it for a second and leaving me panting with anticipation.

"Camden," I whispered, and he laughed softly before he slowly pulled my zipper down, so slowly I thought I would die. "Please," I begged.

He brushed a kiss across my shoulder. "I'm going to take such good care of you, baby girl."

My dress fell to the floor. I hadn't been able to wear a bra since the dress was strapless, and I shivered as I stood there in nothing but a tiny black thong.

"Fuck," he growled, and I yelped as his hand suddenly smacked against my ass cheek, immediately massaging it afterwards as his face fell onto my shoulder. "I've never seen something as perfect as you, Anastasia. I'm not convinced any of this is real yet, because perfection like yours doesn't seem possible."

It was exactly how I felt, and it gave me a heady sensation in my chest that he could feel the same way about me as I felt about him.

"I have to taste you again," he said, pressing gently on my back until I was bent forward, my nipples rubbing against the silk of his gray comforter.

I moaned as he pressed his arousal against my ass, my nipples dragging on the fabric, which might as well have been sandpaper for how much sensation I was feeling.

"Spread your legs," he ordered roughly, and my legs shifted apart like they were puppets on a string.

"Good girl."

I whimpered at his words, taking a step wider because I wanted to be that. His good girl. I wanted to give him everything he desired. Just as long as he fulfilled this *ache* inside me.

He kneaded my ass for a moment, his breaths heavy as he fingered the edge of my thong. "This needs to come off," he said, a second before he snapped it off me like it was nothing, leaving me completely bare.

I sobbed, so turned on, my words falling out of my mouth in a nonsensical stream.

His body slid down until his knees hit the wooden floor with a light thud.

"Relax, baby girl," he murmured, right before his tongue slid between my legs.

I came immediately, so aroused from the anticipation that all I'd needed was the slightest touch to fall apart.

He chuckled as he lapped up my cum. "So fucking responsive," he growled as he pushed two fingers in, finding that perfect spot immediately as another finger circled my clit.

I ground against him, and his free hand slapped the globe of my ass once again. "Hold still for me, Anastasia. I don't want you to move . . . I just want you to *feel*."

"Yes, sir," I cried, faintly aware of his hitched breath and the way his tongue sucked and licked, separating my folds as he continued to thrust his fingers into my dripping core.

My hands fisted the covers as his hands squeezed my ass, pulling my cheeks apart as his tongue slid up, circling my . . . other hole.

"Oh," I cried, jerking forward from the shock of him rimming my asshole. I'd never even imagined that. But, ugh . . . fuck. It felt so good.

His tongue moved back down, his stubble scratching my thighs as he pulled me back so I was almost sitting on his face.

My core was making a wet, embarrassing, squelching sound every time he withdrew his fingers, but he seemed to love it. He was whispering praises against my skin, sucking and biting and licking and turning me into a throbbing mess.

My whimpered pleas echoed around the room, and I couldn't stay still. I fucked myself back against his face as he tongued my clit and then . . . I was coming again. Pleasure tearing through me.

Tears slid down my face as I convulsed.

"Fuck," he huffed, his tongue sliding through my folds desperately like he couldn't bear to let one drop go to waste.

He stayed there, breathing me in, for so long that I squirmed uncomfortably because having someone between your legs, even if you were over-the-top crazy about them like I was about Camden James . . . well, it was a very intimate moment.

Camden took a deep inhale, like he wanted to breathe me in one more time, and then he slowly got up off the floor.

I was still panting against the bed, and I totally didn't expect him to suddenly flip me over to my back so I was staring up at him.

"Look what you did to me," he said in a silky voice, gesturing to the front of his pants, a large wet spot visible . . . had he just come?

"You tasted so good, I came in my pants like an errant schoolboy." His eyes glittered as they slid down my body, stopping on my chest as he eyed my breasts hungrily.

Oh, I guess we were going to be done. "I'll just get cleaned up, then," I told him, trying to keep the disappointment out of my voice. It's not like I hadn't just come several times on his tongue. I'm sure we would get to the main event of me losing my virginity . . . some time.

He laughed darkly, putting a palm between my breasts to keep me on my back and on the bed.

"The thing is, baby girl. You're *not* dealing with an errant schoolboy. You just helped me take the edge off . . . so I can really make you enjoy this next part."

He unbuckled his dress pants and then slid them down, and I realized right away he'd been going commando.

I mean, I wasn't sure that he *could* wear boxers or briefs . . . I didn't even know how he was wearing pants. How had that monster even fit in there?

His cock was beautiful. Was that appropriate to say? The red, mushroomed head was gushing precum . . . or maybe that was residual cum from his orgasm.

And I wanted it.

I licked my lips and watched as he fisted it from root to tip, his gaze still locked on me. He was fully erect, as if he hadn't come at all.

Maybe Camden James really was a superhero after all.

At least in the dick department.

I squeezed my legs together as a thought hit me. Don't get me wrong. I wanted that dick. But if I was in awe that it had fit in his pants . . . how in the world was it going to fit in *me*?

"Trust me, Anastasia, let me take care of you," he whispered gruffly and I nodded.

Because I *did* trust him. I'd follow him off a cliff at this point if he told me that's where I should go. I trusted him like I'd never trusted anyone before.

I'm sure feminists all over the world were weeping at that kind of thought process.

But it was true.

He grabbed my thighs and pushed them open, staring at my pussy worshipfully like it held the key to the universe.

"My beautiful girl," he said as he pressed the gleaming head to my dripping center, taking a moment to glide it through my folds, shock waves of pleasure floating through me until I was shaking against him—and he hadn't even done anything yet.

"Breathe," he ordered, and I let out a huge exhale, unaware of how long I'd been holding it in.

Camden finally began to press in, slowly. I could feel every inch, and I was stretched way beyond my comfort.

"Camden," I cried out desperately. I didn't know if I could do this.

"You're doing so well, baby girl," he soothed, his hand brushing off the tears that were slipping down my face. "You're so tight, Anastasia, best thing I've ever felt. You're literally *choking* my cock."

I sobbed as he pushed in more, and Camden groaned, his eyes squeezing shut for a moment before he reached between us and expertly worked my clit, sending a needy hunger thrashing through my veins.

"Fuck," he growled.

"What?" I gasped, feeling like I'd entered an alternate realm because the world seemed hazy and glittering around us.

"It's just so good. And I'm not even all the way in," he said as he stopped.

His gaze darkened, and he moved his hand from my clit to my chin, gripping it softly so I had to focus on him.

I mewled under his possessive stare. "This is it, baby. It's going to hurt for just a second, and then I'm going to make you feel so good." His voice was velvet as he spoke and it only added to the out-of-body experience I was having.

"Okay," I whispered. I thought I was prepared for what came next, but then Camden thrust in with one hard, smooth motion, tearing through my barrier. I cried out at the pain, losing my breath as I thrashed and sobbed underneath him, the fullness too much for me to handle.

Camden's breathing was harsh and uneven as he stayed there inside me, buried to the hilt.

"Are you alright?" he finally asked after a moment, his voice pure gravel. Camden's lips soothed over my skin, making his way down to my chest where he suckled each nipple. He licked the underside of my breasts, covering every inch of my chest with his tongue and sometimes his teeth. I writhed against his dick, trying to breathe.

The more time he spent on my breasts though, the more I relaxed, pleasure chasing away any residual pain. He continued on and on, until I was finally ready for him to move.

"Please, fuck me," I moaned, and Camden sucked on each tip one more time before he finally lifted his head, his eyes a wildfire of need and desire.

"Thank fuck."

His first thrust was hard and fast, and with each following thrust, pleasure built in my core.

His gold-rimmed eyes stared intensely as he moved in and out, a myriad of emotions in their depths that I was scared I was just imagining.

It was too much, I was *feeling* too much.

My eyes slammed shut, and he slid a hand to my throat, gently squeezing until I opened them back up.

"Eyes on me," he growled, and I nodded, a harsh sob ripping out of my mouth as an orgasm flushed through me, short but significant.

How many was that now?

Camden pulled almost all the way out and I opened my mouth to beg him to stay. His eyes glimmered for a moment before he pounded back into me, starting up a relentless pace.

My nails dug into his shoulders, doing my best to obey him and keep my eyes focused on his face.

He held me in place as he pushed inside of me, sometimes grinding against my clit and sending pleasure sparking through me.

"Fucking perfect, Ana," he breathed at one point. "You feel so fucking good. You're going to come all over my big dick, aren't you, baby girl? You're going to let me fuck this pretty pussy every day."

Our faces were inches apart as I clung to him, and I could only imagine what he saw when he looked at me.

I was obsessed, addicted, and completely under his spell.

"I love you," he growled as he buried himself to the hilt, the cords in his neck standing out in stark relief as he filled me with warm bursts of cum.

My eyes widened, because . . . what did he just say?

I followed him over the cliff, sobbing at the exquisite feeling surging through me. My eyes finally closed, white light sparking at my eyelids. I didn't know it was possible to feel this good.

A second later, his hand was circling my neck again, forcing me to pay attention. "You are fucking mine. I own this body. I own this soul. Mine," he growled, burying his face in my neck.

"Yes," I whispered. Over and over again as he stayed sheathed inside of me.

Camden gave me slow, drugging kisses, and my eyes fluttered closed again, my body completely worn out.

"I'm going to keep you forever," I think he muttered as I fell asleep, a smile on my lips as I slipped into the best dreams I'd ever had.

Camden

I pulled out of her sleeping body, staring down at the blood streaked across my dick, across my sheets . . . down her thighs.

I was still hard, even after the two most intense, *best* fucking orgasms of my life. It felt like my dick was the Energizer Bunny, as long as Anastasia was nearby, it could go on and on.

I wanted to remember this forever. I didn't have a blood kink or anything . . . or at least I was going to ignore that part of me if I did. But seeing her blood coating my skin, mixed with my cum . . .

I'd never seen anything so right in my life.

Something that perfect needed to be documented, I decided, quietly reaching over and grabbing my phone from off the end table . . . before snapping a picture of my dick.

I needed to be able to look at this whenever I wanted. Maybe it would help me control this insanity throbbing through my insides. The insanity that had my dick begging to get back inside her, ready for round two even though she had to be sore. The insanity that wanted to remind me that she was mine, that no matter what, I'd have this part of her.

No matter what, she'd belong to me.

"Okay, crazy," I muttered to myself, cursing when she shifted and let out a soft sigh at the sound of my voice.

I set my phone down and carefully settled beside her, hungrily taking in her perfect features.

I wanted to take care of my baby, but I also couldn't resist just *one* more taste.

Okay, one or two more tastes. I was addicted and I didn't have any intention of curing that anytime soon.

I slid down the bed, carefully pushing between her legs, pausing as she softly sighed. Lapping at her perfect pussy, it was all I could do not to moan. I loved the taste of the two of us combined. I wanted to keep her pumped full of me. I wanted her to feel me inside of her, for her thighs to be constantly sticky with my cum.

Anastasia was softly moaning and writhing under my tongue . . . but somehow she didn't wake up. I watched in satisfaction as her body bent, and she sighed as she came, her pussy clenching my fingers that I'd slipped in so that my tongue could focus on her clit.

A rush of her essence poured out, and I was fucking into the bed, giving my dick much needed friction as I licked and sucked up *every* single drop.

I got on my knees and stroked my dick, over and over again as I stared in awe at her perfect pussy.

Grunting, my seed spilled out all over her folds, sliding down and soaking the sheets underneath her.

I rubbed my cum into her skin, feeding it into her core and spreading it all over her stomach and up to her breasts. I circled her clit, using the cum to get her off one more time.

And still she slept.

My poor baby girl. I'd fucked her to sleep.

She probably needed to get used to it. I had no plans of stopping any time soon.

Sitting back on my haunches, I admired my handiwork. Her skin was coated with me, my white, milky cum was everywhere. I may never let her shower again.

She was perfect.

An idea came to me then, a way to immortalize that moment forever and ever.

Anastasia was going to love it.

Sliding to the side of her, I texted my tattoo artist about scheduling an appointment.

That done, I lay down next to her, memorizing every detail of her face. Her long lashes, the cute curve of her nose, the light freckles that dotted her cheeks . . . the golden glow of her skin. I took in the pink of her nipples and every perfect curve of her body.

I'd told her I loved her. I wasn't sure that she'd actually heard me, but that didn't matter much. I would just tell her that every day for the rest of our lives.

CHAPTER 26

CAMDEN

I was propped up on one elbow, watching her, when she woke up the next morning, blinking open those crystal eyes of hers as she stared at the ceiling for a moment.

"Mmmh," she murmured, stretching her long arms above her head.

I saw when it hit her—when she remembered all that had happened last night. Her eyes widened and she turned her head, her mouth opened in a cute little *o*.

"Hi, baby girl," I murmured, admiring the blush that spread from her cheeks down to her chest.

"Hi," she whispered, her gaze darting down to my . . . very erect dick.

I'd had an erection all fucking night as I'd watched her. While not comfortable, I'd gotten used to it.

I was pretty sure it was just my state of being now.

"Just ignore him, there's no help for my dick at the moment."

She giggled and then winced.

"Is my baby sore?" I crooned, satisfaction uncurling in my gut.

I'd told her I wanted to ruin her. Ruining her pussy was obviously the first step of that.

Her blush darkened, and she bit down on her lip shyly. "I might be out of commission today—" she began before her eyes flashed. "I mean, not that I'm expecting more!"

"There's going to be more, baby girl," I told her, cutting off the panic building in her voice. "There's going to be *so* much more." I watched as she softened back into her pillow, a dreamy glow in her features like my words were her happy place.

It was actually the perfect time to have the appointment that I'd scheduled this afternoon. It was going to be uncomfortable as fuck during practice tomorrow—and I might die if anyone accidentally hit my dick, but I didn't want to wait another second to have a reminder of her on my skin.

"Do you have dance today?" I asked, wishing that she didn't, and that I didn't have practice and we could spend the rest of the day in bed together.

She might need some rest from sex, but there were plenty of other ways I could make her feel good and still give her sweet pussy a break.

"Yes. The only day I have off is Sunday, and even then, I might need to go in because of the showcase."

A shadow crossed her features at the mention of that, and I frowned. She'd been so excited when she'd texted me, but I realized she hadn't mentioned it after that. I made a mental note to follow up with her about it—another time—when she wasn't naked in my arms, and we weren't both bathing in the afterglow of the perfection of last night.

"What time is it?" she asked lazily, as if she didn't really care. I liked that; it meant I had done something right. It was how I felt, too, like all my other obligations could wait. It hit me again, the fact that I'd never felt that way about anything before. Nothing had ever been more important than hockey.

"It's eight," I answered, glancing at the clock.

She nodded and sighed. "I need to shower." She rubbed at her stomach, looking thoughtful, and I admired the view of my dried cum all over her skin.

The idea of her rubbing that off made me growly. "I'd rather you not," I said, using my most convincing voice. "I like the idea of you smelling like me all day, baby girl. Of everyone being reminded that you belong to me now." I moved on top of her, dropping soft kisses down her neck and getting that sigh out of her that I loved. "Will you do that for me, Anastasia? Will you dance all day just like *this*?"

She moaned, and I savored the sound. "Well, I don't think you want me to dance just like this," she teased, gesturing to her current state.

I glanced at the blood I'd left on her thighs. I guess I could wipe that off. But nothing else.

Growling, I bit gently on her earlobe, causing her to inhale sharply. "What do you think? Are you going to give me what I want?"

"Yes, sir," she whimpered as I trailed a finger through her folds, which were already soaking wet.

"Good girl," I answered, trying to ignore the way my dick had become like a fucking iron pole when she'd said that.

I brought my finger to my mouth and sucked off her taste, groaning because I loved it so much.

Fuck, I didn't want to get out of this bed.

At least my hand would smell like her for the rest of the day.

I finally forced myself to move off her, and she pouted as I did.

"You need to rest that sweet pussy, baby girl. I'll give you exactly what you need . . . later. But right now you're going to be my good girl and get *all* better for me."

Her eyes got all dreamy, like they always did when I took charge.

"Promise?" she finally asked throatily, stretching her arms above her head. I tracked her lithe lines like a man obsessed.

"Mmmh. Most definitely," I murmured, giving her one more kiss before I helped her off the bed.

She stayed covered in my cum for the entire day at dance.

And I got a new tattoo in her honor.

So, I would call the day a win.

"Look, we need to talk about your dicks," Logan said the next day after practice, emerging from the communal showers with a vaguely sick look on his face.

"Rookie, what the hell are you talking about?" Lincoln snapped, his face scrunched up in concern.

Logan waved his hand at Lincoln, Ari, and Walker standing there with towels wrapped around their waists.

"Enough is enough. It's called self-mutilation. This is setting a bad example for the rest of us."

"It's actually called 'symbolizing our devotion,'" Ari said, looking completely unconcerned as he whipped off his towel and began to pull on his briefs—showcasing the . . . unusual piercings on his dick.

Not that I was trying to look. It was just hard to miss.

"Fuck, Lancaster," Lincoln growled, turning away from Ari's dick. "Can you not?"

"I can't help it," Ari said lightly. "*Maximus 5000* likes to be a free man."

"Camden, tell them the multitude of dick decorations is too much. And really, guys, didn't that fucking hurt? Especially you, Disney. That's just . . . " He waved at Walker's towel-covered groin, keeping his eyes averted. "I mean, how did you not die?"

I was silent. I was pretty sure that the new tattoo I'd gotten in Anastasia's honor would be "too much" in Logan's eyes.

I mean it would probably be "too much" in everyone's eyes.

It was just right for me, though.

It was also still very . . . fragile at the moment, so I'd decided on a shower at home where I could properly unwrap it and sanitize it as necessary. I'd kept Anastasia busy with my mouth, but I didn't think me—or her—could hold out nearly as long as recommended before we needed the real thing.

"Noticed you're a little quiet over there, Hero," Ari drawled, and suddenly all four of them were staring at me suspiciously . . . still fully dressed in my practice clothes.

"And why didn't you shower after practice? That's a little . . . odd," mused Walker. "You're usually the first in."

"Watching my shower habits, Disney? I think that's the 'little odd' thing in this conversation."

"He did something," Ari announced, looking me up and down and nodding. "The question is . . . what?"

All of them were staring at me again, their gazes a little too close to my dick for comfort.

"Hey," I snapped. "Focus on your own dicks. Especially you, Logan."

"He definitely did something," commented Lincoln, completely ignoring what I'd just said.

"It's always the grandpappies you gotta watch out for," Walker whisper-yelled, shaking his head.

I scoffed and turned away from the idiots.

But there was a big grin on my face as I did.

I'd once told Logan that "real men had dick tattoos." He just hadn't believed me.

Guess I was a real man now.

Later on, Walker walked with me out to the parking lot. He kept giving me lingering side glances, so I finally raised an eyebrow and turned to him. "What's up, Disney?"

He scoffed, as he usually did whenever anyone but Lincoln called him that nickname. "I was just wondering if Anastasia's going to be making an appearance at the game tomorrow, and if she'll be sitting in the Wives' Club. Because I'll need to let Elaine and Emily know there will be one more in the group.

I didn't like the sound of her name coming out of his mouth, but I controlled myself.

I considered what he'd said. I'd forgotten that Walker had hired two female bodyguards to protect Olivia at games and when he couldn't be there. The bodyguards were both built like trucks and could squat five hundred men. There was absolutely nothing to worry about when they were around. No one was getting past those women.

They were perfect.

"Count her in," I nodded, and he smirked.

"Getting serious?" he asked teasingly, his face growing serious when I nodded.

"She's the one," I said before shrugging. "I just don't think she knows it yet."

Walker laughed. "I know all about that," he said. "Spoiler alert, though, we always win." He flashed me a thumbs-up before heading to his truck.

I was grinning. I *was* going to win this. There was no doubt.

Quickening my pace, I got in my truck and drove out of the parking lot, eager to get to Anastasia's ballet studio and get her home.

Anastasia

The day had been a disaster. Dance practice with Dallon was a nightmare. Between his lingering hands and his constant criticisms, my mind was a mess.

I wanted to quit. This big, life-altering opportunity was in front of me.

And I wanted to quit.

I was also running late for Camden's game. The driver he'd sent had to wait at least half an hour outside the studio as Dallon made me practice fouettés over and over again before he'd let me leave.

"I'm so sorry," I told the driver as I slipped into the town car. I hadn't had time to dry my hair or reapply my makeup in my hurry to get to the car, and I ran my fingers through my hair self-consciously as I glanced in the rearview mirror. I needed to throw it up in a bun.

"Not a problem, miss," she said as she shot me a bright smile.

She thankfully didn't talk to me much during the drive. I tried to regroup and push away the stress of practice, but it was difficult. By the time I reached the arena for Camden's game, my nerves were still frayed.

"I'll just drop you off at the back entrance. That's the closest route to your seat tonight," she told me, nodding her head at a set of double doors as she pulled into a half-circle drive.

Dang. In the stress of the afternoon I'd completely forgotten that Camden had gotten me a seat with Monroe, Blake . . . and Olivia.

"Thank you," I said when she'd come to a stop. Crap, I needed to tip her. I rooted around in my bag, searching for a spare dollar—anything.

"Mr. James took care of my tip," she said gently, and I blushed, nodding and thanking her again profusely as I exited the car.

It took me an embarrassingly long time to pull up the tickets that Camden had sent me. I finally had to shove my phone at the ticket person and ask them to help.

Two seconds later, and the elderly man had pulled it up. "Have fun," he said, giving me a grin with a set of false teeth.

"Thanks," I said, ducking my head because a senior citizen knew more about my phone than I did.

I was just embarrassing myself left and right tonight.

Weaving my way through the crowded concourse, I searched for the entrance I needed to get to my seat.

"There it is," I muttered to myself as I finally found the right letter.

I walked down the tunnel, the chill from the ice growing with every step I took until I'd gotten out into the stands. The countdown clock on the jumbotron said there was only two minutes left until the game.

I'd missed almost all of the warm-ups.

Moving to the side, I watched the ice, quickly spotting Camden skating around. Ari said something to him, and I grinned as they did a fist bump. They were so cute.

The picture on the jumbotron changed, and up popped a video of Monroe, Blake, and Olivia sitting in their seats, laughing and talking as they snacked on popcorn.

My stomach clenched. They looked perfect, effortlessly poised, and stunning.

I glanced at my reflection on the metal pole I was standing next to.

I was a mess. The messy bun I'd put together in the car defined the word "mess," and not the sexy kind. My face was pale and drawn and makeupless, dark circles under my eyes that made me look like a zombie.

The jumbotron briefly flashed to someone else in the crowd before going back to the group of women. Again.

There was no way I was going to sit by them. Monroe and Blake had seemed so nice the other night, and I'm sure Olivia was nice, too. But I didn't need to embarrass myself—or Camden—in front of the whole arena by sitting there like this.

He'd understand. Right?

A hint of guilt threaded its way through my chest. He'd been so excited when he'd told me about the seats and that I'd be hanging with his best friends' wives.

I'd just have to get to know them better later.

Besides, we'd fucked once, I told myself petulantly. I didn't need to be sitting with the wives like this was serious.

Except, I desperately wanted it to be serious.

I thought about that "I love you" that had slipped out of his mouth. I'd been actively trying *not* to think about it. Because he couldn't have meant it, right?

It was too early. He was just playing around with me.

I desperately wanted him to have meant that "I love you," though, too.

Because I was pretty sure I was in love with him.

Heart pounding, I turned and headed back down the tunnel, finding a ticket booth.

"Can you trade this ticket for one higher up?" I asked, showing him the ticket on my phone.

The pimply-faced kid stared at me like I was an idiot. "You want to trade that ticket for one . . . higher up?" he repeated slowly.

"Yes, please," I said, plastering on my dance smile because I really needed him to hurry up. The game was about to start and I didn't want to miss any of it.

"Do you realize this is in the front row? These are the best tickets available."

He was still talking to me like I was slow, and I took a deep breath, trying to find some patience. The crowd's roar filtered out from the tunnel behind me, and I tapped my foot anxiously.

The ticket guy blinked a few times, and I inwardly winced at the color of his eyes. They were watery blue. Just like Michael's.

I shot a glance around me, like he could possibly be lurking around just because someone with similar eyes was here.

I still hadn't figured out how I was going to pay Michael off. It was a subject I kept avoiding thinking about because it made me feel so helpless.

"There's nothing else in the lower bowl," the boy finally said, after he'd typed on his computer for the longest minute known to man. He pushed my phone back toward me.

"The upper bowl is fine," I said, hoping I got the lingo right. There was now a line forming behind me, and it was making me even more anxious.

My phone had buzzed multiple times—and the only person who knew my number was Camden. Of course he would be wondering where I was.

The ticket guy stared at me like I was crazy, his nose scrunching up and his gaze darting around like someone needed to come claim me because I'd obviously lost my mind.

The crowd roared again, and I gritted my teeth. "Anything up there will do," I urged.

He gaped at me for another ten seconds before finally turning back to the computer. After a few clicks, he snorted. "All I have is the top row of the upper bowl. The players are going to look like ants."

He cocked his head as he glanced at my ticket again. "Hey, isn't this where the players' wives and girlfriends sit?"

"The upper bowl is fine," I said quickly. "I'm ready anytime."

Wrinkling his nose again, he printed out the new ticket. "I can't trade that ticket in if it's a player ticket." He clicked something else on his computer. "Which I'm positive it is. So, that'll be twenty dollars."

Fuck. Fuck. Fuck. I didn't have twenty dollars. I didn't have one dollar.

"Oh, for fuck's sake," a man growled suddenly behind me, slamming a twenty on the counter. "Give her the damn ticket. The game's starting!"

The ticket guy shrugged and took the cash, and finally, I got a new ticket.

"Thank you," I squeaked, hustling away and ignoring the stares from the disgruntled people who'd been waiting in line behind me.

I went up an escalator to the next level and then moved through the tunnel to the upper bowl.

He hadn't been kidding. I was literally at the very top. I couldn't really make out jersey numbers from up here.

Those other seats would have been so much better. But I was already relaxing, sitting without the pressure of sitting with the wives and constantly being shown on the screen.

It was much better just being able to watch the jumbotron. It was like watching a movie at a theater, not as much fun as watching it live, but still good.

The cameramen loved Ari, Lincoln, Walker, and Camden, and the screen was constantly showing them. It seemed like Camden kept glancing at the stands.

But maybe that was my imagination.

I pulled out my phone. He wasn't going to see this because he was in the middle of a game, but maybe he'd see it in between periods or something. I was pretty sure they had gone back into the locker room after each period during that first game I'd been to.

Me: I'm here. Just decided to sit somewhere else. I looked a mess after practice and didn't want to embarrass you.

I stared at the text, deciding to add a "Kick Some Ass!" for good measure before I sent it.

The Knights switched shifts, and I watched Camden and Ari climb over the boards on the screen.

A second later, my phone buzzed. My eyes widened seeing he'd texted me back. He was playing a game!

Camden: You are in so much fucking trouble.

Another text followed after that.

Camden: Where are you? I'll send an employee to get you.

Camden: Anastasia! I'm serious.

I frantically typed back an answer before he could send any more texts.

Me: I'm fine. Put your phone away right now!

He didn't answer, and I settled back into the seat with a sigh, trying to relax and focus on the game.

My phone rang the second the period ended and the players left the ice.

"Just tell me where you are," Camden purred, sounding slightly out of breath—because he was just out playing a game in front of tens of thousands of freaking people.

"Get off the phone," I hissed. The person next to me, a wizened old grandma-looking woman, gave me a very unimpressed look.

"I'm not going down there. And you can't make me if I don't tell you where I am."

There was a long pause, long enough that my heartbeat started to race.

"You're being a brat, Anastasia," he finally murmured in a silky, dangerous sounding, terrifying voice. "And you know what happens to brats?"

"What?" I whispered back, my clit throbbing from his sexy tone.

"They get spanked."

With that . . . he hung up.

And I was left with a giant wet spot on my panties.

I was a throbbing, panting mess for the rest of the game, squirming in my seat every time Camden was shown on the jumbotron.

An unfortunate situation when you had a disapproving grandma-type character sniffing every time you moved.

Camden played amazing.

Granted . . . I still knew very little about hockey, but judging by the crowd's reaction every time he got the puck . . . he was on fire out there.

He didn't text me again, and my anticipation only grew. Like there was a direct line from the game clock to my throbbing core.

Embarrassing, really.

The final buzzer sounded, and the Knights won.

The crowd went nuts, streamers pouring down from the ceiling as the team briefly celebrated before filing off the ice.

A text came in then.

Camden: Don't move from your seat until I tell you.

Well then.

I could follow that direction. Now that the game was over and fans were pouring out the exits.

And the jumbotron had switched from the crowd to a final score graphic.

My foot was tapping on the smooth concrete at my feet while I waited for Camden to text me.

And waited.

And waited.

And waited.

Until I was the last person in the whole fucking arena, about to get up because this was getting ridiculous.

My phone buzzed just as I was lifting off my seat to leave, find Camden, and give him a piece of my mind.

Camden: Take the blue door to the left of you, go down those stairs, and then take the first right back into the stands.

I frowned, glancing around, startling when I saw there was indeed a blue door to my left. Camden evidently knew *exactly* where I was now.

An easy thing when you were the last freaking person left in the building.

But I could play along. Make up for the fact that I'd made him text me in the middle of the game.

Although, really, no one was making Camden James do anything.

Okay, maybe I *was* being a brat right now.

I followed his directions, going through the door and down the stairs, then taking the first right, a nervous thrill beating at my pulse with every step.

Until I popped out right behind the Knights bench.

Where Camden was leaning against the wall in a Knights tee and a pair of low-slung gray sweatpants, one foot propped up on the bench he'd been sitting on not that long ago.

Oh . . .

"Anastasia," he said, his voice like velvet as he crooked a finger at me.

My feet had suddenly become glued to the floor, and I stared at him, pulsing heat building between my legs . . .

But I was also nervous. He'd been joking about the spanking thing, right? I mean, maybe no one was in the stands right *now*, but this was still a public place. Someone could walk in at any minute.

And what about the cleaning crew? Wasn't it about time that they showed up?

"Baby girl, don't make me ask you again."

He kept using that same smooth voice . . . the one that made me want to drop to my knees and beg him to fuck me.

With that thought, I was able to move, walking toward him like he was reeling me in with an invisible string.

"Hi." I gulped, once I'd gotten into the players' bench area and was a few steps away.

Camden stayed where he was, lounging against the wall, his arms crossed in front of his chest, making his muscles bulge out decadently.

My mouth watered just looking at him.

"I was fined five thousand dollars tonight, Anastasia," Camden said calmly. "Do you know why that is?"

I shook my head slowly, unable to look away from him.

"Because my girlfriend decided to trade her first row ticket for one up in the nosebleeds . . . without telling me. Which prompted me to pull out my phone for the first time in my professional career . . . during a game."

I put my hands up, losing my breath for a second when he pushed off the wall and slowly stalked toward me.

"In my defense, it all happened rather . . . last minute," I said, my voice pitched much higher than normal as I took a step backward, one step for every one he took forward.

Which worked until I hit the wall behind me.

I trembled at the dirty smirk spreading across his face as he continued to saunter my way, because he knew that he'd caught me.

"You're going to get two spankings for every thousand dollars I lost tonight," he purred.

"When we get home?" I asked hopefully.

He chuckled, and the sound slid across my skin sensually.

"Absolutely not."

Camden stopped right in front of me, his hand gently encircling my throat, his thumb rubbing across my pulse like I'd found he liked to do.

"My baby's feeling unsettled, scared about all the new things happening to her," he crooned, his hand slightly tightening as he spoke.

"I think the word for what I'm feeling is . . . independent, actually," I hissed, unable to stop myself from . . . pushing him.

He laughed again and released my throat, slowly lowering himself to the bench so he was straddled across it.

"Come here, Anastasia," he said in that same, calm voice as he patted his lap.

I stared at him, wide-eyed and shocked. He was taking this really far.

Slowly, hesitantly, I stepped closer, wondering when he was going to pull the plug on this little joke.

"Trust me," he murmured, and some of my unease spilled away.

This was Camden, and I *could* trust him.

I stepped up to him, and his hand pressed gently on my lower back. Before I knew it, he was lowering me across his lap, his touch firm but careful.

This was it. This was when he laughed and pulled me up and—

Camden abruptly ripped down my leggings, the icy air spilling across my bare ass.

"What—" I started to protest, squirming on his lap.

Thwack! His hand came down sharply on my backside. The sting was immediate, surprising, and a gasp escaped my lips.

"Camden!" I squeaked indignantly, struggling to get off him. His grip on me was firm, though, keeping me in place.

"That's one," he said calmly, his tone holding no evidence of the massive erection that was digging into my belly.

"You son of a—" I snarled, my words cut off as he spanked me again, the sound seeming to echo around the empty arena.

"That's two."

My face was flushed with hot shame . . . but something else was building between my legs . . . something I didn't want to admit.

Thwack. Thwack.

"That's four."

My ass was on fire, and when his fingertips softly stroked against my skin right after the stinging burn . . . I moaned.

Spankings five and six felt like a dream. I could feel wetness building on my thighs . . . and I wasn't fighting him anymore.

That was wrong, right?

"I want you to repeat something for me, before the next one. Can you do that for me, baby girl?"

"Yes," I sighed, stiffening when his fingers pushed through my cheeks . . . down, down until he was sliding through the slick practically dripping out of my core.

He withdrew his fingers, and I watched him side-eyed as he sucked my juices off his fingers with a groan.

That made me squirm. I needed those fingers back.

"Brats get spanked. Repeat that, Anastasia."

"What? No," I breathed, but there wasn't much fight in my voice.

Thwack.

I jumped, a soft sob ripping from my mouth as he immediately thrust his fingers inside me, pumping in and out until I was on the verge of coming.

Right before I orgasmed . . . he pulled his fingers out.

"Please!" I immediately begged, feeling slightly hysterical as I hovered in that painful, blissed-out state that you only felt right before you came.

Thwack.

"Say the words, Ana," he said roughly, the first hint that he wasn't as in control of himself as he seemed to be.

"No," I replied sulkily, trying to get some friction on my clit by rubbing against his giant, clothed dick.

"Ana," he said disapprovingly, halting my movements as he slid his fingers into me once more, taking me to the edge again before stilling his hand.

Tears were sliding down my cheeks, wetting his thigh as I tried to *will* some kind of relief.

Thwack.

"Last chance, Anastasia. I'll let you come as soon as you say those three little words." His voice was light and carefree, like he wasn't tearing me apart and remaking me into a breathless, thoughtless creature that just wanted to come. "Brats get spanked."

His hands traced down my seam, and I shivered and sobbed . . . and gave in.

"Brats get spanked," I breathed, and his hand stilled.

"Such a good girl," he rasped.

Thwack!

"That's ten." As soon as the words came out of his mouth, his fingers were back in my pussy, thrusting in and out and rubbing against that perfect spot inside me.

My screams tore through the arena as I came, violently, the edges of my vision darkening from the force of the pleasure.

I was gasping for breath, soft cries coming out of my mouth as he slid me off his lap . . . and onto my knees.

"Open up, my little brat," he growled, and I immediately obeyed, just wanting to please him.

He freed his dick from the band of his sweatpants, the tip of it grazing his belly button as it gleamed under the arena lights.

Without warning, he thrust his cock between my lips, shoving into the wet heat of my mouth.

He cupped my jaw, his eyes glittering possessively as he drove into me.

I couldn't fit him into my mouth, not even the world's foremost expert on deep-throating could . . . but I did my best.

Tears and saliva and precum were slipping from the edges of my mouth as he fucked it, his thrusts quickening as he went.

I was just along for the ride, my gaze locked on his as he slammed in one last time. "Anastasia," he roared as his cum filled my mouth, his dick so far down my throat that I had no choice but to swallow.

Not that I didn't want to.

I needed this man. I wanted every part of him I could get.

His breaths were coming out in gasps as he caressed my jaw and slowly pulled out.

Something red on his length caught my eye, but he pushed his still-hard dick back inside his sweats before I could see what it was, the resulting outline in his pants completely obscene.

"Just a little more," he murmured as he scooped up the cum that was coating my chin and pushed it back in my mouth.

I was staring up at him from my knees like a lovesick fool, still completely shocked about what just happened.

Camden pulled my leggings back up and then lifted me off the ground and into his arms. "Are you ever going to scare me like that again?" he asked, a glimmer in his eyes like he wouldn't mind starting the whole thing over again.

Hell, I was kind of up for that too.

"No, sir," I answered, knowing what it would do to him.

He leaned down and gave me a bruising kiss, his tongue leisurely licking into my mouth.

Camden straightened up, seeming to wince slightly as he adjusted his dick. "Let's go home, baby girl."

I nodded, slumping against him as he led me out of the box and down the tunnel, taking one door and then another, until somehow we popped out into the parking lot, the cold night air pricking at my skin.

As we walked, the words burst across my tongue, and it was all I could do not to say them to him.

It scared me to death, but I had to admit it.

I was in love with Camden James.

CHAPTER 27

CAMDEN

I came slowly to consciousness, and it took me a second to realize that something was different. Usually, Anastasia was wrapped around me like a boa constrictor when I woke up, the most painful kind of wake-up when you were trying to recover from a dick tattoo since I wanted nothing else but to slide inside her soft heat.

But she wasn't lying on my chest. I wasn't breathing in her sweet scent either. I rolled over, reaching out to pull Anastasia back into my arms . . . only for my hand to meet cold sheets.

Immediately, my eyes flew all the way open and I sat up, searching the room for where she'd gone. The bathroom door was open, lights off, and there was no sound of a shower running.

Wait . . . was that the smell of bacon?

An agitated humming sifted through me as I quickly slid out of bed and pulled on a pair of sweatpants. Everything in me was hoping that I was just imagining the smell. Maybe she was just curled up on the couch reading. Sometimes I would find her like that in the evenings.

I followed the smell of breakfast cooking through the penthouse, dread building the closer I got.

And when I turned the corner, there she was, wearing nothing but one of my T-shirts and another messy bun, humming to herself and swaying her hips to a Taylor Swift song that was playing softly through the kitchen speakers. She was scrambling some eggs on the stove.

Bile rose in my throat. Fuck, I was going to throw up.

I must have made a noise, because she spun around, a bright, gorgeous smile on her face.

"Hi," she said shyly, waving her spatula in the air. "I made us breakfast."

For a split second, I was a kid again.

I was six years old, and I could smell the scent of scrambled eggs and bacon from my bedroom. It smelled so good, and my tummy was growling. As I walked into the kitchen, I heard the soft sound of my mommy crying.

"Mom?" I called out, my small voice trembling.

She turned to face me, and I froze. Her right eye was swollen and dark, a large black bruise marring her usually kind face. Her smile, the one she always tried to put on for me, was strained and filled with pain. She quickly wiped away her tears with the back of her hand, trying to compose herself.

"Hey, sweetheart," she said, her voice shaky but gentle. "Breakfast will be ready in just a minute."

"Mom, what happened?" I asked, my eyes wide with worry and confusion. I had seen her hurt before, and I hated it.

She forced another smile, but it didn't reach her eyes. "It's nothing, Camden. I just . . . I bumped into something."

I think she was lying to me.

Dan walked in and sat at the table without saying anything to either of us. Mom quickly made him a plate, trembling as she set it on the table in front of him. I watched as she stood by his chair, her hands clasped in front of her, her shoulders all droopy.

My stepdad never even said thank you.

I came back to the present, a cold sweat breaking out across my skin. My chest tightened, and the room seemed to close in around me.

"What are you doing?" I snapped, louder and harsher than I'd intended.

Anastasia froze, her smile faltering. "I . . . I just thought I'd make us some breakfast. You make it every morning, and I wanted to let you sleep in."

"Don't!" I shouted, my voice cracking. "Just . . . don't do that."

Her eyes widened, filling with tears, and I flinched. Fuck. Guilt washed over me like a tidal wave. "Anastasia, I'm sorry," I said quickly, stepping forward. "I didn't mean to yell."

She wiped at her eyes, her hands trembling. "I was just trying to help, Camden."

I took a deep breath, struggling to steady myself. "I know. It's not your fault. It's just . . . seeing you in the kitchen like that. I can't handle it."

She looked at me, confusion and hurt mingling in her eyes. "You can't handle me making eggs? I'm not that bad of a cook." She was trying to joke, but her voice was still pained.

How had I messed up this badly?

I swallowed hard, the words catching in my throat. The only person I'd told this to was a therapist.

But Anastasia deserved to know.

"My stepdad," I began haltingly, "was abusive. He turned my mom into a maid, forcing her to do everything for him, and he'd hurt her if she didn't. She'd cook breakfast with a black eye, trying to act like everything was normal. I'd find her on the floor as a little boy, black and blue and bleeding. My mom left him once, and when she couldn't find a job, she went back. She just served him her *entire* fucking life."

"She's still with him?" she asked softly, the tears still glistening in her eyes, but her gaze steady.

I glanced at the floor, shaking my head and trying to clear the fog of memories. "She died of cancer when I was fifteen . . . still serving him until the end," I added bitingly.

"Camden, I'm so sorry," she whispered. We hadn't even gotten into what had led her to the streets or what had happened to her family. And here she was trying to comfort me after I'd freaked out.

She was such a freaking sweetheart.

"It's a major trigger—seeing you doing things for me. It brings back all those feelings of helplessness and rage. I don't know how to handle it," I admitted, brushing some moisture out of my eyes that had no business being there.

She stared at me for a second and then rushed over and threw her arms around me, burying her face in my chest. I slowly put my arms around her, giving her a chance to back away if she was still mad that I'd snapped at her.

But she just burrowed closer.

A gut-wrenching moment later, I realized she was sobbing into my shirt.

"Baby girl, I'm so sorry," I murmured, absolutely hating myself. I wanted to reach into my chest and tear out my heart. "I'll never yell again. I swear."

She lifted her gaze, ferociously shaking her head. "It's not that. I just feel so sad for you. Picturing you as a little boy, seeing your mother like that. I wish I had known. I would have never—"

Fuck, she was sad for me.

I peppered her faces with kisses, my tongue dragging along her tears and snatching each one. "Don't cry. It's just something I need to fucking get over . . . but while I do . . . "

"I won't make any eggs," she said wryly, some of her spunk returning.

"I'm sorry," I said again, and she squeezed me for another long moment. The smell of eggs and bacon still filled the air, but now it was mixed with the scent of her shampoo, grounding me in the present.

Anastasia gently pushed away. "There's no need to apologize. I'm sure my trigger list is a mile long. We should probably go over it sometime," she joked.

I nodded seriously, obsessing over every detail of her face as I took her in.

"I'm going to go shower," I told her, feeling calmer, but still wanting to wash off the ghosts of the past that seemed to be lingering on my skin.

She nodded, a thoughtful look on her face. "Okay."

"Thanks for breakfast," I murmured as I walked out, unable to not at least thank her for her work.

Anastasia was throwing the eggs in the trash as I left the room.

I stood in the shower, my hands against the wall, the rain showerhead pelting my skin with scalding hot water. The blistering temperature was helping to block out the past . . . a little.

The shower door opened behind me, and I stiffened.

Anastasia hissed as she stepped into the water, reaching her arm around me to lower the temperature.

A second later, her arms were wrapped around my chest, and I groaned because her touch felt so good.

I don't know why I thought that a shower was what I needed. What I needed was Anastasia.

Always.

Her lips brushed against my skin and my head fell back. She didn't usually instigate things with us; she preferred for me to take the lead. I was fine with that, but this was good. So good.

I moaned as her hands caressed my chest, sliding down my abs and taking a moment to trace each one. She was a little obsessed with my abs. Which was fine.

I was obsessed with everything about her body.

"Turn around," she murmured, and without thinking, I did, immediately finding her beautiful eyes, her lashes beaded with water drops.

Fuck. I loved her. I lowered my head to kiss her, and then her gaze dropped . . . to my dick.

Whoops.

I'd forgotten about that surprise I'd been keeping under wraps—making excuses every time she wanted to do something for me after I'd made her ride my face for an hour. It was also why I'd shoved my dick in her mouth the other night at the arena—not that her mouth was a good place for a fresh tattoo, either, but sometimes it couldn't be helped.

"What happened to your dick?" She gasped in a horror-filled voice, her hands coming up to cover her mouth.

"Surprise . . . " I said bashfully, taking a step away to give her the full shot . . . now that the cat was out of the bag.

She was speechless. That was a good thing, right. Dickmatized, so to speak?

"Is that a tattoo?" she asked shakily once she'd recovered the ability to speak.

It was indeed a tattoo. That picture I'd taken of my blood-streaked dick right after I'd taken her virginity . . . I'd had my tattoo artist replicate it. All the drops and striations of where her blood had stained my dick were now immortalized forever on my skin.

Since that was the most life-changing night of my entire existence—and hers was the only pussy I was going to have for the rest of my life—it only seemed fitting.

"What exactly is all the 'red' stuff supposed to be?" she asked, unable to take her eyes off my cock.

It had risen to the occasion as soon as I'd heard the shower door open, so she was able to see every inch of it.

My tattoo artist had said it was the most unusual request he'd ever had in his twenty-year career.

I didn't doubt that.

"I'll show you," I said eagerly, reaching out the shower door and drying off my hand on the towel hanging on the hook before I grabbed my phone. I pulled up the picture I'd taken that night.

"See. It's almost an exact replica," I told her, showing her the shot.

She blinked slowly, her cheeks reddening as she glanced from the photo to my dick . . . and back again. "Is that—"

"My dick the night you gave me your virginity?" I asked cheekily. "Why yes, yes it is."

I understood it was a bold move, getting evidence of someone's virginity tattooed on your cock. But I was hoping she would think it was impressive. Rumor had it that Ari, Lincoln, and Walker's ladies had been very impressed with their own dick-orations . . . after the shock had worn off.

"I don't think I've ever been as surprised as I am right this very second," she whispered, finally dragging her gaze back up to my face.

"Is this a good surprise or a bad surprise?" I said carefully, feeling faintly nervous for the first time.

She was silent for a long moment before a small smile spread across her lips and she wrinkled her nose at me. "Does this—does this mean that when you said you loved me that night . . . that you actually meant it? Because this seems kind of like a big thing when you just *like* someone." Anastasia feigned, glancing behind me at my ass. "Or is this something you do, tattoo intimate parts of your body for girls you have sex with?"

I grinned then, too. I'd thought she was *never* going to bring that up, and I'd been desperate to say it again. I just hadn't wanted to scare her off.

But if the dick tattoo in her honor didn't do it . . . a little "I love you" wasn't going to, either.

"You love me," she whispered, her eyes growing suspiciously shiny again. My girl was so soft. Everything made her choke up. It was one of my favorite things about her—how deeply she felt. I was sure it was one of the reasons she was such an amazing dancer, because she felt the music and the movements so intensely.

"I love you," I rasped, my voice sounding choked, because I was feeling pretty emotional as well.

"I love you like nothing I could have ever dreamed. I love your laugh, and your smile, and the way you care. I love how you light up every room you walk into. I'm obsessed with your body and your talent, and even the way you breathe. Everything you are, is everything I want, little dancer. Forever."

She sobbed, wiping her eyes, a smile lighting up her entire face. "That's a really big word, Camden James," she sniffed. "A really big word."

"As big as a dick tattoo," I teased, because even when she was crying because she was happy, it still hurt my heart.

She pressed her face against my chest, her tears wetting my front as the rain continued to pelt my back.

"Do you have anything you want to say to me too?" I asked gently, knowing I was being a bit of a jerk for putting her on the spot.

But I couldn't not find out. I was desperate to hear her say it. Besides my mother, she was the only person I'd ever cared about loving me. The only person I'd ever wanted to in fact. It felt wrong to sit in this obsession by myself. I wanted her right along with me for the ride.

If she didn't love me, I knew I would eventually win her over.

But I was pretty sure that she already did.

She took a deep shuddering breath before she lifted her head, staring at me with her star-flecked eyes, a galaxy I wanted to live in forever and ever.

"I love you, Camden," she finally whispered, so much hope in those eyes too . . . but also a plea that was written there as clear as a handwritten note.

Don't hurt me, they were saying. Don't make me regret this.

Only time would prove it to her, so I didn't bother to address what she was silently saying.

"Thank fuck," I said instead, the most eloquent thing I could come up with at the moment because there was so much relief washing through me.

"Kiss me," she begged, and I immediately obeyed, my lips sliding against hers unhurriedly as I tried to take a mental snapshot of this moment.

I wished it was possible to get a tattoo on my heart. Because I'd find a way to tattoo this moment all over it.

Anastasia went to grab my dick, and I winced the second she made contact.

"Oh," she cried, ripping her hand away. "It's probably still healing, isn't it?"

"Yeah," I said, a bit chagrined. "That mind-altering blow job the other day was probably not the best thing for it, but fuck it was worth it."

I grinned at the way her whole body flushed at the reminder of the hottest night of my life.

My dick was definitely on board for celebrating this monumental moment, but I also didn't want to die because of gangrene and have it fall off afterward.

"A few more days, and I'm going to fuck you against this wall," I promised, lightly tapping the tile.

Her eyes gleamed at the prospect.

"As you know, though, there's definitely other things we can do," I growled.

She squeaked as I spun her around. "Put your hands on the wall." Like a good girl, she immediately obeyed.

Not that I could ever compare her to anyone else I'd been with—I'd blocked out everything about them. But she was so much better than any lover I'd had in the past.

I'd never had someone respond to me like she did. I'd been aware that I liked to be in charge during sex, and that it turned me on when my partner listened to me, but the way Anastasia answered to me . . .

It was like I'd been given every sexual gift I could have ever dreamed of.

She was perfect. If she ever left me—not that I would let her—I'd be celibate for the rest of my life because anyone else would just be a disappointment.

Sinking to my knees behind her, I hitched up her leg, opening up her sweet pussy to my mouth.

"Camden," she begged, and I grinned in anticipation right before I licked through her folds.

Our moans combined in the steamy air.

I sucked and licked, knowing exactly what tempo felt the best for her. Every cry that came out of her mouth was my road map to her pleasure.

Thrusting three fingers inside her tight hole, my tongue slid back to her asshole, rimming the edges of it as she trembled against the wall.

Anastasia was still unsure about ass play, but I couldn't wait to take her perfect ass. I'd probably die from happiness as soon as I slipped inside.

"Yes, yes, yes," she begged as I pumped my fingers faster, pushing one more digit inside her as I worked her clit with my thumb. If she could take my cock so beautifully, she could definitely take more of my fingers.

My dick ached from thinking of how perfect she'd felt as I'd pushed in.

A few more days and it was game on. It was going to be impossible to hold out for any longer than that.

I changed the angle of my fingers, reaching around with my other hand to press on a spot just above her pubic bone.

"What are you doing?" she asked breathlessly as I continued to work her over.

"Push down for me," I growled, pleasure shooting straight up my dick when she immediately listened.

She screamed as she came, her cunt clamping down on my fingers the same way that she'd choked my dick.

I groaned as she *squirted* all over my face, so much cum that she soaked my fucking skin. It was like taking the world's most delicious shower.

Growling, I went after *every* last drop. My fingers continued to pump into her, because I wanted her to come one more time.

"Camden, I can't," she cried.

"One more," I demanded. "Just give Daddy one more, baby girl."

The rightness of the word settling in my chest . . . and my dick.

Almost the second I'd said it, she was coming again. Pure nirvana on my tongue.

It was almost selfish of me, how many times I ate her out in a day.

But I'd never tasted anything so amazing in my entire life. I could live in my girl's pussy.

Fuck, my orgasm shot through me, hard and fierce . . . and it fucking hurt as I painted the shower floor with my cum.

Yep, definitely not healed yet.

But soon.

Reluctantly, I pulled away—giving her one last lick for good measure, even though it made my dick twitch—which I definitely did not need right now.

Anastasia slid her leg off my shoulder, and I caught her right before she collapsed.

"Wow," she said in a dazed, dreamy voice that she only gave me after I'd made her come hard . . . or spanked her. "I didn't know my body could do that."

I chuckled, licking my lips at the reminder, searching for any sign of her taste.

"I love you, pretty girl," I murmured a moment later, nuzzling into her soft skin.

"I love you too, Camden," she sighed.

And maybe the heart tattoo thing wasn't really necessary . . . I was pretty sure she'd already marked me—permanently—on the inside.

CHAPTER 28

ANASTASIA

The next week passed in perfect bliss. Not even practices with Dallon could get to me . . . until they did.

I hit the ground hard, a sharp pain shooting through my leg. Dallon's face was pale as he hovered over me. "Fuck. I'm sorry. You leapt too soon. It messed up the timing!"

I hadn't leapt too soon. He'd just fucked up. I couldn't call him out on that right now, though, because all I could focus on was the throbbing ache. My leg felt like it was on fire.

"It's not broken. It's not broken," I kept chanting in my head, like positive reinforcement would somehow change whatever Dallon had just done to me.

Panic was clawing at my insides, but I forced myself to stand, biting back the tears. I couldn't afford to break down now.

"Let's get you to Dr. Jenkins," Dallon said, the nicest he'd spoken to me since we'd started practicing. And he wasn't trying to feel me up—apparently, even *he* had a line he wouldn't cross.

The Company's doctor's office was located on-site. It had the same sterile smell and the cold, impersonal lights, though, that every other doctor's office I'd been to had. "Let's get you up here," Dr. Jenkins said. "You can leave, Dallon," he added dismissively. "Thank you for helping Ms. Lennox get to my office."

Dallon scowled, obviously wanting to stay. "Bye, Ana," he finally muttered as he trudged out of the office. My leg hurt so badly that I was able to ignore his continued, annoying use of my nickname.

Dr. Jenkins had excellent bedside manner. It also helped that he looked like Santa Claus with his white hair, rosy cheeks, button nose . . . and a belly that he attributed to his unfortunate love of Twinkies.

The doctor started his exam, poking and prodding at my leg for a few minutes before he had me go into another room with his assistant to take an X-ray.

The entire time my heart was pounding in my chest.

"It's not rebroken," he finally announced, looking up from the X-rays. "But you're not going to be able to walk on it one day if you keep up this pace." Dr. Jenkins frowned, studying the X-ray again. "Surely someone has told you this, Anastasia. After that injury, your leg just can't handle this kind of strain."

Another doctor *had* told me that . . . just a few months ago. I'd ignored that doctor, too.

I kept my voice steady, trying to keep the fact that I was lying from leaking through. "Doctors in the past have said as long as I could handle the pain, I could dance like normal."

He looked at me, his eyes filled with concern. "Are you sure that's what they said?" he finally asked gently.

My lip quivered, and I felt the tears threatening to spill over. "Please, don't say anything to anyone," I begged, my voice cracking. "I'll be fine. I will be more careful. I can't live without dance."

He frowned, clearly conflicted. "Anastasia, you need to start coming in for regular checkups. This isn't something to take lightly."

I nodded eagerly, desperate for him to drop it. "I will, I promise."

He sighed, rubbing his temples. "Alright, but if I see any signs that you're not following through, I'll have to report it. Understood?"

"Understood," I said, my voice barely a whisper.

Leaving the office, a crushing sense of defeat settled over me.

I managed to convince him to keep quiet for now, but how long would that last?

As I limped back to the studio, the pain in my leg was nothing compared to the dread gnawing at my insides.

I hadn't been exaggerating back there. If I couldn't dance . . . I didn't think I could live.

Every part of every day, I had been working on my dream.

What would happen if the only dream I'd ever had in life was dead?

Camden's face filled my head. How he'd looked when he said "I love you," and "forever."

He'd already admitted several times that part of what had drawn him to me was my talent. If that went away . . . I would really be a *nobody*.

And how long would his promise of "forever" last after that?

I had no other talents. I didn't have an education.

I was literally nothing without this place.

What was I going to do?

It was the stupidest thing imaginable, but my sore leg took me into an empty practice room.

I stared at myself in the mirror, taking in the haunted look in my eyes, but also taking in the fact that I had color in my cheeks now.

Camden had given me that.

No, I wasn't going to let my leg ruin everything. I wasn't going to give in. I could still dance. Everything would be fine. I couldn't lose dancing and I couldn't lose Camden.

So I *wouldn't*. It had to be as simple as that.

I limped over, turning on the music before I returned to my spot.

I lifted my hands above me . . . and then I slowly went en pointe.

In the dimly lit studio, I let the music wash over me, each beat a lifeline tethering me to my sanity. With every movement, I poured my heart and soul into the dance, letting the pain and frustration bubble to the surface. I surrendered myself to the rhythm. My movements began with a controlled grace, but as the music swelled, so did the turmoil within me.

My body moved with a fluidity born of years of practice, but tonight, it was different. Tonight, every step was a battle, a desperate struggle to keep the darkness at bay. But still, I danced on, my movements growing more frantic with each passing moment.

The tears blurred my vision as I twirled and spun, the agony of my shattered dreams threatening to consume me whole. I danced. And then I danced some more.

I pushed my body beyond its limits, my muscles protesting with every twist and turn. My arms reached out as if grasping for something just out of reach, while my legs propelled me across the floor, every step like a dagger to my useless leg.

The music crescendoed, and I threw myself into a series of intricate movements, ones I shouldn't have been doing on my best day with the state of my leg. Sweat dripped down my brow, mingling with the tears that streaked my cheeks.

And still, I pressed on.

Until I took a step, and my leg couldn't hold me up.

It buckled, and I collapsed.

My sweat and tears stuck me to the floor as I fell in a heap. Everything was too much. The pain, the grief, the fear.

I was drowning. The edges of my vision blurring from exhaustion. Maybe they'd just find me here in the morning.

I could picture them dancing around me, not bothering to call the police or move my body because I was nothing anymore.

Nothing.

There was the slide of footsteps nearby, and I wearily blinked my eyes, staring in the direction of the door listlessly.

My eyes opened wider when I saw who was standing there.

Camden.

Shame coated my throat, the taste of it bitter and disgusting. Embarrassment lit up my insides. This perfect creature was seeing me at my very worst.

I didn't move, though. I just lay there as we locked eyes. Maybe this was it. Maybe I'd lost my last will.

Or maybe I wanted someone to see me. To see how much I hurt. How much I burned. How much every fucking day zapped my will to keep going.

"Baby girl," he breathed, and there was an ache in his voice, like the sight of my pain was hurting him, too.

That ache burrowed its way inside me, like roots growing beneath a plant.

He walked toward me slowly, like he was approaching a dying animal who was taking its last breaths. He squatted down next to me, brushing his fingers softly against my cheek.

"Oh, baby." His touch warmed me, but I still didn't move.

And I didn't move when he slid his arms around me and pulled me into his chest, lifting me up like I weighed nothing.

I wasn't sure if I was conscious or not. Everything felt like a dream, the world around me a hazy blur of pain and exhaustion. But through the fog, his strong arms lifted me gently off the cold studio floor, cradling me like I was infinitely precious.

I'd never had anyone hold me before but him. Maybe my mother had held me as a baby, but with what I knew of her, I kind of assumed she'd just thrown me into a crib until I stopped crying.

I didn't have it in me to move, or ask him where he was taking me.

I just surrendered, allowed myself to be carried away, the rhythmic sway of Camden's steps lulling me into a state of . . . peace.

The complete opposite of the frenzy I'd been in before.

The night air brushed against my skin, cool and soothing, as we made our way to his truck.

I was still in a daze as he pulled open the door and set me down softly on the seat. He pulled the seatbelt across my chest, and I blinked slowly at him.

Safety. That's what I was feeling. It was washing across my skin, a golden light filling my insides, wiping away the anxiety that had been there the whole afternoon.

"Thank you," I whispered to him.

He smoothed my sweaty, matted hair out of my face.

"Forever," he answered, and I closed my eyes at that word, allowing a tear to slip down my face.

Because I didn't know if that word was real.

I was a mess the next day at dance. Camden had put me right to bed after he'd taken me home, and I'd slept right up until it was time to leave for class again.

He'd tried to cajole me into telling him what was wrong . . . but I'd told him we would talk later. A cop-out if there ever was one.

It had taken five extra-strength Advil for me to be in this room, holding on to the barre as I dipped into a plié.

My leg was so sore. I needed a day off. I probably needed a month off, actually. This was the worst my leg had been in a long time.

"Anastasia," Madame Leclerc's voice cut through the noise of the class. I eyed the doorway, dread pulsing through me as I saw her standing there, her red lips pressed into a severe frown. It never seemed to be a good thing when she needed to talk to me.

The instructor nodded her head at me, and I walked across the room, trying to look elegant and graceful as I did so because Madame Leclerc cared about things like that.

She still eyed me disdainfully the entire way.

"Yes, Madame?" I said, after I'd stepped out into the hallway and closed the door behind me. It wasn't farfetched to think that whatever she wanted to say was not something I wanted the whole class to hear.

"The Company is raising rates," she began, her French accent clipped and cold. "The economy is not what it was and prices have gone up on everything. This means costumes, tuition . . . everything will be going up."

I took a deep breath, my heart sinking. It was already ridiculously expensive to attend here. Only the senior dancers were paid livable allowances for their performances, and for whatever reason, I hadn't been brought up yet.

What I was paid for performing, cleaning, and bussing tables, had barely paid for everything.

Hence, why I had been living in a shelter.

I didn't have a job anymore.

I took a deep breath, thinking of the money that Michael was also expecting in a few weeks.

What was I going to do?

The showcase. I was dancing with a senior dancer—and not just any senior dancer—the male lead for the entire Company. Regardless of how I'd gotten the role, the performance was still happening.

Shouldn't I be paid like a senior dancer then?

I gulped, trying to dig up some bravery. Madame Leclerc had always terrified me. I kept hoping she would be old enough that she'd want to retire, and someone new would come in who would see me as the performer that I was.

"I'm dancing with Dallon in the showcase," I began softly. "I . . . I think that should qualify me for an additional salary for the performance."

Her face curled up in a sneer, but she didn't say anything for a moment. Probably because I had a fair point. Her lips pursed again, though, and I stiffened, preparing myself for whatever misery she was about to throw my way.

"I'm not entirely convinced your performance is even going to take place, Anastasia," she said in a haughty voice. "The reports from Dallon have not been exemplary."

That didn't surprise me at all. It's not like he was going to report that his own poor performance was the thing holding us back. It was much easier to blame the junior dancer that Madame already despised.

"I'm perfectly confident about my performance," I responded, lifting my chin and holding eye contact with her.

It was the only time I'd seen her . . . squirm.

"How about this, Ms. Lennox, if you are able to properly perform *Giselle*, I will promote you. But your performance has to meet *my* standards." She peered down her nose at me. "And I think we both know that you have not met those standards even once yet."

I tried to be a glass half-full kind of person. It was kind of a necessity with what I dealt with on a daily basis—at least until I'd met Camden.

But it seemed to me what she was saying was that no matter what I did at the showcase, there was no hope.

I was fucked, so to speak.

I needed to find a job.

The rest of the day passed in a blur. I even went through the motions during my practice with Dallon. Surprisingly, he didn't comment on it, probably because he'd almost broken my leg yesterday.

At least the day was done. I sank onto the bench in the locker room, rocking my head back against the locker. I was so tired. I could probably fall asleep right there. I sat there for several minutes until my phone buzzed.

Camden was here.

For the first time since we'd met—I was kind of dreading seeing him.

I gathered up my bag and walked slowly outside, taking a deep breath when I saw him standing outside his truck. Some dancers were gathered in groups, and they kept shooting him looks, giggling as they talked about how hot he was.

My hackles immediately rose when I passed one group who were discussing all the ways they wanted him to fuck them.

Mine, I wanted to scream. *He has a freaking dick tattoo in my honor*!

I ran a hand down my face. Seriously, I was falling apart.

"Hi, baby girl," Camden said, meeting me halfway, like he couldn't bear to wait for me to get all the way to him.

"Hi," I answered, and he frowned at the flatness in my voice.

"Everything okay?" He glared at everyone around us like they were responsible for my pissy attitude.

"Just . . . " My shoulders drooped. "I got some bad news today. And now, I really have to find a job. Immediately."

He was quiet as he got me into the truck and then walked around to get in.

"What was the bad news?" he asked after we'd started driving.

I glanced at him. He looked so calm and beautiful. Camden was just as busy as me. I knew he'd had weights today and two team meetings, and yet he still was put together, completely unflappable.

"Anastasia?" he pressed when I hadn't said anything because I was staring at him.

"Madame Leclerc—who's always hated me—she informed me that the Company is raising prices on everything, but not raising salaries for the junior dancers. I told her I thought I should get a raise—be paid something I could actually live on—since I'm dancing with a principal for the showcase. She basically told me it would only happen if she was pleased with my performance . . . and then she followed that up with telling me she hasn't been pleased with *anything* I'd done so far."

"She sounds like a bitch," Camden remarked.

"Unfortunately, bitch or not, she's one of the most famous former prima ballerinas in the United States. People flock to our Company to train with her. It just hasn't worked out for me," I whispered, staring out the window at the city passing by. "But it's a little hard to find a job when, literally, your only training is to dance, and you can only work at night." I laughed to myself. "Actually . . . I think I'm qualified to be a stripper, so I guess there's that."

There was a cracking sound and my gaze shot to Camden, only to see that he looked vaguely panicked . . . and he was gripping the steering wheel really tightly.

"Camden?" I asked cautiously.

"I thought we'd discussed not talking about stripping anymore?" he said roughly.

Except, I wasn't sure that I was actually joking.

"I can cover anything you need, Anastasia. It's not a problem."

I frowned. "Why would you do that?"

Camden glanced over at me, his eyebrows raised. "Because that's what couples do when they're in a relationship, baby girl—they help each other."

You owe me.

You're using me.

Michael and his parents' words echoed in my head.

No, that was *not* happening.

"You're not paying for anything else, Camden," I snapped after a moment, an edge of hysteria in my voice. "You've already done enough. I'm literally sleeping in your house rent-free, eating your food—that you cook for me, by the way, going to fancy performances, and sleeping on satin sheets. You're not giving me anything else!"

An awkward silence descended over us.

"What would you like to do then?" Camden said stiffly.

"I'm going to get a job."

Camden pulled into the parking garage and turned the truck off. "Anastasia, you were almost passed out when I found you last night. The last thing you need is to add more to your plate. What you need is rest."

"Don't tell me what I need, Camden." My voice was bitter and mean, and I hated it.

This was it, this was when he would be done with me. Who wanted an insecure, stubborn street rat when they could have anyone else? It seemed we'd been uncovering each other's triggers really well over the last few days.

Except, mine was in direct opposition to his. He wanted to take care of me . . . and I was *terrified* to let him do it.

The silence continued as he opened up my door and we went into the penthouse, and as we sat through an awkward dinner—because, of course, my perfect boyfriend had delicious baked ziti ready as soon as we got through the door.

I had taken my last bite and had just gotten up to put my plate in the sink when he pounced, pulling me into his lap, not caring as my plate clattered on the table, spilling flecks of tomato sauce all over. I squeaked in surprise, staring at the mess.

"Are you paying attention, baby girl?" he growled.

"It's kind of hard not to when I'm sitting in your lap," I drawled.

His eyes flashed, and I knew he was thinking about the last time I'd been a brat.

"I love you, Anastasia," he said sweetly, gentling his voice. "It would be my privilege to help you, to take care of you, to be there by your side as you work toward your dreams."

He didn't understand. He could say that now, but it would change. Every fucking time I'd depended on someone in my life—it had fallen apart.

"And how do I help *you*, Camden? If I'm not allowed to cook, and I'm certainly not allowed to clean. What am I bringing to the table? What am I contributing to the relationship? If it's about sex, I'm sure there's a million women better at it than me. You can get another *hole*."

I regretted the words as soon as they came out of my mouth. It physically hurt to think about him with another person.

"Don't talk about yourself like that," Camden spat hotly.

Feeling like I was about to burst into tears, I took his beautiful face in both of my hands. He looked so miserable right now.

"What if you do all that, and you decide I'm not worth it? What if you think I'm someone I'm not? What if you wake up one day, and you realize that I'm . . . nothing? I'm nobody." My lips were quivering, because I'd realized that I wouldn't survive.

I wouldn't survive him deciding he didn't want me anymore.

He'd ruined me.

Just like he'd threatened.

I'd survived losing everything else in my life . . . but I couldn't survive losing him.

"It will never happen," he swore fiercely.

I kissed his lips softly and laid my head on his chest, listening to the steady beat of his heart.

If only I could believe him . . .

CHAPTER 29

ANASTASIA

"They can't be serious," snarled Alena, staring at the new announcement on the Company's bulletin board.

When Madame Leclerc had said prices were rising, she hadn't been exaggerating.

This was . . . this was insane.

I'd never heard Alena complain about money before, so for her to be making note about it—I knew it was ridiculous on every level.

"That old hag. It's like she wants all of us to quit," Alena continued scowling at the board with her hands fisted at her sides, like if she stared hard enough, the figures on the paper would magically change.

Finally, she sighed and stepped away, shaking her head before she glanced at me. "Well, at least you won't have to worry about it. Not with that fancy-pants hockey player you're dating."

I shifted uncomfortably. "It's not like that," I quickly said. "I would never ask him to pay for me."

She raised an eyebrow, like she thought I was crazy. "Why the hell not? If I got myself a rich guy, I'd be getting everything I could out of him."

And that's why you aren't with a rich guy, I thought to myself. *They can probably sense you a mile away and go running . . .*

I realized she was waiting for some kind of answer, so I made a noncommittal humming sound—which strangely seemed to work for her.

"So what are you going to do to pay for it?" she asked.

I sighed.

It was the question for the ages at the moment. Between the money I needed to pay Michael . . . and now this . . . it was all I could think about.

"I'm not sure what I can do. I can dance. That's it. Our schedule doesn't allow us to really do anything else." The desperation I'd felt last night was inching up my throat just talking about it again.

Alena glanced up and down the hallway, like she was checking to make sure we were alone, and then she leaned in close. "I know a job that would work. It pays really well, too. I'm doing it until I make the senior company . . . and even then it will be hard to let it go. The money's too good."

I eyed her curiously. "What kind of job is it?"

"A Gentlemen's Club," she said, a challenge in her voice like she expected me to judge her . . . or run away screaming because she thought I was such a goody-two-shoes.

"You . . . strip?" I asked hesitantly.

She rolled her eyes. "I *dance*. It's not so different from what we do here, ya know? Just with a little . . . less clothes. And if you remember that costume we wore last fall . . . it covers about the same amount."

I remembered that costume. She'd had a point. I'd felt like I was dancing naked on stage the entire time. None of us had understood what Madame Leclerc had been thinking.

"I made two thousand dollars last night in tips alone," Alena said proudly, wiggling her eyebrows up and down.

My mouth dropped. "Are you . . . are you serious?"

She nodded with a smirk. "I could get you a job, you know. They'd eat you up. You have that whole angelic thing going on."

I'd mentioned it to Camden because I had thought about it before. I thought about the easy money. How fast I could give Michael the money he wanted.

I couldn't do it, though.

I couldn't become a cliché. My time to strip would have been when I was homeless. But not now.

Where I'd come from, every girl either died of an overdose, got pregnant, or started stripping.

There wasn't really an in-between.

My mother had done the first two.

I wasn't going to do the last.

I also hadn't spent years being upset and sick about Michael's pictures and videos of me, just to throw it all to hell and have a bunch of men see *all* of my body anyway.

"Do they have any other jobs there?" I asked. I guess it was stupid of me, but I'd always just stayed away from those clubs, determined not to give in. It made sense that there would be other jobs there that could actually fit with my schedule.

And not make Camden upset.

"They have waitressing," Alena said with a shrug, like she didn't find that to be a very interesting option.

"Can you get me an interview for that?" I asked.

"Yeah," she said, cocking her head and studying me. "Are you sure, though, that you don't want to try and dance? You won't make nearly as much money."

I nodded. "I'll save that for the experts," I told her.

She grinned and swung her hair around, a mimicry of one of her moves I was sure. "I consider myself as such."

I laughed nervously, smoothing my own hair back into its bun. "When do you think I can interview?" I asked, feeling anxious to start making money—and to get it over with.

"Meet me after class. I happen to have a shift tonight."

"Great," I said nervously, and she winked at me as she walked away.

Camden

My phone buzzed in my pocket while I was spotting for Ari during weights.

I let go immediately to check and make sure it wasn't Anastasia.

"Fuck," Ari griped as the weight bar sunk to his chest.

"Whoops," I said lightly. But I left him there for a second so I could check my text.

> Anastasia: I have a job interview after class today, so I don't need a ride.

I frowned, waiting for another text to come in, some more information.

"A little help over here," Ari grunted. I glanced at him, annoyed, only to see that the weights were still stuck to his chest.

I'd better help with that.

I quickly heaved the bar up and set it on the rack.

"You trying to kill me, Hero? So the more handsome, more talented defenseman is out of the picture?" Ari asked, rubbing his chest with an indignant look on his face.

I rolled my eyes, glancing at my phone again when it buzzed.

But it was just some spam text advertising erectile dysfunction cream. I blinked at that. They had a cream for that?

"Something you want to tell us, Grandpappy?" Logan asked cheekily, reading my text over my shoulder.

I scowled at him. "Did you sign me up for this?"

He grinned unrepentantly and shrugged. "I figured you would appreciate it. You're getting to that time in your life."

"I hate you," I snarled. "I'm doing just *fine* in that department, thank you very little."

"'Just fine'?" Ari said, clicking his tongue. "Not sure if that's good enough. Especially if you want to keep your little ballerina."

I picked up the weights and promptly dropped them.

He huffed as he caught them just in time. "Daniels, he's trying to kill me. Help."

Lincoln, for his part, ignored all of us as he continued doing his weighted lunges.

I typed out a text to Anastasia.

Me: Where's the place? I can take you there. We can celebrate once you get the job :)

There were three text bubbles for a solid minute before she finally texted back.

Anastasia: I have a ride. Thank you, though. XO.

Alright . . . that wasn't suspicious at all.

I glanced at the clock. She'd be out of class in an hour.

"You going to help me with this, or are you just going to stand there contemplating your existence?" Ari snarked.

"Do you want me to drop another weight on you?" I drawled absent-mindedly as I went over where Anastasia could be going tonight that she didn't want me to know about.

"Just make sure not to hurt his face. We'd never hear the end of it," Disney commented as he started jump-roping.

"Or his dick," Lincoln added, finally joining the conversation. "That would probably be even worse."

Ari looked vaguely sick at that comment. "We'd better switch, Hero. Just in case you get some ideas."

I huffed, but switched spots with him, so I could lift weights and think about Anastasia in peace.

The next hour ticked by painfully slow. I was tempted to go wait outside of the ballet studio, but I eventually figured I would just use the tracker to follow her to wherever she went.

"See you guys later," I said finally, not really paying attention to whatever they said in return.

She was on the move.

Anastasia's job interview was at a strip club.

I knew that fucking club. Nick and Matty, two players on the team, went there at least once a week.

Fucking hell.

I didn't want my girl anywhere near that place. All of those men seeing her? I didn't want them seeing her fully dressed . . . let alone with no clothes on.

What was she thinking?

I'D THOUGHT SHE'D BEEN JOKING THE OTHER NIGHT.

Okay . . . what to do.

Besides standing outside and waiting for her . . . something I was already doing . . .

I knew there was a lot of security inside, Matty had told us about being thrown out one night after he'd drank too much—so that ruled out going in and dragging her out.

I dialed the number for the club to see if I could get any information . . . or tell the employees they'd better not hire her or there would be hell to pay.

"Dolly Pockets," a woman answered. She'd been smoking fifteen packs a day for the last forty years judging by the sound of her gravel-filled voice.

"Yes, hi. Can I speak to your manager," I demanded in what I hoped was a very nonthreatening and charming voice.

The woman had the nerve to snort at me. "You don't think we get these calls all the time from jealous boyfriends? Fuck off, asswipe," she snapped, hanging up on me.

I frowned. That was fair. But I liked to differentiate myself from these so-called boyfriends. I was Anastasia's future *husband,* after all.

And I wasn't just doing it because I was jealous. It was because I would literally murder anyone who saw her dancing around a pole. Double murder if they saw a nipple.

Fuck.

I paced back and forth outside the club.

I waited.

And waited some more.

Had they fucking started her right away? It was 7 p.m. for fuck's sake. There were like ten other cars in the parking lot. Surely they weren't that desperate for dancers.

I pulled out my phone and made a frantic text. The guys would tell me if I was being too crazy.

Me: If one wanted to make a large fire, what would one do?

Ari: What's wrong with you?

Linc: Yeah, why are you talking like that?

Me: I'm not talking like anything.

Walker: You're talking like you're going to burn something down.

Me: What?

Linc: He's obviously going to burn something down.

Ari: The question is what?

Ari: Hey look at us, Golden Boy, finishing each other's sentences like true besties.

Walker: I finish sentences all the time.

Ari: Disney, you simp.

Me: This is the most helpful group I've ever been a part of. AND YES, I AM BEING SARCASTIC.

Walker: You literally asked us if we knew anything about burning something down. We didn't know you wanted a real answer.

Ari: Ahh, Disney, you're now talking in the royal "we" for the group.

Linc: That was very smart of you, Lancaster.

Ari: I know.

Me: I was just thinking that the circle of trust would know a little something about burning down a building.

Ari: What circle of trust?

Walker: Yeah, that was very un-circle of trust of you.

I huffed and then my phone was ringing.

It was Lincoln.

"Hello?" I asked, going for casual, even though Lincoln made me nervous.

"What are you burning down?"

"I'm not burning down anything. It was simply a research question—an innocent one—people ask their friends about things like this all the time."

There was a long, exaggerated silence, and if this had been a text conversation, there would definitely have been a " . . . " involved.

"If I were to burn down a building . . . "

"Hypothetically . . . " I interjected.

He snorted. "If I were to burn down a building, *hypothetically*, I'd want to target areas where a fire could take hold easily. Maybe near the entrances or exits, where the airflow is strong, or in the storage room where there might be flammable materials. I'd make sure that all the cameras in the area were disabled first. I'd wear a disguise when I went to the building and start the fire from inside rather than outside. Hypothetically, though, I would hire someone to burn it down using a burner phone that was untraceable so that it could never be linked back to me."

I blinked slowly, even though he couldn't see me.

Because hypothetically . . . hiring someone was a lot better idea than doing it myself.

But also, he sounded like he'd put a lot of thought into that, and that was definitely something to think about.

"Do you . . . *hypothetically* need help with any of that?" Lincoln asked, so casually you'd almost think the golden god really *was* speaking hypothetically.

Before I could say anything, I got a text from him with a phone number. "Call that phone number . . . on one of those prepaid phones from the grocery store. Tell him what you need. You'll be good to go," Lincoln said before he hung up.

Alright then . . . that sounded like encouragement. But it didn't solve the immediate problem of getting her out of there tonight.

Just when I was going to go barging in, she came out the side door, arms crossed in front of herself defensively as she stepped outside.

There was no way she hadn't gotten that job. If I was a club owner, I'd be basing my entire show off her perfection, even if I hadn't seen her dance.

And then when you saw her dance . . .

Well, I imagine whoever had interviewed her was probably seeing gold dollar signs floating in the air around her.

She took a few steps before stopping, her body going rigid as she slowly turned and saw me.

Gotcha.

Anastasia

I sensed him almost the second I'd walked out of that dark, seedy club.

Camden.

He was somehow here.

But . . . I actually wasn't that surprised.

I locked eyes with him.

He looked like a dark god, his eyes glittering as he leaned against a shiny black motorcycle in the shadows of the building—a motorcycle I didn't even know he owned.

"Anastasia," he said calmly, but it was like the calm before a storm. The final breath you took before the gun went off and the race began. "Come here."

A frantic energy filled me, a need to explain . . . it wasn't what it looked like, not really.

But I couldn't seem to form words as I trudged toward him, my mouth dry like it was filled with cotton.

His silence was somehow more intense than if he had yelled. As soon as I'd gotten to the bike, he had a matte-black helmet on my head and was buckling it tightly.

A second later, I was astride the bike.

"Hold on," he growled as he slipped in front of me, pulling my arms around him so that my hands were wrapped around his middle. Camden gunned the engine, and we sped off into the night.

It was freaking cold for a motorcycle ride. Not as cold of a night as it had been last week, but the icy wind still seemed to be taking chunks out of my face as we raced down the streets.

The ride seemed to last forever, and every mile that passed, the anticipation grew. Until I was trembling more from that than the cold whipping at my skin.

At last we pulled into the building. Camden still didn't say anything as he lifted me off the bike and led me toward the elevator.

"Camden—" I began once we'd gotten inside the doors.

"I suggest you don't say anything right now, *little dancer*," he murmured in the velvety tone that I'd learned was his most dangerous tone of all.

"I just wanted to explain that I wasn't—"

Before I could get out another word, I was against the mirrored glass of the elevator, my cheek pressed against the cool wall. Camden crowded me, his lips brushing against my ear as he liked to do when he really wanted me to pay attention.

"You went somewhere unsafe tonight. You tried to hide it from me. You put yourself in a situation where other men could think they could have you. You are in so much fucking trouble, Anastasia."

"I'm sorry," I squeaked as the doors opened into the penthouse.

"Tonight, sorry's not good enough."

He pulled me by my hand into the darkened living room before abruptly letting me go and sitting in one of the tufted armchairs.

"You wanted to dance tonight, little dancer. So dance." He pressed a button on his phone, and a second later, "Guilty as Sin" was playing from the built-in speakers.

I stood there awkwardly because, technically, I hadn't gone there to dance.

"Now," he said roughly, and I jumped at the intensity of his tone.

Fine, I could play along. I *had* really messed up. If a dance was what he wanted—a dance I could give him.

I closed my eyes and let the rhythm take over, moving through me, guiding me. I finally opened them and met Camden's stare across the room, his gaze intense, unblinking. I could see the heat in his eyes, the way they followed every movement I made.

I took a step forward, rolling my hips to the beat, my hands trailing down my sides. His lips parted slightly, and the muscle in his jaw tensed.

I turned slowly, arching my back, letting my hair fall over one shoulder as I moved. Every step, every sway of my hips was deliberate, meant for him. I could feel his eyes on me, burning with a mix of lust and admiration. It was intoxicating to know I had his full attention.

"Anastasia," he murmured, his voice low and rough, barely audible over the music.

I didn't respond with words, just with my body. I spun around, the music lighting up my veins, my movements fluid and sensual. I could see the way his hands gripped the armrests, his knuckles white. He was trying to control himself, but I could see the struggle in his eyes.

As the chorus hit, I dropped to my knees, crawling toward him, my eyes never leaving his. His breath hitched, and I could see the tension in his body, the way he leaned forward, unable to stay still. I reached him, my hands sliding up his legs, feeling the heat of his skin through the fabric of his jeans.

He exhaled sharply, his eyes dark with desire. "Anastasia," he said again, his voice strained.

I stood up slowly, my body brushing against his, and turned around, pressing my back against his chest. His hands came up, almost instinctively, to rest on my hips, his touch sending sparks through me. I leaned back into him, feeling the solid strength of his body against mine.

The music slowed, and I turned to face him, straddling his lap. His eyes were locked on mine, filled with a mix of need and awe. I could feel his heartbeat against my own, a rapid, shared rhythm. I leaned in, my lips brushing his ear.

"Did you like it, Daddy?" I whispered then, my breath hot against his skin.

There was a pause, and his lips moved toward mine. He was finally going to give me what I wanted—what I needed . . .

A second later, I was across his lap, my ass in the air.

Thwack.

"What do I want you to say, baby girl?" he growled as his hand left my ass cheek.

"What?" I groaned, shocked and aroused by what had just happened.

Thwack.

"You know the words."

Thwack.

I blinked, trying to clear my clouded mind. Oh . . . I did know.

"Brats get spanked," I cried out quickly as soon as the words had crossed my mind.

"Good girl."

A second later, I was ripped off his lap. He was moving me easily, like I was nothing but a rag doll.

"Now that you've danced, we're going to move to the second part of the evening you had planned tonight," he rasped darkly. "Where you strip."

Before I could wrap my mind around what was happening, or what had *already* happened, the leggings and blouse I was wearing were ripped off, leaving me in nothing but my bra and underwear. Camden snapped the side of my thong, and I flinched at the pop of pain.

"It makes me crazy to think that anyone else would get to see this," he growled. "It's *mine*." Yanking me toward him, I followed, like I wasn't in control of my body anymore. He arched me backward and bent forward, trailing his tongue over my underwear, pressing into my core and growling as he breathed me. The wet spot on my thong grew as his tongue pressed into my clit through the fabric.

"Mine," he growled again before sliding his tongue and mouth higher, around my belly button and the rest of my abdomen until he was leisurely licking across the globes of my breast.

My breath was coming out in gasps. My chest heaving against his lips.

Pop.

Camden ripped open my bra, and my breasts spilled out. He buried his face in between them, kissing and biting and licking until I was a writhing hopeless mess.

"I warned you, Anastasia," he said, lightly biting my nipple and making me gasp. "I told you who you belonged to. But you don't seem to have gotten it yet. I. Don't. Share."

"I wasn't . . . " I half-heartedly tried to tell him one more time, but then his hand was sliding between my legs, his fingers pushing under the thong and into me. My body buckled forward—my whole being on sensory overload.

"You're going to scream, you're going to come . . . and you might even pass out. And then maybe my little brat will finally learn her lesson."

"Mmmh," I moaned as three of his fingers plunged in and out of me.

He abruptly pulled out. "On your knees," he ordered roughly.

"What?"

"I'm too pent up; I don't want to hurt you. You're going to help me take the edge off before I take you," he growled as he pushed me to the floor. I stared up at him desperately, and for a brief moment, his intensity broke, and I could feel his love for me pouring out of him and coating my skin.

He blinked, and his dark intensity was back. Tangling my hair in his fist, he pulled my head back as his other hand expertly undid his jeans and pulled out his enormous, rigid cock.

My mouth watered for it and he shook his head, smirking as he brushed the head of his swollen dick against my lips. "You want my cock, don't you, my little brat? It makes you wet to swallow my cum."

I moaned in agreement, and he shook his head at me, a smug grin stretched across his beautiful face.

"Well, this isn't for you this time. This is *just* for me." He thrust his dick deep into my throat until I gagged. Using the hand in my hair to keep me still, he fucked my mouth roughly, his delicious pants filling the room.

"You can take more," he said sternly, pushing down my throat until I couldn't breathe. My eyes were watering as his thrusts somehow grew faster. I couldn't help but whimper around his cock, and I was rewarded with his loud moan as he pulled out, his hot cum spraying my chest and the bottom of my chin.

He hadn't even let me taste him.

Camden's chest was heaving, his cock still hard and angry-looking, like he hadn't actually come at all.

"You're still hard," I gasped, wiping at my face.

"I'm always hard nowadays," he said, sounding angry about it. "I could fuck you every second of every day and *still* not get enough of you."

Warmth shot through me at his admission, but before I could think too much on it, Camden had flipped me around and was pushing me down to the ground on all fours.

"Lift up," he growled, tapping my injured leg. A second later he'd slid a soft blanket under it. "You *will* tell me if this is too much."

"Yes, sir," I whispered, and then my thong was ripped, the cold air brushing against my pussy as he lined up his dick and lunged forward until his entire length was sheathed inside me.

I gasped at the fullness, falling to my forearms, my back arched, as he fucked me fast and hard in a brutal pace.

Thwack!

His hand spanked my ass, and I came around his cock, a cry ripping from my lips.

"That's one," he growled, and my eyes widened because I wasn't sure if he was talking about spanks or orgasms.

He kept going, his dick having some kind of superpower because his thrusts never let up, his fingers slipping over my clit at intervals, forcing orgasms when I wasn't coming fast enough for his liking.

Camden spanked me at random, no rhyme or rhythm, catching me off guard every time.

And I came relentlessly. So often that I lost track, that time lost all meaning.

I was nothing but sensation and pleasure, sparks of pain only adding to the experience. The world around me grew blurry and discolored, my cries changing into hoarse gasps as I lost my voice.

And still he fucked me, in every position imagineable. Until my vision darkened, and eventually I lost consciousness.

I woke to him gathering me up in his arms, cradling me against his body as he walked down the hall. I could feel his cum inside of me, sliding down my thighs as we moved. His voice was gentle and soothing as he laid me down on the bed. I briefly passed out again, only coming back when he soothed my aching pussy with a warm washcloth.

"I love you, baby girl," he murmured . . . and then I was out again, slipping into a blissful, deep, dreamless sleep.

I woke up the next morning feeling like I had a hangover. The room felt too bright, my head felt dizzy and out of sorts, and my body was sore . . . especially between my legs.

It was the good kind of pain, though, like after a workout, and something was settled in my chest, something that had felt broken before and I hadn't even realized it.

Rolling over, I wasn't surprised at all that Camden was dressed, laying next to me, his head propped up on his arm as he watched me.

"I kind of feel like you're my stalker at this point," I croaked, and he grinned unrepentantly.

"I'm pretty sure I am."

I took him in, still as amazed as I was the first day I saw him that I was in this beautiful man's presence. I wasn't sure that even time would be able to make that fade. He was just too perfect, all my favorite features in one *sensational* package.

"How are you feeling?" he asked, his gaze roaming over me like he could see under my skin.

"Sore," I admitted, "And I feel like I've been crying for hours or something . . . but I feel good."

"If I was too rough—" he began.

I reached out and grabbed his shirt, shutting him up. "I loved it," I told him honestly. "I'll never forget it . . . I want . . . I want more."

His eyes glimmered. "I have no doubt that your inner brat will rear her head and that will happen again." I wrinkled my nose in response, and he huffed. "I bet you're already thinking of the next thing you can do to drive me crazy."

I sobered at the reminder. "I wasn't going there to apply to be a dancer," I told him, finally getting the words out that he wouldn't let me last night. "I was just going to waitress. They have hours that fit into my schedule, and the pay's really good." Even as the words came out, I felt like I was convincing myself just as much as him. I *really* didn't want to work there. Every inch of the place had been smoke-filled and dark, and the man I had interviewed with had leered at me and said inappropriate things the entire time. I doubted I could last even a week there.

"I can't handle you working there, in any capacity," Camden told me fiercely, last night's madness flickering in his gaze. "I'll go insane. I'll have to camp out there, gouge out the eyes of anyone inside. Do you know how crazy I would get if someone tried to grab you like they do all the time in those sorts of places?" He shook his head. "I would have to kill them."

I scoffed at his ridiculousness—but he didn't laugh.

He stared at me for a moment before his chin stiffened, and a hard glint came to his eyes. "I need you to explain why it's so important that you get a job, why you won't let me take care of you. It's not like you aren't working hard every single fucking day. Too hard in fact. Nothing about you is lazy, or a user. Nothing!"

He reached out and pushed a piece of hair out of my face. "So tell me why you won't let me help you. Why you won't let me take care of you . . . something I'm desperate to do."

My gaze dropped, and I stared at the soft sheets, tracing them lightly with the tips of my fingers. It was hard for me to talk about this. I never had—with anyone.

"For as long as I can remember," I began haltingly, "the men in my life have felt like they were owed something. Like anything they did to provide for me . . . or my mother went on an invisible list that they kept careful records on. My earliest memory is of my mother and father arguing, my father screaming at her that she *owed* him for the work he put in every week. Like taking care of me wasn't enough for him."

I sighed, my hand flattening on the sheets as I took a deep breath. "She left soon after that. She left me. And then I was the one who owed my dad something."

I finally glanced up at his face, instead of the pity I thought for sure he would have, there was just patience . . . and understanding, like everything was becoming clearer to him.

"It continued after that. After . . . after my dad hurt me, and I got placed with the Carvers, they never let me forget how *generous* they were. How I literally owed them everything for taking me in. How they had to help me pay for dance after I lost my scholarship. Michael was especially keen on reminding me how much I owed them."

I took a deep shuddering breath, hoping he was really getting it.

"All my life, the people around me have made me feel like I'm a burden, that anything they give me comes with a price. I . . . I don't want it to be like that with us. I never want you to feel like I'm using you, that I'm not here for the right reasons. Especially when there's such a gap between who you are and . . . me."

It's why I still can't tell you everything, a voice inside me cried.

I couldn't look at him then. I tore my eyes from his face and stared at the sheets again.

"I would die if you ever felt like that. If you ever told me I owed you for the love that you've given me," I whispered.

Camden's fingertips grazed the side of my face, and then he was softly moving my chin up so I had to look at him.

"It seems like me promising I'd never feel that way won't convince you . . . yet. So, how about I promise you that I will *tell* you if I ever start to? Will that work for you, baby girl? Will you at least give me your trust that I will do that?"

I studied him, my mind filled with all that had happened the last few weeks. All the things he had said, all the things he had done.

It was shocking when it hit me. I had spent all this time telling myself I couldn't trust him, but it wasn't true.

I *did* trust him. More than I had anyone else. How careful and gentle he'd been with me from the start. How he'd waited for me to fall in love with him. How he'd already done so much for me without asking for *anything*.

How sure I was that he really loved me.

"Okay," I whispered, and his eyes widened.

"Okay, what?"

"I believe you. I . . . I trust you."

His eyes closed and he let out a sigh, and then he was reaching out and pulling me to him.

"Will you let me take care of you? Let me help you work toward your dreams. *Trust* that I will tell you if I ever start to resent that."

I took a deep breath, because this was big. This was giving him . . . the final piece of me. The piece that he could use to destroy me completely.

"Yes," I finally whispered. "I will."

Camden kissed me softly and then laid us both down. "Get a little more rest for me, baby girl," he murmured as I nuzzled into his shirt, breathing him in. "I'll take care of everything . . ."

CHAPTER 30

ANASTASIA

This felt big. I was going to my first away game since I started dating Camden . . . and I was flying on Lincoln's private jet with Monroe, Blake, and Olivia freaking Davis. Or at least I thought it was Lincoln's jet. Camden had been kind of vague about the details.

I had also taken my first voluntary day off of ballet—ever—to be here.

It felt like a big step in our relationship.

As Camden liked to remind me, not as big as a dick tattoo . . . but close.

He'd had to leave early to fly with the team, so I was waiting in the lobby for the car that was going to take me to the plane. Camden had told me to wait in the penthouse until it got here, but I was too anxious, so I came downstairs. Despite my best efforts . . . I had already started depending on Camden even before our life-altering conversation last week—especially in social situations.

It was going to be fine. The game was going to be great, and when Dallon bitched at me again about missing practice, I was just going to ignore him. Better than I had yesterday at least.

"Are you serious, Anastasia? A fucking day off! Do you even care about this performance? About the Company?" I bit down on my lip, preventing myself from pointing out that he had been thirty minutes late today . . . again. "You think you can just waltz in and out whenever you feel like it? This isn't a hobby, it's your career!"

"I know that, Dallon. I fucking know that!" The ferocity in my voice shocked both of us because it took a second for him to respond.

"Don't ask for another day off, Anastasia. Or I'll find a different partner."

Thinking about that was not going to help me make friends today. I would be in a pissy mood if I was stressing about missing practice. This was a big deal for Camden.

And I wasn't going to let him down.

The car arrived, and I freaked out the entire drive to the private hangar.

Private hangar. I still couldn't believe it.

I'd never even flown a commercial airplane, and now, here I was, about to step onto someone's personal jet.

We got to the hangar, and my heart pounded harder with each passing second. There was the airplane, sleek and imposing. As the driver opened my door, my legs felt like jelly. I slowly walked toward the stairs leading up to the jet, and then I gripped the handrail tightly, willing myself to move forward.

I had just reached the top when a seventy-something-year-old woman wearing a cat apron popped into the entry. She was carrying a tray of cookies. Her silver hair was tied back in a neat bun, and she had the warmest smile I'd ever seen.

"Hello, dear!" she greeted cheerfully as she extended the tray toward me. "Would you like a cookie? Freshly baked."

I blinked, completely taken aback. "A cookie?"

Another grandma-looking woman stepped out from the small hallway to the left. "You must be Anastasia. Aren't you a pretty thing! Although, I guess that's to be expected. Mr. James is a *fine* specimen of a man." I couldn't help but grin as the elderly woman pretended to swoon. "I'm Edna and that's Mabel. And we'll be taking care of you today."

Mabel's smile widened. "Now, why don't you take one of these cookies and settle on in? They're chocolate chip, my specialty."

It took me a moment to stop gaping like a fish. On the plus side, though, my nerves were gone, replaced by sheer bewilderment. Was this how the airline industry was? I'd never heard that the flight attendants were senior citizens. Camden had definitely left this part out when I'd pestered him for details about the flight so I could be prepared.

Probably on purpose. He would be enjoying my reaction if he was here.

"Thank you, Mabel," I finally managed to say, taking a cookie from the tray. As I stepped onto the plane, I had a view into the cockpit—the pilots also seemed to be in the over seventy crowd . . . and female. There were three of them, and they all waved at me when they saw me looking.

I turned to walk down the aisle, only to see Blake, Monroe, and Olivia almost falling out of their seats as they laughed at me.

"Welcome to Grandma Airways," sang Blake.

"Our boys' answer to the *taxing* dangers that come from air travel from the male species." Monroe's voice was dripping with sarcasm, but there was a smirk on her lips that said she didn't really mind.

I absentmindedly took a bite of the cookie and a moan slipped out. It was the best fucking cookie I'd ever tasted. "Holy shit," I gasped.

Olivia nodded knowingly. "Good right? Makes up for the insanity—fortunately for Walker."

I giggled, a little dazed because Olivia Davis was talking to me like we were friends. I needed to get a hold of myself.

I realized then that Olivia was hooked up to some kind of device. There were cords coming out from under her shirt and a computer-looking machine was on the table to the side of her, a heartbeat line beating on its screen.

"Don't mind this," Olivia said, gesturing to the device and looking adorably embarrassed. "Walker won't let me get on a plane without it, so we can make sure the baby is okay. Even though the doctor has told him a million times that air travel is completely fine at this point in my pregnancy."

"That's kind of . . . cute," I mused, thinking I could see Camden doing something like that.

Don't think about having babies with him, Ana. Your ovaries might explode.

Monroe snorted. "You're going to fit right in if that's cute to you. Others might call it overprotective, possessive . . . "

"Crazy," Blake added with a giggle.

Then, we all were laughing at the same time.

I think I was going to like these girls.

"More cookies?" Mabel asked, appearing out of nowhere beside me the second I'd sat down, this time with spectacles perched on her nose.

I glanced at the girls who all looked to be holding in gasping laughter. Blake had a hand over her mouth.

Mabel seemed used to it, her own eyes twinkling like she was definitely in on the joke.

I grabbed a cookie, and then another, and settled into the flight.

I'd missed out when I'd sat in the nosebleeds. The front row was a completely different experience. The players literally crashed into the glass right in front of you. Your seat actually shook with the force of it.

I'd never seen anything so exciting in my entire life.

Although, if I had sat with the girls that day, I would have missed what happened after . . . and I certainly didn't regret *that*.

I shifted in my seat just thinking about his hand palming my ass.

Camden winked at me as he skated by . . . like he could read my mind.

"Oh, we're up there . . . again," Olivia huffed.

Blake slung her arm over our shoulders, reaching farther to grab onto Monroe's shirt. "Smile ladies," she laughed as she pulled us close.

I stared up at the jumbotron now displaying our faces—our *smiling* faces.

I barely recognized the girl up there, with color on her cheeks and a grin so wide it took up her whole face.

I'd never *believed* I could be that girl, either.

So happy that I could barely breathe without smiling.

I glanced at Camden, watching as he slammed someone into the boards, fighting over the puck.

And it was all because of him.

CHAPTER 31

ANASTASIA

I walked down the hallway after class, exhausted and ready to head home. "Anastasia," a voice called. Turning, I saw one of the office admin people walking toward me—Linda, I think was her name—and Michael.

I froze, gaping at the wide smile on his face as she said something to him and pointed over to where I was standing.

"I had no idea you had such a charming brother," Linda cooed as she got closer. "He came to the office looking for you. You really need to answer your phone," she chided lightly.

"Foster brother," I murmured, the synapses in my brain not working correctly because I was used to Michael showing up outside. This was the first time that he'd actually come *inside*, violating an unspoken treaty between us I just now realized I had believed in.

My heart sank, dread twisting in my stomach.

"Thank you, Linda," Michael said charmingly. "My parents will be so grateful for your help. Anastasia has been so busy lately, we've scarcely seen her!"

I felt sick as I watched him play Linda like a fool. This was what he always did, and just like always, I couldn't believe that no one else seemed to see the cockroach that lay under his pleasant surface.

I wanted to scream as I watched her walk away.

"Get over here, Anastasia. We're leaving."

I was stuck in place, unable to move.

I couldn't do it. Not now that I had Camden.

Anger flashed across his face. "Sorry, I should have said that differently. Let's fucking go." The genteel tone dropped, replaced by the one I was used to when I didn't give him what he wanted. "Fight me on this, and I'll release those fucking photos. *Everywhere*. See how much that NHL star wants you when the whole world can see your pussy, and he finds out how much you like to show it off."

My shoulders fell. Camden had been so upset just on the notion that I was interviewing at a strip club. How would he feel when the whole world saw me naked?

Disgusted, obviously.

Trust me. I could hear his voice in my head saying that over and over again.

But in this case, it wasn't about not trusting him. It was about not tainting him. I didn't want him to have anything to do with Michael Carver.

He was way too good for him.

"Move," he hissed, pushing me toward the exit behind me.

One problem with that, though—my phone was still in my locker. Camden would freak out when I didn't text him and didn't come outside after class.

"I need to grab my phone."

Michael snorted. "Like I'm going to give you a chance to let Fancy Pants know there's been a change of plans today. Get fucking moving. I'm getting annoyed, Ana, and you know what happens when I get like this."

I did. Oh, I did. One time, he'd stabbed me with a fire poker just because he decided he didn't like the sound of my voice—I hadn't even been talking. Another time, he'd put his hands around my neck and choked me until I passed out.

There were a million stories in my back pocket like that.

The ride to his childhood house felt like a nightmare, every familiar landmark like a monster waiting to pounce. As we pulled into the Carver's driveway, its familiar worn bricks and perfectly landscaped lawn sent waves of nausea through me. Mrs. Carver even had pink roses blooming this year.

The same roses that Michael used to pick for me, placing them in my hand and making me squeeze the thorny stems until I bled.

"Home sweet home," Michael cooed, shooting me a grin that didn't reach his eyes.

His hand pressed against my back as we walked up the sidewalk to the front door. It felt like a death sentence.

"Hello, Anastasia," Mrs. Carver said when she opened the door, staring at me with the same lifeless eyes she'd had the entire time I was growing up. The house smelled the same, a mix of Pine-Sol and stale air. It made me want to run, but Michael's fingers dug into my skin, pushing me across the living room to the dining table that was already set.

"Look who decided to join us," Mrs. Carver said to her husband, her tone icy.

Mr. Carver sat at the head of the table, his stern face etched with permanent disapproval as he cast me a disinterested glance, eyes cold and calculating behind his glasses. Mrs. Carver settled herself rigidly onto the seat beside him, a tight-lipped smile on her pink-stained lips, the same color she'd worn while I'd lived with them. Her posture was stiff and unwelcoming, but her gaze softened when she stared at her son. It looked like her blind spot for the psychopath hadn't gone away.

It was obvious, as usual, whose idea it had been for me to come to dinner.

Michael's hand slid down to the curve of my ass, and I lunged forward, sitting in a chair before he could do anything else.

After dinner, would he have something to show me in his old room? Would his camera be sitting on the desk? Would a silk blanket be draped across his bed? I was on the verge of a panic attack just sitting here.

There was a baked chicken on the middle of the table, expertly made I was sure because Mrs. Carver had always been a good cook.

I wanted to throw up all over it.

Suddenly, the doorbell rang. We all glanced at it, like a doorbell ringing was the oddest thing that could ever happen.

Mrs. Carver sniffed when it rang again. "That package is two hours late," she huffed. She finally stood, her expression irritated as she went to answer it. I heard the faint murmur of voices—and one sounded awfully familiar. Sitting up straighter in my seat, my eyes darted toward the doorway.

But surely not . . . I had to be imagining his voice out of pure longing because I wanted him to be here so badly . . . protecting me like he had with everything else.

Her footsteps echoed on the tile floor, signaling her return—but there was another set of footsteps that had joined hers.

My heart nearly stopped when I saw Camden behind her, looking completely at ease and confident and flawless . . . despite the fact that he'd just walked into a house of horrors.

It was all I could do not to burst into tears. How had he found me?

How was he always able to save me?

"Hi, baby girl," Camden said cheerfully, coming over and placing a soft kiss on my cheek, his hand warm and comforting and perfect as he gently squeezed my shoulder. He glanced at the food laid out on the table. "This looks amazing, Mrs. Carver. My mouth is literally watering."

"Who are you?" Mr. Carver asked, the first words he'd spoken since I'd arrived. He was eying Camden like he was an alien who'd landed from space.

In this family, he might as well have been.

"I'm Camden, Mr. Carver. Anastasia's boyfriend. I'm sorry for the surprise visit; I was held up with hockey practice. It was so *nice* that Ana was able to get a ride." I didn't miss his inflection on the word nice, but Mr. and Mrs. Carver seemed to.

"Hockey practice?" Mr. Carver asked, the first time I'd heard him sound interested in something since I'd met him.

"Anastasia hasn't mentioned it? I'm a defenseman for the Knights."

Mr. Carver leaned forward. "The Dallas Knights?"

"Yes, sir."

And just like that, I watched as Mr. and Mrs. Carver turned into putty in Camden's hands.

"This is Michael, our son," Mrs. Carver said, gesturing to the sonofabitch as Camden settled on my other side.

Camden was silent for a moment, and I saw his gaze was focused on where Michael's fingers were digging into my thigh. I'd forgotten his nails were even hurting me—I was just so fucking relieved Camden was here.

"Hello, Michael," Camden said evenly, his stare slowly dragging to Michael's face. I shivered at the underlying threat in his voice. Michael must have heard it, too, because he yanked his hand away from my leg.

I couldn't help but look at Michael—not surprised at the look of pure fury in his eyes. Michael had probably been planning this dinner for months, and Camden was ruining everything for him.

Camden leaned back, his arm draped casually over my shoulders. "Can you grab the potatoes for me, Michael? I'm *starving*."

Michael stared at him for a moment, a menacing snarl on his lips, as he finally *slowly* reached for the bowl. But Mrs. Carver got to it before he could, practically shoving the potatoes at Camden in her effort to get them to him.

It would have been funny if anyone but the Carvers were the ones doing it. There just wasn't anything funny about them.

We began to eat—or at least everyone else did. I couldn't stomach a single bite, even with Camden here. Now that my initial surge of dopamine at his arrival had leveled, I was getting anxious again.

Camden was going to find out about the pictures.

And he was going to be so *disappointed* in me. Cheeks burning, I glanced at Camden, expecting to see a scowl on his handsome face. But when he saw me looking, he gave me a reassuring smile, like everything was fine.

"So, Michael, how's work treating you?" Camden said lightly.

Michael stiffened next to me.

"Oh, Michael's in between jobs, right now. His manager was just awful," Mrs. Carver commented. "He'll find something soon, though. He's such a smart boy."

I almost gagged on the small bite of mashed potatoes I'd just put into my mouth at the idea of Michael being called a "boy." He was far too evil to ever resemble that word.

"Thanks, Mom," Michael said through gritted teeth, not sounding thankful at all.

I didn't speak a word for the rest of dinner. Neither did Michael.

Camden, meanwhile, ate every bite on his plate, and entertained Mr. and Mrs. Carver with NHL stories the entire time. It felt like forever had passed when he finally pushed back from his chair. "Well, we'd better get going. I'm sure Anastasia's exhausted from dance today. This was amazing, though."

Mrs. Carver blinked at me like she'd forgotten I was there. "Oh, you can't stay for dessert?" she asked disappointedly.

Camden patted his stomach. "I couldn't eat another bite, ma'am. That was the best chicken I've ever had."

It was almost fascinating, watching Camden turn Mrs. Carver into a tittering version of herself.

It didn't escape my attention that Mrs. Carver didn't offer me dessert. It also didn't surprise me in the slightest.

"Come on, baby girl," Camden said, helping me out of my chair.

"Thank you," I said, every nerve on edge. Was this it? Were we really going to walk out of here unscathed, and it would be done?

"I'll show you out," Michael said then, dashing all my hopes.

"Oh that's—" I started to say, but Camden cut me off.

"Sounds good."

Shit.

Camden said his goodbyes, artfully evading Mrs. Carver's invitation to come back soon. She and her husband had a much cooler farewell for me, but it was still infinitely less icy than it usually was.

And then we were walking out, Michael silently stalking behind us.

None of us said anything until we were outside, the door to the house firmly closed.

"Go get in the truck," Camden suddenly murmured to me, and I glanced up at him, only to see the full weight of his feelings.

He was absolutely furious.

"Let's just go," I whispered back, not because I was scared that in a fair fight Camden couldn't beat Michael to a pulp . . . but because never in the history of the world would Michael ever engage in a fair fight.

"Are you sure she's worth it?" Michael called from behind us.

Camden stiffened and slowly turned to face him. "Excuse me?" he said, in a chilly voice that should have sent Michael running, if Michael had any normal human emotions left in him.

Instead, Michael stood his ground, his arms folded in front of him, a wide grin stretched across his serial killer face. "She obviously doesn't care about you if she won't even give me what I want for the pictures."

Fuck.

This was it.

A terrifying heat was settling over Camden as he stared at the man who had tormented me from the time I was just a girl.

"What pictures?"

Michael laughed, looking delighted as his gaze bounced between us like a demonic ping-pong ball.

"Well, she can't be that in love with you if she hasn't told you about *that*."

"What pictures, Anastasia?" Camden turned to look at me, completely ignoring Michael. His body was stiff, a dark expression in his gaze that I couldn't quite read.

I squeezed my eyes shut, a tremor passing over my skin. I wished this wasn't happening in the front yard of the house that *still* gave me nightmares to this day. My throat was clogged, anxiety clawing at my spine. My pulse was racing so fast, I thought my heart might explode.

"Smile, little bunny. Arch your back. Pinch your nipple. Yes, that's it. You like that, you little slut."

Memory after memory assaulted my brain. Fuck. I was going to throw up. Leaning over, my breath came out in short, panicked gasps.

I didn't want to give Michael a show. He'd love that, me sick over him.

Frantically inhaling, I tried to make myself brave enough to talk about this—my darkest secret, my biggest shame. *This* was where I would lose him, though.

I forced myself to straighten, dragging my eyes to meet Camden's face. I just needed to get the words out, to get it done.

Slowly I began . . . every syllable halting and *painful*.

"Growing up, Michael would take . . . pictures of me . . . without my consent. And since then, every time I've come here, he's forced me to take *more*." I took in a deep, shuddering breath. "I know I shouldn't have let him, but I'm terrified of him," I tried to explain.

My excuses sounded stupid coming out of my mouth, but I didn't know how else to explain the sheer psychological terror that I experienced because of Michael. He was the bogeyman in the closet for me. And he knew it.

Michael had never given a threat that he hadn't followed through with.

"Now that you're here, though, you can give me the money that your little girlfriend couldn't. And this whole thing can be over with," Michael said gleefully.

Camden was still looking at me, a blank expression on his face. Why wasn't he reacting to what I'd said? What was he thinking?

He was disgusted by me, I knew it.

I *knew* this was how it was going to be.

"He's been blackmailing me since you and I met. I . . . I didn't want to embarrass you." The words came out in a choked whisper, shame so thick in my voice that I could taste it on my tongue.

Camden slowly turned to give Michael his attention, not acknowledging what I'd said at all. I squeezed my eyes shut in pain, a tear sliding down my cheek.

"You ever study cockroaches, Michael?" he asked, and I blinked, because that's what Michael was. A cockroach.

"Can't say I have, *Camden*."

"Well, the thing about them is that if you kill one, there's always another one that's waiting in the wings. I'm sure someone has described you as one before, so you should get that allegory."

Michael lifted his chin, his cheeks reddening.

"I'm not paying you that money. Cockroaches like you never give up. There's really only one way to get rid of them. Do you know what that is?"

There was a tic in Michael's cheek, and he didn't answer, his pale blue eyes darkening like clouds right before a storm.

"Extermination." Camden leaned forward, his lips curling into a menacing smile that gave me goosebumps.

Michael's eyes widened in shock, and my heart was pounding . . . I was pretty sure Camden had just threatened to kill Michael.

The thing was, I wasn't sure what method of death could possibly be enough to pay Michael back for what he'd done.

The door opened then, and Mrs. Carver peeked her head out, her gaze darting between us all, like she'd just noticed the tension that had been present all of dinner. "Everything okay out here?"

"Of course, Mrs. Carver. We were just talking about *pest* control."

"Oh," Mrs. Carver said, clearly confused since it was the dead of winter and bugs weren't a problem at the moment. "Well, have a safe drive." She lifted her hand in farewell.

"See you, ma'am," Camden nodded, his palm on my back as he led me toward the truck.

I could feel Michael's gaze digging into my spinal cord, probably planning all the terrible things he was going to do to me.

We drove off, and I kept my eyes on the road in front of us, not daring to look back and lock eyes with Michael.

I could only breathe after we'd turned a corner and we were no longer in his sights.

The silence was stifling, though, and I couldn't handle it. I was so damn grateful that Camden came for me, but I was sure I'd fucked it all up—again.

I glanced at him, flinching when I saw how *livid* he was. His teeth were gritted together and he was clenching the steering wheel so tight, his knuckles were white. My heart was squeezing in my chest. I knew he'd be angry at me for this. I knew he'd hate me.

"Thank you for coming to get me. I'm *so* sorry," I finally sobbed brokenly. "I understand if you don't want to see me again . . . "

"What the fuck are you talking about?" Camden's face snapped toward me. "You're not going anywhere."

"What?" I whispered, confused. "But you're . . . furious."

Camden growled, beating on the steering wheel with one of his palms. "Of course, I'm furious! I just found out that a disgusting monster has been torturing you for your entire life. He was taking intimate pictures of you. He was violating you! And no one fucking did anything about it! I'm trying not to turn the truck around and kill him."

I started crying harder as his eyes softened, the look in them turning tender and loving as he focused on me.

How could he look at me like that after what I'd just admitted?

"It's okay, baby girl," he soothed. I blinked, my hands shaking as I brought them to my face in disbelief. Was he serious? He couldn't be? Could he?

A thread of hope . . . and relief began to twist its way along my insides.

"I *wish* you had trusted me. But I understand. I do. You're fucking terrified of that motherfucker, that's obvious. I realized it that day when I saw him standing on the street corner outside of Charlie's. But you're not going to have to deal with him anymore. *I'm* going to take care of him. I told you the other night that I'm going to take care of *everything*." He sounded so confident, like all of this was easy.

"You don't understand, Camden. He's . . . he's not normal. The pictures are only one of his *things*. He used to torture me after I moved in, crazy stuff—things I can't even talk about because it's so freaking traumatic to even say them out loud. And embarrassing, too . . . " My last words came out in a whisper.

"Why is it embarrassing?" Camden asked, his voice careful, like he could sense I was falling apart.

"Because I . . . I just let it all happen. I told his parents the first few times, and they called me a liar, so I never brought it up again. I never told anyone—not my teachers or my caseworker . . . no one. I was too afraid of them not believing me . . . or of being placed somewhere even worse." I swiped at my eyes, furious that any of my tears were attached to Michael.

Camden abruptly pulled to the side of the road, threw the truck in park, and then faced me fully. "You were a young girl, recovering from a horrific injury, who was all by herself. I think you're the bravest, most incredible person I've ever met, Anastasia."

I scoffed. "You don't have to say that."

He reached across the seat, cradling my face with both hands as he pulled me closer to him. "I'm fucking serious. Anastasia Lennox, I am in complete *awe* of you, and that only grows with every passing day."

I closed my eyes as he placed the most heartbreakingly sweet kiss on my lips.

Every time I thought it would be too much, that this would be when we broke, he fixed us.

Or maybe the better way to say it was . . . he fixed *me*.

A thought hit me as he let me go and pulled the truck back on the road.

"How did you find me?" I asked.

"When you weren't there when I came to pick you up, and you weren't answering your phone—" he added, casting me an exasperated look. "I went into the studio and asked if anyone had seen you. Some front office lady said that your brother . . . *Michael* . . . had come to get you."

His hands tensed on the steering wheel before he took a deep breath and relaxed them. "I had the address of your foster parents already . . . it had come up when I had done some *research* on you when I was trying to figure you out."

"Some research?" I asked, my cheeks flushed because I was guessing that meant he knew a lot more about me than I'd thought. I was more embarrassed than upset. He was technically famous . . . sometimes I forgot about that. I would think someone, his agent, his publicist . . . *someone* was looking at who these guys dated.

Camden reached over and squeezed my hand. "I'm glad I knew what I did. What exactly was your plan tonight? What happened?"

I told him how I'd been cornered after practice and basically forced to the house.

We pulled into the parking garage, and Camden turned off the truck, sitting so silently that I began to fidget in my seat with nervousness.

Finally, he looked at me, and I got lost in the fire in his gaze, twin flames of warning. "You are not going to worry about Michael Carver anymore, do you understand, baby girl?" he vowed. "I'm going to *destroy* him if he ever comes close to you again. He doesn't exist in your world. The monster is dead, okay?"

I nodded, a touch of hope filling my chest. I wanted to believe him. I wanted it desperately.

Maybe it should have scared me what he was promising, but it didn't, not at all.

Because like he'd said, the only way to *truly* get rid of a cockroach . . . was complete extermination.

CHAPTER 32

CAMDEN

I listened to the recording I'd taken on Anastasia's phone.

And then I listened to it again.

Dallon Holmes was an asshole of the highest order, and as soon as I'd heard how he was speaking to her, he was done.

Anastasia was never in a good mood when she came home from practice, and she never wanted to talk about it.

Now, I understood why.

I'd listened as he'd gone back and forth between verbally berating her and coming on to her.

Absolutely unacceptable.

I'd promised Anastasia that I would take care of her problems, and this fucker was now firmly on that list.

But I needed to handle it delicately. I was not going to ruin the opportunity she'd been working so hard for.

I pulled out my phone to consult . . . the brain trust.

Me: So, Lancaster . . .

He responded back immediately, like he always did. I was a little worried that he had sex holding his phone in one hand. I kind of wanted Anastasia to ask Blake.

Ari: Go on . . .

Ari: Are you texting about my report?

I snorted at the phone.

Walker: What report?

Ari: Oh, look who's decided to join the conversation. The offender himself.

Me: This has nothing to do with what I was texting about.

Ari: Quiet, Hero. This is important.

Logan: What did Disney do?

Ari: Do you mean what did Señor Buttkiss do?

Walker: . . .

Walker: What?

Ari: Who did you congratulate tonight when we won, Disney?

Me: This feels like a trap.

Walker: It really does.

Ari: See, right there! Butt-kisser.

Linc: Alright, let's get the drama queen's rant over with. Lancaster, I'm pretty sure he gave me a high-five after the game.

Me: I was not watching Walker, because I had better things to do. So I will defer to Lincoln.

Ari: Children. I SCORED A FUCKING GOAL TONIGHT.

Walker: Good boy?

Ari: Sorry, Disney, that's your kink, not mine.

Logan: Can I point out that Lincoln scored two . . .

Ari: Can I point out that you didn't score one?

Ari Lancaster removed Logan York from the chat.

I could literally picture the steam coming out of Ari's ears right then. Wish I had a picture. Maybe I could get one.

Me: Could you, by chance, have Blake take a picture of you right now?

Ari: First, Hero, you're so far out of the circle of trust right now, I can't even see you. Also, my wife's name is never allowed to come out of your mouth or your keyboard. I'm pretty sure we've gone over this. Second, Disney, Lincoln always scores. I scored a goal and defended your ass all fucking night. I got dick punched by Donovan at some point. You know what that would have done to Blake if there was permanent injury to her favorite part of my body.

Linc: Technically, Camden is beating you this year in goals scored.

Ari: Technically, you've been officially replaced as my best friend by Geraldine, but we aren't talking about that.

Linc: . . .

Walker: Ari Lancaster, you are a god among hockey players. All hail you.

Ari: Thank you. That was the proper response to my magnificent performance tonight.

Linc: I think he was being sarcastic.

Me: Only because I need Ari to help me, I'm going to say Disney meant that text from the bottom of his heart.

Ari: Your offering is accepted.

Ari: Hero, if this one involves dogs, I'm out.

Walker: What about cats?

Me: Can we focus, please?

Me: I need a replacement dancer person . . . who is not an asshole. Oh, and he has to be one of the best and able to dance with Anastasia's Company for her showcase.

Whoops. I'd missed the most important requirement for this unicorn of a dancer.

Me: Just a small thing really, but he also has to be gay.

Linc: . . .

Ari: Anything else? And just in case you can't sense the sarcasm in my text, because sometimes that's hard for you in person—I was being sarcastic.

Me: Can you help me?

Linc: Why do you need this?

Me: Anastasia has a problem. The principal she's dancing with . . . is an asshole.

Linc: Should we just kill him instead?

I blinked at the phone. I was *pretty* sure that he was joking.

Walker: I don't know that I got the sarcasm on that one.

Ari: Yeah, me neither.

Ari: But also, Hero, you do realize that I said I took ballet in college, right?

My shoulders dropped. I mean it had been a long shot.

Ari: Just kidding. I have the perfect guy. I'll send you his contact info. Just tell him you're friends with me. He owes me.

Ari: And now you will, too. Even more than after the toe incident.

I did a fist pump. But of course, Lancaster couldn't stop there.

> Ari: But, just so we're clear, we're just friends. Not circle of trust members and not besties. Only Geraldine . . . and Monroe hold that honor.

I smirked.

My phone rang. It was Lincoln. "Hello?"

"I've got a guy . . . " he said immediately.

Why did that not surprise me? He seemed to have a guy for everything actually, kind of unusual for a high-profile hockey player . . .

"Does your fire guy also specialize in ballet?" I asked, only half joking.

Not that I hadn't used the fire guy. He'd actually taken care of the strip club last Friday, just in case Anastasia got any more wild ideas. I'd made sure to turn off the news the other night when they'd started talking about the random fire that had burned down the whole place.

"No, but he *can* arrange for a tire iron to hit Mr. Asshole's leg while he walks to his car," Lincoln said casually, like we were talking about the weather, or the game tonight . . . instead of maiming someone.

That seemed . . . extreme. But he'd also called my sweet baby girl a fucking train wreck. It didn't take an expert to know that Anastasia was ten times the dancer that he was. He then had touched her enough she had to say, "please don't touch me there" a few minutes later . . .

I'd been listening in on her practices now that she had started bringing her phone everywhere after the Michael incident.

Which reminded me . . . I still needed to deal with him. One of Walker and Olivia's bodyguards had a friend—female, of course—who I'd hired to stand guard outside the Company when I had hockey obligations. She'd reported that Michael had still been lurking outside the studio almost every day, leaving right before Anastasia came out of class.

The Dallon situation needed to be handled so I could move on to solving that.

"Actually . . . that sounds good. I'll take it," I said a moment later.

"Cool," Lincoln responded, and he hung up without another word.

I stared at the phone for a second. I think I just hired a guy to bust out someone's knees. Had that really happened?

My phone buzzed with a text from Ari. He'd sent me contact information for a dancer named Rudolf Fedorov. Typing in the guy's name on Google, I became more and more impressed as I went through his resume. He was one of the top principal dancers in the country, and his contract allowed him to perform with various companies over the years.

He also was married to a man named Ted.

I was wondering if Ari was just fucking with me at this point. Rudolf fit my *exact* specifications.

I still dialed the number that Ari had sent, and thank fuck, Lancaster had come through. Twenty minutes later, Anastasia had a new partner for the showcase, assuming Dallon's leg met its planned end.

Whatever Rudolf owed Ari . . . it must've been a lot.

CHAPTER 33

ANASTASIA

I was on top of the world as I watched the game with Monroe, Blake, and a very pregnant Olivia.

It had been one of the best weeks of my life.

A strange week . . . but one of the best weeks.

Dallon had gotten jumped coming out of his apartment one morning a few weeks ago. The police thought it had been a targeted attack by a rival dancer or something because they'd gone after his leg with a tire iron.

Everyone at the Company was speculating about who could have done it.

Personally, I wasn't sure that it *had* been a dancer—Dallon's personality would lead to a lot of enemies. I imagined there were a lot of people who would wish him harm. On the plus side for Dallon, his injury wasn't anywhere near as serious as mine had been—it was just a bone bruise. Of course, though, Dallon had declared himself *unable* to perform in the showcase. Leaving me without a partner after I'd endured his torture for months.

A miraculous thing had happened then. Rudolf Fedorov, one of the top principal dancers in the country, had decided to come teach and perform at *our* company for a year. He had a reputation for getting bored, and had done year long stints on leave from his New York company before. I had literally screamed when I heard the news. The opportunity to learn from him and watch him dance was a once in a lifetime opportunity.

When I didn't think it could get better, for some unknown reason, Rudolf had volunteered to take Dallon's spot in the pas de deux. I had almost fainted. I'd started my first practice with him on Monday. He was everything that Dallon was not. Professional, prompt, humble, kind, encouraging . . . the list went on and on. And on top of that, he was one of the most incredible dancers I'd ever seen.

He was also gay and happily married to a man named Ted.

So, the perfect partner for me to dance with in Camden's eyes.

I'd been gushing about our practices every day. Camden would just smile fondly and listen patiently to every word that came out of my mouth.

I loved him so much.

"This baby needs to stay in here," Olivia muttered, bringing me back to the present as her face scrunched up in pain. She'd been getting Braxton-Hicks for the past few weeks. I didn't know much about pregnancy, but I was wondering if maybe her Braxton-Hicks had turned into real contractions.

"Should we get you to the hospital?" I asked anxiously, patting her shoulder awkwardly. I had become fast friends with all of the girls, but I was still timid around Olivia. I wasn't sure that was going to change. She had been an idol of mine for too long.

"Absolutely not," she said through gritted teeth. "This baby is staying inside until after this playoff round."

I shared a look with Monroe and Blake.

The Knights were currently playing Nashville in the second game of the first round, and all of the guys were very focused on winning the Cup. They were the favorites to win—how could they not be with Lincoln, Ari, Walker, and Camden on the team? Walker was not going to go anywhere without Olivia, though, so the Knights could be down a goalie if the baby came soon.

It seemed Olivia was determined for that not to happen.

The crowd was a sea of blue and silver tonight, all of them screaming and waving banners. I sat on the edge of my seat, my heart pounding in my chest. I'd thought the regular season games were intense, but the playoffs were on a whole other level. The air was thick with tension and excitement, every cheer and chant vibrating through me.

I watched Camden, my eyes following his every move. He was a force out there, focused and determined, his eyes never leaving the puck. The crowd roared as he checked a Nashville player into the boards, reclaiming possession for the Knights.

Logan was also on fire tonight. He was playing much more sharp and aggressive, like the playoffs had pushed him to another level. He streaked down the ice, weaving through the Nashville defense. The puck glided from his stick to another player's in a seamless play. My breath caught as Logan positioned himself in front of the net, waiting. The pass came, and with a swift flick of his wrist, the puck soared past the goalie and into the net.

"Yes!" I screamed, jumping to my feet as the arena exploded in cheers.

Logan's face lit up with pure joy as he was mobbed by his teammates. His first playoff goal. The scoreboard flashed, and the Knights' lead extended. I glanced at Camden, who raised his stick in a salute to Logan, pride evident in his eyes. The game clock showed there was still five minutes left in the period . . . and I really had to pee. I would just slip out right now to use the bathroom before the lines got long. Even the bathroom lines for the special ticket holders got long in between periods.

"I'm going to go to the bathroom," I told Freya, the bodyguard Camden had hired for me after he'd learned how serious the Michael issue was. It was still weird to me that I had a bodyguard . . . I'd literally been homeless not so long ago. But I could admit that it made me feel safer whenever I was out of Camden's presence.

She got up out of her seat, and I followed her up the stands and down the tunnel to the bathrooms. "Give me one second to check them," she said, and I nodded as she looked through the stalls one by one, finally clearing me to pee.

Which I was thankful for since I really had to go.

"I'll be waiting right outside the doors." I nodded and slipped into the stall, hearing the sound of the bathroom door thudding shut after her. The bathroom was quiet, the hum of the arena muffled by the thick walls.

Half a minute later, I heard the door open again.

"Everything okay?" I asked her, feeling awkward to be talking to her while I peed. I'd never had that experience of going to the bathroom with my girlfriends.

She didn't answer, and the silence stretched on, now unsettling. My heart skipped a beat, and I peeked through the crack in the stall door. I didn't see anyone . . .

I flushed and then opened the door cautiously, stepping out into the empty bathroom.

A second later, I was slammed against the wall, a hand gripping my throat. Michael's face loomed over me, his eyes wild and crazed.

"Hello, little bunny," he hissed, his voice sending a chill down my spine. "It's been really hard to get a hold of you."

Panic surged through me, and I clawed at his hand, struggling to breathe. His grip tightened, cutting off my air. Spots danced in my vision as I kicked and writhed, desperate to get free. "Let . . . me . . . go," I gasped, my voice barely a whisper.

He smirked, enjoying my terror. "You think you can hide from me? You're mine, Anastasia. You'll always be mine."

Just as I felt myself slipping into unconsciousness, the bathroom door burst open. Freya stumbled in. She lunged at Michael, her fists flying. Michael released me, and I collapsed to the floor, gulping in air.

The two of them struggled, Michael trying to fend off my bodyguard's relentless attacks. He was no match for her, though, and I watched as she landed a solid punch to his jaw. He staggered back, blood trickling from his lip, and then he turned and bolted out the door.

Freya rushed to my side, her eyes filled with concern. "Anastasia, are you okay?"

I nodded weakly, still catching my breath. "I'm . . . I'm fine. Thank you."

She helped me to my feet, her grip steady and reassuring. "He came at me from behind, hit me with something. I'm so sorry."

I waved her off, still struggling to breathe. I leaned over the sink, my pulse wild and out of control. Glancing in the mirror, I winced when I saw how red my neck was, and how some of the capillaries in my eyes had burst.

Crap.

"I'll get a message to Mr. James," she said, watching me with wide, concerned eyes.

"No," I gasped, my voice a little hysterical. "I don't want to distract him from the game."

"He'll want to know," she said chidingly. "We need to have a doctor look at you, and we need to report this to the authorities as well."

"I'm fine. I promise. All of that can wait until after the game. Let's just get back out there."

She stared at me disapprovingly.

"Please," I pleaded.

Finally, she reluctantly nodded. "But the second the game's over, I'm reporting this."

I nodded thankfully.

As we left the bathroom, the noise of the arena washed over me again, a stark contrast to the terrifying encounter I had just endured. My mind raced, trying to process what had happened. Freya was visibly nervous as we walked, her head bouncing around like a bobblehead as she checked for threats. I was the same way, sure that I was going to see Michael in the crowd at any moment. Neither of us breathed until we were back in the stands, going down to our seats.

I bit down on my lip when she touched the back of her head and winced. She needed to get looked at, too.

Zipping my jacket all the way to my neck, I settled into my seat, pulling my hair around my shoulders in hopes I could hide the marks for as long as possible.

My neck was aching, though, and I really wanted to cry.

"Anastasia, are you alright?" Blake asked next to me. I smiled and nodded knowing they would want me to tell Camden right now, too, if I told them what happened.

"Yep," I said instead, ignoring the side eye that Freya was giving me and trying to avoid eye contact with anyone else.

I must not have done a good job of faking because at one point Camden stopped in front of us mouthing "what's wrong?" through the glass.

Pasting my dance smile on my face, I gave him a thumbs-up and he finally skated off.

But I didn't think he believed me.

I couldn't help but glance around right along with Freya, continuing to look for Michael in the crowd.

The game raged on, the intensity never letting up. Nashville fought back hard, their players pushing and shoving, desperate to even the score. Walker seemed to take up the whole net, blocking every shot that came his way, and making it look easy. Nashville was relentless though, and the puck found its way to an open player, who lined up for a clear shot at the goal.

Before the puck could fly toward Walker, Camden dove in front of it, his body a blur of motion. The puck slammed into his shin pads and ricocheted away, the danger averted.

I jumped out of my seat, ignoring the flash of pain in my neck as the crowd roared. He was so freaking good.

The final minutes of the game were a blur of frantic action. The Knights held their ground, every player giving their all. When the final buzzer sounded, the crowd erupted, the noise absolutely deafening—we'd won.

"I'm calling the police now," Freya snapped in my ear, clearly irritated she'd given into me. I nodded. I definitely wanted them to get Michael—I just hadn't wanted to mess up Camden's big night.

Michael had already messed up a million of mine.

I walked with the girls down the tunnel that led to the locker room, Olivia waddling the entire way because her belly was so huge. We waited around the locker room doors with some of the other wives and girlfriends.

Camden was the first one out. He took one look at me up close and it was all over.

"Who the hell did that to you?" he growled.

I immediately burst into tears.

CHAPTER 34

ANASTASIA

Camden was standing in the closet with me, watching me closely while I got dressed . . . like Michael was going to pop out of my clothes and take me if he left.

He'd been like this since the bathroom incident, watching me every second as if I was going to disappear if he even blinked. Freya had ended up being diagnosed with a concussion that night, so she'd been on leave for the last week. Camden had gone everywhere with me, not leaving my side unless Olivia's bodyguards were also present.

I was also on a peeing ban at games unless all the girls—and the bodyguards—were with me. Under no circumstances did I want a repeat of that night, so I wasn't pushing back on anything. It was clear that Michael was losing it, becoming even more unhinged and desperate. It made him even more terrifying than before.

For Camden's away playoff games, I'd taken off from practice to go with him. He'd said he wasn't going if I didn't come, too. He'd gone to Madame Leclerc himself about the situation, and whatever he'd said . . . had been very convincing. She'd started being way nicer to me. Which I guess was a perk of having the hottest, most charming man alive as your boyfriend—especially if he was an NHL star who was sponsoring the Company.

Her change in attitude didn't bother me as much as I would have thought. I needed a breather from the stress and the drama and the constant ridicule.

However it came.

"You look beautiful, baby girl," Camden said, his eyes heating as he slowly took me in. We were having a dinner party at Geraldine's to celebrate the Knights' first round playoff win. They'd won four games in a row and finished early. The two teams battling it out to play them next looked to be headed for a seventh game, so the Knights would be home for a few extra days before the next round began.

I wasn't sure about meeting Geraldine. She'd evidently been in Europe for the last month, which is why I hadn't met her even though she lived across the hall. I kept imagining this gorgeous modelesque woman trying to sweep in and hit on my man.

I may have become a touch possessive myself.

"What are you thinking about?" he murmured, crowding me against the wall as he dipped his lips to my shoulder and dropped decadent kisses across my skin.

I gasped, losing the ability to talk for a moment. Camden had been very careful with me since the incident, and I missed the hair-pulling, spanking, fingertips-digging-into-my-skin *Daddy* that he usually was.

"Just tonight," I finally whispered as his fingers slid down my stomach and between my legs, sliding over the damp silk of my underwear—I was pretty sure I was always wet around him.

His fingers had just started to dip beneath my panty line when the doorbell rang . . . at least five times in a row. Camden groaned, his forehead falling to my shoulder. "I'm guessing that's Ari," I said in a raspy voice, and his head snapped up.

"I don't want to hear another man's name coming out of your mouth when you sound like that. Do you understand?" he commanded in his silky, dangerous voice that could get me to do whatever he wanted.

"Yes, sir," I whispered.

"Better remind you just in case." His fingers finally pushed under my panty line, thrusting inside me as he expertly worked my clit. I was a trembling, panting mess by the time he was done with me.

And the only name I obviously screamed as I came . . . was his.

Camden left the closet to answer the door, still licking my essence off his fingers.

I stood there for a second, my insides fluttering from the orgasm he'd just given me.

And then I finally got dressed.

I was way more nervous than I should have been as our group stood at Geraldine's door, waiting for her to open it.

"Are you sure this is good enough wine?" I whispered, staring at the bottle clenched in my hands.

"Relax, baby girl," Camden murmured, smacking my butt and making me jump. "She's going to love you."

"Rookie, you must be really excited to see your girlfriend again," Ari said with an especially evil grin.

I glanced back at Logan who was looking unusually pale. He was staring at the wall with wide eyes. "You have no idea what you're in for," he muttered to me, his voice filled with dread.

I shot him a quizzical look, but before I could ask, the door flew open with a flourish. There stood a woman, resplendent in a peacock-blue turban adorned with jeweled pins and a matching caftan that flowed around her like a regal robe. Silver hair peeked out from beneath the turban, and her eyes sparkled with mischief. She had to be pushing eighty. Was this . . .

"Welcome, darlings!" she exclaimed, her voice booming with delight. "Come in, come in!"

We stepped inside, and the woman's eyes immediately landed on Walker. A devilish grin spread across her face. "Well, who is this handsome young man?" She sauntered over to him with a sway in her hips that belied her age.

Walker's eyes widened in shock, but he managed a polite smile. "I'm Walker, nice to meet you, ma'am."

"Ma'am?" Geraldine echoed, her eyebrows arching dramatically. "Call me Geraldine, darling. Or better yet, call me *anytime*." She winked, her fingers trailing lightly along his arm. "Tell me, Walker, have you ever been with an older woman before?"

Walker chuckled nervously, glancing at Olivia for support, but Olivia was no help, she was laughing so hard I was afraid the baby was going to pop right out.

This was the famous Geraldine?

I glanced up at Camden with a scowl. His face was stretched with a wide grin, obviously eating every minute of this up. "You enjoyed me being jealous over a senior citizen, didn't you?" I hissed.

He winked. "I always enjoy you being jealous, baby girl. Makes me not seem so crazy."

Ari had been standing a little to the side, and he huffed loudly, frowning as he stared at Geraldine fawning over Walker. "Geraldine, baby cakes, don't I get a greeting?"

Geraldine glanced disinterestedly at Ari. "*Oh*, they brought you along again." Her face dripped with condescension as she looked him up and down. "Still not interested," she sniffed.

Ari was staring at Geraldine like the ground had fallen out from under him. I imagined that this was one of the first times a woman hadn't been charmed by him.

Monroe and Lincoln exchanged amused glances, while Blake and Olivia tried to stifle their laughter. Camden squeezed my hand, his eyes twinkling.

Geraldine spotted Logan then—trying to hide behind Lincoln . . . unsuccessfully since they were about the same height and build.

"I see you, pet," she cooed at Logan, waving a finger at him before she clasped her hands in front of her face. "We're going to have *so* much fun tonight!"

"And who is this lovely young lady?" Geraldine turned her attention to me, her gaze sharp and assessing.

"Mimi, this is my Anastasia," Camden introduced. "Anastasia, meet Geraldine."

Geraldine's eyes softened slightly as she looked at me. "*Your* Anastasia. She's the stunning dancer, isn't she? My, my, our boy moves fast when he knows what he wants." She wiggled her eyebrows at me. "I like that in a man, don't you?"

I grinned awkwardly.

Camden leaned close. "Geraldine was with me the night that I first saw you."

Oh! I nodded at that, feeling a bit more at ease now that I knew who he took to the performance that night. "It's nice to meet you. I've heard so much about you."

"All good things, I hope," she said with a wink, then turned her attention back to Walker. "Now, Walker, do tell me all about yourself. How do you feel about rope play?"

Walker choked, his eyes wide and terrified.

Geraldine laughed, a rich, throaty sound. "Oh, I'm just kidding, darling. I prefer handcuffs." She winked at him again and glided ahead of us down the hall into a . . . very unusual living room filled with statues of what appeared to be the same man.

"Her late husband, Harold," Camden murmured, noting the expression on my face as I stared at the statues. "I'll explain later."

I nodded, sure it was going to be an interesting tale . . .

Ari had hustled up to Geraldine's side, clearly trying to get her attention. "How do *you* feel about Batman, Geraldine?"

She glanced at him and sniffed. "Superman was the superior hero, everyone knows that."

Ari's mouth opened and closed like a fish out of water as she continued to flirt with Walker, not giving him a second look. Blake linked arms with him and whispered something in his ear about *letting him be Batman when they got home* . . . and he seemed to perk right up.

I wasn't going to ask.

Logan was walking along beside us now, a huge frown stretched across his face as he glared at where Geraldine was still flirting with Walker.

"What's wrong, Rookie?" Camden teased.

"It's like I'm not even here," he growled, gesturing forward. "I'm just as interesting as Disney!" He huffed as Geraldine patted Walker's bicep, acting so impressed. "You know what, I'm going to show her *my* bicep . . . maybe my quad, too. That will really get her going."

Logan hustled ahead and started doing just that. Monroe was laughing so hard she was crying as Lincoln held her up.

"I think Logan has left out a few details from the other night," Ari mused, his eyes mischievous as he cocked his head, no doubt planning how he was going to torture Logan about this later.

We moved to the dining room where a long table was set with fine china, gleaming silverware, and crystal glasses. A chandelier with pink crystals hung overhead, casting a warm, pink glow around the room.

Dinner was served, and the conversation flowed, mostly led by Geraldine. She regaled us with tales of her younger days, her flirtations with famous men, and her various escapades. Throughout it all, she kept her focus on Walker, who handled her advances with increasing awkwardness.

"Walker, dear, how long have you been playing hockey?" she asked, her eyes twinkling.

"For basically all my life," Walker replied, scooting closer to Olivia like Geraldine was going to reach across the table and snatch him up.

"It's such an exciting sport!" Geraldine crooned. "Maybe you can teach me a thing or two about handling a stick."

Logan nearly choked on his drink, while the rest of us struggled to contain our laughter.

"I like her," I whispered to Camden and he snorted.

"She definitely never fails to make things interesting . . . "

"I play hockey too, Geraldine, remember?" Logan inserted suddenly, leaning toward her eagerly like he wanted her to scratch his head or something. "I'm *very* good at handling a stick."

There was a beat of silence, and Ari's face was literally going red from the effort it was taking for him to hold himself back.

"Go ahead, Lancaster. Just get it out," Lincoln finally sighed.

"I–I don't even know what to say first. 'That's what she said' or 'good to know' or . . . "

Logan had realized by then what he'd just said. "I meant I could *show* her how to handle a stick!" he huffed, throwing his hands up.

We were all silent again, and then the group burst into laughter, Geraldine staring at all of us with a twinkle in her blue gaze. "Sounds good to me," she said, finally stroking Logan's bicep. He preened, like he'd just won some kind of medal.

I had to set down my soup, or I was going to choke on it because I'd never laughed so hard in my life.

"Pinch me, Golden Boy. Because I'm obviously in some kind of nightmare where people like Disney and the *rookie* are better than me. I'd like to wake up now," Ari hissed.

"You're my favorite, Lancaster," Blake flirted, and Ari got a starry look in his eyes as he gazed at her, completely forgetting anything else.

So cute.

The rest of the evening passed in a blur of laughter and stories. Geraldine continued to flirt outrageously with Walker, occasionally throwing Logan a bone . . . and Ari continued to be offended about it.

Until she brought up how useful her fake teeth were.

Then Ari seemed *quite* content that she wasn't paying attention to him.

As we left, Geraldine softly touched my arm before pulling me into a clove and cinnamon scented hug. "Camden is a lucky man to have you. Don't let anyone tell you otherwise," she whispered in my ear.

I pulled back, feeling strangely emotional. "I won't."

She turned to the group, her gaze focusing on Walker as she blew him a kiss. "Come and give me a hug, you big lug." Walker looked a little terrified as he carefully bent over to pat her back awkwardly. "Do come back and visit, Walker, dear." Geraldine gave him a flirty smile, batting her eyelashes.

"Arrgh!" We all glanced at Walker and he was rubbing his butt, his eyes wide in horror. "She just pinched my ass," he hissed. Geraldine winked at Olivia like a Cheshire cat. "Good job," she mouthed at her. Olivia hadn't really stopped laughing the entire night, and she was still laughing now. Walker shot her a dangerously sexy grin, and she abruptly stopped giggling, a blush rising on her cheeks about it.

I pretended not to notice that Logan seemed to be angling his ass toward Geraldine, like he wanted in on the action, too.

"Cheeky boy," she finally cooed at Logan, giving him a kiss on his cheek—the one on his face thankfully. "I'll be seeing *you* soon."

Logan grinned down at her. "Looking forward to it."

She leaned forward. "You can show me how you handle those sticks."

Logan's face was red, and he was coughing and sputtering as he exited the penthouse—much to Ari's delight.

"Bye, Geraldine!" Ari called in his most flirtatious tone.

She huffed . . . and closed the door.

Ari turned on Walker. "Don't get any big ideas, Disney. You're still a simp," he snarled.

Walker grinned, looking far more confident than he had at the dinner amidst Geraldine's advances. "But evidently Geraldine's a simp for me, so I think *that's* what counts."

Ari was cursing at Walker hilariously as Camden began leading me across the hall to our home. "I can think of something more interesting to do than listen to Ari bitch, can't you, baby girl?"

I grinned, my core getting wet at just the *thought* of what he could do to my body. "Yes, Daddy," I whispered, enjoying the way his eyes flashed with heat.

Camden pushed me into the penthouse without saying goodbye to anyone, and the rest of the night was definitely more *interesting* than anything that had happened tonight.

CHAPTER 35

CAMDEN

Walker: It's happening. Man your stations. My baby is coming.

Linc: I'm pretty sure that my job was to stay away so that the baby doesn't think I'm her Daddy.

Ari: I'm pretty sure Golden Boy just told his first joke. I'm going to write this down in my diary.

Me: What's my job again?

Walker: Chicken tenders! You're going to bring Cain's chicken tenders because that's what Olivia has requested for her post birth meal.

Ari: You know there's a thing called Door-Dash, Disney. You should try it sometime.

Walker: You think I'm going to let some stranger have access to food that my wife is going to eat?

Me: Don't worry, I'll bring the chicken, Disney. And I'll make sure that no strangers have access to it. I'll watch them at the restaurant like a hawk.

Ari: Hawk and chicken in the same sentence. Fascinating.

Walker: You're a man above men, Hero.

Walker: Lincoln, on second thought . . . maybe you should be a second-day visitor. You've brought up a valid concern.

Ari: Just because you secretly call him "Daddy" doesn't mean that the baby will.

Walker: . . .

Linc: . . .

Ari: . . .

Me: . . .

Walker: I think we're fine with you visiting on the first day, Lancaster. ;)

Ari: 🖕

I heard the elevator ding and I stood up from the couch, eager to see Anastasia. Freya had to bring her back from the studio today because I had a mandatory practice that ended at the same time. I'd fucking missed her every second.

"Hey, baby girl, did you check your texts? There are more pictures of the baby. Walker also said Olivia is begging for chicken strips. We should go pick some up and get to the hospital," I called as I walked toward the elevators.

Anastasia was stepping out as I got there, her hair still up in a bun and sweatpants pulled up over her leotard. When she didn't reply, I glanced closer, noticing she had a completely blank look on her face.

I'd never seen her look like this before.

Especially not when I was talking to her about Olivia's new baby. She was already obsessed with her, and she'd just been born.

"What's wrong?" I asked, taking a step toward her.

Anastasia took an answering step back.

"Anastasia," I growled, not liking what was happening.

"Is this true?" she whispered in a trembling voice, holding up a crumpled piece of paper in her hand.

Frowning, I reached out and grabbed the piece of paper, unwrinkling it.

Well, shit.

Call Charlie. You should ask him if your boyfriend got you fired. Maybe he will tell you the truth this time . . .

I was betting that Michael had struck again.

"Where did you get this from?"

"Linda from the front office gave it to me as I was leaving the studio."

Of course, she did. Linda was obviously an idiot. We'd already informed the front office Michael wasn't allowed anywhere near Anastasia. Linda must want to be fired. Badly.

"Answer me, and don't *lie* like you did about the shopping trip and how it came with your sponsorship," she snapped before I could even open my mouth.

Mmmh, I guess she'd figured that one out.

I sighed, trying to think of what to do.

On the bright side, considering everything I had done to get us to this point, this was honestly the one I was *least* worried about her finding out.

On the other hand, she was obviously still very upset about it.

Which I didn't like for us. At all.

"Yes or no. I want to hear you say it." Her chin was up and her fists were clenched.

"I did have something to do with that," I finally said, not ashamed of anything I'd done, least of all that.

She slowly closed her eyes, squeezing them like she was trying to hold all of her emotion in. I hated this.

Even without all of the other things Michael had done, I would have destroyed him for this.

"I just don't understand how you could do that," she said, a tear sliding down her cheek that felt like a knife in my fucking gut.

"You really can't?" I asked gently.

My phone buzzed in my pocket as a text came in, and then another. Walker was probably pleading for Olivia's chicken. The food that Anastasia and I were supposed to deliver—together.

"You were working yourself to the bone, being paid practically nothing. You weren't listening to reason," I told her. "You would have worked there until you passed out and they had to scrape your body off the floor."

She winced at that. "It was still my choice, though! You took that away!"

I had taken a lot of choices away from her. But in my defense . . . she was making a lot of bad ones at that point in time.

My phone buzzed again.

"I want to talk about this with you. We can talk about it all night until you feel better," I told her softly. "But we should go give Olivia the food she wants. You were really excited about that . . . remember?"

Her chin lifted even higher, and I sighed because her inner brat had decided to rear her head.

"I think—I think I just need some time to think. Maybe I'll go back to the studio for a bit." She held up her hand like she knew what I was thinking. "I'll bring Freya with me, of course." She bit down on her lip, shifting on her feet anxiously. "I'm just going to change into some clean dance clothes."

I rubbed my face tiredly because this next part wasn't going to be fun.

Following her into the closet, I tried to reason with her one more time. "You've been desperate to see the baby. Just come with me and we can talk about this."

She shook her head. "I'm so mad at you," she said in a broken voice. "I . . . I can't be around you right now."

I sighed. "Alright, baby girl. I'll give you some time." I walked over to try and brush a kiss against her cheek, and she flinched away.

Anastasia obviously wanted to be spanked.

I walked out of the closet and bedroom, and locked the door behind me.

I'd thought it was a construction defect that the lock was put on the wrong way on the master bedroom.

Turns out it was divine providence.

I was halfway down the hall when she realized the door was locked.

"Camden!" she yelled through the door, and I had to take a deep, calming breath to keep walking toward the elevator.

"Here's your time to get your head on straight," I called behind me.

She screamed in response.

Then the banging began. She alternated between yelling and hitting the door.

It was fucking awful.

I forced myself on the elevator, locking the floor entry behind me for good measure.

I would give her some time, just like she'd asked, and then she'd understand. And if she didn't . . .

I'd spank her until she did.

Anastasia

I sat in the dark hunched over, my back against the door. My voice was hoarse and my hands were tired from beating on the wood.

He'd locked me in the freaking room. Like an errant child. How could he?

Usually, I didn't like the dark. In the shelter I'd gotten used to sleeping with low overhead lights on at all times. Camden always left the closet light on with the door cracked when we slept.

I guess that was childlike, too.

I groaned as I wiped my eyes. They felt like sandpaper after I'd spent the last hour crying.

And for what?

That was what I was really struggling with as I sat there. Charlie's had been important to me because it had been a symbol of my independence. It was attached to my fear of not owing something to someone.

Camden was right—I *had* been working myself to death. I'd been working so hard that I'd been miserable. Now that I was *just* doing ballet, I was still exhausted, but I was satisfied every day. While I'd been working at Charlie's, I'd just been exhausted. And it had seemed like no matter how hard I worked, I never got ahead.

I think part of it was how genuine he'd seemed after I told him I was fired. His anger had seemed real. All of his emotions had seemed real.

There'd been no sign that he was the one responsible for it in the first place.

He'd shown he was trustworthy in every other way, though, hadn't he?

Michael was behind the note. I knew he was. This was his goal, to push Camden and I apart, so I'd be alone . . . and he could get to me. He loved psychological things like this, things that would twist up my insides, make me second-guess myself and everyone around me.

I tried to picture what it would have been like over the last few months if I'd still been at Charlie's.

Misery.

That's what it would have been like. I still wouldn't have been making enough to get my own place.

I would have just continued to go . . . nowhere.

Even my leg had begun to improve since I'd stopped working there. Being able to rest it at night rather than work on it—it had made a huge difference. I'd been able to push much harder as I practiced for the showcase.

Every day since I'd known him, Camden had wanted what was best for me. He'd just wanted to love and take care of me.

Getting someone fired . . . that was crazy. I couldn't deny that. But it had come from a place of love. Right? I could at least be confident in that.

Could I forgive him, knowing that he'd done it because he loved me?

It felt like I could.

My eyes were getting drowsy, and I pushed off the floor and got onto the bed, burying my face in his pillow because even mad at him, I wished he was here.

Eventually, I fell asleep.

I woke to an orgasm, gasping as pleasure surged through my entire body. My eyes flew open to the sight of Camden between my legs, leisurely eating me out.

I wasn't sure how I'd slept through the start of this, but *oh my gosh*, it felt so good.

My head fell back into the pillow as my hips began rocking against his face, chasing the high that his mouth was so good at giving me.

"I love you," he murmured right before he spread my cum all over my asshole and slowly pushed his fingers inside, his tongue pressing on my clit.

"Camden!" I cried out as he stretched my hole, his lips sensually sucking and licking my core at the same time.

This felt like a dream—an incredibly erotic dream—but a dream nonetheless.

"Taste so good, baby girl," he murmured as my head thrashed from all the nerves he was brushing up against with every thrust of his fingers.

"Come, Anastasia," Camden growled, and I screamed as another orgasm burst through me, goosebumps exploding across my skin as he continued to finger fuck me through my pleasure.

My breath was coming out in frantic pants as he pulled his fingers out and slipped off the bed, walking to the bathroom.

I was faintly aware of the sound of running water, my eyes growing heavy again.

I was *so* tired.

"Go to sleep, little dancer," he whispered when he returned, pulling me onto his chest. I buried my face in his neck and breathed him in, and once again, I slept.

CHAPTER 36

ANASTASIA

Camden was still asleep when I woke up, wrapped around him like I had been every morning since I'd started sleeping in his bed.

He was so freaking beautiful. There wasn't anything about him that I wasn't completely obsessed with.

Except maybe the fact that he'd locked me in our bedroom and got me fired behind my back . . . I was still debating how I felt about that.

"Who's stalking who now, baby girl?" he said in a growly, sleepy voice before his eyes flicked open, revealing those tornado-green eyes that I loved so much. My breath caught, because I'd never get used to what I saw when I looked in them. Love and devotion and obsession . . . everything I wanted from him.

"How are you feeling?" he asked carefully, and I continued to stare at him as I considered his question.

Shifting, I realized that my . . . ass was a little sore. My eyes widened.

Oh, that hadn't been a dream!

Blushing, I sighed. "Are you asking how my body is feeling . . . or my heart?"

He huffed and pushed some hair out of his face, his bulging bicep catching my eye as he moved.

I was definitely on the horny side this morning, not the best state of being for the important conversation we needed to have.

"I'm always worried about both, baby girl," he said.

I closed my eyes and fell back on the pillow with a huff. "Are you even sorry?"

Now it was his turn to huff. He took so long to answer that I finally glanced over at him.

He was studying me like I was a puzzle he was desperate to figure out. "No," he finally said.

Not shocking me at all.

"And I'd do it again, and again, and again. As long as it got you here in my bed like this."

I considered that statement. It made me feel good. Really good. I'd never been wanted. Ever. So the way Camden James wanted me, it was like heroin—a high I would be desperate for, for the rest of my life.

"Let me ask you a question, baby girl," Camden said, reaching over to pull me back onto his chest.

"What?" I asked, tracing the tattoos inked across his skin.

"What would *you* do to get me into your bed like this?"

I blinked, not expecting that question.

The answer came easily, though, like it had been waiting on the tip of my tongue for him to ask.

"Anything," I answered softly. "Absolutely anything."

His hands tangled in my hair, and he pulled me toward him for a bruising kiss that seemed to touch my soul.

I broke away so that I could look him in the eyes. "Don't lock me up again, Camden James."

"Don't try to run from me, Anastasia Lennox," he combated easily.

I wrinkled my nose. "Deal," I said, returning to his lips for another perfect kiss.

Only later did I realize he'd never made the same promise back.

And only later did I realize that I really didn't care.

Camden

"She's beautiful," Anastasia cried as she lifted Isabella from Olivia's arms. Her lower lip was quivering adorably as she cooed and brought the baby to her chest.

Walker hadn't allowed me to hold his baby. He'd muttered something about radiuses and ten feet, and then Olivia had offered the baby to Anastasia.

"Mind her head," Walker said frantically, even though I was pretty sure Anastasia had it perfectly covered. She was a natural, in fact.

Olivia was staring at her baby in awe, like she'd never seen something so beautiful in her entire life.

Suddenly, Olivia burst into tears. Walker froze, a frantic look on his face as his gaze darted between his baby and his wife, like he wasn't sure what to do.

He practically lunged toward Anastasia. "I need my baby back," he said in a crazy person voice.

"It's okay," Olivia cried, still sobbing and just staring at her baby. "I just love her so much."

Anastasia had a goofy grin on her face as she reluctantly handed the baby back. My hands twitched when I saw Walker's hand brush hers, the insane urge to cut his fingers off flashing through my mind for a minute.

That was . . . weird.

I *had* locked Anastasia in a room last night, so maybe it wasn't that weird.

Anastasia looked good with that baby, though, food for thought for another day. Logan might call me a grandpappy, but the only "Daddy" I wanted to be at the moment . . . was hers.

Walker slid the baby back into Olivia's arms, and I watched as she pressed a gentle kiss on her forehead. It felt like we were intruding on a sacred moment as I watched the three of them together. Olivia had come from a really tough childhood; she and Anastasia could probably tell stories for days—all of them equally awful.

Olivia glanced up at Anastasia with glossy eyes. "I can't believe she's really here."

Anastasia nodded, her own eyes growing shiny.

Olivia started singing to the baby then, and I pulled Anastasia into my chest as she started to weep, too.

Walker and I exchanged looks, like what the fuck were we supposed to do?

Later, as we were walking through the parking lot, Anastasia was softly humming the song Olivia had been singing.

I smiled down at her, glancing up to make sure we were going in the direction the truck was parked, and then I stiffened.

Michael was standing about a hundred feet away, a feral grin on his face.

I gave him one back and hoped he saw the promise in my gaze. Whatever he saw was at least enough for his smile to fade and for him to start walking away.

I wasn't going to fuck him up in a hospital parking lot, though. What I had planned for him needed to be done in private, where I wouldn't make the headlines. I couldn't exactly take care of Anastasia from *jail.*

Anastasia hadn't noticed him, and I preferred that.

Michael was living on borrowed time.

He just didn't know it yet.

CHAPTER 37

ANASTASIA

Michael was following me.

It was all part of the plan, but it was terrifying.

Even knowing that Camden was watching over me, my heart was going a million miles a minute, so fast that I was worried I might be having a heart attack.

We'd tried this three times over the past week after Freya had seen him lurking near my dance studio—but Michael hadn't taken the bait.

Tonight, apparently, he had.

We could have called the police—there was a warrant out for his arrest because of the bathroom attack. But Camden and I had both decided that it wasn't good enough. It wouldn't be enough to make up for all he'd done to me all these years.

He'd probably get a couple of months probation, or if he was sentenced to jail, he'd get early release.

Michael Carver had tortured me since the day I'd woken up in the hospital. He'd cut my skin—marked me with his blades and his teeth, he'd haunted my nights, he'd locked me in a cage, he'd stalked me through the streets, he'd forced me to take pictures for him and violated my body and my soul. He had blackmailed me and then strangled me for fun . . .

For all of that, the justice that I needed to sleep at night had to be done ourselves.

Like the other nights, I pretended I was walking home from dance by myself, Camden staying out of sight so Michael would think I was truly alone.

My breath was coming out in gasps as I walked along the sidewalk, trying to keep my steps controlled and not break out into the run that I wanted to.

I would catch glimpses of Michael every time I turned a corner—he wasn't trying to hide from me at all. He was enjoying this right now, the predator hunting his little bunny.

I knew the plan, we'd gone over it again and again, but I still felt too much like prey as Michael stalked me through the streets.

Turning the corner, I went down a road I wouldn't usually take, that *no one* usually took. I stopped in front of an alleyway, pretending to look at my phone.

Camden: I love you.

I read the text over and over, trying to prepare for what was coming next.

Michael's footsteps sounded behind me, making me sick. I felt violated just having him within ten feet of me.

"Hello, *Ana*," he purred as he walked up behind me, smug satisfaction coming off him in waves.

Because he thought he'd won.

"Michael," I whispered, my bravado failing as I slowly turned to stare at him, just like it always did. I was shivering as we looked at each other, his watery blue eyes that starred in all of my nightmares taking in every inch of me.

I backed up into the alley, my hands in front of me like I was trying to ward him off.

His footsteps were slow and measured as he stalked me, past the piles of trash and decay that lined the sides of the building, his shiny shoes crunching dead leaves and debris as he walked. In my mind, this was where he belonged. There was no amount of nice clothes or expensive hair products that could hide what he was—the worst kind of trash.

A little scream popped out of my mouth when my back hit the chain metal fence at the end of the alley—unplanned, of course—but I'd never been great at controlling my reaction to him.

Michael grinned, and it felt like the mask had fallen. Like his demonic inside had finally leaked out to his face.

"You should leave," I told him, as usual hating the tremble in my voice.

"But little bunny, you would miss me too much," he mocked.

"What's the end game here?" I asked. "You grab me . . . and then what?"

"End game?" he asked, raising an eyebrow. I wanted to reach out and rip off that eyebrow, mark that face up. "You know what the end game is, little bunny. You know what the end game was always going to be. Ever since I saw you walking home that first day."

Michael held out his hand, like he expected me to take it and walk out of here with him.

I scoffed, straightening off the fence and holding my chin high, trying to hold on to all the bravery Camden had been instilling me with since I'd met him.

"Ana . . . I've got a special little cage set up for you. So you can be my bunny forever and ever. Won't you like that? I've got a place on my own again. So I'm the only one who can hear your pretty little cries. I've prepared it just for you. You're going to love it." There was a singsong lilt to his voice, and my eyes widened in horror as he pulled a long serrated knife out of his coat. "Come here, little bunny."

He was six feet away when, apparently, Camden decided that was close enough.

Camden appeared at the entrance of the alleyway behind Michael, a small cooler in his hand.

"Hello, Michael," he taunted, and a little part of me unclenched as I watched fear seep into Michael's eyes for the first time before he jerked toward him in surprise.

Camden

Michael blinked several times, staring at the cooler as he recovered from the shock of seeing me.

"You planned this," he growled, like *we* were the ones in the wrong here.

"Yeah, well obviously," I said with a grin that hopefully Anastasia would forget, because I was sure it was incredibly sadistic.

"What's your plan then, *Hero*?" he sneered, showing that he'd been looking into me as well. "Did you bring me lunch?" Michael gestured at the cooler.

I chuckled before I used my free hand to pull out the gun from inside my jacket, aiming it at his chest.

His eyes flashed, a chuckle escaping his lips. "This is hilarious," he taunted Anastasia who was still plastered against the fence, her attention rapt on the gun in my hand.

Without hesitation, I pulled the trigger, and Michael flinched, his mouth dropping as the gun released a stream of water that soaked his shirt and the front of his pants. I squirted some on his face for good measure.

"What the hell?" he muttered, as he looked down at himself, confusion and shock contorting his features, his hands shaking as he touched the wet stain.

I couldn't help the smirk that tugged at my lips. "Oops, I must've grabbed the wrong gun," I said lightly.

I'd actually struck him dumb. That seemed like an accomplishment for how much the guy liked to talk.

"I actually meant to do this." Opening the cooler, I reached in with a gloved hand and started throwing chunks of meat at Michael as I stalked closer to him. He was so surprised by the meat suddenly hitting his chest, that he didn't really react to my movements until I was just a few feet away. Ana slowly inched to the side—knowing what was going to happen next.

I lunged forward and punched him in the face, enjoying the way he crumbled to the ground. For good measure, I dumped the entire contents of the cooler over his head, the bloody mixture coating his face and hair like a horror movie.

"Motherfucker," he growled, fumbling with his knife, the blade now streaked with blood.

"Forgot one more thing," I said, holding up a hand as Anastasia tossed me the wire cutters she'd been hiding. Ripping off the glove, I threw it at Michael, and snapped the wire that had been holding up part of the fence. I whistled, and a few seconds later, Fluffy and Midas bounded into the alley through the hole. Their usual friendly demeanor had vanished, replaced by a fierce hunger as they zeroed in on Michael.

Geraldine had wanted to be part of the plan when I'd asked to borrow the dogs again—after winking at me and telling me she'd keep my first outing with the dogs "on the down-low."

She'd had them in their kennels on the other side of the fence.

Michael's bravado crumbled in an instant. "What the—"

Before he could react, the dogs were on him. Midas latched onto his arm, growling and shaking his head. Fluffy, the giant poodle, went for his legs, his powerful jaws clamping down hard. Michael screamed, a high-pitched, panicked sound that echoed throughout the alley, and his knife fell to the ground as he tried to scramble away from the animals.

"Get them off me! Get them off!" he shrieked, trying to shake the dogs off, but they held firm, biting chunks off as they tried to get to the steak blood.

Fluffy let go of his arm, and a second later, Michael's high-pitched screams filled the air as Fluffy bit into his dick. Michael's screams turned into sobs under the relentless attack.

He had always been the predator, but now, he was nothing more than prey.

For good measure, Darcy, Geraldine's Saint Bernard, came bounding out through the fence, too—it hadn't surprised me that Geraldine had even more feral, meat-addicted dogs as pets. Darcy lunged forward, her jaws outstretched, and a second later, Michael's nose had disappeared.

I watched, a grim satisfaction settling over me as I watched the carnage.

Anastasia's hand slid into mine. She was pale and shaking, her fear of the dogs very present, but her eyes were glimmering as she watched the nightmare that had haunted her for so long, get torn to shreds.

"That's probably enough," she murmured when he passed out from blood loss. I was pretty sure the lump on the ground was part of his tongue. It would seem the dogs had gotten a little aggressive.

"Probably," I said after Midas took another bite out of Michael's dick.

Geraldine appeared in the entrance, carrying a jar of peanut butter. She stared at Michael's limp body on the dirty ground, a small smile on her face . . . which was a little scary. "What good little puppies," she cooed. "Let's go take a bath, darlings." She leaned over and whistled sharply, holding out the jar, and the dogs immediately leapt from Michael to get their treat.

Blood and peanut butter . . . quite the diet.

"Got the cages," Ari huffed as he and Lincoln appeared behind Geraldine, lugging three enormous crates.

"You're a good boy," Geraldine told Ari, patting his face before she lured the dogs into the crates with the peanut butter.

Ari was glowing, literally preening under her praise.

"A little help, Lancaster," Lincoln grunted as he lifted one of the huge crates. Midas whined, and Lincoln eyed him carefully, like he was going to escape from the cage and decide to attack.

Anastasia was still frozen, staring at Michael and his blood pooling on the ground.

Her lips twitched, and then she started to giggle. At first, it was soft, almost a whisper of laughter, but it quickly grew louder, hysterical, her eyes wild and unfocused. The giggles turned into sobs, wracking her body with the force of her emotions. She began to collapse, and I grabbed her, pulling her into my arms. I didn't want the dirt and grime of this alley to even touch my baby girl.

"Is it really over, Camden?" she choked out between sobs. "Or is this just a dream? I need to know he can't come after me anymore."

I held her tightly, feeling her tears soak through my shirt. "It's over, baby girl," I whispered, my voice as steady and reassuring as I could make it. "He won't hurt you anymore."

Her sobs quieted a bit, but she clung to me still. I stroked her hair, whispering soothing words, trying to anchor her in the present, away from the horrors of the past.

"My guy's coming for cleanup." Lincoln locked eyes with me, giving me a chin nod that was almost as good as a "good boy" coming from him. "He'll take care of any cameras, and he'll make sure some junkyard dogs are found with some of his scraps and blood," he said, gesturing toward Michael. "Fluffy and Midas will be *blame-free*." He grinned. "He also wiped that asshole's computer and phone—he hadn't made any other copies of the pictures. They're *all* gone."

Anastasia reared her head back and gasped. "Really?" she whispered, her eyes filling with more tears. My poor baby girl. Those pictures had been haunting her for years—of course I was going to make sure they were destroyed.

She snuggled back into me, whispering a soft "thank you."

I gave Lincoln a thumbs-up and he smirked.

I no longer wanted to know how Daniels had so many *guys* . . . or what he needed them for.

But I was pretty sure that I was now in the circle of trust.

"Do you think Michael will say anything?" Anastasia whispered to me as Ari, Lincoln, and Geraldine disappeared around the corner . . .

I glanced over at Michael's body disinterestedly. "I think he's missing most of his tongue . . . and fingers. So no."

She pulled back slightly, her tear-streaked face searching mine for any sign of doubt. "Are you sure? What if he finds a way?"

I cupped her face in my hands, looking directly into her eyes. "He won't. He can't. Trust me, Anastasia, it's over."

She nodded slowly, the tension in her body starting to ease. I could see the relief in her eyes, but also the exhaustion.

"Come on," I said softly, helping her to her feet. "Let's get you out of here."

She was shaking for the entire drive back to the penthouse—adrenaline and residual fear still raging inside her.

Once in our place, I carried Anastasia into the bathroom. With one hand, I started a warm bath, the steam filling the room. Then I set her down and helped her undress, my movements gentle and careful. She slipped into the water, a sigh of relief escaping her lips as the warmth enveloped her.

I quickly stripped and slid in behind her, tucking her against me as she laid her head back against my shoulder. I traced her features obsessively as her eyes fluttered closed

"Thank you, Camden. You're like my own personal superhero," she whispered. "I love you so much."

We stayed like that until the water turned cool, the silence between us filled with a newfound peace. When we finally climbed out, I wrapped her in a towel and led her to the bedroom, tucking her into the soft, warm sheets.

Laying down beside her, I pulled her close. Her breathing slowed, her body relaxing against mine. As she drifted off to sleep, I stared at the ceiling, the events of the night replaying in my mind.

Michael was out of the picture, and for the first time, it felt like Anastasia could truly heal.

CHAPTER 38

ANASTASIA

One Month Later

The lights dimmed, and the hush of the audience settled over the theater. I took a deep breath, feeling the familiar rush of adrenaline. Rudolf stood beside me, his presence steady and reassuring.

Considering we'd had such a short time to practice together, I'd never been more confident in one of my partners.

I'd also never been more confident in *myself.*

The music began, soft and haunting, and we moved as one, our bodies perfectly in sync.

As the first notes filled the theater, I felt the music seep into my bones, guiding my every movement. Rudolf and I began with a series of graceful, sweeping steps, our feet gliding effortlessly across the stage. The connection between us was electric, every glance and touch filled with the story of Giselle and Albrecht.

Rudolf's hand found mine, and he spun me out, our fingertips brushing as we separated. I twirled, my tutu fluttering around me like petals in the wind. As I came back to him, he lifted me high into the air, the spotlight catching the sparkles in my costume. For a moment, I felt like I was flying, weightless and free, suspended above the stage.

"Beautiful, Anastasia," Rudolf whispered as he lowered me back to the ground, his voice filled with admiration.

Our bodies intertwined in a series of intricate lifts and turns. I could feel the energy of the audience, their rapt attention adding to the magic of the performance. Rudolf's hands were strong and sure, guiding me through each lift with ease. The chemistry between us was undeniable, so different from how it had been with Dallon. Every movement was perfectly timed, every expression mirroring the emotions of our characters.

As the music swelled, Rudolf lifted me into a grand arabesque, my leg extending behind me as I balanced on his hand. The world outside the stage faded away, and all that existed was the dance. The emotions of Giselle poured through me—love, betrayal, forgiveness—each one expressed through the precise, elegant movements.

The final sequence was an arrangement of delicate, flowing steps that brought us closer together. Rudolf's eyes locked onto mine, and I felt a surge of emotion. This was the essence of ballet—the silent communication, the unspoken connection that transcended words. My heart pounded in time with the music, every beat resonating in my chest.

When the final notes played, I struck the last pose, holding my breath, waiting for the audience's response. No matter if Camden was the only one who clapped for me, I knew it was the best I had ever danced.

There was a beat of silence, and then the theater erupted into applause, the sound washing over me like a flood of warm water. I looked out into the crowd, searching for the one face that meant everything to me.

And then I found him.

Camden's eyes were shining with pride, his smile wide, our friends seated all around him. He jumped to his feet, leading the standing ovation, and my heart felt like it might burst.

I hadn't known it was possible to be this happy.

I turned to Rudolf, and he gave me a knowing nod. "You nailed it," he said, grinning as he pushed his sweaty, black hair out of his face.

As we took our bows, the applause grew even louder. The spotlight was blinding, but I soaked it in, the thrill of the performance still coursing through me. I felt amazing, alive, and utterly triumphant.

The curtain closed, and Rudolf and I left the stage so the crew could clear the props for the next showcase performance.

"If you aren't a principal in the next couple of months, that lady needs her head checked," Rudolf muttered as Madame Leclerc gave us a nod that was as good as a "Bravo" coming from her.

I smiled at him, not really sure if that would happen. My leg was aching, and even though it was doing better than in the past, I had begun to accept it for what it was—I wasn't sure my leg was capable of performing an entire ballet as the lead.

The realization had come, but I wasn't as devastated as I would've been before. I'd found a new dream.

And his name was Camden James.

Camden stepped out from behind a curtain, his arms filled with the biggest bouquet of flowers I'd ever seen. I swooned for him, just like I always did, and the sight of him filled another hole inside of me.

It was the *first* time I'd ever received flowers from a loved one after a performance.

He pulled me into a kiss, the flowers pressing against me and filling my senses with their fragrance.

I preferred *his* scent much more.

He wrapped me in a tight hug, lifting me off my feet. "In awe of you, baby girl," he murmured, his voice filled with emotion. "I'm so fucking proud of you."

I held on to him, everything inside me *beaming* with happiness. "Thank you," I whispered.

Camden straightened, his arms loosening around my waist. "Want to go see everyone? Geraldine even brought her *card group* so she could brag about knowing you."

I huffed, pressing up on my tiptoes, my face tipping to his ear. "Not quite. You know how . . . on edge you get after a game?" I whispered. "Where you can't wait to tear my clothes off and fuck me . . . "

Camden stilled, his hand pressing down on my lower back. "Go on," he urged, his voice suddenly rough.

"It seems ballerinas get that way, too . . . *Daddy*."

He growled, licking his bottom lip slowly, hunger in his gaze as I slowly stepped away.

"Anastasia . . . " he rasped.

I giggled as I tugged at his hand and he followed me with a sexy grin. We rushed past dancers and crew members, ducking down a hallway when we thought no one was looking, opening random doors as we tried to find a place to go.

Perfect. A cleaning closet.

My heart was racing in excitement as we squished into the little room, stocked with shelves of cleaning supplies, mops and brooms stashed in the corners. Camden grabbed a cart and shoved it against the door. I wasn't sure that would actually prevent anyone from coming in if they wanted to, though. I also didn't care.

I *needed* him.

Camden stalked toward me, pushing me against the wall. A bottle skittered across the floor as he kicked it away.

The darkness heightened everything.

I'd said before that I didn't like the dark, but I'd gladly be in the dark with him like this . . . any time. Even surrounded by the scent of cleaning supplies, I was able to let go and succumb to my body's sensations as his mouth trailed down my neck.

His hand roamed over my breast through the thin leotard I had worn for the pas de deux as he bit down gently in the spot where my shoulder and my neck met.

I moaned, my thighs rubbing together, the seam of my tights straining against my clit, but not giving me what I needed. I wanted his hand, his fingers, his *cock* inside me. It was the only thing that was going to help satisfy my ache.

"Camden," I whimpered.

"I know, baby girl," he soothed. "I want to live inside you. It feels like my life is spent just waiting to fuck you."

"Yes," I gasped as he pulled at my top, sliding it past my shoulders and then my waist, grabbing my tutu and my tights so they were down, too . . . until I was completely bared to the chilled air.

He left the tights gathered around my knees, though, so that it was difficult to move.

Camden's finger slipped into my soaked core.

"Your cunt is so fucking wet, baby girl. I love this." His finger was agonizingly slow as it thrust inside me, and my fingers dug into his shoulders, trying to spur him on.

I wanted to cry when he pulled his finger out, making a big show of licking it like it was the most delicious treat he'd ever tasted.

"I think I need more," he growled into my ear.

Camden pushed me against the wall and dropped to his knees. Only then, did I remember how . . . sweaty I was. I tried to push him away, but he wasn't having it, burying his face in my core, and breathing deeply.

My eyes squeezed shut as his mouth sealed over my clit, and then he parted my folds with his tongue, licking and sucking until my hips were fucking against his face. I forgot all about worrying, and just thought about how good he felt.

Hungry noises were spilling out of his glorious mouth, and I soaked them all in, my fingers threading through his hair as he jerked me closer.

Camden pushed two fingers in my core, curling them so he could hit that special spot inside of me. “Yes,” I moaned as he greedily sucked on my clit, his fingers pumping in and out, faster and faster.

I was blind with lust, not caring that anyone could come in. I just wanted him to keep eating me like this.

Fisting his hair, my orgasm built, my entire body beginning to convulse as I came all over his face.

Camden pushed his tongue into my slit, growling as he drank me in.

My head fell back against the wall, enjoying his leisurely licks through my folds as I came down from my pleasure.

It still wasn’t enough, though, not even close.

“Turn around,” he ordered, and a dark thrill ran down my spine at the greedy possession in his voice. “Hands on the wall. Arch your back.”

I liked this position, glancing back over my shoulder, he did, too. He was staring at my bare ass in rapt wonderment.

“This fucking body,” he growled, his hands massaging my ass cheeks for a moment as he continued to stare.

Thwack! I whimpered as he suddenly spanked me before leaning over and soothing the sting with his tongue.

“You were a fucking goddess on the stage tonight,” he breathed against my skin. He straightened, his hands caressing my back. “I can’t believe your talent.”

A moment of doubt flashed inside me at his words. “You would love me without it, though, right?” I whispered as he pulled out his cock and rubbed it through my dripping folds. “Even if I didn’t dance.”

Camden abruptly thrust his cock inside me, and a low moan tore from my chest as he pushed and pushed until his hips were flush against my ass. He slid a hand to my throat, holding it possessively as he arched my back even more, until his lips could brush my ear.

“I would love you no matter what, baby girl,” he growled. “If I had to give up everything to have one day with you—one minute—I would do it. I worship the ground you walk on, not just for your beauty or your talent, but for *you*. The way you fixed something inside me the second I saw you. The way you complete me in a way I never could have imagined. I love the way you smile, the way you breathe . . . fucking everything. You own my soul, Anastasia. And if you decided to never dance again right this fucking second . . . none of that would change.”

His grip tightened on my throat, and a solitary tear slid down my face. Somehow, every day with him was better than the last.

"Do you trust me yet?" he rasped as he slowly slid his dick in and out, root to tip so I felt every single inch of him. "I know I have this body now, but do I have all of this perfect fucking heart?"

He thrust in hard, catching me off guard with the sudden change in rhythm.

"Do I, baby girl?"

My breathing turned ragged and harsh as his hips slammed against mine in earnest. "I own this body, but you own *all* of me. Everything I do, I do for you, Anastasia. So tell me, please," he growled, "do I own you, too?"

The dark room was filled with the sounds of flesh smacking together. My hips pushed back at him, wanting everything he was willing to give me. His words were like drugs, spreading pleasure through my veins.

His hand tightened on my throat, and I came, my core tightening around his cock, sparks of ecstasy shooting across my skin.

"Answer me," he rumbled over my hoarse cries.

"Yes, yes, you own me, every part of me," I gasped.

"Forever?" He thrust hard, one, two more times, and then his low groan filled the room as his cock pulsed inside me, pumping his warm cum into my desperate pussy.

"Forever." I sank back against him, content for him to hold me up. I'd just put up the performance of a lifetime and then gotten fucked against a wall—my legs, especially my injured one, could use a break.

"I love you," Camden whispered, and we both moaned as he slowly pulled out of me.

I immediately felt empty without him. I felt the same way that he did, like I lived for the moments he was inside me.

His hand was still around my throat. Camden's fingers slid through my folds, pushing the cum back inside that had begun to drip out of me.

I soaked in his leisurely movements; the feral edge I'd had, finally sated. I barely moved when he slid his fingers over my asshole, using our combined essence to push inside with just his fingertip.

"I'm going to take this next, baby girl," he murmured, slowly fucking in and out. "Are you ready for that?"

"Yes, Daddy," I gasped, a smile spreading across my face at his answering groan.

He gave me another orgasm, this time with his finger in my ass and his lips devouring my breasts. Then he flipped on the lights to make sure my costume was put back into place and my hair was smoothed before we walked out of the closet hand in hand.

Our friends were waiting for us in the lobby, and I swore they all gave us identical grins when we walked in.

"Well, well, well, Anastasia's performance ended thirty minutes ago. A lot to handle backstage?" Ari hummed, his eyebrows wagging up and down.

I went to make an excuse, but Camden beat me to it. "We were *celebrating*," he answered, completely unapologetic. My whole body flushed red as the group burst into laughter.

"You were amazing!" Olivia's voice said from somewhere. Blake lifted up her phone, showing Olivia and Walker on FaceTime with baby Isabella. "I was crying the entire time!" she squealed.

Walker pressed a kiss against the side of her head. "She's stopped crying all the time, so that actually *is* a big deal," he commented fondly.

I grinned at them, choked up that they cared enough to watch even with the new baby.

Everyone came up to congratulate me.

And they all had flowers.

"Radiuses," Camden sternly reminded Ari when he stepped up to hug me. He backed up dramatically, his hands up in front of him.

My eyes were shiny as I stared at the new family Camden had given me—by themselves, more than I could have ever dreamed of.

Together, though, they seemed like a miracle.

Camden's arms slid around me, and he buried his face against my neck. "Are you happy, baby girl?" he murmured, his lips caressing my skin.

It was amazing how much I wanted him, even though I'd just *had* him.

I had a feeling it was always going to be like this. A never-ending desire for Camden James.

I'd lain on that cot all those months ago, night after night, and wondered if life was always going to be like that. If all I would ever know was struggle. I didn't know when all of me would believe my new life was real.

"How's your leg?" Camden asked, his arms stroking up and down my back as the elevator began its ascent to the penthouse.

"Pretty good," I murmured lazily, enjoying the feel of his hands. I'd definitely need to ice my leg before falling asleep, but for now I was okay. "I think I'm ready to get into bed, though."

"I'm hoping you can wait up for just a little longer," he said, an edge to his voice as the elevator doors dinged and then opened. I glanced up at his face, but a flickering light caught my attention from inside.

Peering curiously into the penthouse, I gasped, my breath catching in my throat.

The living room was bathed in a warm, golden glow. Candles were set up all over, their flames dancing and flickering from every surface.

Pictures of Camden and me adorned the walls and tables everywhere, capturing months of laughter, love, and the most extreme happiness that was possible.

"Camden?" I whispered, my voice barely audible over the pounding of my heart.

I turned to look at him, and he was down on one knee, a small velvet box in his hand. My heart stopped as I stared down at him.

"Anastasia," he began, his voice soft but filled with emotion. "From the moment I saw you, I knew my life would never be the same. You are the reason I breathe. You're inside me; I can't even remember what life was like without you. I can't *live* without you."

Tears welled up in my eyes, and I struggled to keep my breathing steady. I took a step forward, and then another, eventually falling to my knees in front of where he was kneeling. Because I just wanted to be wherever he was.

He opened the box, revealing a stunning diamond ring that sparkled in the candlelight. "I want to spend the rest of my life with you. I want to make you happy every single day. Marry me, baby girl."

"It sounds like you're telling me to marry you, rather than asking me, Camden James," I said with a hitched laugh because I was *feeling* so much.

He grinned, and the sight of it took my breath away. "That's because the only acceptable answer is yes."

I was crying then, my body wracked with happy sobs as I stared up at him. "You know you're completely wrong for me," I whispered.

He wrinkled his brow, immediately beginning to protest, and I silenced him with a kiss before pulling back.

"But only because I was completely wrong for you . . . until you made everything right. You're my hero. Perfectly imperfect. You say you're obsessed with me, Camden. But I'm obsessed with you right back. All of you."

"So, I'm assuming that's a yes," he growled, rubbing his nose cutely against mine.

"Yes, Camden. Yes, a thousand times, yes."

He slipped the ring onto my finger, and I threw my arms around him, pulling him into a tight embrace. He stood, lifting me off my feet, and spun me around as we both laughed through our tears.

“I love you so much,” I whispered into his ear, my voice choked with emotion.

“I guarantee I love you more,” he replied, setting me down gently and pressing his forehead against mine. “I am now the happiest man in the world.”

That was the key, wasn’t it?

Apparently, that was what I’d been missing all those years.

I’d been doing my best to find my own happiness, and I’d been failing miserably.

I’d tried to do everything right, on my own, thinking it would give me results.

I thought when Camden James came swooping in, that it wasn’t going to work.

I’d been so sure he was all wrong for my disaster of a life.

Evidently, what I’d been missing . . .

A possessive, intense, overwhelming NHL star willing to battle all my demons in whatever way was necessary.

The pucking wrong man . . . turned out to be the right one.

EPILOGUE

CAMDEN

The crowd's roar was deafening. The tension in the air tasted like ash on my tongue.

This was what I lived for.

Well, this and Anastasia *James*, but that one was obvious.

It was Game 7 of the Western Conference Championship against Denver, and we were down by one. The clock was ticking, each second a reminder of how close we were to the end.

I wanted this. I wanted this so fucking bad. If we could win, we'd be playing Tampa Bay in the finals. And I knew we could beat them. I could almost feel the Stanley Cup in my hands.

I chased the puck into the corner, just reaching it before I got slammed by fucking Jenkins, his shoulder driving me into the boards.

Fuck.

Sharp pain exploded in my shoulder . . . and my thigh. My thigh had been a constant nuisance the whole round, though, thanks to my darling little *wife*.

I took a deep breath, trying to focus on the ice in front of me. The memory of that night with the gang flashed through my mind, and I couldn't help but smirk. We'd gotten drunk, celebrating winning the round, and somehow, Anastasia had convinced me to get "mine" tattooed on my upper thigh . . . in her handwriting. She'd said she wanted us to have a reminder of the night she'd danced for me, straddling my thighs before I'd forced her to her knees.

In my extremely drunken state, it had seemed like a great idea.

She had laughed hysterically when she sobered up the next morning and saw it.

The joke was on her, though, because the tattoo had been in exchange for her eloping with me, and *I* was now a married man.

Now, the sting of the tattoo was just a further reminder of how I was wrapped around her little finger.

And that was definitely okay with me.

The puck dropped, and I was back in the game. Logan was flying down the ice, his eyes sharp and focused. He weaved through Denver's defense, and I shot the puck toward him, my heart pounding.

"Fucking shoot!" I shouted, but he didn't need my call. He saw the opening and took it, his stick slicing through the air. The puck soared past the goalie and into the net, the red light flashing.

"Fuck, yes!" I yelled, pumping my fist as the crowd erupted. Logan skated over, a huge grin on his face.

"Good job, Rookie," Ari screamed, pounding on his back as he skated by.

"Let's finish this, boys," Lincoln growled, and I was pretty confident that meant game over. Daniels was going to get us the last one.

He'd never let Logan show him up.

We lined up for the face-off, twenty seconds left on the clock.

Logan skated beside me, his eyes locked onto the puck. He took control as soon as it fell. Dancing around the defenders, he weaved in and out, finally passing it to Lincoln who was waiting right in front of the net. Lincoln did some crazy move and pushed the puck backward toward the goal—never even facing it.

Denver's goalie lunged, but it was too late, he hadn't been expecting a shot like that.

The puck hit the back of the net, and the arena exploded. A second later the buzzer sounded.

We'd won. Victory!

Lincoln collapsed to the ice as we toppled onto him, celebrating the win.

"We're going to the Cup! We're going to the Cup!" the crowd chanted.

Logan grinned up at me from the giant pile of players. "Hell yeah, we are!"

I was emotional as I took in the moment, breathing deeply for a second before searching for Anastasia's face in the stands. She was up against the glass, her hands clasped in front of her, and even from here I could see that her eyes were shining with pride and joy.

I skated over to the boards near her, leaning in close.

"What did you think, Mrs. James?" I called out, grinning like an idiot.

She rolled her eyes because I used every excuse to say her new last name at least a million times since I'd gotten her to marry me. "That was hot . . . " she began, leaning close to the glass and mouthing the next word. "Sir."

Daddy, Sir, *Love of her fucking life*, they all made me feral. Everything about her did.

I turned back to my teammates, the adrenaline pumping through my veins as I thought about what was next. I knew we could do it. We'd be celebrating like this again soon.

After we'd hoisted up the divisional championship trophy at the end of our award ceremony, I skated off the ice to grab my stuff from the locker room, wincing as I stretched my thigh to climb over the boards. Logan clapped me on the back. "That tattoo still feeling like a good idea?"

I grinned. "The dick one was always a good idea, Rookie."

Logan's jaw dropped and I winked. "Oh, was that not the one you were asking about?" I said innocently as Lincoln was passing by, making googly eyes at Monroe as he went.

"We talk way too much about dicks in this group," Lincoln commented.

I huffed out a laugh. That was probably true.

Glancing back at Anastasia, still on the ice with the girls, I saw she was laughing at something one of them had said.

It was the really good kind of laugh, where you threw your head back and you felt it all the way down into your bones.

And even though Logan had already gone down the tunnel, I still answered him to myself.

"Best idea ever."

Anastasia

The sunlight streaming through the window was unforgiving, piercing right through my pounding head. I groaned, rolling over to shield my eyes from the brightness. Camden was there, propped up on one elbow, freshly showered, eyes clear—like we hadn't drunk our weight last night.

It was a little unfair.

"Good morning," I rasped, my voice thick with the remnants of last night's celebration. "I may have overdone it."

He chuckled softly, pressing a kiss against my cheek as he handed me an orange juice and two painkillers, forever taking care of me. "*We* did. But it was worth it."

It took me some time to shake off my hangover. Camden eating me out before my shower, like a starving man helped, though. I was actually feeling human as we got into his truck to head out.

Today was Camden's day to volunteer at the community kitchen.

And *today* was the first time I'd be *volunteering* with him.

I was quiet for the entire drive, already choked up from the emotion sitting in my chest as I thought about how much things had changed from that day I'd first met him in line.

Like how I didn't have nightmares anymore.

Michael was gone, destroyed. Camden had been keeping tabs on him, and he'd told me they'd put Michael in a special care facility because he couldn't do anything for himself. Talking, eating, using the restroom, *taking pictures* . . . they were all out of his reach now.

It felt like the sweetest ending possible.

And I hadn't felt a second of guilt.

Dance had also become amazing again. I was partnering with Rudolf on another show and I'd finally been promoted to the senior ranks after the showcase. Dallon had returned, a more humble version of himself, thanks to the tire iron, and I hadn't had to speak with him once. And Madame Leclerc, she still hated me, but she was more civil about it. I could work with that.

I still wasn't sure that my leg could handle being the lead for an entire ballet, but being the lead in the Company's smaller showcases was still a dream come true.

Shaking my head, I thought about the biggest changes in my life . . .

Like how I was married to my soulmate, living in a penthouse, every day a dream.

I still wasn't sure how I'd gotten here . . .

Camden let me be lost in my thoughts until we pulled into the parking lot. "Baby girl, you don't have to do this. If you need some time . . . "

I was already shaking my head before he'd finished talking. "I want to do this," I said fiercely. "It's just a lot to process, you know? Just a few months ago, I was the one coming here to get food, and now I'm coming here to hand it out. I . . . I just can't understand how I've gotten so lucky." My face crumpled, tears sliding down my cheeks. "You saved my life, Camden James."

"Baby girl. I hate when you cry," Camden groaned, pulling me into his arms. I sobbed into his chest for a good five minutes until I was finally able to get a hold of myself, furiously wiping at my face because this was important, damn it. I could do this.

"Are you ready?" he asked gently, and I nodded, staring at the building through my window.

"Let's go."

The community kitchen was already bustling with activity as we walked in. The other volunteers greeted Camden, all of them casting me furtive looks, probably wondering where they recognized me from. Now that I was getting three meals a day, I'd filled out, not looking as bedraggled and desperate as I had when I'd come here weekly for food.

Freddie recognized me, though. "Ms. Anastasia!" he cooed, coming over to give me a hug before Camden let out a low growl that stopped him in his tracks.

Freddie's answering grin was hilarious as he raised his eyebrows up and down. "You got your girl after all, Mr. Hockey Star. Not sure what she sees in you, but I'll allow it."

I giggled at Camden when he scoffed. "We have to get to work, old man. Let us pass."

Freddie gasped dramatically, and I knew I'd spent too much time around Ari Lancaster, because it totally reminded me of him.

"Get to work then, both of you. Just try not to get jealous that I've got the turkey sub station today, Anastasia."

I laughed. "Deal." I was still grinning as Camden and I walked to our station.

"Love that smile on you, baby girl," he murmured, sliding my hair off my shoulder so he could press a kiss to my neck. "Even if it was because of another man. Let's just not make that a habit."

"Yes, sir," I purred, rolling my eyes at his possessiveness. My husband's eyes glittered dangerously.

Husband. I was never going to get over that word.

I breathed in the familiar scent, memories flooding back. This place had been a lifeline for me, that was for sure.

"Ready?" Camden asked, squeezing my hand gently.

I nodded, feeling a lump form in my throat. "Yeah, let's do this."

We donned our aprons and got to work. Camden and I were assigned to the stew station. He served while I handed out bread and fruits and tried not to cry because my heart was so full the entire time we worked.

I recognized some of the regulars that had eaten here each week with me. They looked past me, probably not even thinking of the possibility that I could have been one of them not that long ago.

But I remembered them, the struggle etched into their faces was a reflection of *my* past. It was overwhelming. I wanted to help *more*, as much as I could.

"Mr. James!" a young boy said as he bounced toward us wearing one of Camden's jerseys. His exhausted-looking mother trailed behind him, a small smile on her lips as she watched her son's excitement.

"Hey buddy," Camden smiled. "How were those seats the other night?"

Oh, this must be Sean! Camden had told me about him. He'd given him playoff tickets.

"It was the best night everrrrr," Sean practically roared. Everyone around him turned, smiling at the happy little kid.

"Good to hear," Camden laughed. "Have I replaced Lincoln as your favorite player yet?"

Sean looked torn, biting on his lip. "Well, maybeee. But that last goal was really, really good."

Camden winked at him. "I get it. One of these days I'll win you over."

Sean gave him a high five and then headed to the next station where there were cookies waiting for him.

"Thank you," his mom said softly, accepting bowls for the both of them. "It really makes his day seeing you."

"Of course," Camden said easily.

She smiled a soft, sad smile at the two of us and moved to the next station.

My heart felt like it was going to break just watching her walk away. Tears pricked at the corners of my eyes, but I blinked them back.

The hours passed quickly. Camden and I worked side by side, our movements in sync, like the perfect little team. And when the day was finished, and we'd stepped outside, the cool air a welcome relief after the heat of the kitchen, I'd somehow fallen even more in love with him.

"I want you," Camden breathed as we stepped into the elevator to get up to our home. "You're so fucking sweet. So fucking good. I'm *desperate* to fuck you."

"Hmmm," I murmured as his lips tortured my skin. "I'm desperate for that, too. I might even have a surprise for you."

He inhaled sharply at that little reveal. "I like the sound of that," he growled. "And when do I get my prize?"

"If you're good, Daddy, you can get it right now."

He moaned and bit down on my shoulder. "I can be *very* good, baby girl."

The doors slid open and I stepped out into our entry. "I'm just going to make myself a bit more comfortable first," I told him casually, pulling away and beginning to strip off my shirt . . . and then my leggings, so that it was easy to see the fact that his jersey number was now tattooed on the base of my spine.

"Fuck," he rasped, and I began to count down silently in my head. The girls and I had gotten the tattoos as a surprise yesterday before the game. He'd gotten two tattoos for me . . . it only seemed fitting that I get one for him. Thanks to our drunken escapades last night, I'd been able to hide it from him until now.

One, two . . . I'd just gotten to *three* when he pounced.

And he must have really liked my surprise . . . because we didn't stop making love all night.

SECOND EPILOGUE

CAMDEN

"Now that girl knows how to make an entrance," Logan purred, staring at a dark-haired woman walking toward a seat next to the visitor's bench.

"I'm sure you want to become very familiar with her entrances," mused Ari, his attention not even on the woman in question.

I snorted. "That was a good one."

Ari huffed, his head snapping to look at me, his gaze kind of *crazy*-looking. "Why do you sound surprised at that, Hero? If anyone is funny in this group, it's me." He elbowed Lincoln who was making moon-eyes at Monroe and Lincoln growled.

Literally growled.

That guy was kind of scary.

"Golden Boy, tell them how funny I am."

"It seems like you're doing a good job of that yourself," Lincoln mused, rubbing at where Ari had hit him.

"I think I'm in love," Logan groaned, almost sounding serious as he stared at the woman lustfully.

I glanced around to see if Anastasia had gotten here yet, grinning when I saw her coming down the steps with Monroe, Blake, and Olivia.

"Tell me I'm not seeing things," Logan elbowed me, and I snarled at him before reluctantly glancing over to where Logan was drooling. The girl was probably what most would consider "objectively attractive," but she might as well have been paint drying on the wall for how interested *I* was in her.

"Fuck," Logan snarled, sounding slightly . . . unhinged.

That caught Lincoln's attention, and then we were all staring at the rookie as he glared at where one of the Tampa Bay players had leaned over the glass and was smiling down at the woman in question.

"Fuck, fuck, fuck."

With that *dramatic* display, he skated off, shooting at the net angrily. Walker hit the goal post, annoyed with the rookie. But Logan didn't seem to notice.

First period ended, and we were down by one, and playing like complete shit.

"Fucking hell," Logan muttered, eyeing that same Tampa defender he'd gotten pissed about before the game. Logan's *mood* had continued throughout the period. He hadn't called me *Grandpappy* once.

I would have said that it was the stress of being in Game 1 of the Stanley Cup Finals, but . . . it was obviously more than that.

"Hey, Rookie, is there a reason you keep checking Number 45? And was that fight really necessary?" Lincoln spit as we walked back to the locker room for the break. "I'd rather not be one man down the *entire* fucking game."

Logan gritted his teeth, looking like he was debating whether he wanted to fight Lincoln right now.

"*That* was fucking Tyler Miller. The biggest motherfucking asshole you will ever meet. We played together in college." Logan was pacing the locker room, looking like he was possessed as he clomped around in his skates.

"As enthralling as this story is—get your fucking head on straight, Rookie," Lincoln snapped, right as Coach Porter came in to *also* rip us a new one for how we were playing.

"This is the fucking Stanley Cup Finals, gentlemen," Coach barked. "How about you start fucking playing like it!"

Lincoln was still chewing Logan out when we got back onto the ice.

Play began again, and Lincoln's little "pep talk" hadn't seemed to work. Logan's aggression was still ramped up, his usual precision replaced by raw, unfocused anger. He and Tyler collided against the boards, and I winced as Logan took a particularly hard hit.

Tyler gave him a thumbs-up, and Logan responded with a vicious check. Ari grabbed him by the jersey and ripped him off before he got *another* penalty.

During a break in play, I saw Logan glance up into the stands. His face lit up with a mischievous grin as he waved at the girl he'd been talking about before the game started. Tyler snarled at Logan and shoulder checked him as he passed.

Fucking great.

When we got back on the ice, Logan's intensity only increased. He took every opportunity to slam into Tyler.

When he was sent to the penalty box for the third time of the night . . . I was ready to kill him.

The game was slipping away from us. Tampa Bay scored on Walker, and despite our best efforts, we couldn't catch up. When we lost by one, it wasn't a surprise.

We hadn't deserved to win.

What was a surprise, was Tyler's girl, or whatever she was, had come onto the ice with some of the other WAGs to celebrate. As I watched, Logan skated over, grabbed her by the waist . . . and kissed her, bending her backward theatrically like we were in a fucking Hollywood movie.

"What the fuck?" Tyler snarled, shoving Logan away from the girl. Tyler didn't seem to notice when she slipped on the ice and fell.

But Logan did.

Logan's eyes flashed, and a second later, he and Tyler were crashing to the ice, fists flying. The crowd erupted, the noise deafening. Teammates from both sides rushed in, pulling them apart.

Logan's face was red, his lip bloody as Lincoln dragged him toward our bench.

"You're fucking dead, York," Tyler screamed over the ice.

Logan flipped him off with both hands, a maniacal grin on his face.

Fuck.

This was going to be quite the Finals.

BONUS SCENE

Want more Camden and Anastasia? Come hang out in C.R's Fated Realm for an exclusive bonus scene:

Get it here: https://www.facebook.com/groups C.R.FatedRealm

Camden's Baked Ziti

SERVINGS: 10 SERVINGS

INGREDIENTS

- 1 POUND DRY ZITI PASTA
- 1 ONION, CHOPPED
- 1 TSP CRUSHED RED PEPPER
- 3 CLOVES GARLIC
- 1 POUND LEAN GROUND BEEF
- 2 (26 OUNCE) JARS SPAGHETTI SAUCE
- 6 OUNCES PROVOLONE CHEESE, SLICED
- 1 CUP RICOTTA CHEESE
- 6 OUNCES MOZZARELLA CHEESE, SHREDDED
- 2 TABLESPOONS GRATED PARMESAN CHEESE

INSTRUCTIONS

BRING A LARGE POT OF LIGHTLY SALTED WATER TO A BOIL. ADD ZITI PASTA, AND COOK UNTIL AL DENTE, ABOUT 8 MINUTES; DRAIN.

MEANWHILE, BROWN GROUND BEEF, ONION, CRUSHED RED PEPPER, AND GARLIC IN A LARGE SKILLET OVER MEDIUM HEAT; STIR IN SPAGHETTI SAUCE AND SIMMER FOR 15 MINUTES. PREHEAT THE OVEN TO 350 DEGREES F (175 DEGREES C). BUTTER A 9X13-INCH BAKING DISH.

SPREAD 1/2 OF THE ZITI IN THE BOTTOM OF THE PREPARED DISH; TOP WITH PROVOLONE CHEESE, RICOTTA CHEESE, 1/2 OF THE MEAT SAUCE, REMAINING ZITI, MOZZARELLA CHEESE, AND REMAINING MEAT SAUCE. TOP WITH GRATED PARMESAN CHEESE.

BAKE IN THE PREHEATED OVEN UNTIL HEATED THROUGH AND CHEESES HAVE MELTED, ABOUT 30 MINUTES.

ACKNOWLEDGMENTS

We all need some "Daddy" energy in our life, am I right? Camden James and his baby girl are some of my favorite characters I've ever written. You'll notice this book turned out quite a bit longer than the others in the series, and it was because I just couldn't get myself to let them go. This world has become my new personality and I'm so grateful to you all that I get to keep writing in it. The Dallas Knights and the Circle of Trust are my versions of warm hugs to you all. Obsessive, red flag carrying, d*ck decorated hugs . . .

A few thank-yous . . .

To Raven, One of my greatest blessings in this author journey has been our friendship. This book would not have gotten done without your unwavering support, encouragement, memes, brainstorming, songs, and sprinting with me around the clock. Not only are you the most talented writer I know, but you are also kind and true and trustworthy, and the kind of friend every woman dreams of. ILY.

To Alexis, Thank you for bringing my characters to life and being the ultimate cheerleader in my corner. I can't remember what life was like without you. You're a tier 1 friend for sure. Xoxox.

To my beta readers, Crystal, Blair, and Lisa, You three are such a huge support system for me. I'm so grateful for your comments, videos, support, and steady presence. You are all my dear friends. Thank you for being there for me so selflessly and wonderfully.

To Stephanie, my editor, your dedication to me and this book was incredible. Your willingness to work was an inspiration. You treated my baby like it was precious, and I'm so appreciative of your hard work. Thank you for making Camden and Anastasia shine.

To my PAs and bffs, Caitlin & Sarah. Couldn't survive without you guys. I love you forever.

And to you, the readers who allow me to live my dream. I love you more than you will ever know. You've brought a gift to my life that I still can't believe is real. Thank you.

ABOUT C.R. JANE

A Texas girl living in Utah now, C.R. Jane is a mother, lawyer, and now author. Her stories have been floating around in her head for years, and it has been a relief to finally get them down on paper. Jane is a huge Dallas Cowboys fan and primarily listens to Taylor Swift and hip hop (. . . don't lie and say you don't, too.)

Her love of reading started when she was three, and it only made sense that she would start to create her own worlds, since she was always getting lost in others'.

Jane likes heroines who have to grow in order to become badasses, happy endings, and swoon-worthy, devoted (and hot) male characters. If this sounds like you, I'm pretty sure we'll be friends.

Visit her C.R.'s Fated Realm Facebook page to get updates, and sign up for her newsletter at **www.crjanebooks.com** to stay updated on new releases, find out random facts about her, and get access to different points of view from her characters.